A Trumpet Sounds

O black and unknown bards of long ago,
How come your lips to touch the sacred fire?
How, in your darkness did you come to know
The power and the beauty of the minstrel's lyre?

. . . . . .

What merely living clod, what captive thing
Could up toward God with all its darkness grope,
And find within its deadened heart to sing
These songs of sorrow, love and faith, and hope?

From *O Black and Unknown Bards*
by James Weldon Johnson

A Trumpet Sounds

A Novel Based on the Life of Roland Hayes

Eunice Young Smith

LAWRENCE HILL & COMPANY

Westport, Connecticut

Copyright © 1985 Eunice Young Smith
All Rights Reserved

1 2 3 4 5 6 7 8 9 10

Lawrence Hill & Company, Publishers, Inc.
Westport, Connecticut 06880

Library of Congress Cataloging-in-Publication Data
Smith, Eunice Young, 1902–
  A trumpet sounds.
  1. Hayes, Roland, 1887–1977—Fiction. I. Title.
PS3537.M385T7 1985   813'.54   85-17596
ISBN 0-88208-198-5

Manufactured in the United States of America

Contents

Foreword	vii
Part One	1
Part Two	107
Part Three	181
Afterword	259

Foreword

WHEN I first met Roland Hayes and heard him sing I wanted greatly to do a study of him. But at that time it would have been impossible to pin him down long enough for a biography. He was at the peak of his singing career, booked solidly for exhaustive tours with merciless demands on his time and endurance. I calculated my chances of obtaining the material I would need and was dissuaded.

I decided instead to follow the progression of his struggles as best I could and then simply to tell a story, elaborating episodes where I had only fragments, enlarging on my intuitive understanding of the shy little boy who wanted so much to sing to America, and gathering a miscellany into a cohesive plot structure.

To do this with acuity I felt it was necessary to steep myself in those elements of Roland's growing years that discernibly would have influenced his character, his way of thinking, his ambitions. I had to know his people, his family, his teachers, his friends, where and how they lived, the cultural milieu in which they labored.

I went south to the little town where he was born, Curryville, Georgia, and sat on a porch facing Horn Mountain. I housed in an unpainted, hearth heated, unmodern cabin similar to the one he described to me. I worked in the cotton fields, filling my bag along with the others, talking while I worked with whoever might be in the next row. I went home at night to cook and eat the kind of food

A Trumpet Sounds

common to all Negro families, beans and side meat and corn bread flavored with sorgum—for the lucky ones. I went to the little piney woods school, and attended the Zion Church in the Flatwoods and sang and listened to the endless sermons. I listened . . listened . . . . listened to their talk, listened to its rhythms, its melodious alliterations, its slurrings and contractions and witty distortions. I listened to the old tales, the fanciful inventions braided with scriptural fibers. I became enamored of my subject and longed to picture everything, the lore, the customs, the history, the rich heritage of poetry and song. I found myself writing the exposition of a people—an unruly tome. The dramatic story of one person got lost.

It took me years to revise and cut ruthlessly enough, years in which other facets of my life took over. I wrote other books; I painted and exhibited; I learned to etch and was careless with nitric acid fumes which had me for a while playing hide and seek with death. I reared a family.

But at no time did I contemplate abandoning A Trumpet Sounds. I rewrote it finally, only loosely following Roland's career (Amon in my story). That he learned to mimic musical sounds from his father, that his family moved after his father's death to Chattanooga, that he went to work in a sashweight foundry, was seriously injured there, after which his mother insisted on his reassuming his education even though he was offered a foremanship by the company, his studies at Fisk, his joining the Jubilee Singers, his move to Boston—all are historically based. His sister, Mattie, (Leah in my story) did marry a teamster and go to live on Buzzard's Roost where she was intolerably lonely, and for a season Roland went up there to stay with her. She was neglected and unhappy and came home to wither and die. In my story Amon's sister dies on the mountain.

Mine is a story. It aspires no further. It is an account of a gifted black American determined to fulfil his potential, his destiny against a multiplicity of obstacles. It concludes at the crest of a first wave of success, only indicating the future it presaged.

Part One

Chapter 1

"DAYCLEAN, you boys. Git up!" Sabina called from the doorway. Amon, still caught in the web of sleep, turned, drawing his feet in under the quilt and closer to the warmth of Willy sleeping next to him. Then consciousness seeped slowly forward and washed him free of the mesh of dreams.

Across the room the window was a dim gray square. Amon could hear the first plaintive twitter of birds, a rooster crowing back the dark, a cow lowing away off in a pasture. He shut his eyes again, the ease of bed giving him a sense of weightlessness, as though he could float, airy as milkweed down, and all about him came a singing . . . In that great gettin'-up mornin'-. . . . Huuummmmmm uummm . . . . Golden slippers I'm gonna wear . . . . Huuu-mmmm-ummmm . . . . Hallelujah . . . . Hummmm-ummmm . . .

He didn't sing the words aloud. It was unlucky to sing before breakfast. He squirmed, and the cornshucks mattress rustled faintly. Willy threw out an arm in his sleep and struck Amon across the forehead. On the other side of him fat little Jebiah curled like a warm kitten. Ma had called them to get up, but he was the only one who had heard. Willy and Jeb were in deep sleep and across the room where his two older brothers slept no sound came to indicate they had heard their mother's summons.

Amon stretched, conscious of the ease of his bed. Not all the boys in the Flatlands had beds. He knew many who slept on

A Trumpet Sounds

straw-filled ticks on the floor. Pa had made their beds of good strong hickory. Pa had carpenter tools, and he knew how to use them. He could build most anything he had a mind to, Amon thought. He had made all the furniture in their cabin. He had built the cabin too, felling the straightest pines in the woods, grooving and notching them and fitting them together to make a sound framework. He had chinked the cracks with yellow clay and had split pine boards for the roof. Then he'd gathered stones for the chimney, cleaving them together with clay mortar. Theirs was a fine house, Amon thought. They had a deal table and chairs with split cane seats out there in the big room where the fireplace was, and where Ma and Pa's bed was, and the big oak chest. The windows of their house had glass to see through. Many of the houses in the Flatlands had only square openings with shutters that at night or in the winter or when it rained had to be closed and kept it dark inside except for the firelight from the hearth. Pa had made a real pretty trim around their chimney place, and an extra long mantel above it.

Amon could hear his mother moving around now in the next room, hear the low rumble of her voice speaking to Pa, the pat-pat of her feet crossing the bare floor as she went inside. When she returned, Amon knew, she would rout them out. He rolled over and pulled the quilt above his head. The early morning was cool and the mosquitoes had left off their pesky searching-out hum. His body felt loose with rest, his feet separate from his legs, his arms adangle, his head an air bubble, all of him held together only by the hunger in his stomach.

Presently his mother came to the door again and called impatiently: "Gettin' up time, you boys." And when no one stirred, she raised her voice. "Yunnah fixin to eat best stir youselfs and fetch me some wood. Come along. Git a hump on." A moment's wait and then, "Asa, you hearin' me?"

No answer.

"Obie! Amon! I de-clare!"

The quilt moved and Amon's head emerged.

"I needs wood," she said crossly. "You hear me, one of you? Nobody cut none yesterday. Come along, one of you. Your pa's half milked by now."

Eunice Young Smith

Amon rolled out of bed, now eager for breakfast. He pulled on his shirt and overalls and went to the woodlot. It was barely light. A thin streak of pink pushed up along the tops of the trees in the east. Mist still clung to the hollows, swam along the ground. Everything seemed to be floating on a great still pond; the cabin floated there beside the road moored to the gnarled old mulberry tree. The rail fence around the truck patch was drowned in mist and only the tops of some posts by the gate rose above it like so many ducks on a pond.

Moisture lay beaded everywhere. It felt slippery cool to his feet, cool and wet on the handle of the axe. It steeped odors from rotting bark and pine needles and old leaves in the woods, and the grasses and matted weeds at his feet, the manure piled by the barn, and the honeysuckle that grew thickly everywhere. A longing stirred Amon, half joyous, half painful, a reaching out for something he almost knew, nameless, as intangible as the morning mist.

His mother screamed from the doorway, "Amon! When you fetchin' that wood?"

He jumped as from a clout. He swung the axe, and the pieces flew from the pine chunk. He gathered an armload, and padding back to the kitchen dropped it beside the stove. His mother, grumbling, laid dried leaves and small bits of fatwood together and struck a match to them. A tongue of blue flame leaped, and she fed it more chips.

His father brought in the milk, foam curling on the lip of the pail. He poured some into a pitcher and took the rest to the springhouse. The smell of the warm milk made Amon's mouth water. Even the smell of the burning wood was appetizing. He went out into the yard to be free of it. Asa and Obey came out, heading for the outhouse, and shortly Willy and Jebiah followed.

When they returned, smoke was rising steadily from the chimney, and the smell of frying side meat drifted from the cabin door. Sabina called again: "Jordan, I needs water."

The man came to the door of the springhouse and barked to anyone within earshot, "You ma needs water."

Asa sauntered to the well and lowered a bucket, then pulled it up so slowly the pail felt scarcely a quiver and the water was level with the top of it when he lifted it out.

"You all hear you ma?" Jordan roared again.

Obey caught one side of the pail, and together he and Asa carried the water to the kitchen.

"You boys gonna die one these days, but it sure ain't gonna be from overhurry," their father growled, jerking the pail from them, slopping the water over the doorsill and the boards of the floor. Amon and Willy and Jeb clustered near the door, hunger drawing them.

"I want my wash pots filled," Sabina flung across her shoulder as she stirred corn batter into pork drippings. "You kin lay into that soon as you've et. I got two big washes plaguin' me today."

"Obie and Willy kin fetch you water," Jordan said. "Asa goin' to Jackson's to chop cotton. Me and Amon'll work our patch today."

"I don't aim to chop cotton at Jackson's today," Asa muttered, darting a rancorous look at his father.

Jordan caught the look and the words. He swung his lank body around, and his head jutted toward Asa. "How come you ain't aimin' to chop, eh?"

"I jes ain't." Asa stood in surly defiance near the door.

"Who say you ain't?"

"I do." It was hesitant, yet assertive. "Me an Bobo goin' to Lockwood's."

Amon quivered hearing the brazen words. That was where Asa had been last night when he had told ma after church that he was going to Uncle Zeke's. They'd followed him, he and Obie had. They had been scared but they'd followed. Obie said the music they had at those breakdowns of Lockwood's was "Ummm-uummm!" And it was. Even from the edge of the woodlot back of the house the sounds of fiddle and drum and quills were exciting, so shrill all the dogs had slunk off and the boys had shivered listening and wanting to go up closer for a better look. Once in a while they could see figures dancing by the open window and they could hear old Rip Lockwood calling the sets. They'd been creeping up for a sharper view when they were startled by a shadow moving against the house. Clutching each other, they had sunk to the ground, to follow the crablike figure of Fez Babber shadowed on the wall. The boys recognized it and knew they were not the only ones spying on the Lockwoods.

Amon knew it was not only the wild dancing and the music his parents objected to. There was another reason, something his mother referred to as "that there devil talk." He knew it had to do with white folks, but why this should disturb his parents so greatly he did not see. Everybody talked about the white folks, poked fun at them, made sly nasty remarks, lied to them. How different the devil talk at Lockwood's was from all the rest Amon did not know. But he had a deep awareness of his family's apprehension concerning Asa and the goings-on at Lockwood's.

"You do as I say," Jordan bellowed.

"I don't gotta listen to you," Asa snarled. "I'm fifteen—'bout time I was my own boss." His feet were planted far apart, his thin brown hands clamped on his hips. But his eyes shifted warily.

"Son," Sabina put in, coming to the door with the bowl and spoon, "don't you talk like that. Hear the 'struction of you father. The Bible say that."

Asa turned away, and she followed him, pointing the spoon at his back. "Them Lockwoods ain't no good for you, son. They purely ain't. What you aim to do there a day like this? It choppin' time. You knows that. Ain't them Lockwoods got honest work to do same as the rest of us? I don't hold with them and their ways a-tall. You know what the Bible say. You gotta come out from amongst them."

Asa walked out, not heeding her. Jordan followed, his fists drawn up in front of him, his face mean with fury. Amon and Willy and Jeb huddled near the door, anxious and fearful.

"You choppin' today, hear me!" Jordan ranted. "I'll cut the hide clean offen you do I have to. I know that Bobo Sutton. And I knows you and what goes on over there. It ain't all dancin' and drum beatin'. I know. I got ears in the back of my head. They hatchin' plots goin' to get us all hanged. You wanna get us all in trouble—" He grabbed Asa and flung him around and waved a fist in his face. "Why you wanna do it, huh?"

"I don't aim to work for that white bastard no more."

"You want I should tell that to Jeff Jackson—jes like that?"

A Trumpet Sounds

"I don't care what you tell him."

"Maybe you don't want to eat, neither. Maybe you'd as leave none of us eats."

"You kin work for him, but not me."

"What you gonna do? Work for Lockwood? He gonna feed you?"

"I'm going to clear out of these parts. You can't breathe around here but somebody ready to knife you or hang you to a tree."

"That ain't so."

"It is so," Asa screamed, "and you know it. You plain don't wanna see. You won't listen to nobody has an idea how to get out from under."

"That ain't so."

"It is."

"They ain't no way out from under."

"They is iffen you got guts to take it." Asa saw his father's anger falter. "Someday us Negroes is gonna rise up and say our say and ain't nobody gonna stop us."

"What you wanna say, huh?"

"I wanna say we got some rights."

"Nobody done stop you now."

Asa sneered. "You know that ain't true. You scared right now 'cause you know Hank Lockwood talks bold. You can't see—"

"They's things you can't see neither. What you aim to do with all that talk, huh?"

"I wanna clear outta here."

"Outta here? And where you aimin' to go?"

"Up north maybe."

"You gotta eat there, same as here."

"I'll get me a job."

"Who gonna pay you? Another white man. He ain't gonna be no better than they is around here. Jeff Jackson's a good man."

"Good! My God! We work his fields. We pick his cotton. We make him rich—and he *sooo* good to us." Asa spit. "He let us get in debt to the store and to him—so far in debt we can't never be free of it. Ain't no place we kin turn where it ain't debt and work. You and Ma so old you can't see—"

Eunice Young Smith

"I kin see plenty maybe you cain't."

"You ain't seein' further than the next crop." He whirled and ran toward the woods. Amon wanted to run somewhere himself so he couldn't see his father's flustered and thwarted rage, couldn't feel Asa's thick and roiling hate.

As far back as he could remember Pa had been riding Asa like a man on a stubborn mule. Often Pa whipped him, and Asa went into a sullen mope, brooding and dark, lasting for days. Twice he had run away, no one knew where. Then he had come home, sick, taciturn, his anger dried up in him, to bend again to Pa's demands and Ma's preaching, and Jeff Jackson's field work.

Jordan didn't follow Asa now into the woods. He came back and sat down at the table with the rest of them and ate his breakfast. Afterward he told Amon to get his hoe, and he went to hitch Lightning, the mule, to the plow. Amon saw Asa returning from the woods then, get his hoe, and without a word stalk off along the road toward Jackson's. Amon wondered that he could head into a day of hard work without breakfast.

Obey and Willy bickered over turns at the windlass until Sabina called sharply to them, "When you boys get them kettles filled, I'll be needin' a right smart of wood hauled. And I want you should run up to Farabaugh's and fetch Miss Nancy's wash for me."

Amon saw Obey whisper something in Willy's ear. If he had plans to go fishing today, he might as well change his mind right now. Ma would keep them busy all day. Even young Jeb would be given a job. Ma'd make him sweep the yard or pull weeds or shell corn. After a Sunday of rest Ma was rarin' to go. He went back into the house to get his hat. It was woven of corn shucks and rushes, badly frayed and with a hole in the crown, but it was better than no hat. When the sun rose high, no one could work a field bareheaded.

His mother said to him, her voice now less strident, "Lemme hear Lightnin's bell ring steady till you-all walk outta that field. We got to make a crop this year for certain, else we ain't got the money to pay Mist' Jackson. The ceegar box 'most empty since you pa took out for the plow blade. I's plain worrified, Amon." Her voice wheedled. "You get along now, son, and see you pa and

A Trumpet Sounds

Lightnin' keep a-movin'. I be harkin' for that bell."

Then an uncommon gentleness seemed to invade her. She touched the boy's arm and looked into his face with troubled, pleading eyes. "Be a good boy, Amon. Your brother purely tears my heart out."

Chapter 2

"ANYBODY can impitate a lil ol' quail," Jordan drawled.

He lay with his head against a sweet gum trunk, legs straight out before him, hands, limp as half-dried tobacco leaves, folded across his belly. His lips moved slowly, working a grass stem gradually up into his mouth. He was completely relaxed except for the slight exertion of his feet. Wound around the big toe of the right foot was a piece of soiled string that had been knotted to a long strand of wild grape vine. This was thrown up over a branch of the sweet gum, and from the end of it dangled the bell that a few minutes before had hung from the mule's collar. The mule, resting too, cropped the grass a short distance away along the fence row.

Out in the sunny field Amon leaned against his hoe and rubbed one bare foot up and down against the other. He listened intently. From the thicket at the far end of the field a partridge called, "Bob-white, bob-white."

Amon whistled an answer, "Bob-white . . . bob-white."

A woodpecker hammered, and from the brush close by a brown thrasher insisted lyrically, "Drop-it . . . drop-it . . . cover-it . . . cover-it . . . I'll pull it up."

"Sass that there plantin' bird," Jordan urged.

Amon seemed not to hear. He dropped his hoe in the furrow and joined his father under the tree. "The bell's too dingy. Can't scarce hear nothin' but that ol' peckerwood drummin'."

He flung himself in the dusty grass, rolling away from a shaft

A Trumpet Sounds

of sunlight that penetrated the thick foliage above him.

"I used to could drum like a peckerwood," Jordan said leisurely, selecting another grass to chew. "Reckon I still kin. My grandpappy knowed when it gonna rain jes hearin' the way the drummin' go. Leastwise he 'llowed he could. I reckon not, me. I been hearin' them birds long time now, and they drums when it dry same as when it wet. I'm bound I don't favor the peckerwood none. They's witched."

"How so, Pa?"

"Ain't I never told you that?"

Amon squirmed. He had heard the tale more than once, but he said, "I disremember. Lemme hear it."

"Well, now, they say there's a curse on the peckerwood, and I reckon it's so. They don't sing; they rob other birds' nests; they drums holes in trees and kills 'em. They jes no good. They got wings and tail black as soot, and they got a red head. You know how they got thataway?"

"Unh-unh." Amon turned on his side and propped his head with his hand.

"Seems they was an ol' saint a-travelin' round the world preachin'—course, this were a long time ago—and he come to a cabin where a woman was bakin' cakes. She had a red cap on her head and she live all alone and she was rich. Preacher, he say to her, 'Ma'am, I is real hungry. Might could I have a cake?' An' she say, 'I'll bake you one.' So she took some dough and made a cake and put it in the ashes to bake. Byemby, it done, and she take it out. But she say to herself, 'This too big for that ol' beggar. I'll make him another one.' So she set that one in the cupboard and she take a smaller piece of dough and she make another cake. But when that done and come out the ashes, she look at it and say to herself, 'This too big for that ol' beggar. I make him another one.' So she take a weenie-teenie lil scrap a dough—scarce can't see it, an' she roll it an' roll it, real flat and thin and squingy, and then she put it in the ashes. Course, it burn up black and hard, and she give that to the saint. He all faint and weak from hunger, and when he see that lil ol' burned-up cake, he sure as certain mad. He say, 'From now on I reckon you kin git your food the hard way.' The old woman never said a word, jes went up in smoke through the chimbly. And out the top of the chimbly come a bird, all sooty black 'cept for the white apron on e front, and the red cap on e head. And that the peckerwood, and he always goes a-drillin' in hard wood that way ever since."

"Pa, you reckon that's for true?"

"Sure enough it's true." Jordan emphasized his words with a jerk of the bell cord. "Ain't I heared it from my grandpappy? And ain't he heared it from his grandpappy?"

What stories Pa could tell, Amon thought to himself. But he had to admit storying didn't get fields plowed or seeds in. Pa didn't take easy to farming, that was for certain. If it weren't for Ma, most likely none of their twenty acres would be in crops. It would be left a happy hunting ground undisturbed by hoe or plow. Amon tried to imagine their farm in such a state. He stared out across the cotton field to the wide thickety fence rows where scrub pine and persimmon and locust crowded a tangle of muscadine and honeysuckle and blackberry cane. Ma complained at the ground left so when it could, she said, be better put to cotton or corn. Pa claimed the wide fence rows sheltered birds and birds fed on the crop pests. Besides, they gave them fowl for eating; he could not be persuaded to narrow them. It was a thin excuse, it seemed to Amon, for making the fields to work as small as possible, for hunting land lay all about them. Woodland stood thick to the west beyond the barn and corncrib; it hugged the eastern borders of their cotton field; it crowded their acres to the north and marched up Horn Mountain. From where Amon sat, he could see little beyond their cotton field, for trees almost encircled it. One side was bordered by a creek, fed by springs that bubbled out of the mountain and tumbled down into their valley, meandering through brush and scrub and dividing their land into irregular fields and pastures.

When Sabina and Jordan had come to the Flatlands after an unsuccessful attempt to make a living in Chattanooga, Tennessee, Jordan had purchased on contract from Jefferson Jackson this timbered stretch along the west border of his plantation. With the help of Sabina and one mule and a good set of carpenter tools, Jordan had cut trees, built their cabin and shed, and sold enough pine to make a substantial payment on the land.

A Trumpet Sounds

They had grubbed out stumps and planted corn and cotton. Leah, their first child, was just a little girl then. Asa was perhaps two, and Maisy, the child that had died, just a lap baby. Sabina often told how she had left Leah to tend Asa and Maisy in the poll shelter, which was all they had to live in at first, while she and Jordan cut trees and cleared land and built their cabin. A neighbor had helped them. The cabin was only one room at first; but it had seemed, after the exposure of the poll shelter, a splendid home.

The earth had been rich and fertile, and the crops were good. Jordan paid on their land after each harvest. And each year during lay-by, when work in the fields slackened, he labored to construct a barn and a corncrib and a small chicken coop.

When Leah was eight and Obey and Amon had been born, Jordan added another room to the cabin. Still later he built a weatherboard lean-to kitchen. Amon could remember the building of that, for he had been six or seven years old then, and Will and Jeb were the set-along babies.

Then, when Amon was ten, Leah had married Harp Bracket, a lumberjack who had been stationed with a gang cutting trees on the mountain behind their place. He could remember Harp's songs coming to them down the mountain. He could remember Harp and Leah singing together, his voice low and thick and Leah's soft and high. They sang together all the time, he calling to her across the fields or from the woods and she answering. Then Harp married Leah and carried her away when he left, and they lived in different places, wherever Harp happened to be lumbering, until now she was settled in a cabin at Buzzard's Roost, on a mountain up north of Dalton.

Jordan pushed his hat up and said now, as though he had been pondering the matter all this time, "I didn't buy this here land along back when me and you ma come from Tennessee 'cause I study it be good cropland. Course, it right kind it turn out that way 'cause I ain't found the treasure yet. But that's why I done have a hankerin' for this here stretch. The treasure. I knowed from my pappy it air buried somewheres in these hills. Might could be right yonder on old Horn Mountain. I been searchin', but I ain't found it yet. One these days you an' me gonna find that treasure, Amon, and then we all be rich. My granpappy say the old chief took that treasure chest and hid it deep in a cave in the hills when he makin' a last battle and re-treat. He was killed, and so he never could tell nobody where he buried it."

"What kind of treasure, Pa?"

"Well, it were powerful valuable in them days. It were all the treasure the whole tribe done have."

"Were it money, Pa? Might could be gold, huh?"

"Yeah. One of these days when you an' me's out huntin' we gonna find out. We could stumble right on the place."

Amon thought about the times he had gone with Pa, tramping the forest, discovering bear dens in the cliffs and fox holes and caves where wolves lived. He thought about the times when he had been allowed to go hunting with Pa and some of his friends, not to do any shooting, for he had no gun, but to tag along and learn the ways of the forest and the wild creatures and to carry the catch. Hunting at night was always a fearsome experience for Amon, made doubly awful because he dared not show his terror lest he be found lacking and denied the company of men, perhaps even denied a share of his father's secret life in the woods.

The bell, which had been rhythmically tolled by Jordan's foot, stilled abruptly. The man eased himself up on an elbow. He pursed his lips and whistled—a warble, a soft chuckle, then a string of flutelike call notes. For a moment all was still; then the birds broke into song again—all save the mockingbird.

Jordan said, "He's a-lookin' right now for the feller has come chargin' in on his campground. You mark. He make his next sing up closer. He 'spicious right now. He lookin' all round." Jordan chuckled softly, pulling his hat down over his face and sinking back into the grass.

Amon whistled, calling the mockingbird, trying for his father's texture of sound. He longed to imitate the bird notes faithfully, as his father did. The bell jangled.

"Amon," Jordan's words seeped out from under the hat, "you aim to talk like a mocker, you purely gotta be a mocker. Ain't no other way, son. You gotta be one way down under. Ain't I told you that?"

Amon waited a moment and tried again—whistle, warble, and call notes. He listened, cocking his head. Then he tried again.

A Trumpet Sounds

"Was that better?"

Jordan shook his head. "You makin' love to that bird, son. You singin' the matin' call and he knows it ain't the truth. You has to say the right things if you 'spect to fool that bird. You has to set on a limb and sweet-talk you mate about the babies be hatched purty quick . . . how you gonna feed 'em an' all."

The man talked deliberately, and for a moment the toe stopped twitching the bell cord. "You gotta flap your tail," he went on, "and comb your wings with you bill, an' catch a flea maybe. Then you looks all round to see no hawk a-sneakin' up. You study bout that lil ol she-bird settin' on that there nest jes as nice. You fixin' to tell her everything's fine. Tell her how swell you is. Tell her you better'n a jaybird . . . clack-clack . . . you better'n a titmouse . . . whreep-whreep . . . better'n a redbird . . . peter-peter-pete . . . better even than that there thrasher bird." Here Jordan shoved his hat back and whistled a long series of warbling, burbling, rippling notes. "You jes gotta be that there mocker a-settin' up in that tree iffen you aim to sing like he do."

Amon yearned for the dull gray coat of the mockingbird, yearned to press himself into the bird's sinew and flesh and feeling. What did the mocker think about? What kind of feeling did he have? Was he jealous of the other birds with brighter colors? Would a bird try to make up for his dull coat by trying to sing sweeter? Did he maybe say to himself: "I ain't got pretty blue feathers, nor orangy ones like that oriole, nor red ones like the cardinal feller. But none of them birds can sing worth shucks. I can sing red and I can sing blue, and I can sing speckledy iffen I've a mind to. I certain sure can sing better than that redbird . . . 'peter-peter-pete'. . . and that plantin' bird. He's a fine one with his spotty vest and brown coat. But I can do everything he can and more."

The notes of the thrush flowed from Amon's lips as spontaneously as from the bird's throat. He whistled gay liquid notes. They rippled along his tongue and out his pursed lips and hung in the shimmering heat.

Then from the branches high overhead came a shrill scolding. The boy erupted into laughter, bending double and slapping his knees.

Eunice Young Smith

"I made him mad, Pa. I purely did. He's lookin' for me, Pa. I made that there mocker mad as mad. He thinks there's a lil ol' he-mocker come here to steal his home place. I fooled him, Pa. I purely did." He turned to the man, quivering with delight at his success. Then his laughter subsided. "Pa! You-all make out not to hear?"

The foot had ceased to twitch the bell cord. The steady rise and fall of the hat was disturbed only by a flutter of the brim as a gurgling snore issued from beneath. Amon sighed. His success had gone unwitnessed. Only the mockingbird could say how truly he had spoken. It didn't matter. He had done it once, he could do it again.

Out in the neglected field the sun blazed down relentlessly. Amon thought he should go back out there and pick up his hoe and start chopping again. But the heat, the drowsy sound of insects, the overpowering sweetness of the honeysuckle, the snoring man beside him, made exertion impossible. He lay back in the grass and pillowed his head on his arm. He'd snooze a spell and then go back to chopping.

A twig snapped on the other side of the fence row that separated the cotton field from the vegetable patch and the cabin. The boy's quick ear caught it and translated its meaning instantly. He jerked Jordan awake. "Hey! Ma's comin'!"

Jordan came upright, pushing his hat to the back of his head. The bell jangled as the vine jerked it down.

"Git the mule."

Amon was already at the mule, leading it toward the plow. "Back up, Lightning. Whoa . . . gee . . . back up . . . gee."

Jordan snatched the bell from the vine and was fastening it again to the mule's collar when Sabina broke through the thicket and came stamping across the field toward them. She carried a jug. Her face was wrathful and her voice shrill with vexation.

"You-all loafin'. I jes knowed what you up to . . . a-layin' down there in the shade when they's work to do. I hear that there bell stop ringin'. You don't fool me none. I knowed what you up to. How you aim to get them weeds out, man? Snore 'em out?" Her anger turned to Amon. "You, boy . . . that the way you get the choppin' done? Sittin' under a tree? You knows what the good

17

A Trumpet Sounds

book say. The Lord loves the worker man. He cain't abide a loafer, nohow." She glared at Amon, then shook her fist at the unheeding head of the man. "How I gonna rear up this boy the way he gotta go when all the time you jes show him how to loll around? The Lord say you reaps what you sows . . . an' you ain't sowin' nohow . . . You, Jordan Sayre . . ." She waggled her head at the man, and her mouth was a grim line across her face. "You hear me? What you gonna say to Mist' Jackson when we don't make a crop and you can't pay him no money?"

Jordan picked up the reins and slapped them listlessly on the mule's back. "We pays Jeff Jackson most from us working his crop, not ours."

"Maybe so, but we needs to make this crop too, and you knows it. That's the only cash money we gets, 'cept for my washes, and it gotta spread a powerful long way."

Amon drank thirstily from the jug before he went back to where he had dropped his hoe. He took it up, the handle burning hot from lying in the sun, and resumed chopping out the unwanted cotton plants. From under the jagged brim of his hat he watched his mother, standing astride one of the rows, her hands on her hips, yelling abuse at them. She was thin and straight as a poplar sapling, her dress hanging formless from square, boney shoulders, her waist wide and flat under her patched and faded apron. Her feet were long and thin as paddles. Under her sunbonnet she wore a checkered headcloth, and it stuck out now in two ears that bobbed around from the steam of her scolding.

Amon felt a quick pity for his mother. She was so fierce yet so funny standing there like a scrappy bantam hen. He knew it was worry that itched her into the bitter scoldings, but a needless worry, he felt. He favored his father's way of regarding their problems. They would get along. But Ma couldn't see it that way. She wanted things. She seemed to be driven under a whip trying to get them. She passed the sting of it on to all those around her. He tried to shut her words out. Lord, how hot it is! Could fry chitlins smack on a stonetop . . . Sun found that hole in my hat . . . burns like a branding iron. . . . Ol' sun beatin' down . . . dancing on the rows up and down . . . up and down . . . I kin see it away off there a-shimmerin' and a-glimmerin' . . . Can't watch . . .

Eunice Young Smith

Gotta chop cotton. . . . *chop-chop* . . . hack out those two-three there . . . leave the next lil clump . . . *chop-chop* . . . Take out the next four . . . *chop-chop* . . . push one back out the next clump . . . . wiggle this one out here . . . don't leave 'em too thick or Ma'll make you do it over . . . *chop-chop* . . . don't cut 'em too thin or we won't get us a crop . . . Here's a skip . . . Ma'll make me plant peas in all the skips . . . Sort of sad hackin' out all the healthy lil green plants . . . *chop-chop* . . . funny how cotton likes it so hot . . . I'm purely fryin' . . . *chop-chop* . . . feet say ol' Satan laid a fire on this here red clay . . . my arms is all mush . . . all melted down . . . *chop-chop* . . . Ain't no use talkin' so sad . . . you can't never stop . . .

His father passed him, Lightning sending up puffs of dust where his feet hit the dry earth, dragging the plow, cutting down the weeds between the rows, throwing the dirt up around the cotton plants. His father was mumbling. Amon opened his ears again. Ma had gone and Jordan was at the end of a row. He turned the mule and started back and then suddenly he lifted his head and began to sing: "Oh, bury me down . . . oh, bury me down . . . Comin' for to bury me down. Ol' sun got me firebound . . . My feet gonna stumble over prickery ground . . ."

Amon flipped a cotton plant into the air and his spirit took wing. Pa was shouting now, mixing up the words of songs but rolling a heady melody out over the field. Amon picked up the last line and repeated it. Then lifting his voice high and clear, he sang two more lines:

> *Sometimes up and sometimes down*
> *Still my soul is a-heavenly bound.*

And together they chorused, prolonging the refrain,

> *Comin' for to carry me home . . .*
> *Coooommmmiiiinnnn' for to carrrryyyyy meee home.*

Chapter 3

OBEY came from the back room fastening the strap of his clean overalls. His blue shirt was buttoned to the chin, and his cheeks glistened from recent scrubbing. He looked to his mother for approval.

"Chase that hound dog outta here," she said, "and go hep Jebbie. Them boys'll foolish round in the yard for an hour don't I holler 'em. All that screechin' I hear ain't dirt rollin' off. See Jebbie gets rinsed good or he wiggle all during church with the soap itchin' him. Go long. I got all I kin do fixin' the victuals we totin'."

Out behind the lean-to the younger boys made a lark of scrubbing themselves, slapping the water at each other, screaming and prancing.

"Hey," Obey said. "You purely makin' a mudhole, you. Ain't enough water to get shed of the dirt you puttin' on right now. Ma'll whup you."

Willy and Amon sobered. They looked at themselves and then at the nearly empty bucket.

"Come on, we gotta wind up more water." Amon caught the other side of the pail and they ran to the well. When they returned they began scrubbing in earnest, rubbing Ma's strong lye soap all over their bodies, then rinsing, letting the water run in puddles at their feet.

Obey said, "Amon, you scrub Jeb. He'll get me all wet if I do it."

"I kin do it myself," Jeb protested. "You-all get soap in my eyes."

Amon grabbed the little boy and sloshed water over him. Then he soaped and rinsed while Jeb screamed and struggled. A few minutes in the sun and they were all dry. They trooped in for their mother's inspection.

"You get all that field dirt off you?"

"Yes, ma'am."

"Come here. I kin tell."

They came and she sniffed them closely. "Umhum, you smells bad of soap. I reckon you slick enough for the Lord. And recollect now, you all make your nice smile to the preacher today, and speak like he learn you to. He takin' a big pride in you boys. Willy, smooth your hair back. I de-clare, I'm bound I'm gonna have to cut it off or let you braid it up like your pa."

"Cut it off, Ma," Willy pleaded, "so's I look like Obie and Amon. I the onliest one ain't with kinky hair."

"That's so. You like your pa. You the spit of him." She smoothed Willy's straight black hair up from his forehead, putting it flat to his head.

Jeb pushed Willy, crying, "Who am I the spit of, Ma? Hey? Say it, Ma."

Sabina gave him a gentle shove. "You ain't the spit of nobody but youself. Ain't nobody in this family fat as you is. I plain musta picked you offen a gooseberry bush. Go 'long."

"Come on, gooseberry." Obey grabbed the little boy by the back of the neck and rushed him toward the back bedroom. "Get your clothes on 'fore somebody eats you raw."

Sabina finished tidying the kitchen. Mumbling, she put a pan of cold beans and cornbread on the table for Pa and Asa's dinner. It was a sore point with her that she could not get Jordan to go to church on Sundays, and a still sorer one that he kept Asa from going, whom she felt needed the chastening even worse than his father. Jordan insisted he required the service of Asa to comb and plait his long hair and that it was a tedious, all-morning ceremony. While Asa disliked doing Pa's hair and openly chafed against any request of his father's, he disliked going to church even more, and so submitted to this chore as furnishing a better excuse than none at all.

Jordan reclined under the mulberry tree in the front yard

A Trumpet Sounds

smoking his corncob pipe and patiently waiting for the Ellums to come along.

Sabina's sister, Lowillo, and her husband Ezekial Ellum, and their six children lived a mile or two up the Takearun Road in a leaning house with a leaky roof and three broken windows which Zeke claimed he had not found the time to mend. Lowillo put pans under the leaks in wet weather and Zeke stuffed the gaping windows with paper and rags. Unlike Jordan, Zeke was not handy with tools. Nor did he enjoy farming. He preferred to hunt and fish or, instead of either of these, to sit. On weekdays when he yearned for sociability or to elude the harsh call of duty, he sometimes would appear at the Sayre farm on the pretext of asking Jordan's advice on mending an implement or drenching a hog, and the two of them would go off, not to be seen for the rest of the day.

But Sunday was the official day of rest. No pretext was necessary to recline at ease under the mulberry and enjoy conversation. Zeke and his family approached the Sayre farm now in high spirits. Lowillo, fat, loud, and flamboyant, was full of bluff drollery and, while she did not vocally abet Zeke in his laziness, she did little to discourage it except to yell at him occasionally when one of the children was not handy to do the minimum of chores that got done around their place.

Lowillo saw little sense in steaming over things one couldn't change anyway, either as to the nature of husbands or the conditions of life. Things went to rack and ruin on their farm in a climate of cheerful unconcern.

Lowillo was cook for the Jackson's at the big house, a job she thoroughly enjoyed, because of the pleasant surroundings in which she worked and the plenitude of food always available, as well as for the money she earned and other emoluments incident to her employ. Mrs. Jackson was somewhat of Lowillo's shape and size, a woman of affable nature. She often gave Lowillo dresses and hats and beads that she no longer used. These adornments Lowillo wore to church, giving herself jaunty airs and earning some envious glances and considerable gossip.

The Ellum children came boiling in off the road, Sarah and Buck and Panty and Starlena and Daniel and Fry. Lowillo came up with a flourish. She was wearing a floppy brimmed hat with a big red feather in it and she carried a red purse. Her blue silk dress was of a once fashionable cut. She looked totally unrelated to the man and the tatterdemalion children.

Jordan appraised her through several quick puffs of smoke. "You cuttin' one fancy figger this mornin,' gal."

Lowillo put one hand on her hip, fingered her feather and gave him an arch look. Zeke sniggered. "She clean roll you eyeballs, man. Don't she?"

Jordan conceded with a sideways nod. "That dress sure do blend with your figure, sister."

"Umm-uuumh!" Zeke agreed with fervor.

The Sayre boys came running from the cabin. They welcomed their cousins, chattering together like sparrows in a haymow. Sarah and Buck and Asa were near enough in age to have views in common. Starlena and Panty were close to the age of Obey. Daniel was ten, and Fry, just turned seven, was regarded by fat Jebiah with grave admiration.

Zeke had already eased himself to the ground beside Jordan while Lowillo stood before them, preening. "Hey," she said, "I study to look over the congregation this mornin and see what I sees 'mongst the men. Two sorry loafers under the tree to home. Me an Sabina needs a escort. Heh!"

"Go long, gal. You ain't temptin' us nohow."

"Heh! Satan the one do the temptin' round here. He gonna tempt you two right out you tickets."

"What tickets, gal?"

"You knows what I mean, brother. You losin' you ticket for the Jubilee Train."

"Go 'long, Willo. Everybody talkin' 'bout that train ain't gonna be on it." He laughed. It was an old saw.

"Heh! Least I goes to church and tries to get on. That's more'n some folks do."

Sabina emerged from the cabin all ready to go. She said, "I left food on the table for Pa and Asa and Zeke. Don't you go unpackin' your basket."

"I ain't unpackin' nothin'. If they wants ham and sweet potato pie, they kin come to church. They don't need much strength to set at home all day." She hoisted her basket as the children came spilling out onto the dusty road. Sabina screamed after the boys, "You keep clean now. Hear?"

A Trumpet Sounds

Lowillo flung a parting rebuke at the men. "Gonna come a day when you won't wanna set. You gonna crave to board that golden chariot and the Lord gonna say: 'You kin fry you tails right outta here, 'cause they ain't no room in heaven to set when you done been settin' all you days on earth. Scram!' "

Amon shivered, clearly seeing Pa and Uncle Zeke being banished from heaven. He and Starlena lingered behind, always fascinated by the adult talk. They let the other children scramble on ahead while they walked sedately, ears pricked for their mothers' words. Aunt Lowillo was saying: "I don't study them Lockwoods—an' it ain't the prancin' and dancin' bothers me. It's the talk goes on afterwards."

"I know," Sabina said. "They ain't jes breakdowns."

"No they ain't. They jes plain yellin' for trouble. Somebody gonna hear—and then you knows what's gonna happen. 'Twernt but talk got that Collins boy drowned."

"And Fez Babber—"

Amon knew about Fez. Everybody did. Because of what had been deemed high-and-mighty talk, Fez, only a boy at the time, had been beaten so that he was never able to walk straight or to stand upright again. Fez was a living reminder of the risks of free speech.

"It purely frightens me. But how come you go to them breakdowns, Willo?"

"I don't go to them," Willo denied hotly. "I goes over there to yank my Sarah and Buck home. They sneak off and go. Seems like all the young folk wanna go over there. I don't know what they think they cookin' up—but it ain't chitlins."

"One of these days somebody gonna turn up at Lockwood's ain't invited."

"That's what I tells Buck. I says, 'Why you wanna get mixed up with them? You gets knowed for keepin' that kind of company, you bound to come in for trouble when they do, and they plain bound to.' All that hate talk. What good it do anyway? Jes gets 'em riled up and they don't wanna work for the white folks a-tall . . . And then the white folks gonna start wonderin'—"

"Miz Jackson say anything?"

"No, not yet. But Zeke say Jeff Jackson ride some of the boys about the way they don't take no interest in what they doin'. He notice. Sometimes I get real scared."

Sabina's mouth set in a stern line, and she stared straight ahead. Amon sensed her vexation. He knew she did not want to be vexed on this day. Weekdays were filled with fretting things. Sunday was the Lord's day, when the spirit should find ease. Ma was gentler on Sundays. She wore her best black calico dress and white apron and a spotless headcloth and her shoes. She wanted her spirit clothed as beautifully.

Up ahead they could see where the other children had reached a crossroads. A wagon pulled out from the sideroad and stopped.

"That's Wazzy Stengel and his ma and pa," Amon said.

"We could have ketched us a ride iffen we'd been up there," Starlena said, and Amon nodded, watching the other children pile into the wagon. But he really didn't mind not getting a ride. He and Starlena were both content to be with their mothers and taking a long time on the way. It made Amon feel good when the talk came around to his sister, Leah. He knew his mother liked to speak of her, to tell of getting a letter from her. Asa had read the letter when it arrived. Then later Ma had asked him to read it to her again. Several times he had seen her take it down from the mantel and finger it and put it back. He too liked to feel the letter. It seemed to bring Leah closer, down off her mountain and into their lives again.

"How she doin' up there on Buzzard's Roost?"

"I dunno," Sabina said hesitantly. "I dunno. She sound piney to me, Willo."

"Huh!" Lowillo snorted. "That figures. Why ain't she be piney? Up there on that mountain all alone, no chick or child, no close neighbor."

"That's it, and her Harp gone so much of the time. 'Tain't right for a woman to be left alone so much like that, Willo. She say Harp ain't never to home for long."

Amon saw his mother's hands tighten on the basket. In the way of sensitive children he was aware of his mother's yearning for Leah. She set a heap of store by Leah, he thought.

Lowillo said, "Pity Leah couldn't have married one of the

A Trumpet Sounds

boys in the Flatlands and settled down closer to home. Bein' your only girl, it sure would've been a comfort."

"I don't want her married to nobody in these here Flatlands. I wanted she should get outta here. But not up on Buzzard's Roost. She were right smart in school, Leah were. Iffen she could've jes gone a bit longer she might could—"

"Might could what? Ain't nothin' she kin do but get married. What good it gonna do her gettin' more schoolin'?"

Sabina sighed deeply. "I used to study 'bout sendin' Leah to school in Atlanta. She might could have been a teacher. She so smart, and she purely knowin' with younguns. But I dunno. Jordan and me, we ain't never seem to get money for more'n we has to pay out to live. Seems they ain't nothin' left to work you hopes on."

"Well, iffen she did be a teacher, she might could have gone away to teach—somewheres way off. You wouldn't see her no more than you do now."

"That's true," Sabina conceded. "But I reckon that wouldn't be such a hurt to me as this."

"Nobody can keep they chicks under wing when they growed. Might as well make up you mind to let 'em scratch where they got a mind to."

Some friends coming from a lane joined them. They exchanged greetings and walked toward the church. By the time everyone had gathered, it was almost eleven o'clock. They went into the modest clapboard building and sat down on the benches to await the preacher, Ross Sheppard.

Chapter 4

The windows of the Zion Baptist Church of the Flatlands were wide open, and the sounds of the singing voices swelled through in exuberant tides:

> *Oh, by an' by . . . by an' by . . .*
> *I'm a-goin' to lay down my heavy load . . .*
> *By an' by . . .*

The benches were all filled, the men sitting on one side of the room and the women and children on the other, the deacons occupying the Amen Corner. The building served as school, when it was in session, as well as church, and as social headquarters for the whole Negro community. Ross Sheppard was preacher and teacher. He had been graduated from a primary school in Dalton and for a small stipend taught the children of the Flatlands for three months of the year and held church services every other Sunday. The rest of the time he spent working his small impoverished farm and trying to keep track of his numerous brood.

Ross Sheppard was a good minister to the people of the Flatlands. He was a big man, better than six feet tall, with broad shoulders and loose-swinging, long arms and powerful hands, equally facile with axe or hymnbook. Behind the plow on weekdays he resembled a great lumbering bear; before the congregation on Sundays, a Jehovah. His mobile face and resonant voice could command attention at any time. But on Sundays, when the fire of the gospel spirit moved him, he could stir his people immoderately.

A Trumpet Sounds

His arms rose now in benediction. He closed his eyes and his face took on a rapt expression as he began to pray. He prayed for the welfare of them all, "Lord, take care of my people. Bless them. Let them know your word—"

After the first few words the congregation caught the spirit of his plea and murmured amens at any pause in the flow. His benediction had scarcely concluded when Rafe Bassam's quavery voice rose from near the deacons' corner. The crumpled, frail old man, stirred as always by the preacher's opening words, felt impelled to add his special prayer. His clouded eyes peered from beneath woolly white brows as he lurched forward onto his knees.

"Lord, I jes wanna say a thanks prayer," he began, then straightened and clasped his hands before him. "I jes wanna tell about the good things. I got lotsa good things to thank You for. I wanna say 'em. I wanna tell You I sure 'nough grateful, me. I'm so thankful this mornin', Jesus. When I gets up and see the sun shinin' and the birds singin' I so thankful. I say to my wife, 'Penny, we kin thank the Lord Jesus we here. We kin thank Him 'cause last night we sleep in soundness.' Oh, I jes pray out all my thanks. I got lots of 'em, Lord Jesus. Thanks for all my blessings—"

His voice rose and fell, some words clear and loud, some only a murmur, sliding together, whispered emotion. The congregation began to sway and hum softly.

"Lord Jesus, I knows I's in you hands . . ."

The hum became louder.

"I knows You won't forget ol' Rafe . . . Don't know what I'd do iffen You did . . ."

The humming was cadent, melodic.

"I sure don't, Lord Jesus . . . I likes to call on You name . . ."

The humming swelled and diminished. The prayer went on and on, interspersed generously with amens and humming—on and on until the old man's voice tapered off into a tired, wispy sigh. Then, without pause, the humming swelled into a spiritual, sweet, haunting, laced with harmonies:

> *The gospel train a-comin' . . . to carry us away . . .*
>   *For to carry us away . . .*
> *Oh, the gospel train a-comin', for to carry us away.*

Eunice Young Smith

Hands clapped, feet beat time. Amon sat on the edge of his bench, his feet patting out the rhythm, and clapped and sang. The long prayer, the intoning congregation, the spun-out refrain, stirred him with excitement. He felt merged with the robust sounds. No longer a puny boy too scared and shy of everything, he was a huge joyous feeling. He was part of that peopled train heading for heaven. When the last notes of the song drifted away through the open windows into the summer sunshine, Amon sat back, sighing deeply. He looked into his mother's face and she reached to touch his limp hands. The congregation coughed and shuffled and settled itself for the sermon.

Preacher Sheppard opened his Bible to Leviticus. He stretched his neck up from his collar and squared his jaw. For a moment his eyes rested on the row of children, his children, on the front bench. His wife held a baby on her lap. Next to her sat their oldest girl holding another baby. The rest of the children ranged like steps to the count of seven.

He was reading now, his voice low and musical: " 'And the Lord spake unto Moses. Speak unto all of the children of Isreal and say unto them, "Ye shall be holy, for I the Lord your God am holy".' "

From the deacons' bench came the response, "Hear the word."

" 'Ye shall fear every man his father and mother and keep my Sabbath. I am the Lord.' "

"Amen, amen."

" 'Keep my Sabbath,' He says. You all know what that means? It means for us to keep it in the right mind. It's the day of rest. It's the day to come to church and praise the Lord."

"Amen to that, brother."

"Of course, I don't need to urge some folks to take their rest on Sunday. Some folks just naturally rest on Sunday same as they do any other day."

"Hallelujah!" It was a chuckle.

" 'Now the Lord said to Moses: "When you reap the harvest of the land you shall not reap the corners of the fields. And you shall not glean the vineyard nor gather every grape of the harvest. Thou shalt leave them for the poor and the stranger. I am the Lord".' "

A Trumpet Sounds

"Amen, amen. Tell us about it." Sometimes the deacons responded, sometimes the whole congregation. If they did not, Ross reminded them with, "Join in, brothers, sisters. Praise the Lord."

He continued: "That means we aren't supposed to take everything for ourselves, even if it all belongs to us. The Lord expects us to share our good stuff, some of our food and some of our cheer, too. He doesn't want us to keep it all to ourselves. We gotta give to our neighbor sometimes. That's good for the soul."

"Hallelujah."

"Praise the Lord."

Preacher Sheppard cleared his throat. "And the Lord says to Moses: 'Go tell all the people: "Ye shall not go up and down as a talebearer, neither shall ye stand against the blood of thy neighbor. I am the Lord".' "

"I am the Lord. I am the Lord."

"Hallelujah."

Ross looked out over the upturned faces before him, and his next words came softly and slowly. "Do you know what that means? That ye shall not stand against the blood of thy neighbor? God never said nothing about if you have cause or not. Maybe there be cause. But He says ye shall not give back in kind. Maybe if God was here right now He'd say something else too. He'd like as not say you might bring down a wrath on your heads and on the heads of your families you ain't reckoned on. He says a soft word turneth away wrath. . . . Not a hate word. God never preached us to use hate words. And I want to tell you now there are words being spoken in this here county could stir up more hell than heaven."

Amon shivered and thought about Asa. Asa ought to hear Ross's words, maybe ought to pay attention. But I reckon it wouldn't do much good, he concluded.

"It's a foolishment," Ross went on. "Retribution comes to them as is not cautious of their tongue and their talk. Hate don't get us nowhere, folks. Just turns inside and eats us up. We all living here in these Flatlands, one brother with another, dark or white, and we got to live peaceable. We all dependent on one another. We gotta take what comes and make the best of it. Jesus taught us to be meek and mild and loving . . . yes, even loving to our enemies. It is a hard row to hoe, no arguing there. We got many temptations. We need to pray all the time for strength to bear what we gotta bear. But we have to use the brains God gave us to stay alive. . . ."

The sermon continued, Ross all but naming names of those not present whom he felt needed to be forewarned, hinting broadly of dangers other than those incurred in violating the Lord's edicts. He promised that injustices would all be straightened out one day, in God's world and in God's time.

And they sang "Hallelujah" and nodded agreement.

Then preacher Sheppard swung into the part of his sermon all awaited most eagerly. His voice rose to a shout as he exhorted his people to repent. There would come a day when everyone would be called to judgment: "The thunder'll roll. . . . The lightening'll tear open the heavens . . . The wind'll roar through and the earth'll shake . . . The whole world will come afire . . . The sun'll fall down and scorch the earth black . . . The moon'll turn red and the stars go out . . . and all the graves will open up and the bones'll start to crawl . . . And they'll creep and they'll crawl . . . And the roads will be packed with us sinners aimin' for heaven . . . a-crowdin' and a-shovin' along that road . . . and trampin' each other tryin' to get there . . . An Ol' Satan . . . he'll be right there in the thick of us with his pitchfork . . . raspin' this way and that to get his share of the poor souls that wants awful bad to go up that road toward the angels . . . toward the music and the golden gates."

He threw out his arms toward a hypnotized assemblage and shouted: "You wanna go in the gates?" He paused. "Or do you wanna be pitched off the road into hell by Satan?"

To Amon it was clearer than the room in which he sat, every detail outlined and colored. He cowered, fearful and little. Then preacher Sheppard described heaven, making the golden streets and the bright robes and the crowns of glory beautiful and real. These, too, Amon saw.

With groans and shouts and cries, everyone participated in the rhapsody. "Listen to him, brothers, sisters . . . Lord have mercy! . . . Hallelujah! . . . Join in all! . . . Halleluah!"

A Trumpet Sounds

Bodies swayed, hands clapped, feet stamped, women moaned. The responses swelled and ebbed with separate rhythm. Ross shouted the first few words of a sentence, then murmured through the rest. The shout, the roll of mumbled words . . . the intoning congregation . . . always interwoven with the surging responses.

Amon pressed his hands together until they hurt. His mouth hung open and he gasped for air. His head got bigger and bigger, and something kept pushing at his temples. The voices had become a roar in his ears, and he felt dizzy. He closed his eyes and fell against his mother.

And then suddenly there was no great noise at all. Preacher Ross had stopped talking. Other voices simmered into silence. Slowly Amon revived. Preacher was seated, wiping his face with a red handkerchief. There was a rustle among the benches. Everyone felt exhausted and happy, freed of stored-up tension, unburdened of angers and sorrows and pity and hate. They lifted their voices and sang:

Down by the river side . . . ummm . . . down by the river side . . .
Oh, we'll wait till Jesus comes . . . down by the river side.

Amon sang from his soul and felt alive and new again. How he loved to sing. He wished that singing was a duty like hoeing corn or picking cotton and he was made to do it all day long.

When the service was over, men, women and children walked slowly out the front door, speaking to one another, laughing, shaking hands. They joked with Ross, who greeted them at the door, told him he gave them a fine service. They invited Ross and his family to share the food they had brought.

Out in the churchyard under the trees baskets were opened and food was distributed. Some of those who lived nearby went home to eat this meal, but those who had come a long way, and practically all of the children, stayed to enjoy the picnic in the churchyard.

It seemed only a short interval, and then church took up again for the afternoon and evening services. Business matters were discussed. The church roof leaked badly and had to be mended before fall rains came. It was agreed that if Walt Logan and Matt Kershall would do the work of putting them on, the Dolson boys would split the shakes. Some new desks were needed for the children before the new school term. Twang Stebbins agreed to make them.

Ross raised the matter of books for the school children. "We need something besides spelling books and a few readers. If each one of us tosses in a little, we maybe could start a library."

This statement met a mingled reaction.

"Our kids don't need no libery."

"Yes, they does."

"I don't hold with book learnin'. I ain't had none; I don't hold with my kids havin' what I ain't."

"You send 'em to school, I notice."

"No, I don't. They jes goes is all."

"You could stand with a lil learnin', Jake."

"Who, me?"

"You might could come out the long end of a deal onct could you count."

"Would Sam not hinder me, I'd take a spot of learnin' myself."

"I wisht I could read a paper now and then."

"Papers only tells of troubles and white folks."

"I seed a paper onct. Wasn't nothin' in it for black folks."

"Well, we don't want our kids raised up ignorant, do we?"

"What good a libery do, heh?"

"Quit you blab," Lowillo shouted, waving her arms, "and maybe Ross kin explain."

There was a hush and Ross spoke. "The schools in town have libraries."

"For free?"

"Yes, for free . . . free for any child to read who wants to."

"Don't they got their readers and geography?"

"Yes, but that's not enough. They should have books to tell them something besides a reading lesson. They need to know history, about what happens in the world. They—"

"Why they gotta know that, Ross? Don't do us no good knowin' what happen down in 'Lanty or up north somewheres. Why our kids gotta know that?"

A Trumpet Sounds

Ross frowned. Before he could go on, Sabina pushed Lowillo aside, thrust several women from her way, and planted herself before the questioning crowd.

"I tell you why. Cause we bound to raise up our children better than what we is. We ain't long outta slavery and we don't know how to go, nor how to do. We come out a dark place into the light. We gotta make the most of the light. You wants your children should be field hands all they life? And your children's children . . . and their children . . . on and on like that? How they gonna do any better 'less they has some learnin', and 'less they knows what doin' in the world, like Ross say. I knows that. The book say that. It say we gotta strive for wisdom, don't it? A lotta wisdom done come outta books. I knows that. You-all ought to know it too."

Granny Rachel said, "We ain't money for the new Bibles yet."

"You couldn't read it if you had it," Sabina retorted. "Why you so hept on gettin' a Bible? Eh? To stick in your chest drawer and brag you got it? Won't do you a mite of good there. But maybe, could your children read good, then when you does get you Bible they kin read it to you. Eh?"

There was a murmur of approval for this logic, and after a little more wrangling it was decided to take a collection for the purpose of buying some books for the school, brother Sheppard to be the purchaser next time he went to the city. The hat was passed and coins emerged from pockets and shoes and from little bags tied around necks and hidden in bosoms.

The evening was devoted to reading the psalms and singing. For Amon this was the best part of the Sunday service. He sat between his mother and Sadie Markham and sang every song. Sadie smiled down at him. "You likes the singin'?"

Amon nodded, unable to say how much he liked it.

"You gotta lot of voice for sech a lil skinny kid," she said. "It sweet, too."

Later, walking home along the dusty, winding road in the moonlight Amon did not feel like singing. He tried to recall some of the psalms—"Thou shalt not be afraid for the terror by night."

Eunice Young Smith

"There shall no evil befall thee." "When the wicked spring up from the grass, it shall be they destroyed." But would they be? Could he depend on the Lord? Might not some crawling thing work out of the black shadows and grab him before God noticed? It would be easy for the Lord to overlook him down here on the dark road and God way up there where the moon was. Suddenly he felt forsaken, terrified of the lonely road at night. He crowded his mother's skirts. Sabina shoved him away.

"Go long, son. Leave me room to move."

Aunt Willo said, "Run up ahead with the other children, Amon. You ma and me wants to talk."

But Amon stuck obstinately at her side. Sabina sucked her teeth. "He ain't the same as the others," she said. "He born with a veil. Makes him different. He sees things makes him feared and nervish." She shoved him again. "Sakes alive, boy, what ails you? Go long now. Go up there and take care of Jebbie."

Rejected by the women, reluctant to join the other children, Amon felt abandoned. He caught snatches of talk before and behind him. Aunt Willo was saying, "How you suppose Ross hear all 'bout Lockwood's breakdown so quick? He sure catch up with the news, don't he? You know what Caddy Phelps told me?"

The rest was lost in shrieks of laughter from the children. As they came over the rise near Dean's Hill Corner, the moon was driven under a bank of cloud, and the road became a dimly seen streak through a dark trough. The children's voices hushed, and they waited for the women to catch up with them. For a little way they all walked in silence. Far off a hound wailed. The frogs stopped clacking in one of their inexplicable silences. Then to those acutely listening ears came a sound that seemed louder than thunder. From the woods bordering the road came the staccato crack of a breaking branch. It galvanized the huddled group of women and children. There was a gurgling scream, "A hant! . . . I seen it! . . . Run!"

As though Satan himself were at their heels, they bolted down the road, skirts flying, feet scarcely touching the ground. Lowillo yanked off her hat and waved it frantically as she moved her heft with amazing speed. Sarah and Buck each held a hand of Jeb, and the little boy was sailed along at such a clip his feet trod

A Trumpet Sounds

air. Even Obey's bad leg was no deterrent to flight. They covered the remaining half mile in an incredibly short time and came tearing around the bend and into the Sayre yard breathless and bug-eyed, just as the moon came out from behind the clouds.

Amon was thankful to be home, to see Pa and Asa and Uncle Zeke sitting calmly on the front porch. Jordan took his pipe from his lips and stared at them.

"Nice night like this—how come you hurry?"

"We seen a ghost," Sarah said.

"Where you see a ghost?"

"By Faulkner's place. Sarah seen it."

"We all heard it," Panty gasped. "Didn't we?"

"Pah. Ghosts don't make no noise."

"This one did."

"Man alive!" Lowillo said, fanning herself with her hat. "Did we light outta there!"

"Ain't nothin gonna eat a tough ol' bird like you."

"I ain't tough this minute. I's plain melted to mush. Oh, me, how I run!"

"My feet ain't touched nothin' all the way," Jeb crowed. "The ghost hang onto 'em."

Buck said, "Boy, if we'd let go you arms, you'd knowed who hangin' on to 'em." He tittered and pinched the little boy.

"We sure run fast. I never look back. No suh."

"Then you don't know were it follerin?"

"Not me. I don't look."

"Haw, you might have seen a deer iffen you had."

Amon wanted to say, "I looked back. I saw something." But in the babble and confusion he could not. He felt no one would believe him anyway, any more than they really believed Sarah. But in that second when the branch snapped, when utter terror had rooted him to the ground, Amon had seen something between the trunks of the dark trees. The drifting cloud had partly uncovered the moon, and he knew instantly what he was seeing. It was no ghost. It was the grotesque shape of Fez Babber.

Chapter 5

Amon lay on his belly staring down into the still, shallow water of a little cove. Cress grew thickly along its edge, in flower and bitter to the tongue. A frog leaped, making a solitary splash, rippling the water out in a widening circle. When it cleared, Amon could see holes in the mud at the bottom, hoofprints made by deer coming to drink. Minnows darted in and out of the holes. "Fixin' to find them a nice quiet cave to squiggle into and lay their eggs," he thought. "They like it better in there than out where the current runs fast." For a long time he lay with his hand cupped above the water. Then it shot down quick as thought and he had captured a tiny fish.

"Little ol' minnie," he chuckled, "you ain't scarce no bigger'n a tadpole. Ma'd whup me to a fare-thee-well iffen I brung you home for supper." Mirth rippled for a moment along his ribs as he visualized Pa staring at the minnow on his plate. Then he flipped the fish back into the water. He glanced at his pole, the end pushed into the soft earth of the bank and propped with a rock, the line dangling into the stream unteased by so much as a nibble.

"We ain't found ourselves a good spot," he told himself. "Not onct today." And the thought was tinctured with apprehension, for when Ma allowed them to go fishing she expected results. Obey had caught four or five bream, but his own string held only two small pout. They had come further along the branch than usual searching for a likely spot, penetrating deep into the woods at the

A Trumpet Sounds

foot of the mountain, more than two miles from their farm. The boys had followed a deer path that wound for a way along the stream until they came to the little backwater, where Amon said he would try his luck again. Obey was a couple of rods further along, around a bend, where a clump of locust and witch hazel hid him from view.

The late afternoon sun slanted through sweet gum and willow, throwing a fretwork of light and shadow on the water and on the boy's back. Peering below the grasses that overhung the bank, Amon discovered periwinkles and washed some of them and put them in his pocket. Dried and strung on a piece of gut, they would make a charm. Panty had told him once how to make such a talisman, and how good it was for warding off warts and hants and measles and bad luck in general. She told him hers was always bringing her good luck, like the time she stubbed her toe so bad she got out of a job of potato hoeing after she had rubbed the charm properly. And anyway, whether potent or not, the periwinkles were pretty, and Amon liked them. If Leah were still at home, he would have searched for enough to make her a necklace.

His thought drifted, gathering pictures of his sister. He saw her moving about their cabin, slow, hands touching things soft and easy—never snatching—never cuffing—laughing hands—laughing voice—sweet-talking voice—saying things made you feel good—telling stories. Ever since he was a little set-along child Leah had told him stories. He could remember all the stories and the play songs . . . funny little old play tunes you could skip-hop to. Leah was a thrush in a treetop, singing . . . singing everywhere . . . out in the fields. . . driving up the cows at daybreak . . . over the wash pots . . . in church . . .

He rolled on his side, resting his head on his arm, aware of the breeze that set the trees sighing. Over and over a towhee whistled the same few notes, and tree toads whirred incessantly. The sounds came to him mingled, a wildwood chorus, and his thought lay along the wind, knowing its impatient push, its voice among the thickets, a melody accented by the zzzt-zzzt-zzzt of a fly and the steady buzz of a bumblebee. The sounds flowed about him, stirring his senses, certain notes repeating over and over. Words flowed into his mind, a tune with them:

> *All a little bees comes a-buzzin' round,*
> *Buzzin' round, buzzin' round.*

The wind hummed an accompaniment. The rhythm pleased him, and he repeated: "All a little bees comes a-buzzin' round. ." Then, to balance the refrain, he added, "And me a-sittin' 'long here."

Surprised at his own creation his voice rose in confidence:

> *All a little birds comes a-singin' round,*
> *Singin' round, singin' round.*
> *All a little birds comes a-singin' round,*
> *And me a-sittin' right here.*

He rolled onto his back and flung out his arms.

> *All a little winds comes whirlin' round,*
> *Whirlin' round, whirlin' round.*
> *All a little winds comes whirlin' round,*
> *And me a-lyin' right here.*
> *All a little—*

The words broke off sharply. Amon's ear, close to the ground, had caught the sound of hoofs. Not cattle this far back in the woods, he knew. It didn't sound like hogs. A deer, maybe. Something had started it, and it was coming swiftly, crashing through the underbrush. The boys were downwind, giving the animal no warning scent. In a moment the deer flashed past and disappeared into the forest again, the sounds of hoofs diminishing quickly.

Around the end of the stream Amon saw the bushes part and Obey pick his way along, carrying his pole and string of fish. He ducked down behind the bushes where Amon lay. His voice was cautious. "What you reckon started that deer?"

"I dunno." Amon sat up.

"It were scart-like, weren't it?"

"It were goin' mighty fast."

"Yeah."

"Don't go that fast lessen somethin' tailin' it."

"Somebody huntin', you reckon?"

"I ain't heared shots."

"Might could be a painter."

A Trumpet Sounds

"Painters don't hunt daytimes."
"Might could be somebody jes goin' through."
"That scared that deer?"
"Yeah."
"Who you reckon be goin' through?"
"Dunno. Let's lay low."
"Pull your pole down. It stickin' up above the bushes."
"You reckon somebody might could be comin' here to fish?"
"Naw."
"Nobody can't see us lessen they drop they line right smack to this here spot."
"I don't study it nobody goin' fishin'."

The boys crouched, listening intently. Straining ears caught a new sound. Mumbled noises drew nearer. Both boys knew the owners of the voices—the growl of Fez Babber and the slur, like water running through grasses, of Pula Kemp. The man and the woman, believing themselves alone in the woods, were taking no pains to guard their words.

"Them stinkin' rats, them God-damned stinkin' bitches." The words, not the tone, bit. "Why they wanna say I done it? Why? I ain't never gone near Noah Thoman, and I wouldn't let the filthy polecat near me."

"Sure, sure," Fez agreed. "I know that. They jes wanna lay blame somewheres."

"Why me? Why they wanna pick on me?"

"You jes happen to be handy is all, and they've heard things about—"

"Me makin' conjures? Well, maybe I does. But not the kind they say."

"White folks is always suspicious. And them Thomans is purely trash. They say anything."

"What I gonna do, Fez? They gonna ride me for sure."

"You best hide for a spell. Go up where my still is. Nobody don't bother nothin' up there."

The two had slowed almost to a halt, Pula studying the path uncertainly, then shifting her gaze to the hunchback at her side.

"They try to make up to you for what they done, don't they?"

"Naw," Fez denied. "I pay 'em to see nothin'."

"Well, I dunno."

"You best get outta their way for a spell. There's trouble brewin'. I hear talk. Ain't only the Thomans."

"How you hear so much, Fez?"

"I get around."

"What else you hear?"

"Hank Lockwood's got hisself noticed and . . ."

The voices blended and blurred as the man and woman went out of hearing. When they had gone, Obey whispered, "What you reckon she done?"

"She said she didn't do it."

"Conjured. She say Noah Thoman!" Obey gasped, and his mouth dropped open. "You recollect all the fuss when Les died? They blamed Pula for that, remember?"

"Oh, Lordy! You reckon Pula witched Noah?"

"Preacher say there ain't no witches hereabouts."

"He might could be wrong. Pula could fool 'em if she's a witch."

"That's so. You scared?"

"Boy, I's putrified."

Obey fumbled in his pocket and brought out a mangy rabbit's foot. He rubbed it over his head and down both sides of his nose and arms, then handed it to Amon.

"Rub this on you. It'll sic off the bad luck."

"You hear what Fez said about Lockwood?"

"Yeah, he's got hisself noticed."

"Yeah."

"Iffen he's noticed, maybe Asa's noticed too. Lordy, Amon, them riders'll be after Asa maybe. Jesus, what we do?"

"We best go tell 'im, and fast."

They picked up their poles and fish and ran along the path toward home. At the western edge of the Jackson plantation they emerged from the woods by a cornfield. Keeping well to the cover of the fence rows, they gained the road about a quarter of a mile above the Thoman place.

Of the seven workers' houses on the Jackson plantation, the one in which the Thomans lived sat nearest the Takearun Road along which the Sayres and Ellums and Lockwoods had their

A Trumpet Sounds

small farms. The Thomans were the only whites who worked for Jeff Jackson, and because there were so many of them, Jeff had given them the biggest cabin on the place, one with four rooms, a gallery around three sides, and two front doors.

Les and Noah Thoman were twins, considered good-enough workers when sober, given to brawling only when the cotton was in and their pockets jingled with cash.

The twins had married Marie and Sheba Ware, cousins who got along well together, and who wanted to live side by side, or better—since Jeff Jackson would let them have the big cabin—all under one roof. In the three years they had nested on Jackson land six more children had been born into a household already creaking from the strain of ten people. Somehow they managed to live, always in debt, always borrowing, always with sickness and malnutrition.

Then without warning or apparent cause, Les had been stricken. He fought and raved and tossed and struggled and died, throwing his wife and brother and children into a frenzy of grief. Their lamentations and distress were the talk of the valley, not so much because they had a grief—that was legitimate and understandable and shared by all—but because in their bewilderment, in their need for a simple explanation for strong, roistering Les to be so stricken, they sought a scapegoat on whom to spend their misery. Even though the doctor said Les had died of typhoid, they said Pula Kemp had laid a curse on him.

Noah had bitterly mourned his brother's death. He became apathetic. He drank more than ever, and was practically useless in the fields. Jeff Jackson tried to reason with Noah, tried to reconcile him to his loss, but without noticeable effect.

So when Noah took sick about a week ago, instead of concluding that without doubt Noah, too, had typhoid, the women asserted Pula had witched Noah, that she had thrown a conjure in their well and poisoned the water. Even the Negroes in the Flatlands wagged their heads, and they shunned the Thomans because it was one of their own people was accused.

Only Sabina, of their close neighbors, strove to help. She brewed calamus root tea and herb concoctions for Noah, but they

Eunice Young Smith

were totally unavailing. She made big kettles of soup and fed the children.

Now, as the boys approached, screams issued from the house, and a long shrill wail. It sent Amon's nerves tripping. His first impulse was to run for home. But to run for home meant running directly in front of the Thoman house. His instinct betrayed him and bore him ineluctably toward the source of his terror.

The sounds coming from the house were dreadful. He saw his mother emerge from one of the front doors, pushing two little girls ahead of her. He heard her call to Walt Logan, who was standing in the yard, "Keep these kids out from under foot, can you? And send somebody up to the big house."

"To tell Mister Jackson?"

"Yes."

Noah was dead! The news chilled Amon. This was what Fez and Pula had been talking about. The second Thoman twin had died. It was a devil sign sure.

His mother caught sight of him then, standing there in the road with Obey. She waved them on, her arms flailing the air in an unmistakable directive. Two more stupefied children added to the sobbing, yelling, hysterical families was not to be borne.

Amon turned and ran, wails following him down the road. "Run fast . . . run fast . . . run fast . . . faster," his brain babbled. "Don't listen . . . run faster . . . faster . . . can't hear the crying . . . can't hear the screams . . . can't hear . . . run."

It was almost dark. Home was in sight. Who would be there? Willy? Jeb? Maybe Pa and Asa. He had to warn Asa. Asa had to stay away from the Lockwoods . . . the Lockwoods were in danger . . . He had to tell Asa.

Chapter 6

PELTING down the road ahead of Obey, Amon hit home ground breathless and with one fish missing. His bare feet spurned the stubbly yard and he took the porch in a leap. A candle burned in the lean-to. Pa was likely home, or Asa. Someone was singing, "Put on de kettle, put on de lid, My lil baby want shortenin' bread."

His senses were assailed by the odor of cooking and the singing. In his excitement he did not see things clearly inside the dimly lit cabin, only that Jeb and Willy were there chattering to a woman who stood by the stove in the kitchen. Wasn't Aunt Willo, nor Aunt Candy. The shape wasn't right. As the woman turned, he saw her face in the candlelight. He dropped his pole and fish line and lunged for her and clamped his arms around her. "Leah! Leah! Leah!"

She held him tight, putting her cheek down on his head. They swayed back and forth, hugging, Amon breathing in the good smells of her, road dust and sweat and starched calico and warm loving flesh.

"Where you been, boy?" Her voice rippled, sweet as fresh-churned butter. "I come home and ain't nobody here 'cept Willy and Jeb. Where you all go to?"

"Me an Obey been fishin'."

"Look." Jeb hoisted Amon's fish line. "Big catch!"

"I lost one, running." He turned back to Leah. "When you

come? Why didn't you say you was coming? Heh? Ma's to Thomans . . . Noah, he's dead."

"How you know that? How you know?" Willy and Jeb demanded.

"We seen Ma over there." Amon shoved the little boys aside. He wanted to look at Leah. Pretty as a cotton blossom, he thought, only pindly, maybe, but smiling, just like she used to . . . her hands patting . . . slow, gentle hands . . . not slappy or pinchy. "Hey, when you get here, huh?"

"Since a couple hours."

"How you come?"

"On my feet. How else? Boy, you lookin' mighty good to me, you purely do."

"Leah, how long kin you stay, huh? Kin you stay a long time?" Willy tugged on one arm and Jeb on the other. "You kin sleep in my bed," Jeb offered. "Will you tell us a story, Leah? Will you?"

Amon grabbed the fat, bouncing little boy and pulled him away from Leah. "Leave her be a minute, can't you? Hey, ain't Pa home yet?"

"Not as I see."

"Who done the milking?" It was full dark now and way past milking time.

"Asa milked."

"Asa! Where is Asa?"

"Lettin' the cows out, I reckon. You hungry, honey? I cooked supper."

"Yeah, oh, yeah. It smell powerful good, but I gotta see Asa first."

"He be in in a little bit. Whatsa hurry?"

"I gotta find him."

The stress in Amon's voice was sensed by Leah and the younger boys. "What's the trouble? What's Asa done? Why you gotta find him?"

Obey burst in through the door as though shot in from the dark, breathless and popeyed. "Why didn't you wait for me? You—" Then he saw Leah, dropped his pole and fish and ran to her.

A Trumpet Sounds

Amon went out to find Asa. It would be better to tell him what he had to say in private; it would give Asa a little time before the whole family jumped him with questions. He found his brother at the barnyard gate, and his words came stumblingly and faltering.

"Asa, Lockwood is in trouble."
"Why you say that?"
"I heared it."
"Where?"
"From Fez."
"When you been talkin' with Fez?"
"I ain't. I jes heared him."
"Where?"
"In the woods . . . with Pula Kemp."
"How come you in the woods with Fez and Pula?"
"Me an Obie was fishin' and they come by. But they didn't see us."
"Well, what did he say?"
"He says Lockwood's is noticed."

Asa was struck silent. He stared at the younger boy as though trying to ascertain how much he knew, how much he could believe from someone given to jitters and hiding from thunderstorms.

Amon said, "Why do you go to Lockwood's, Asa? Why do you take up with trouble? Ma says they is purely—"

"Oh, hell, don't I know what she says? She don't know what she's talkin' 'bout."

"She knows they stir up folks an' make 'em mad."

"Maybe they do and maybe they don't. Maybe they want to stir folks up. Maybe folks needs to be stirred up."

"Ma says it don't do no good. Jes gets the white folks down on us more." Amon shivered, feeling sure of it.

"You don't know. You ain't never been to a meet. You don't know what we talk about."

"It's hate talk, Ma says."
"I like it."
"Why you like it, Asa?"

"'Cause it makes me feel good, that's why. I kin go over to Lockwood's—and lots of other folks goes there, too—and we can

Eunice Young Smith

talk about how maybe one day we get to vote, how we figger we can get the white people to listen to us, to give us a chance at something."

Amon looked incredulous. He didn't understand. "What kind of chance, Asa? What you mean?"

"We can talk over there about the way we feel inside," Asa went on, "about all the low-down things the whites do to us . . . how they push us off the streets, off the sidewalks . . . make us use back doors into stores . . . how we don't dare try to buy a cup of coffee in a public eatin' place. We talk about how polite we is and how we smile real nice and say 'Yes, ma'am' and 'No, sir' and how we would like to spit in their faces. We talk about how they take our money and cheat us and make us work their fields for a lil stinkin' nothin' we can't make do on nohow, and we have to go into debt to 'em so they kin keep us workin' and workin' for 'em. And ain't never no chance to get free. We ain't free, Amon, no more than Pa and Ma was in slavery days. We burdened down jes the same. We scared like they was. We don't dare stand up straight an' say our say . . . or we get lynched or beaten. They ain't no place we can get a fair trial or any kind of justice. Don't you know how low down we are? Don't you ever think about what gonna come of you . . . of all of us? Ma talks the Bible. She twists things. She pulls out jes the meek words to flash around. Theys other words in the Bible. I can read. Why don't she shout how the wrath of God gonna descend on the unjust and the oppressor? Why don't she talk about the Lord smitin' the wicked? Why don't she talk about how somebody ought to smite them white jackasses that thinks they owns the earth and all on it. I hate 'em, Amon. I hate 'em all, every last bitchy bastard of 'em. You hear! I'd like to push every white face down in cow plops."

"Don't yell." Amon giggled nervously.

"I wanna yell. When we go to Lockwood's, we all yell. We say what we think and we like the talk."

Amon could understand that. All the Negroes liked to downtalk the whites. They did it all the time, even though they knew that not all white people were mean and patronizing. Why was what Asa and the Lockwoods did so different? And then Asa answered Amon's unvoiced question.

47

A Trumpet Sounds

"It ain't all we do." He bent his face close to Amon's, and even in the darkness his features seemed lined with fury. "We make plans."

"What kinda plans, Asa?"

"To get back at the whites."

"How you gonna do that?"

"I don't know, but Hank got ideas. They take a spell to work out. He wants to work things out real legal an' all . . . go round and get everybody to sign this here paper sayin if they let Negroes vote, we'll all vote for Kruptney for sheriff. And then we take the paper to Kruptney and we say we'll get him put in office do he keep a tight hand on the riders and the Kluxers. See? It takes a while to work out. Me, I'd go for a few burnings and beatings of our own. I reckon we ought to give back as good as we get, beatin' for beatin', life for life. I'd like nothin' better than to march on the sheriff's house, drag him outta bed in the middle of the night, jes like they do to us, and string him up to a tree. I'd as leave whip the skin off them Schneider skunks as peel a willow. If we'd stand up and quit bein' scared all the time and give back like we get, maybe the white folks would slow down a little before they murders."

Amon's head whirled. He began to see why Ma worried about Asa's going over to Lockwood's. But he wondered if she really had any idea what went on over there, of the ideas Asa came away with, or went over there with. New fear for Asa overwhelmed him.

"It ain't gonna do you no good dead," he blurted.

"What ain't?"

"Gettin' even."

"I'd as leave be dead as ground down all the time."

"You can't do no good an' you can't get even iffen you dead," he repeated. "They get you sure, Asa. If you at Lockwood's and they come for them, they gonna take you too, sure as sure."

"How they gonna know? They ain't no stoolie at Lockwood's."

"It gets out."

"How?"

"Fez knows. He knows all about Lockwood's. He spies. Obey and me seen him one night."

"How come you seen him?"

Eunice Young Smith

"We was there too, the night of the breakdown."

Asa had turned toward the house and Amon followed, feeling a rising terror and his own ineffectuality. Tell Leah, his thought said. Maybe she could persuade Asa, make him see that he was in danger.

But Asa needed nothing further. A deep fear had settled on him. His gestures were wooden, his voice heavy, as he spoke to Leah on reentering the cabin. "Ain't Ma home yet from Thomans?"

"Didn't Amon tell you? Noah died. Ma'll stay over there most the night now, I reckon. But where's Pa?" She turned to face Asa. "Why didn't he come home with you?"

"He won't be home," Asa threw over his shoulder as he went to close the shutters of the window.

"Why not? Pa go to Thomans too?"

"Not Pa."

"Where then?"

"How should I know? He jes head for the woods. You ought to know what that means."

The treasure, Amon thought. He's gone off again after the treasure, just as he had so many times before. Unpredictably, without good-by or concern for crops or responsibility, when the burdens of farm and family weighed his spirit, the lure of the lost treasure beckoned irresistibly and Jordan would leave, to be gone a week or many weeks. When he returned after these absences, he never told where he had been. Sabina, the whole family, accepted them as they did the rain and the drouth and the dust storms and the insect plagues.

Obey prodded Asa. "Did Amon tell you 'bout Fez and Pula?"

"Yeah."

"You reckon Pula conjured Noah?"

"Oh, shut up."

"Well, he's dead."

"That's a foolishment," Leah said.

But Obey was not to be silenced. "She makes 'em, them mojo dolls—to look like white folks, an' then she spits on 'em and rubs 'em with cow plop and sticks 'em with pins all over an'—"

"How you know that?" Jeb's curiosity was aflame. "You see

'em, huh?"

"Panty told me. She saw one onct."

"Asa," Leah bent over her brother, thoughtful and serious, "Amon says the Lockwoods is in trouble."

"So what!"

"They your friends, ain't they?"

"I reckon."

"You reckon they know?"

"About what?"

"I don't know, but whatever Fez was talking about. You might could warn Hank."

"What I warn him about? Fez Babber talk? He's in cahoots with the revenuers. Maybe he's in cahoots with the riders too."

"All the more reason to pay a mind to what he says."

Asa scowled.

"You want your supper now?" Leah asked. "I don't 'spect Ma be comin' home till late."

"How come you kids up the creek in that pine land?" Asa flung angrily at Obey and Amon. "Ma said you had to hoe potatoes this afternoon."

"We hoed 'em and then went." Amon knew Asa was worried and this was just hitting out at random.

"Come and eat, boys," Leah urged, putting bowls of chitterlings and gravy on the table. The younger boys gathered around and fell to the meal hungrily. Only Asa seemed not to relish food. He stared at his plate and fiddled with his spoon, his eyes hooded and sullen. After a time he got up, looking nervously at the shuttered window and the door. He cast one strange glance at Leah and went out into the night.

"He goin' to warn 'em," Amon whispered. "He purely gotta warn 'em."

Leah nodded. "I heard things comin' out from town."

"What things?"

"Tate's men are out to scare any Negroes that aim to try to vote for a new sheriff." She tried to describe the local politics so that the boys would understand, but most of it they failed to comprehend. After a while Leah cleared the table. She warmed water and washed the pans and spoons. Amon dried them for her.

Eunice Young Smith

He asked her then about Harp and about her life at Buzzard's Roost. But Leah seemed not to want to dwell on these matters and changed the talk to things about himself and the other boys and Ma and Pa and how the cotton was doing.

Later, they all sat on the gallery steps in the moonlight waiting for Ma to come home. Occasionally, across the still night air, fragments of a high wailing came to them. Rube, the old spotted hound, whined and came and lay down beside Leah, and she stroked his ears. Amon thought maybe she would sing, but she didn't. She grew silent, pulling her knees up and tying them with her arms, staring at the moon as it climbed up the sky.

Willy and Jeb and Obey chattered sociably, making a big thing out of every least event they told her of. Amon became unbearably sleepy, and although he had no desire to go to sleep and leave Leah there, his head nodded and nodded. He had only a hazy notion of Leah's rousing him to guide him in to bed, where he fell asleep immediately.

It was dawn when he woke. He lay close to the warmth of Willy and groped for remembrance. What had happened? Why was the house so still? Why did he not hear Ma slapping around in the kitchen? Oh, yes, Leah. He hadn't dreamed Leah, had he?"

He leaped out of bed. Maybe he had dreamed it all . . . the words of Fez . . . the death of Noah . . . Asa . . . Leah . . . the whole awful day. He padded across the bare floor toward the outside door. It was open and he could hear soft voices, like the early rustling of birds. Ma and Leah sat on the cabin steps. Ma drooped wearily, and her voice was a dull monotone.

"Miz Jackson come. She kind and she wanna help, but she don't stay long. After a bit she dust outta there like a strong wind on her tail. She mean well, but she ain't never seed nothing like them Thomans. All them lil kids with they snotty noses and they pants filled, cryin' and carryin' on and gettin' in the way so's you can't move. And that leastest boy of Les's, the one that simple in the head—nobody can't do nothin' with him, and he howl and howl like a hant. He no notion why he doin' it. But everybody else howlin', so he howl too. He jes lay in the middle of the floor and yell that way. Make you blood 'jeel hearin' him. Marie tried to stop him. Granny woman, she try. He right there in the way.

51

A Trumpet Sounds

Nobody can't seem to do nothin' but scream. The hounds set up a wailin'. Cows come bellerin' at the yard gate . . . Somebody gotta go milk . . . Somebody gotta cook food and tend them bawlin' babies . . . Walt, he come back from takin' some of the kids away, and—"

"Oh, Ma, you plumb wore out. Come rest now," Leah urged.

"Where's Pa? He might coulda come and spell me a bit."

"Pa didn't come home. Asa said he went off to the woods."

Sabina's shoulders seemed to droop further, but she said nothing.

"Asa didn't come back last night either."

"Where'd he go?"

"To Lockwood's, I think. Amon and Obey heard some talk between Fez and Pula Kemp that the riders are out."

"Oh, Leah." It was a groan. "I's plain feared for Asa. He been over to that place too much. Pa and me knowed it were dangerous. We tried and tried to warn him." She shook her head. "I don't know what's gonna happen."

Leah put her arm around the older woman, who continued to shake her head despairingly. "Pa gone . . . Asa gone . . ."

"Harp's gone too, Ma, most the time," Leah offered as comfort. "He's off three four weeks at a stretch, lumberin'. I get so lonesome I nigh about go crazy up there on that mountain all alone. No neighbors real close, no kids, no nothin' but a few chickens—and panther and bear at night in the woods all around. I get a wishin' for you all so bad I like to die. I jes couldn't stand it no more. I run down the mountain and I keep on running, and when I get to Dalton, Matt gave me a ride on the caboose of old 29 comin this way; and I walk out from Dalton and come home. I ain't no call to go back right off. I can help you with the hayin' and the cotton till lay-by. I can stay and help you, Ma, till Pa gets back maybe."

Sabina rose, throwing up her head. "I jes rest a spell. Get them boys up to the chores, will you?" She laid a hand on her daughter's arm, and there was a faint tremor in her voice as she added, "I sure happy you home again, honey. I sure enough happy about that."

Chapter 7

AMON, Asa, Obey, and Leah all were working in the Jackson fields, and all were aware of the growing tensions and suspicions. Across the miles of cotton and potatoes and peanuts backs bent above the red clay and hoes scraped and chopped, and the talk went on endlessly about Noah's burying and the desperate plight of the two widows and the twelve children. What would Jeff Jackson do with them? Let them stay on in the house with the two front doors? . . . He'd need the house for other workers now with Les and Noah both dead . . . He might could send them to relatives down near Rome . . . Would Miz Jackson take the oldest girl up to work in the big house? . . . She'd have to soak the lice off first . . . Why did Marie and Sheba go on accusing Pula Kemp? . . . They hadn't found any conjure in the well . . . They's purely scared silly is all and don't know what to set they minds to . . . They talk so bad they done got folks edgy . . . The riders is gathering . . . That's what Fez says . . . He knows . . . He's got ears to all that double-talk goes on . . . Yeah, he says don't none of us to go near no voting place, not even near . . .

Accepted, of course, was the knowledge that not all the white folks in the valley were riders or white trash like the Thomans. But their concern was diluted, constrained by the pressures for conformity, and their sense of justice was timorous. Apathy governed the well-meaning, while the more violent elements of white society favored action—coercive, destructive, and cruel.

A Trumpet Sounds

The sun burned hotter and hotter on the bent heads and backs. Beloved work songs swelled from throats parched with thirst. The spirit of the people grew dull with weariness, and slow-moving feet walked out of the field at sundown.

When the boys and Leah returned home, Sabina's washes were piled in neat stacks ready for delivery the next day. Supper was ready and bedtime came with full dark. With sleep Amon's fears, like oblique shadows, swelled and became nightmares: A knock coming to the door . . . a great banging and voices outside in the night calling . . . calling . . . his mother rising from her bed, fumbling in the dark for a candle . . . Leah sitting up on her cot . . . her mouth open and eyes staring wildly in the faint light from the window . . . the banging growing louder . . . voices thundering . . . "Come out!" they were shouting . . . "Come out or we break down the door" . . . and Ma going to the door and opening it . . . Oh, how could she open it when she knew it was the riders! . . . And they were saying . . . "We want Asa . . . Send out Asa." . . . and Asa getting up and going out the door before they could lay hands on Ma . . . and there were the masked men and they had a rope . . . and they dragged Asa out and swung the rope round his head and down on his neck and dragged him off . . . and Ma pleaded . . . and Leah pleaded . . . and he, Amon, rushed out and pleaded . . . "Don't take Asa . . . Please don't take Asa . . . He ain't done nothin'!"

"He ain't done nothin'!' He ain't!' He ain't!" It was a shriek, and it filled the cabin. It woke the other boys, and it brought Leah, padding like a wraith in her nightdress from the other room. She sat on the side of the bed and held Amon.

"That's all right, honey. You've had a bad dream. Don't cry, don't cry."

And then there was a lightening of the window square from the outside. Leah noticed it, and Asa did too, and they went to see what made the sky red in the north.

"Fire," Asa said. "Something's on fire."

Amon stopped weeping. Sabina had roused and was at the door with Obey and Willy and Jeb.

"That's over Ellum's way."

"Beyond," Asa said. "More like Lockwood's." He was pulling on his pants fast. "Jeb, Willy, go get Uncle Zeke and Walt and Uncle Ben. Get everbody you kin find, and hurry." He ran out the door.

Neighbors came from all around, from as far away as Lone Dog Branch and the Forks and Barnum Gulch, came in haste with pails and shovels, to attend what was a foregone disaster. A fire well started could only burn itself out.

They helped Hank salvage what they could from the cabin before the roof fell in and dragged the wagon away from the inferno of the barn. Hank's mules were safe in the pasture, and somebody managed to turn the hogs loose.

Hank Lockwood and his wife and two sons watched with the rest while everything he possessed went up in billows of black smoke. The talk was the same over and over:

"You know how it started?"

"Sure I know, coal oil and torch."

"You seen who done it?"

"I seen them ride away. I come out when the dogs start yelpin'."

"They shot one dog."

"We knowed Schneider's sorel mare right enough. Ain't no mistakin' it."

"I sure as hell woulda liked to take a bead on them."

"They'd got you for certain then, like the dog."

"Fez said the riders was gatherin'."

"I heard."

"We didn't think they'd do nothin' like this."

"Iffen they think you talkin' too big, they never leave you be."

"I know. I ain't got a chance now. They turn all the planters against us. We ain't gonna work nowheres."

Everybody agreed. Lockwood had been singled out to be persecuted as a warning to all the others who thought or spoke as he did. He would be harassed and hounded out of the county.

All night through, the talk went on in whispers and in rueful head-shaking. Some talked louder than others, and there were many who wished to retaliate. "We ought to burn one of their barns . . . We might could set that coop of Bates . . . or set their hayfield . . . Naw, they got more dogs to that place than you kin

A Trumpet Sounds

count. . . . We might could go see Judge Persons. . . . Ha, what he do for you? He say you got to have evidence. Then where are you? You ain't got no evidence, not that you kin mention out loud."

Hank agreed. He had best load the belongings he had salvaged onto his wagon and leave, head north. The Flatlands could no longer be his home.

"Them stinkin' bastards!" Asa exploded for the hundredth time, as he stood beside Sabina, watching the flames sink slowly into gray ash in the early dawn. "I can't abide to live amongst them, I purely can't. I wanna get out. There gotta be somewheres they ain't so cussed mean and ornery. Hank talkin' of goin' north. Where? I dunno. Chattanooga or Knoxville or maybe up further. I wanna go, too, Ma. I plain gotta get away from here."

"Son, what good it gonna do you to run away. You might could run into somethin' worse."

"How could it be worse. Ma, you ain't lookin' at things straight. You don't let yourself see things as they are. If we'd all up and pull out, leave them cold with their field work—nobody round to cut hay or dig potatoes or pick cotton maybe they'd pay us some kinda mind and say we got some rights. Maybe they'd not grind us down. Maybe—"

"How we gonna do that? All of us pull out? Where we all go? Eh? That foolish talk."

"No, it ain't. We gotta rise up and fight back and show em we got guts and we gonna use em."

"Fightin' back ain't no way to settle a argument."

"It's one way. How you figger to settle it then? How?" It was a scream.

"Shussssh."

He lowered his voice, but it hissed with tension. "You talk about dignity. How we gonna have it when we take this sort of thing all the time? We gonna jes lie down and take it and say nothin' on and on all of our days? And no hope of gettin' up ever. All our lives we gonna eat dirt from them white devils?"

"I dunno," Sabina shook her head woefully. "I plain don't know. But they jes gotta be another way."

"Maybe they is. Maybe you find it. But me—I wanna get out

from under now. I wanna go up north with the Lockwoods. Say I can go, Ma. Say you want me to get out from under."

Amon, standing close by, felt the urgency of Asa's plea. He wondered if Asa's way might not be the right way. The thought of bloodshed and brutal fighting was abhorrent to him. In stumbling, little-boy fashion his mind searched round for some other means by which to gain a fair and rightful regard from the white people. Hard work maybe, like Ma urged, or getting real smart, like preacher wanted the books for. He didn't know how, but he wished mightily for some peaceful easement of the awful hurt white people caused.

Sabina was silent, thinking deeply. Presently Leah came and stood beside her, and then Lowillo came and Candy, and they talked around and around this dreadful happening. The sun rose, red and then yellow and hot, and the day began. There was work to do, and if they wanted to earn money, they had to betake themselves to it.

Hay was in and cotton in flower. The corn was waist-high. It was lay-by time and one could ease up a little on the hoe. For the next six weeks there would be school. Hands folded in her lap, Sabina rocked in her creaky chair, both feet flat on the boards of the gallery, creak-pat, creak-pat, back and forth.

She stared out across the moonlit yard, her mind withdrawn, seeing distances beyond the road and the tangled fence row and the field. Now, until cotton picking time, her sons could go to school, could take up their learning where they had left off in the spring. She anticipated each session of school with passionate eagerness, and her heart had ached when Asa had gone as far as one could go in the small Flatlands school. When she had finally consented to Asa's going with the Lockwoods up north, she had urged him to find a means if at all possible to go to one "of them places called college, like Booker Washington talked about."

Schooling for her sons was the goal of all her striving, the bedrock on which she built her hopes for the future. Lay-by meant rest for a spell from concern over crops, but it never meant rest from toil for Sabina. With the boys all in school she would have to draw her own wash water, would have to fetch and tote bundles of

A Trumpet Sounds

laundry and tend the garden patch.

The boys sat on the steps now with Leah, listening to her fairy tales.

"They's better things to study on than them hoodoos and goblins," she protested when Willy screamed with pretended fright over jack-me-lanterns Leah said danced at night in the swamps and tried to lure travelers to their deaths.

"You tell Bible stories, Ma," Obey said. "They's scary too."

"I ain't studyin' 'bout Bible stories now. I'm studyin' 'bout school. It starts tomorrow, and I'm right glad."

"Oh, Ma, why you gotta bring that up? School ain't fun."

"School's a fine thing."

"How you know? You never went."

"I never had no chanct to go to school. When I was a youngun on the plantation, they ain't no school for slave childern. But when I works in the big house, I used to give the master's little George and Mary cookies out in the pantry and then coax 'em to tell me what they learns in school that day. They tells me and I remember every word. That's the only lessons I got. I do craves to read a book, but I ain't never had no chanct to learn. When freedom come, I work hard jes to eat. Ain't day-time left to study or go to school."

She ruminated, her rocker going creak-pat, creak-pat. "We the ignorantest folks. I study on it long and long. Sure as shelled corn, ain't none of us goin' nowheres till we get some learnin'. You can't battle this world with ignorance, and I knows it."

"What good the learnin' do us, Ma? What good?"

"Didn't preacher tell us about that man Booker Washington? Didn't he say freedom can't be give to folks. We all gotta pay for this here freedom. Yes, ma'am, we does. And the price is dear. God knows we gotta pray and pray for strength to meet this price. But law! Ain't it somethin' worth payin' dear for? It like walkin' straight up to the Promise Land and knockin' at the door. You children don't know how sweet this is, this life like you knows. You think it hard. Maybe it be hard, maybe theys a lot ain't rightly honest and just and fair. But you don't rightly know what hard is. You ain't seen the rocks you pappy and mammy done stumble over. Maybe we don't see the rocks up ahead either. This man,

Eunice Young Smith

Washington, he sees them. He say they is plenty of rocks. He knows we gonna fall down. But he wavin' a light to show us the way. He say right off there two things we gotta study on hard. We gotta put brains in our work. That's what he say—put brains in our work."

"What's that mean, Ma, put brains in our work?"

"I reckon he means get all the schoolin' you kin. I study on them words a smart spell. Theys lots of folks do their work jes like they pa did, or they granpa. They don't stop to figger is there a better way to do it. They maybe don't figger a-tall. Now iffen they put brains in what they do, they might could come up with a better way to do it, see?"

"That's easy to say, Ma," Leah objected. "But you can't read a book on how some big planter does and then you go ahead and do it. The big planter starts with more money and more land and more cattle, more hogs, more hands to do the work, and what's more, he got nobody on his neck holdin' him back."

"Don't you steer me off the track. I knows what I mean. This man Washington didn't start off with it easy. He was a slave jes like me. It were worse when he tried to get started, I kin tell you, plenty worse. But that boy learn to read, and then he read and read and the more he read the more his brains growed and the more they growed—"

"You jes makin' all that up, Ma," Willy interrupted. "You don't know all that for certain."

"Yes, I do so know it. And I knows another thing. All over this land, all the places where they reads them newspapers, folks is hearin' that man's words, and harkin' to them too. And that about brains ain't all he say. He say we gotta make our work dignify. We gotta know we childern of God and do our work proudful."

"What we got to be proud of, Ma?" Leah's quiet words stabbed the shadows. "Because we work till we drop for a few dollars? Because we gotta do what some white man say or we starve? We proud because we kin crawl on our bellies up to somebody's back door and say: 'Kin I please pick your cotton? Kin I please cut your trees? I take any pay you wanna give me for the honor of workin' for you.' Is that doing it proudful?"

59

A Trumpet Sounds

"I ain't never heard you talk like that, Leah."

"It's the truth."

"Maybe it is, and maybe it ain't. I ain't thinkin' along them furrows." Sabina's mouth slid around on her face as she strove to clarify her thoughts. "We can't show nobody nothin' when we so ignorant. That clear as day. We jes don't know enough to battle them smart folks. We gotta get schoolin'." She clenched her hands hard between her bony knees, and her eyes glowed in the dark sadness of her face. "We got a right to be self-respectin', no matter what. We can be proud we childern of God. We can be proud do we live decent and be forgivin' and kind. We can be proud iffen we do what's right."

"Why should we be proud to do what's right. The white folks ain't."

"We can set them a mold to copy."

"Oh, Ma! You reckon the white folks gonna pattern on us?"

"They might could do worse."

She stopped rocking and the creak-pat ceased while the frogs and the crickets became boisterous. The children quieted and sat staring out into the moonlight. Like the rest, Amon was still, but his thoughts were a tangle of question and puzzlement. It was strange to him that his mother became so riled by words read to her from a newspaper. Maybe they were nice words, maybe they did make sense. But what did it have to do with them? With Ma and Pa and his brothers and Leah and himself? Booker Washington was just a name, somebody way off somewhere who got something printed in a newspaper. It did not seem to touch his life. What did it have to do with his eating and sleeping and getting up and going to the fields and milking the cow and slopping the hogs? What did it have to do with the sky full of clouds and the moon making long arms in the yard or the hooty owl or the sliver in his finger? Yet this man's words had the power to disturb his mother, to rile her up about school and all. So they scratched him too. His mother's next words disturbed him further.

"I long to see our people better off," she said. "I can't do much 'cept tend them when they gets sick and help bury them when they dies. But I got five sons, an' I wanna see them do somethin'."

Eunice Young Smith

"You didn't talk that way to Asa," Obey mumbled. "He wanna do something."

Leah added, "That's what Asa said Lockwood wanted, a chance to get up off our rumps and show we have the right to dignity and pride."

"But not their way," Sabina snapped. "Not their way—by givin' back with hate and cruelness. There's another way—" She broke off, floundering in uncertainty.

"How, Ma?"

"I dunno. I dunno." It was almost a groan. "But they must be another way to lead the childern out of the land of bondage. One of you boys maybe find it, God willin' . . . and you set our feet on the right path. Maybe you, Jeb. Maybe Amon here. Maybe he be a preacher."

"Oh, Ma." A preacher! The very word made Amon shiver. It hit at him like the pronouncement of doom.

Chapter 8

PA came home finally, thin as a scarecrow, his clothes filthy and ragged. With no fuss at all he settled back into the familiar routine of the farm. He took over the chores of milking and fence fixing as though he had never been away. No one questioned him. He accepted Leah's presence with complacent good will, as though she were permanently once again one of the family.

He heard about the Lockwoods' ruin and Asa's going but declined to be drawn into a discussion of either. At such times he withdrew into Indian enigmatic silence.

Then Leah said she had to return to her cabin on the mountain.

"Harp be comin' home soon now. I best be there. Ma, let me take Amon back with me for a spell."

Much as her heart hovered over Leah, Sabina had been reluctant to consent to Amon's going when school was in session and was won over only when Leah promised to teach him, "same as the school would," while he was with her.

So Sabina had said he could go "until pickin' time anyways." She had folded his clean shirt and overalls and put them in a crocus sack with his shoes and a cake of soap. She had given him a quilt, too, saying Leah might be short of covers. She filled a sack with potatoes and another with ripe tomatoes and wrapped up some dried peas and meal and the last chunk of smoked meat in the springhouse. Sabina fussed over Leah, urging things on her until Leah protested they could carry no more.

The bundles had been a penance all along the way, lightened only by their eating the tomatoes and Amon's wearing his shoes. After the seven-mile walk from the farm into Calhoun, the ride in the empty boxcar had been blissful. Amon had never gone so fast in his life.

When the train neared Dalton, Leah gathered up their packages, making one big bundle wrapped in the quilt, and made ready to jump. Amon would always remember with a gasp his plunge off the slackening train, his feet racing out from under him, his big shoes plowing the wind until the earth came up and hit him in a sliding slap. Leah tossed the bundle off and he heard it hit the ground with a *smack-thud,* and then he saw Leah leap after it and run and fall too.

They scrambled together after the bundle and lugged it along the tracks and across a place where there were high board fences and heaps of coal. Amon's shoes kept sliding around and rubbing his heels into sores and the bundle seemed impossible for them to lift up the steep bank above the rails.

Then at last they were out on a street where there were stores and houses lined up one right after another. Near an alley they set the bundle down and Leah separated the bags and parcels for them to carry. Going through Dalton there had been so much to see, so many people and wagons and buggies and buildings, he had been distracted from his fatigue. Now they were outside of the town on the road going north toward the mountain. They sat under a hickory tree by the side of the road to eat the corn bread and sweet potato Ma had given them for lunch.

Amon licked the crumbs from his fingers. The front of him was covered with cinders and his shirt was torn. It was muggy hot, and sweat mixed with dirt to encrust him.

"I'm dry as a wood tick in a drouth."

"Maybe we'll come to a branch."

"Could we stop at a farmhouse an' ask?"

"Dogs is mean to strangers."

They picked up their bundles and started on again. Amon carried his shoes hanging from their laces around his neck and his

A Trumpet Sounds

feet were thankful. The sun had gone under and a heaviness lay in the air. Not a leaf stirred. It took exertion of will to move. Even without the sun, sweat trickled down their faces and necks and between their shoulder blades. Leah studied the sky, singing to herself, "I'm gonna lay down my heavy load . . . Jesus . . . some day . . . some day . . ."

"It feels like rain, don't it?" Amon said.

"Corn need it bad."

"Cotton looks good though. Cotton sure one dry-weather plant."

They stared at a farmer's vast cotton stand, and Leah said, "Nobody raises cotton up mountain. I miss a sight of the fields spreadin' wide an' the rows taperin' to a point way off yonder and the pickers with their bags takin' off the puffs of white."

"What mountain folks do if they ain't got cotton?"

"It's a marvel how they make out."

"What folks do to eat?"

"Some of them don't hardly. Some raises a few apples or cabbages maybe. They grub out a little ledge and plant a little truck. Some of the women weaves and knits. They make right pretty cloth. That's the trouble livin' in the mountain. Land's cheap and the people buy it, and they don't figger how they gonna make out from that poor land. Nobody has enough to do with on the mountain, except maybe the moonshiners. Liquor is about the one money crop. If they kin keep a still hid from the revenuers, they do all right."

"Where they got their stills?"

"Oh, round in caves and such. The agents don't find too many. Sometimes I think they blind on purpose 'cause they know the mountain folk ain't got much to do with."

"You reckon anybody'll ever find Fez Babber's still?"

Leah shrugged. "Ain't so far. You know where it's hid?"

"No, but Pa do. He's been there. But he wouldn't tell nobody on Fez."

"Sun ain't come back yet; air so heavy. Sure look like rain, don't it?"

They had turned off the pike and were traveling a narrow dirt road. Amon lagged. His arms ached painfully. Leah stopped and put her bundles down. "Give me the quilt," she said.

She spread it out on the ground and put the bundles of clothes and the sacks of food in the center. "I can tie it all together and tote it on my head. It be easier than arm carryin'."

"You can't carry it all," Amon protested, but he hoped she could.

"You tote the meat then, and your shoes." She lapped the quilt up over the bundles and tied the four corners together as tightly as she could, then hoisted the pack to her head. She balanced it for a moment with her hands, then walked poised and steady, her arms swinging. Amon grinned up into her face, half-hidden by the sagging folds of the quilt.

"Kin you pack that on your head all the way up mountain?"

"I reckon not the last half. It gets pretty steep."

"It ain't so hot now no more."

"They's a breeze stirrin'. It gonna rain."

"It best hold off till we get to Buzzard's Roost."

"Ain't rained in so long it'll take a spell to work up a good wet."

"Will Harp be home when we get there?"

"Might could be. Can't never tell when he get back. When the foreman say they got enough cut for a while, the men go home." She shrugged. "Few days, then they goes off again. You tired, honey?"

"It's a powerful long way, ain't it?"

Leah half-spoke, half-sang: "Lord, I don't feel no ways tired . . . Children! . . . I hope to shout glory . . . Children! . . . Ain't no ways tired . . . ain't no ways . . . huuummmm hummm." Amon did not join in, and after a few hummed bars she stopped.

They had left the dirt road for a lane now narrowed by weeds and vines to a pair of wheel tracks. Walking was difficult. they passed a deserted cabin, its doors and windows gaping holes, the ground around it planted to the steps in drouth-sick cowpeas. The wheel ruts wound on through dry pastures and scrub and patches of woodland and long stretches of parched clay supporting little besides vetch and sandspurs.

Presently the trail began to climb. It still was wide enough for a mule and wagon, but rough and eroded in places. The sky had

A Trumpet Sounds

grown steadily darker and in the somber light the country around seemed to Amon sad and forsaken. His legs ached. Leah was now holding the bundle with one hand for the way was rutty and ascending.

She said, "This is where we take the nigh cut, this path here. It goes straight up. The road goes round."

It was dark beneath the trees and a wind worried them, complaining. The path climbed steeply, skirting projecting rock, bridging a stream by means of a fallen log. Leah tripped across this and came up so short on the other side Amon collided with her. She stood motionless. He peered around her. What he saw made his hair stiffen. Six feet in front of them a weird struggle was taking place; a still writhing black snake was being devoured by a rattler. The meal was only half engorged, the jaws of the rattler working slowly, now top, now bottom, while the body of its hapless victim, fully as big as the rattlesnake, still whipped about in the dust.

Cautiously, so slowly she seemed hardly to move at all, Leah backed, pushing Amon off the path and behind a rocky ledge. She eased the bundle from her head. Her eyes scanned the ground nearby. She found a fallen branch, overlong, but stout, and holding it aloft went stealthily back to the path. High above her head she raised the cudgel and then with furious force brought it down on the head of the rattler. The impact bounced both snakes into the air—just as lightning cracked and thunder roared. Horrified, Amon watched the two snakes plunge and coil and thrash under Leah's frenzied pounding until at last they lay quiet and the thunder petered out into a low grumbling.

Leah stood back then and threw the pole from her. She rubbed her hands down her thighs, then wiped her arm across her dripping face.

"Judas," Amon whimpered. "Judas—a snake in the home path. That one awful bad sign." He felt a sudden wave of sickness.

"Ain't as bad a sign as it would have been iffen we'd stepped on it. The bundle kept my eyes lookin' down is why I seen 'em so quick." She went to gather up the bundle again. She was winded and her hands shook. Amon faltered at the sight. He said, "Leah, let's get us another pole and tie the bundle on it, and then you kin

Eunice Young Smith

tote one end and I'll take the other."

Leah sighed gratefully. "That's a right smart idea. We get us a branch with a crotch still on. It'll keep the bundle from sliding down the back end as we goin up. We best hurry now. Rain gonna break any minute."

They skirted the rock escarpment and came to the path above where the snakes lay. Up and up now they had fought their way against a tattering wind, lifting and dragging and bumping the bundle. Every muscle was taxed to the utmost. It had become very dark. In the flashes of lightning Amon could see Leah up ahead, bending into the onrushing storm, one arm flung across her face, guarding it from whipping branches, the other holding tightly to the pole. Big raindrops spattered the leaves like shot. More lightning and a crash of thunder sent Amon sprawling, dropping his end of the pole. He pulled himself up, scrambled for the pole end, fear making him clumsy.

"How far we gotta go, Leah?" He screamed to be heard above the rushing wind and thrashing branches. "Ain't we nigh there?"

Leah dragged at the pole with both hands, pulling Amon, lifting their burden over a fallen tree. Then she disappeared behind a wall of water.

A cloud had burst. They were drenched in seconds, the quilt and all that was in it soaked and weighted to the ground. They staggered against the sodden bundle. Trees thrashed over and around them, moaning. It was dark except when lightning ripped open the sky and lit the rocking trees.

Amon screamed in terror. Had there been a cave, a hole, any cover at all, panic would have driven him to it. But there was no protection here, only the wind-beaten, battling girl up ahead.

Leah's feet slid out from under her. Again and again she went to her knees, then pulled up again, rocks rolling away under her feet. Like a tiny skiff in an angry sea she battled into the face of the storm. Up and up. She caught at a waving branch and held fast while water plunged beneath her. On again, up and up, inch by inch she dragged the waterlogged bundle, the pole, and the boy the last hundred feet onto the ledge which was, to her, home ground. Yonder, through a curtain of rain, was the cabin.

A Trumpet Sounds

The gale rushed at them across the clearing, forcing them to fight for every step ahead. The wind billowed Leah's dress like a sail and threw Amon off his feet. He crawled the last few yards of open ground.

At last, exhausted, they reached the door. Leah opened it and dragged pole, bundle, and boy within. The wind whipped the door to, and Leah put the bar in place. They stood panting in the shadowy cabin. Then Amon slid to his knees, numb, emptied of thought and fear. He put his head on the soggy bundle and closed his eyes. He knew he could never move again.

Chapter 9

When Amon awoke next morning, sunlight filled the open cabin door. He stretched stiff muscles and rolled on his side, adjusting his mind to new surroundings, recalling the events of yesterday. A shaft of light lay across the muddied place on the floor where he and Leah had dropped their mired clothes and the bundle the night before. Somewhere outside he could hear Leah singing: "Sister Mary, Mary Jane . . . Why'nt you come along . . . Why'nt you come along . . . Ummm . . ."

He rolled out of bed and went to the door. The air was washed clean and cool, and the forest smelled pungent sweet. He ran behind the bushes at the back of the cabin to where Leah was swinging an axe, making chunks fly from a pine log.

"Howdy, boy," she greeted him. "You sure sleep like the dead. You hungry?"

Amon took the axe from her. "I'll chop. It'll limber me. You had breakfast?"

"Not yet. I sleep late too. We come a far piece yesterday. Soon as I get a fire goin' I'll make us some porridge." She gathered up some of the chopped sticks.

Amon lifted the axe, then stood and grinned at his sister. "No cows to fetch and milk, no fowl scratchin' round, no mule to feed, no dogs even smellin' round-" He shrugged and shook his head.

"There will be after today, boy. I'm fetchin' home the goats."

"Goats! Where you got 'em?"

A Trumpet Sounds

"To a neighbor's. I'll carry you along when I go for 'em." She stood for a moment looking at the frowzy garden patch. "Everything sure go to pot when your back is turned. Look at them weeds in the squash vines. But it ain't all bad. Weeds make good feed for the goats." She started to walk away and then turned to Amon again. "You fill my wash kettle and make me a fire under it and I'll wash them filthy things ornamenting the line there. I don't aim to carry you round the mountain with no pants on."

Amon looked down at himself in Harp's old coat that Leah had put on him last night when she had stripped off his wet and muddy clothes. What a sorry sight he was for sure. He picked up the axe and went to work with vigor. "I'll fill the kettle," he called after her, "do you wash my pants first thing."

"Sure," she laughed as she went to the cabin singing:

You naked as a lil ol' jay bird
  The day that he was born . . . the day that he was born
But you get feathers by an by
  Iffen you eat your corn . . . iffen you eat your corn . . .

As they were eating breakfast, Amon spied the guitar hanging above the mantelpiece. "Hey, Leah, you didn't tell me you had one of them. Can you play on it?"

"Sure, I can play. It's Harp's. He showed me how to work it. I can't make it wail like he can, but I can pick a tune from those strings. You want to hear it?" She smiled at his eagerness. "I figured you would. Finish your mush and I'll take it down."

Amon emptied the bowl with a rush. Leah took the guitar down then and rubbed her thumb over the strings, making a sweet chord. Fascinated, Amon watched his sister's long fingers pluck music from the strings while she sang, "Mammy's lil baby loves shortenin', shortenin'—Mammy's lil baby loves shortenin' bread."

She threw back her head, laughing, patting one foot as she sang loud and free and Amon, with delight, joined in:

Put on de kettle, put on de lid
My lil baby wants shortenin' bread.

Together they sang several verses. Then, still patting her foot, her body swaying, Leah began an old religious song: "Goin' to

Eunice Young Smith

have a happy meetin' . . . Goin' to shout an' never tire . . . Goin' to the promised land . . . mmmm."

The guitar so enthralled Amon he could not contain his joy. He sprang up and threw himself round and round until he was dizzy. The sleeves of Harp's coat flapped beyond the end of his hands, his skinny legs looked like the point of a top as he whirled. At last he pulled up in front of Leah, panting. "Can I touch it, Leah? Please, say I can touch it."

"Sure you can touch it."

With trembling fingers he touched the strings, the keys and the smooth wood of the box. "Boy-man! I purely craves to play on that thing."

"It's not hard to learn. I reckon if I can, you can."

"Would you show me, Leah? Would you for real?"

"Sit down," she said, "and roll them sleeves up. Now, hold it like I did, and put your fingers so." She laid her fingers on the fretted board. "Now, go across the strings with your thumb. There. See, you made a chord. Now put your fingers so and so and make another chord." He placed his fingers as Leah showed him and he played the chords over and over. His quick ear caught the tones and branded in his memory the position of his fingers on the strings that produced them.

Leah said, "Now play the chords one after another faster and sing, 'Jimmy crack corn—' Go on."

He did. Over and over he played the chords and sang: "Jimmy crack corn an' I don't care . . . Jimmy crack corn an' I don't care . . . Ol' master's gone away." His accomplishment excited him.

And his readiness to learn pleased Leah. She said, "You won't have no trouble playin' the guitar, Amon. All the trouble you gonna have is gettin' anything done around here but the playin'. And it ain't all guitar playin' when we get them goats home. It takes a heap of the day tending them."

She took the guitar from Amon and placed it back on its hook. "We'll play some more tonight. But right now we got work to do. You can scrub up this dirty floor while I wash our clothes."

She gave him a corn-shuck mop and Amon went to fill a bucket with water from a spring that bubbled out of the rocks behind the cabin and ran in a shallow ditch across the clearing before it tumbled down the mountain side.

"There's a nice bank of clean sand out there," she called after him, "to scour with. But first fill my wash kettle and light the fire."

Amon scrubbed the floor conscientiously, rinsing it afterwards with buckets of fresh water and swishing all out the door. When the floor dried, certain areas appeared lighter than the rest. Amon shook his head over this, unaware of those moments when, lost in contemplation of the guitar, he had scrubbed back and forth endlessly in one spot.

With the cabin clean again and the clothes hanging fresh on the line, Leah said, "Your overalls will dry quick in the sun. Then we go after the goats. Reckon Eulie and Nora will be glad to see me back. They been keepin' my goats 'most a month now."

With clean shirt and overalls on, Amon felt renewed. He skipped and hopped along beside Leah as they made their way around the mountain to a more open section where the land leveled to a narrow plateau. Here Eulie Tuggs and his wife Nora lived alone, their children having married and gone away from the mountain. They had kept Leah's goats with their herd, for they were fond of Leah as though she had been a daughter.

When Amon and Leah came from the trees into open ground a dog raced, barking, to meet them in a delirium of welcome. He pounced on her, licking her face and hands. He fawned, then rolled over on the ground. He tore madly around the yard in wide circles, then came with a rush to Leah with slobbering affection.

Nora, too, was overjoyed to see Leah and to meet Amon. She hugged them both to her broad bosom and her shiny round face creased with pleasant folds. She urged them into the cabin and immediately set about brewing a pot of coffee. She called Eulie in from the barn, and they all sat down at the kitchen table over freshly baked bread and cheese, and exchanged news and gossip. Nora wanted to know everything about Leah's family and everything that had happened to her on her visit home. They in turn told her all about the happenings on the mountain.

Eulie said he lost one of his kids. "Bear got him. Yep. Seen the tracks plain. That lil kid was easy to ketch though. It were a pindly lil ol' one, always layin' down sort of tired-like. Reckon he got shortchanged on milk right from the start. Didn't have a show with them two doe kids beatin' him to rations every meal. Reckon I'd have eaten him myself iffen the bear didn't beat me to it."

Leah's two does and two kids were doing fine, he said. After they had finished eating, they went to the field where Eulie's dog, Rinx, was guarding the herd. Leah found her goats without trouble and went to them. They seemed to know her, for they licked her hands and nuzzled her. The two kids, born in May, were husky youngsters, frisky and playful. Leah considered the little buck, mindful that shortly he would be a nuisance in her small flock. She said, "Nora, you any hens you cravin' to sell?"

"Maybe. What you got in mind?"

"I'd favor a hen or two that's layin' so's I could give this here boy an egg now and then. Maybe make him a sweeten cake too." She pulled Amon against her and fondled his head. "Eulie, would you make a swap? My little buck for three hens and a clutch of settin' eggs?"

Nora looked at Eulie and they both nodded, but Eulie said, "That ain't a fittin' swap, gal. But I tell you what. I'll throw in some feed, a little grain, and some good hay and we'll call it square, eh?"

It was agreed that they should drive the goats home, but that Eulie would bring the hens and the grain and the hay by mule. Nora gave Leah fifteen eggs and the speckled hen she said had already raised one brood and was hankering to set on another. "She's a good mother, that one. Eulie'll fetch the hens to your place, but you best tote the eggs yourself do you want they should arrive whole." She laughed and slapped Amon on the back. "I shore glad you brung your little brother back to keep you company for a spell." Her gaze rested on Leah with unabashed affection. "When your man comin' home?"

"Any day, I reckon. We lookin' for him any day now."

Goats, Amon was soon to learn, were more trouble than cows. They had to be watched constantly. It was not safe to let them stray too far. Sometimes they were staked out in grassy

A Trumpet Sounds

places in the hills, the stakes being moved as soon as an area was grazed clean. Sometimes the tethers caught on brambles or wound around small trees and the foolish goats would stand shackled to their chins and bleat unceasingly until rescued. And so, when other work permitted, Amon stayed with them. He liked this, for it was a leisure when he could dream, could practice bird calls and, holding an imaginary guitar, could pick out tunes of songs he knew.

But there was more work to be done around Leah's small farm than he had thought possible that first day of arrival. Hoeing the vegetable patch free of weeds had kept him busy for days. All the weeds were shaken clean and put in the racks for the goats. Leah kept their shed scrupulously clean. The does, she said, were fussy creatures, wanting always to be clean.

Amon scrubbed out the pig house and readied it for the hens. He cut poles for roosts and gathered grass for the laying nests. He fixed a corner for the speckled hen, building a partition with locust saplings so the other hens could not eat her grain and water.

In the days that followed he helped Leah repair loose shingles on the roof, and he cut wood until his arms ached. Nights in the mountain were cold, even in summer. Together they hunted foxgrape and huckleberries, and together they set snares for wild turkey and squirrel, which Leah made into savory stews, cooking them slowly over the coals in the fireplace.

Leah found an old pair of Harp's trousers and washed them and cut them to size for Amon. They were of a soft cloth, not duck, and Amon liked them. One day he and Leah had gone down mountain to the Forks where the nearest store and post office were. They bought salt and meal and molasses, Leah counting out the nickels and pennies carefully. She had only what she had earned while working in the Jackson fields, and it would have to last them until Harp got home. She asked at the postal window for a letter, but there was none. Harp, she said, was a poor one at letters, though he could read and wrote a beautiful hand. But he was always moving from place to place with the gang of rough men and had little opportunity to write letters or to get them.

Eunice Young Smith

Sometimes Amon spent whole afternoons herding the goats, moving them from one place of forage to another. Then he would guide them home at evening, waiting patiently while they sipped water at the trough before he milked the does.

He would wash outside and come to the cabin door adrip, savoring the good smells of okra and corncakes. Then a wave of joy would half-drown him, a deep thankfulness for food and firelight and Leah; and then for something more—that delight that always came with the lifting down of the guitar. He knew Leah would make him study his spelling words first and his writing and reading, but afterward there would always be time for them to sing and play.

Over their meal now they talked of what they would do on the morrow.

"Maybe Harp come tomorrow." Amon had been saying that every day since he'd been there.

"Maybe. Can't never tell when he come. He best get here before our money runs out."

"We kin catch us another squirrel."

"There's still stuff in the garden."

"We got milk and cheese. You make real good cheese."

"We might could sell some down to the Forks."

They often talked of the guitar and how Harp came by it from a man who owed him money and couldn't pay and so gave the guitar instead, and how easy it had been for Harp to learn to play.

"He's full of music," Leah said. "That's how come he got his call name. Folks say he makes music like the harp of an angel. And he sure do. When he comes home, he'll play for you and sing. You like he is, Amon. You're full up of music too. You sing so sweet." She paused, looking at him fondly, her head tilted. "Wouldn't it be something iffen you be a real good singer one day—maybe sing in one of them concert halls in the city?"

"What's a concert hall, Leah?"

"Harp's been to one, up in Chattanooga. Lots and lots of people come—oh, hundreds of people—and they pay money to go there to hear the singin'."

"Sure enough?"

75

"It must be a fair sight—everyone all dressed up beautiful, and the carriages and all—and they comes to hear the singin'."

"Who do the singin'?"

"Oh, different people I reckon."

"How they get to do them songs in a concert, huh?"

"I dunno exactly, but I reckon you have to be purely smart."

"I could never sing in one of them places, Leah." Amon was seeing all the crowd, all the faces staring.

"Why not?"

"I'd be plum scared silly of all them people." He thought for a moment, then added, "But I sure would like to sing to 'em if I could."

"You jes a little boy now. When you get growed, you be different. But you have to go to school and get an education first, like Ma says."

"She purely hept on schoolin', ain't she?"

"She's right, Amon. I do a lot of thinkin' when I'm alone up here. I think a lot about us—not jes you and me—all of us colored people down here in the South. It seem to me we like men in a road gang, fastened together with chains round our necks—workin' along, workin' along, with our backs bent and lashed. We hungry and some of us is sick but we can't do nothin' 'bout it. We get so tired and so discouraged but we can't do nothin' but jes go along—all the time. Can't look up at the sky. Can't hope it goin' to be any different. Can't step outta line. We jes like the road gang. We ain't got the chains round our necks as you can touch, but we got them right enough. And who gonna break them chains, Amon? Nobody gonna break them lessen we do it ourselves. Jes like Ma say . . ."

"How we gonna break chains, Leah? Do you reckon Asa gonna break some? You reckon that's why he gets so mad and talks rash-like? He wants to fight the white people, wants all the Negroes to gather together and march out like soldiers and really fight. He says the Civil War done free the slaves but now we got something jes as bad laid on us. I can't figure all that Asa means when he talks—he gets so wrathy. He purely hates the white folks."

"I know. He gotta lot of spirit, but I'm not sure it's aimed right. It don't seem to me hate gets anybody very far. Mostly it gets back hate, don't it?"

"Asa says the white folks got no conscience, and iffen we wasn't good to work for them they'd be shed of us right off."

"I don't know, Amon. Seems like we should be able to live side by side without so much sorrow and hurt. We all jes human beings, all sort of sorry and weak and unseeing. Maybe could something sweet and gentle get mixed in with all the other feelings."

"Like what, Leah?"

"Like singin' maybe. When folks sing together, they feel good. Music unhates people."

"Let's sing now, Leah. Get down the guitar and let's us sing."

So they sang, drifting from the work songs to the blues songs Leah had learned from Harp, to the spirituals they loved to sing together. They devised harmonies and spun out refrains until the sounds became hypnotic. When they sang the words of the old song:

> *Green tree a-bendin',*
> *Ol' sinner done a-tremblin'*
> *A trumpet sounds within-a my soul.*

Amon said fervently, "That how I feel when I sing, Leah—like a trumpet goin' off inside me."

"I know," she said, patting his hand. "But now it's time for bed. And you had no lessons tonight. We make up for it tomorrow. Tomorrow we do double."

It seemed to Amon that he had scarcely got to sleep when Bruno set up a fierce barking. There was a heavy thud against the door and a gutteral growl. Bear, Amon thought, as he saw Leah rise, her figure ghostly in her long white gown. Bear! And we got no gun. What would they do if the latch gave? He saw her creep toward the door hesitantly, listening. Then the thumping came again and she said, "Who's there?"

A man's voice bellowed, "It's me, Harp. Let me in."

In a moment the door was thrown wide and Harp stepped

A Trumpet Sounds

across the threshold and engulfed Leah in a smothering hug. He lifted her off her feet and whirled her around.

"Lady, lady, lady! Am I glad to be home." He kissed her and Leah clung to him, making funny choked sounds. They held together and rocked back and forth, Harp's big arms crushing her close. Then he saw Amon standing like a stump in the middle of the room.

He roared, "Great Jehoshaphat! Who's that?"

Leah twisted in his arms, laughing through tears. "It's Amon, silly. Don't you recollect my little brother?"

"Too dark in here. Can't see." He strode to the fire and threw on some fatwood sticks. "Light the candle, sugar-bun. Build up the fire. Put on the kettle. I'm home. Your Harp's home. It's fair dayclean and I been travelin' the night through. I'm done up there for three weeks, and I ain't wastin' no daylight to come home." His laughter filled the cabin. He banged the table with his fist and all the dishes bounced and rattled. Amon stood agape, relief and joy drowning him. Harp tweaked his ear.

"Get you pants on, boy, and come alive. This is a great day in the morning!"

Chapter 10

Cotton was bursting from the bolls when Amon made his way home in August. He could see pickers in the fields everywhere as he stumped the last weary miles out from Calhoun, his shoes dangling from their laces around his neck, his new breeches tied securely in his bundle. It was late in the day and the sun was lowering. Singing voices carried far on the still air. Amon felt a soaring joy. It seemed to him that he had been gone a long time and that he was somehow changed. Everything seemed familiar, yet different, himself different also, as though he had grown beyond certain things he formerly knew and could see them clearly in a new light.

He kicked at the dust and whistled the tune of "Little Liza Jane." At the edge of their land he startled a guinea hen feeding with her brood in the weeds beside the road. She flew up with a clatter of voice and wing, followed by the young fowl, and they wheeled across the road and over some low bushes into a cornfield. The brittle clack of her cry had an astringent effect on his spirit, dissipating his weariness and sharpening his pleasure in being home. As he turned into the yard, Race and Lulu lifted from their slumber by the gallery steps, stretching forward from their hind legs and giving an unenthusiastic "wuff wuff." Amon spoke to them.

The sun, slanting low through the mulberry tree, dappled a triangle on the gallery boards. The house was deserted. Everyone,

A Trumpet Sounds

Amon knew, would be in the fields until sundown. He carried his bundle into the cabin, his eyes athirst for the sight of familiar hearth and kettle and table and chest and the box with Ma's mending. He saw a letter against the candle on the mantel and took it down to examine it. It was addressed to his mother and he recognized Asa's writing. There was no return address, but the postmark was Nashville, Tennessee.

He went into the bedroom where he had slept all his life until he had gone with Leah to Buzzard's Roost. He touched the hickory board of the bed head and ran his fingers down the covers. He remembered then that he had forgotten to bring home the quilt. It did not alarm him; his gladness was too large to be spoiled by regrets.

"I'm home," he told himself. "I'm home." He hummed a few bars as he went across the front room to the shed kitchen. "Lord, I'm comin' home . . . Gonna lay down my heavy load . . . huuum-mmm." He stood there in the kitchen, his senses feeding greedily on the peaceful order, the lingering odors of ironed clothes and scrub water. Even the shadows seemed friendly, and he became impatient to see Ma and Pa and all his brothers, to hear the family chatter, to learn what was in the letter from Asa. Ma would tell him to open it and read it to them all, although Obey had no doubt read it to them already many times.

The sun lowered and evening shadows gathered swiftly. Old Lightning stood at the barnyard gate, his head hanging loosely over the rails. A few hens scratched in the yard, and Amon could hear Betsy mooing for someone to come and milk her.

Then they came trooping in, and once again he was surrounded by his family, being asked a thousand questions, hearing all the gossip of the Flatlands, all the nonsense of the younger boys, hearing that Asa had a job with the railroad in Nashville. Ma was proudful in the telling and seemed eased of her anxiety over Asa, although Asa's letter, when Amon read it to himself later, hinted of activity other than laying ties and rails.

Then the days slipped into the pattern of the usual, the relentless labor, the sizzling heat, the bottomless sleep at night. Each morning after their breakfast of mush and milk and syrup, when the day was barely light, Sabina had the boys up and at the chores. There was much work at home to do before the sun had dried the dew off the cotton and they could head for the fields.

Every family in the Flatlands picked cotton, even children younger than Jeb, even old people like Granny Rachel, even mothers with nursing babies who had to leave the infants under the trees in the charge of other infants only slightly larger. Even Uncle Zeke picked cotton. His back, which made its protest to every other demand, subsided before the lure of cash money—and cotton was cash money.

Hour after hour, men, women, and children bent above the cotton plants in the blazing sun. Throats dried and thickened, vision blurred, backs screamed, shoulders ached under the load of picksacks. But the people sang. Above the waves of heat the old melodies and refrains flowed and ebbed away across the fields, away into endless distances, into endless silences and back again.

Amon picked with the rest, lifting the fat white bolls and stuffing them into his sack, over and over endlessly. It was numbing, thought-sapping, yet once an inexplicable rapture had possessed him. The searing heat, the deadly tiredness, were for a moment submerged in a strange ecstasy. His heavy, light-blinded eyes stared down the vanishing rows of cotton plants narrowing to a point at the horizon. Some ancient, wind-bent water oaks silhouetted against the glowing sky away off at the end of the field appeared to him like people plodding onward across a great distance—forever bent, forever stumbling, but going onward and upward toward that descending white ball in the sky. It touched something in the boy's mind, the bordering of a dream, a dim knowing of these people in the fields, a knowing of them as a part of himself, yet a part of the whole universe, and he a part of both. The twisted shapes of the trees seemed like giant figures representing a limitless number of humankind, staggering, groping, falling and getting up and plodding on—upward toward a great gathering—a heavenly choir. And the music that swelled from that choir out over the earth and out among the stars was beautiful beyond words to tell. The sun lowered slowly, golden pillars of light reaching pink-edged clouds, dispersing them, turning them to violet and fiery red before it faded. The vision vanished.

A Trumpet Sounds

Sundown and supper, home and bed. Amon went about his usual chores knowing an elation apart from his deadly weariness, a strange mixture of feelings unaccountable to him, a remnant of his ecstasy in the cotton field. He let the cows out to pasture after Pa milked, moving behind them patiently, not caring to hurry them, absorbed in his thought. Nightjars called, their plaintive cries coming thinly from the woods behind the barn. Dark descended.

Another day was gone, another link in the chain of days . . . getting up and eating and then chores and going to the fields and coming home and more chores and eating and then sleep . . . and then getting up and starting another day . . . and you went away on a certain morning and you climbed a mountain . . . and there your days were filled with the sounds of a guitar . . . and you came back down off the mountain and things didn't seem the same quite . . . yet they were the same . . . nothing changed . . . picking cotton just the same as always . . . folks bickering over silly things . . . same as always . . . singing, too, same as always . . . songs that eased the back and lifted the heart . . . singing sweet as birds at dayclean . . . folks singing all over a cotton field . . . folks bent over but still singing . . . dragging heavy picksacks but still singing . . . singing red and singing blue and singing purple sometimes . . . and gold like in the sunset . . . sounds like colors . . . like the things you felt . . . like something you didn't know, only felt deep down under . . . singing . . . singing . . . Leah singing with the guitar . . . Leah saying maybe singing was important . . . me singing . . . singing . . . singing . . . *me singing!*

Chapter 11

Hunched against a whittling wind, Jordan plunged after his harrow. It was a right time for planting winter grain Sabina had said and, protesting, he had cleared a small field for oats. His breath came in gusty white streams as he sang and shouted at Lightning, "Gonna go up there on de judgment day . . . Gee there, mule . . . Haw! . . . ummm on a judgment day . . . hummm te tummm te tum . . . Hallelujah! . . . Oh, the chariot's a-comin' . . . the chariot's a-comin' . . . Hallelujah to the lamb! . . . Gee there, mule . . . gee! Move, you ol' fool . . . Hallelujah!"

Amon, broadcasting the seed, giggled, forgetting momentarily the wind that haggled his thin coat. There had been rain and sleet for two days and then a light fall of snow. The newly turned earth, brittle with ice, was sharp as needles against his feet. His fingers were stiff with cold, but his insides mirthed warm to his father's silly jargon. At the edge of the field Jordan halted, studying the sky, then shifting his gaze to the woods, then to the ground at his feet. "Coon track round here thick, boy," he observed. "Them varmints is plain wastin' for the stewpot."

"You study on a hunt, Pa?"

Jordan turned Lightning and adjusted the harrow. "Well, we might could get us a passel of meat for Christmas. We sell the hides and make us a lil extra money, eh, boy?" He spoke quietly, but Amon detected an undercurrent of eagerness. "You go ketch your Uncle Zeke's ear. He been a-pesterin' me for a hunt. Tell him

A Trumpet Sounds

to come along over here 'bout nine-ten tonight iffen he favors coon or possum for Christmas dinner. Then you skittle over to Uncle Effam and have him fetch up Yorks and Matt Stengel. Matt got three the best coon hounds in the county. Set the seed there. I'll walk outta this here field."

By the time Amon had covered the ground to these scattered neighbors and returned home, it was dark. The lighted cabin window was a welcome sight as Amon streaked across the yard and bounded in at the door. Sabina was folding the last of her ironed clothes into the basket. Jeb was playing on the hearth. Amon held his hands to the blaze.

"Where you been?" his mother questioned.

"Pa sent me to Uncle Zeke's. We goin' on a coon hunt tonight."

"Well, that's good. We could bear with some fresh meat."

"Where's Willy and Obie?"

"They ain't back yet from totin' Jackson's wash."

Jordan came in shortly and soon after him Willy and Obie. They sat down at the table, and Amon ate ravenously, his hunger sharpened by the miles of running in the cold.

By nine o'clock a surprising number of men and boys and dogs had gathered in the Sayre yard. If Pa felt any astonishment at their number, he gave no sign. He greeted one and all with gruff hospitality. He counted the dogs.

"Thirteen hounds, one mean brute of Walt's, and Stengel's yeller bitch. You mighty short on dogs, men. If we run outta coons and possum, I allows we kin shoot a couple a curs."

The fifteen dogs gamboled, snuffing and barking and pawing, aware of the night's prospects and eager to get started. Matt said, "I was fixin' jes to fetch along Ashes here; but Sack and Cloth, they lose they minds stayin' behind—so here they is too."

"Thas the same way with Howler and Sneeze," York said. "They don't work good separate. Didn't figure you'd favor havin' one dog settin' down on a hot scent." His look was innocent, but his eyes glittered in the dancing light of the pine torch Jordan held.

Uncle Effam agreed, "That sure as sin the truff. Dogs always works best in pairs. That's why I brung Biff and Pansy."

Raillery and laughter larked among the men as frisky as the

dogs. Everyone felt in good spirits. Pine knots were lighted, guns shouldered, axes hoisted. They all trooped out behind the corn-crib, where Jordan said the dogs would quickly strike a scent. Only moments and they were hot on a trail, yipping and baying, the men after them, torches careening, away over the new-plowed field, through thorny fence rows, across a stalky cotton patch, down along the branch, up a little gully, and into the woods.

The dogs ran as though hornets were after them. The ground being moist and the scent fresh, it was no time at all before they came to a treed raccoon, and there they howled and yammered in a frenzy until men and boys caught up. The coon's eyes glinted in the torchlight, making him an easy target. Matt shot him, and when he fell to the ground Buck caught him up from the snapping dogs and tossed him to Lijah to carry.

The dogs were on another scent almost immediately, and after them the men streamed, holding torches high to find the easiest way through the vine-snarled woods.

They came to a low, boggy place and had to pick their way around it. A thin coat of ice covered the area, but beneath it the ooze was soft and miring. Amon, bringing up the rear with his wavering torch, plunged into the sticky mud. He caught himself back quickly, but not quickly enough. His right foot sank deep, and the viscous muck sucked at his shoe when he wrenched his foot free. Surprise and confusion hit him as his bare foot felt the cold earth. In the wavering light he saw the ooze slowly coming together over his shoe. He looked for some place to press the flaming pine knot and then fell to his knees beside the bog just as the sticky mass was smoothing above his shoe. He plunged his hand into the muck, feeling frantically for the leather. It had gone deep; the mud was to his elbow. He had a moment of terror when he thought he might fall face forward into the slime and never be able to pull himself out. Then his fingers touched the tongue of the shoe and slowly he pulled it free. He emptied it, using leaves to wipe away as much of the mud as he could before he put it back on his foot.

The hunt had left him far behind; he could no longer hear voices of either hounds or men. A stillness was all about him and fear clutched him. He took the torch from the crotch of the tree,

A Trumpet Sounds

the leaping light seeming only to accent the blackness beyond its wavering circle. He hallooed. He ran distractedly—away from the bog and away from the direction of the hunt. He thought he heard a distant baying and ran that way for a while, making wide circuits around thick stands of underbrush. Then he thought he heard the hounds off at an angle and frantically ran that way. He lost the sound but ran on, not knowing where he was. He yelled again and again, but the deep forest seemed to swallow his cries. He ran into thickets and had to back out. Blinded by tears he bashed into a tree and the torch was jerked from his hand and fell spluttering into the wet mast. He grabbed it up in panic lest it be extinguished and he left in utter blackness.

And then suddenly there was Jordan, axe in hand, looking only a little annoyed.

"Keep up with us, boy," he said. "We needs that light."

He took the torch from Amon, and soon they were back with the other hunters and the yowling dogs. A raccoon had been treed but was hiding in a hole halfway up the rotted trunk. Axes swung, and soon the men called to stand from under as with a loud crack and a noisy struggle of branches the tree fell. The dogs went into a delirium at the mouth of the hole. It seemed to Amon a grimly unfair fight, one raccoon to fifteen dogs. But the whirling, biting mass of claw and fur told of an admirable courage in the victim. The savage Lambie gripped the raccoon by the throat and shook him like a piece of rag.

A needling cold descended and the hunters built a fire to warm themselves. The men swapped yarns about their dogs and their prowess in remembered hunts. Matt told about chasing a sheeshee through the forest all one night with dog and gun but never once getting close enough for a shot. It was a tale all had heard before, but it still could make Amon's hair stand on end. York and Effam got into an argument over the relative merits of trapping possum and hunting them with a gun. Effam said he didn't rightly favor possum hunting nohow, for a devil went along with that. "Possums is too danged easy to ketch. They's a pure devil temptation."

York said, "Well, I don't crave to strike up no friendship with Satan, but iffen he want to put a lil temptation in my path all wrop

Eunice Young Smith

up in possum fur, I ain't gonna argue with him."

"Call in the dogs and leave us get on the trail of a possum," Jordan said. "Devil or not, we aims to ketch us a few."

They tramped out the fire and started off again, walking now, and after they had covered a mile or so Jordan's Lulu, specially trained for possum hunting, picked up a scent, and away they all went as fast as bushes and briars would let them. The trail led out of the forested area down into bottom land and across a creek, then hugged a fence row for a quarter of a mile to an old spreading hickory tree. There the dogs gathered. The torches revealed a possum hanging by its tail from a fairly low branch.

"Let's take this feller alive," Uncle Zeke panted, as he grabbed a torch from one of the boys and held it aloft to see the animal better. "We kin tote him home on a pole and fatten him up a bit. He be tastier that way."

It was agreed. Jordan said, laughing, "This is too easy. Jes like Effam say, a plain devil temptation." He laughed again. "I'll get up on the rail and pull that limb down a ways and you-all grab him before the dogs jump him."

Amon felt suddenly that it was too easy, as though the possum had been planted there as a lure, a temptation, as Uncle Effam said. Jordan climbed on the top rail of the fence and leaped for the trailing branch of the limb that held the possum out toward its end. He balanced for a moment holding onto the branch. Then Walt's big brute, Lambie, got too excited and threw himself, howling, against the top rail of the fence. Amon saw his father sway for only a second; then there was a crack and the branch snapped off sharp at the end. The limb with the dangling possum sprang back up. Jordan's feet seemed to shoot out from under him. There was another loud crack as he came down on the rail in the center of his back. It seemed to Amon his father broke like splintering wood. He rolled backward over the rail onto the ground and lay still.

The possum hung high in the air again, the branch swaying a little. Buck said, "I'll get a pole and knock him off." Trout Stengel said, "No, climb up the tree and shake him down." And the dogs were yelping and howling like mad and the wind blew the torches every which way—and there was Pa and he wasn't getting up.

Amon ran to the fence and held his light high. "What's the

A Trumpet Sounds

matter, Pa? You hurt?" Then he saw Pa's face and he screamed for Uncle Zeke.

They came then, all of them, and bent over Jordan, puzzled and concerned. They lifted him and laid him out straight, for Jordan could not seem to move at all. All he could gasp was, "My back—is broke." It seemed hard for him to breathe, and in a few minutes he was unconscious.

Afterward all Amon could remember were those words of Uncle Effam going over and over in his head—"a devil temptation . . . a devil temptation . . . possum are too easy to catch." And he remembered that the men had chopped poles and fastened them together somehow with vines and socks and belts and so had made a stretcher and carried Pa the ten miles home.

They carried him in and Sabina rose from the bed, and they laid Jordan down on it gently, still unconscious. Sabina rubbed his hands and feet, trying to bring warmth back into the cold body, and asked again and again how it had happened. They all tried to explain what they did not themselves understand. They said they thought Jordan had fallen on the rails in such a way as to break his back. That was what he had said before he lost consciousness. The men talked in low voices, going over and over the happening.

Toward morning someone went to fetch Granny Rachel. She poured whisky between Jordan's tight teeth and lifted back the lids of his eyes and told Sabina to keep hot bricks all around his body.

The hunting party finally dispersed and went sadly home. There was nothing more they could do. Obey and Willy and Jeb, wakened and frightened, stood by and stared at Pa. Sabina put her head down in her lap and rocked back and forth, and Amon did not know how to comfort her. All he could think of was: It were a devil temptation . . . It were . . . It were.

Chapter 12

JORDAN was paralyzed from the neck down, and he lived, brain befogged, for only a week. While he moaned in pain or lay rigid in stupor Sabina cared for him tenderly, bathing his face, keeping him warm with flannel-wrapped bricks, trying to spoon broth between his unreceiving lips. Amon, getting up to go outside in the night, sometimes found his mother asleep on her knees beside the bed.

When Pa died he wondered that Ma did not give way to grief as Marie and Sheba had done over Les and Noah. Remembering that fearful wailing and the demented antics of those families, he was thankful that she did not. Grief, it seemed to him, was a deep-down sickness that you couldn't lose by yelling, although some folks eased themselves that way.

Relatives and friends came with comfort and help. They urged Sabina and the boys to their homes for Christmas dinner. Walt came and chopped wood. Uncle Effam offered to come and do chores, and he and Uncle Zeke sat all night with the neighbors who came to sustain Sabina the night before the funeral.

The usual festivity of the season was curtailed, no one wishing to seem gay in the face of Sabina's sorrow. Amon did Pa's chores although Buck and Danny Ellum both said they would do them for him. But Amon only repeated what he had heard his mother say to Aunt Willo: "Thanks kindly, but theys four boys here and we can manage. Everybody got troubles. We kin bear ours."

A Trumpet Sounds

He tried to act as Ma did, not making a fuss, hanging on tight to his feelings and getting busy on jobs that had to be done. "If you keep movin'," he told himself, "swing an axe, lug water, anything, the harder the better, you keep the sad thoughts from knocking you down." He milked old Betsy, his head pressed against her warm flank, and talked to her reassuringly, as Pa always did. He fed the animals, remembering Pa's sudden gusts of song. He chopped wood and recalled when he and Pa had found the quail nest with the new hatched chicks and how Pa knelt in the grass making noises like the mother to quiet them. He remembered how Pa grew angry at times trying to teach him to mimic sounds. He remembered, too, Pa's anger at Asa. He tried saying to himself, "Pa ain't here no more. He ain't gone on no treasure hunt. This is for real. Asa ain't here—only Obie and Willy and Jeb and me and Ma. You gotta know—Pa ain't here." Even before Ma said the words, he had said them to himself: "You the man now. Pa's dead and Asa's gone and Obie, he ain't strong. You the man here now."

The day after Christmas Ull Sonderson came and measured Jordan for a coffin. They laid him out in his Sunday suit, which few had ever seen him wear on a Sunday, and Ross Sheppard came and said prayers over the body. For a night and a day there had been no sleep in the Sayre cabin while friends and family kept mournful vigil. Then Matt and Uncle Effam and Uncle Zeke and Walt and Trout and Lem carried the smooth poplar box to the waiting wagon, and slowly over the frozen ground in the still December morning Lightning bore his master to the graveyard beside the Zion Baptist Church in the Flatlands.

In wagons and on foot relatives and friends followed, singing the well-loved hymns, the songs so often distorted but triumphant on Jordan's lips, "Oh, Lord, tell me what to do . . . Keep me from sinkin' down . . . uuummm . . ."

At the lip of the grave, standing close beside Ross, Amon had been surprised to see Fez Babber, his head bent low, his hat crushed between his hands. His crooked back seemed to lift above his head and tears coursed unchecked down his cheeks. Was he thinking maybe of some time when Pa had saved him from the revenuers, Amon wondered.

Eunice Young Smith

Snow began to fall as the coffin was lowered into the hole, a thick slow falling snow that blunted the sound of shovels in gravel and the earth falling on the lid. Then, because of the Christmas season and because Ross wanted them to think of death as a rebirth, he suggested they sing. As they turned from the grave and retraced their steps homeward, their voices rang out like bells.

> *Go tell it on the mountain*
> *Over the hills and everywhere . . .*
> *Go tell it on the mountain*
> *That Jesus Christ is born.*

Amon rose earlier now mornings without urging from his mother. He cared for the cows, feeding the heifers, milking old Betsy, carrying the milk to the kitchen and pouring some into the pitcher before taking the rest to the springhouse, as Pa had always done. Obey helped to feed and water the pigs and chickens and the mule and to clean the stalls and pens and spread fresh straw. Together the boys dragged logs from the woodlot and chopped wood for hearth and stove. They carried water for the kitchen and for Sabina's wash kettle. They cut down all the corn and cotton stalks in the fields. They knew that the work Pa had done, albeit unwillingly, must now be done by them. Sabina had made this plain when, a few days after the funeral, she had spoken to them long and seriously. Obie and Amon were the men in the family now, she said, and they would have to shoulder the burdens of men. They would all have to work hard. Besides, it was time for school to start again and all four boys had to go to school. To Amon's protest that she needed him at home she said: "I'd rather you went to school than doin' ary work round here. I kin manage. There's a new teacher this year, come from Atlanta, and I reckon he goin' to learn you boys somethin' good."

Thinking about it afterward, Amon decided it had not been so bad as he expected, meeting the new teacher and starting school again. Roger Fullmer was a young man, not much older than Asa Amon guessed, and he wasn't like anybody you'd run from. He wasn't very tall, but he had wide square shoulders that looked hard with muscles under his rough brown coat. "I reckon he could

A Trumpet Sounds

whup Buck or Bobo easy do they get to cuttin' up," Amon thought. "But he don't look mean a-tall. His eyes is sort of sad like . . . like maybe he wished you was goin to be smart or something. But he ain't gonna lick you iffen you can't answer."

Amon shared a reader with Panty Ellum that first day, and for half an hour the fourth grade stumbled and halted and was prompted through the first few pages. Then Mr. Fullmer said, "That's enough for today. We'll go back over it tomorrow and it should go faster. You'll want to become good readers as quick as possible. I see the school has some new books, and I think you are going to like them. You've all heard about Abraham Lincoln and Frederick Douglass?" His brows raised in a questioning glance and then lowered at the reassuring nods of some of the children. "But do you know what they were like when they were your age? They were farm boys, very much like yourselves. They had all kinds of troubles and adventures before they grew up to be such famous men." He fingered the bright-covered books standing between two polished stones on his table. "These books tell the stories of their lives. Then there is another book here which tells about a farm boy who learned how to make his father's land produce more than it ever had before. It helped his family make bigger crops so they got more money and could live better and eat better. It's all in this book, and you're going to want to read it. You'll want to read all of these books and many more besides, I hope." He smiled at them and Amon felt friendly and decided he would study hard so he could read the books Mr. Fullmer praised.

Toward the end of the day the pupils were asked to put away their work and Roger Fullmer talked to them. He said he was glad to be teaching in their school and he hoped they would all be friends and enjoy their work together. He said, "That's important, that we should enjoy our work."

He paused, his gaze roving the upturned faces before him. "Some of you may enjoy studying so much you will want to go further in school, on to a university perhaps."

Amon could only guess what a university might be. He could see by the looks on their faces and the shifting in seats that Bobo and Elijah and Buck and most of the other kids didn't know what teacher meant either. But he went right on as though they did.

Eunice Young Smith

"Some of you might want to become nurses or doctors, or even teachers." He grinned here. "We don't all have to be farmers, you know. It's a big world outside the Flatlands."

Amon could tell from the looks on almost everyone's face that the kids liked Mr. Fullmer and liked what he'd said about having fun in school. Friday afternoons wood be special. "That's going to be talk time—for everybody in the upper grades."

"We will discuss all sorts of things at these periods, anything you want to talk about. Perhaps to start with, next Friday, we could each tell about some place we have been, or some place we would like to visit."

No one seemed disturbed by this announcement. Some even displayed a furtive eagerness. All except Amon. The teacher's words had struck terror to his heart. Stand up before all the kids in the room and this new teacher and speak! He couldn't do it—not ever. Already his mind was a blank, his tongue fat and dry.

All week the thought of the approaching Friday soured Amon's waking time and troubled his sleep, blotted out words he should know in the reading lessons and fouled up his multiplication tables. When Friday finally came, he had a strong temptation to run into the woods and hide until it was over. Only the even greater dread of facing up to his mother afterward brought him to the schoolhouse and kept him there.

Most of the boys and girls were eager for the afternoon talk time. Even Danny and Jeb had ideas about places they would like to visit and hoped they would be called on to speak their minds, even though teacher had said this period was for the older children.

First one boy or girl and then another was asked to stand and speak. The teacher and all the other pupils listened attentively and when the speaker sat down questions might be asked and certain aspects of the talk discussed. Amon was amazed when Sarah Ellum told about going to Chattanooga, for he knew she had never been to the city and only knew of it from hearing Uncle Zeke and Aunt Willo talk about it. But her mental image of the place was so vivid and her recounting so lively that all her listeners were beguiled. Lijah stared at her with a silly grin and across the room Amon could see Perk Parsals raise his brows and tilt his head in appreciation. Amon kicked his feet back and forth and was quite enjoying himself when Sarah's talk ended abruptly and she sat down.

Before he could collect his wits he heard Mr. Fullmer saying, "Amon Sayre, where would you like to go on a visit?" His smile was engaging, but his words were doom. Every day for the past week Amon had rehearsed in his mind what he might possibly say if he were called on. He thought he might tell of going to Buzzard's Roost, about the snakes and the storm. He would like to tell about the guitar and the night he and Leah thought there was a bear at the door and how it turned out to be Harp. He hoped he would not ever be called on, but if he were, he longed to respond to the teacher's request, to show Mr. Fullmer that he liked him and wanted to do what he asked. Now his resolve vanished and terror possessed him. His mind went blank and he could not remember one thing he had meant to say.

"Isn't there some special place you have always wanted to see, Amon?" Mr. Fullmer prompted. "Some place perhaps that you have been once and would like to visit again? Come, get up and tell us. Make something up if you prefer. It doesn't have to be real."

Amon clasped his hands between his knees and sweat sprang out across his brow.

"Come, come," the teacher urged. "You must have some kind of an idea."

Amon had—to sink into the floor and disappear. Now, by Danny on one side and Elijah on the other, he was elbowed to his feet, where he stood, mouth open, eyes glassy, unable to utter a word.

Mr. Fullmer mercifully passed to Missouri Dunham, who was waving a frantic hand, eager to have a turn. Amon sat down. At the end of the recitation period Mr. Fullmer said, "Well, this has been fun, hasn't it? We'll do it every week. You may recite a poem if you wish. Or you can just get up and talk about milking the cows or hunting rabbits—anything you want. Then we will discuss it and see if we can improve. That's the idea, you see, to improve."

At home in the evenings Obey and Willy and Jeb recounted for Sabina all that happened at school every day. She would put aside what she was doing and sit down, her back straight, hands on her knees, eyes alight, and listen closely to all they had to say. Pride bristled in her comments. "Jebbie, you learnin' you ABCs, Willy, you makin' words outta them letters, and Obie and Amon, you learnin' to make sense outta the words. Ain't that a powerful fine somethin'? I de-clare!"

When Obey told her about the Friday talks, she slapped her knees and her face stirred with one of her rare smiles. "Tell me 'bout 'em," she urged. "What you get up and speechify, Obie, heh?"

"It didn't get around to my turn," Obey said. "But Amon got called on."

Jeb said, "Teacher don't call on us little kids, but I coulda spoke Goosey Gander iffen he did."

"You'll get your turn one day, honey. Then you speak up nice like that. Amon, what you talk about?"

Willy laughed. "He got up and talk like a pout. You know, Ma." And Willy opened and closed his mouth fishwise, soundlessly.

"What the matter ails you, Amon? Why don't you speak out when the teacher asks you?"

"I dunno."

"He's scared," Obey said.

"Nonsense! What you-all scared for, son? You got no call to be scared. That new teacher's a right nice man. He's your friend. He wanna help you. It ain't fittin' to refuse him. What you wanna be scared for, heh?"

Amon didn't know; he wished he did. He had asked himself the same question again and again. School, which in time might have become a half pleasant chore, became instead a progression toward the day of execution—Fridays and the dreaded speakings. He prayed to be sick on Friday or for something to happen that would save him from his ordeal. And then something did happen.

The fateful day came and there were many recitations, several of which drew admiration from both teacher and the room. Amon was not called on. At the end of the period there was singing. Mr. Fullmer asked them to stand and sing "America," which they all knew the words of well, and he went about among

A Trumpet Sounds

them waving the air with arms and hands to help them keep time.

Amon was happy in any singing, loosed from self-consciousness, knowing an identity with melody and the words of a song. This slow, majestic strain evoked pictures in his imagination: "My country, 'tis of thee, sweet land of liberty . . ." He saw the land he knew, the Flatlands, the branch flowing through the valley, the wooded hills, the cotton fields and the cabins, the sun coming up red in the mornings, mist lying white in the hollows, the cows plodding the lanes at dusk. . . . "Of thee I sing. Land where my fathers died" . . . Yeah, fathers and grandfathers, back and back . . . Pa too, buried in the graveyard alongside the church . . . "Land of the pilgrims' pride. . ." Land of my pride, where I was born . . . where our farm is . . .Land I love . . . "From every mountain side . . ." Where the trees march green and secret, up and up, where the deer and the fox live . . . where a million birds shelter . . . where Pa's treasure is . . . where Leah lives . . . "Let freedom ring . . . Sweet freedom's song". . . song . . . song . . . He was a song, no body . . . only sound . . . a high, swervy sound . . . a song . . .

The words winged from him, high and sweet. His eyes closed, his lips apart and smiling, he sang. When he returned to sensibility, everyone was seated, and he alone remained standing. Mr. Fullmer stared at him, a puzzled look in his kind eyes. Amon snapped his mouth shut and sat down.

Later, as the children prepared to leave, Mr. Fullmer asked Amon to remain. When everyone had left the building, he picked up the wastebasket and emptied its contents into the potbellied stove. He erased the arithmetic problems from the blackboard and then came and sat down on the bench beside Amon.

"You like to sing, Amon?" he asked.

"Yes, sir."

"Has anyone ever told you that you have a very good voice?"

Amon said hesitantly, "My sister did, and one of the ladies at church did once."

"Would you like to make something of your voice? Develop it? Train it?"

"I dunno. Reckon I ain't thought about it none."

Roger Fullmer shook his head in a bewildered way. "Do you

like school?"

Amon studied the floor. Finally he managed. "N-not Fridays."

"Why not Fridays? You haven't spoken a word since school commenced. I thought most of the boys and girls enjoyed Fridays."

Amon hung his head, miserable. He liked Mr. Fullmer. He didn't want him to think he was stubborn or mean-headed.

"You can't be afraid of the boys and girls. You've known them all your life. What is it that bothers you? Are you afraid of me?"

"N-no, sir."

"Then what is it?"

"I dunno. I get scared and can't say nothin'."

"But you like to sing?"

Amon nodded.

"You don't feel scared when you sing?"

Amon shook his head.

"Then on Fridays why don't you sing for us instead of speaking? Would you like that better?"

Amon's face brightened and he nodded again.

Mr. Fullmer seemed relieved, too, as though he had solved a stubborn problem. "Very well," he said. "Next Friday you may sing. Sing anything you choose." He hesitated a moment and then went on. "I won't ask you any more to get up and speak." He studied the boy's sensitive face for a little before he added gravely, "Some of us are born more thin-skinned and high-strung than others. We can't help that. We can't help having fears. Some of them are part of our surroundings, some are fed to us as babies. We didn't ask for them any more than a cotton patch asks for weeds." He studied his hands for a while, silent. Then, "We can't help getting the weeds. But I think we can help keeping them. Do you know what I mean?"

Amon shook his head, bewildered, thinking, "He talks like Ma."

"Of course not." He got up and strode across the room, his hands deep in his pockets, mumbling, "I get ahead of myself . . . want to go too fast." He turned and came back to the boy. "I only mean to say, don't worry about being scared of things, people—

A Trumpet Sounds

everything. You'll grow out of that, I'm sure. I just want you to like school, Amon. I believe very deeply that schooling—learning—can be our salvation. I mean it can be the solution to many things. It can—Well, anyway we've solved one problem, haven't we?" He smiled and held out his hand. "From now on your way to speak will be through songs."

Once outside Amon kicked up his heels and raced across the schoolyard like a spring colt. The other boys and girls were far out of sight. He whirled round and round in the road. He leaped and capered. He ran, his coat flapping in the cold wind, his neckcloth flying into his face, his arms flailing. Joy bubbled in him, his sense of liberation explosive. He felt like Elijah mounting the chariot for Paradise, and so he shouted as he ran:

> *He's a-rollin' on the thunder*
> *He make-a the lightning come . . .*
> *My Lord is on the mountain . . .*
> *My soul is a-shaaaakin' down!*

Chapter 13

January turned brittle cold, sleet and snow falling frequently from heavy skies, and riddling winds scudded across the valley. Amon could not remember when the cold had hurt so much or the wind endured so long. It blasted his face and hands raw whenever he went outside. It drove down the chimney in billows if the fire burned low, and it whiffed in around the windows and the crack under the door. It came up through the floor boards at night and penetrated the shuck mattress, and Amon curled himself close to Jeb and wished for more covers to his bed.

When the wind died, a harsh cold settled over the land. There was no forage for the stock. The cow and heifer stayed close to the barn, sharing a poor, huddled comfort with Lightning and the sow. The hens moped inside the coop, slow to move, indifferent to the grain thrown to them.

The fuel needed to keep the fires was prodigious. Night and morning the boys chopped and carried to keep the woodbox filled. Sabina heated water inside now and did her washings in the shedroom, carrying endless buckets of water from well to kitchen, throwing the water into the yard when she had finished, where it froze in a smooth gray sheet.

Death rode the Flatlands and carried off old and young. Granny Rachel died toward the end of January and old Thebe Stengel, Matt's father, in February. It was Matt who found Bayou Thoman, the idiot child, frozen to death in the stone pit back of his woods.

A Trumpet Sounds

One morning Sabina drove Lightning to Calhoun to have meal ground and to deliver a wash and pick up another. When she returned, she put hay in the manger and threw a blanket of old sacks over the mule's gaunt frame, shaking her head. "Poor ol' Lightning, you 'bout done for. I 'llow you ain't gonna last till spring. I don't see how we gonna get along without you, nohow."

The next morning, when Amon went to milk Betsy, he found Lightning stretched out on the straw of his stall, quite dead. Sabina wrung her hands over this loss, even though she had expected it. There was no money for another mule. How were they to get the spring planting done?

Uncle Zeke came and skinned the mule. The gaunt frame held meat for little more than a few meals for the dogs. Obey and Amon and Uncle Zeke dug a pit and buried the entrails. The hide would be dried and put to many uses, mending harness and making shoes.

"I don't see how we gonna mount this fix," Sabina lamented. "We might could work our own fields by hand with all of us pitchin' in and workin' dayclean to dark. But where we gonna find time for Jackson's fields? And our own crop ain't gonna pay no mortgage and buy marl and salt. How we'll make out I plain can't see."

School closed at the end of March, the help of all the children being needed at home at planting time. Roger Fullmer had made school so enjoyable they were all sorry to have the term end. Before he left to go back to Atlanta, he spoke to Amon again about his singing, urging him to study hard and think about developing his voice. Amon wondered how he was to go about that. Anyone could sing in church whether his voice was developed or not. Everyone sang everywhere, but no one thought of doing anything in particular about it. God gave you a nice voice: there it was and you sang. Even Mr. Fullmer had fumbled trying to answer Amon's questions. He told him about a group of singers who had gone out from Fisk University and had sung before large audiences in different cities of the world. They were young people with fine voices who had a far, high goal in life. He said, "Amon, I believe you have an unusual voice, good enough, if trained, to take you places."

"Where would it take me, Mr. Fullmer? I ain't goin' no place I knows of. How my voice take me?"

Roger Fullmer had seemed abashed, not knowing how to present a large idea to the boy. He said, "I mean, if your voice is what I think, and if it were trained, you might be a great singer some day. You might sing on the concert stage."

The concert stage. That was what Leah had talked about. But himself, singing on a stage in front of a lot of people—that was plain silly. He was just a farm boy of the Flatlands, head of a family. He wasn't going anywhere. Ma needed him bad right here. And he had turned his thoughts inward toward other things.

With spring the rains softened the hard clay of the fields. Pastures turned green again, buds opened, the branch rose. The field of winter wheat that Jordan had planted was lush and thrifty. It was time to groom the land for another season.

Sabina said one morning, "We gotta get our peas and taters in. The moon's right."

She hitched herself and Amon to the plow, and with Obey guiding it, they turned the softened earth of the truck patch. They had dragged the plow back and forth over half the small field and Amon had begun to stagger against the makeshift harness and wonder if he could endure to the end, when they heard a clink of metal on stone that spoke of hooves, and heard a man's voice. "Haw, Bruno! Come along, boy, look where you goin'." And presently Fez Babber turned into their yard, riding a mule.

"Mornin', Sabina," he called politely as he continued toward the garden patch while the woman and the boy stood in the lumpy field and stared.

"I reckon you could use this here mule."

Sabina pressed her hands against her hips and studied the mule and the man on its back. "It right neighborly of you, Fez, but I ain't got the money to hire no mule."

"I ain't ask you to hire him. You go ahead and use him."

"How you make out on your own fields? Ain't you need your mule to plow?"

"I got another mule."

"He's rich," Amon thought. "He has a still. He don't need to care do he plant cotton or nothin'."

A Trumpet Sounds

"I 'llow as we'd be powerful in you debt, brother Fez," Sabina said as she eased the leather from across her shoulder and straightened her headcloth. "I don't rightly see how we can repay you."

"I been paid," he said.

"How come?"

"Jordan helped me more'n once."

Sabina walked up to the strapping young animal and stroked its nose. "I nigh 'bout made up my mind we ain't walkin' outta this here field today. I ain't done much plowin' when Jordan alive."

"I seed at the buryin' your mule wa'n't good for long, and I says to myself, come plantin' time Sabina Sayre gonna need a lil help. I'm right proud I gotta mule to offer you."

"Brother Fez," Sabina said gratefully, "you a real kind-hearted man."

So the fields were plowed then for cotton and corn, and when, in May, the cotton plants were about four inches high, Amon and Bruno plowed furrows and threw the dirt up close to the plants. Amon took Bruno through the corn again and again, keeping the field as clean as ever his father had. All the boys and Sabina too worked at chopping, both at home and up at the plantation.

Old Betsy had dropped a bull calf in May, and Sabina said they would keep it, let it suck through the summer, and they would slaughter it at Christmas time. The sow farrowed, crushing two of her small litter by rolling on them the first night. Sabina set hens, putting a clutch of duck eggs under one of them.

By lay-by the season had become alarmingly dry. The corn was curling, and even the cotton withered in the heat. The vegetable garden was a wretched mass of wilting vines and desiccated fruit. Beans dried up before they could mature, and the squash never developed. Sabina and the boys carried water from the branch in a futile effort to keep the plants alive.

Pastures scorched brown, so the pigs and cows had to be turned into the woods to forage as best they could. There was no hay fit for cutting. The well went dry in August, along with those of many of their neighbors, and then water had to be carried from the branch for all purposes—a back-racking haul for Sabina's washes.

Dust lay like a smothering yellow pall on trees and weeds and along the roadways. It rose in choking clouds whenever a wagon passed. The earth of the yard packed into a hard yellow floor, little puffs of dust fluttering whenever one of the dogs or children ran across it.

No teacher was engaged for the summer session of school, for money was nonexistent. People gathered to shake their heads and condole with one another. Cattle had to be sold, for there was no feed. The animals, thin and impoverished, on a glutted market, brought a poor price. The cotton was sparse and everyone suffered, plantation owner and small farmer alike. All who depended on the land for their living were made desperate when the land suffered. Each day turned into a vigil, a studying of the sky and a weary, fruitless praying.

By September disaster was plain. Mere survival meant that many would have to seek help, would have to borrow to stay alive, would have to heap themselves with additional debt against their future ability to work and repay. Sabina held a council with her sons.

"We ain't gonna be able to meet the payment for our farm this year," she said. "What we gonna do? If Mist' Jackson let us go over to next year with our debt, an I 'llow as how he would, we gonna have to pay double then. How we gonna do that? We jes get deeper and deeper in debt is all. An' how we gonna eat this winter? We scarce got nothin' from the row crops, and they ain't but mighty little in the ce-gar box. The cotton so poor we never gonna make a crop. What we gonna do I plain can't see. I got a good mind to pull up outta here 'fore we gets so deep in debt we can't never climb out."

Ma's talk was shocking to Amon. He knew that things were bad, but he hadn't known Ma was desperate. Leave the farm! Where on earth would they go? What could they do? How could there be a life for them away from the farm?

"What we do, Ma?" Obey whimpered. "What you got a mind to do?"

A Trumpet Sounds

"I dunno zactly. I ain't got it all sorted out in my mind yet. But we best get away from here while we can."

"But where can we go?"

"I study on it some. We might could go to Chattanooga. Your Aunt Tatty Lou Collins live up there. She'd help us, I reckon, till we got planted fresh. I figure they is washes to do in the city same as here. Theys jobs you boys kin do, too. We won't be at the behest of the land and the rains nor payin' on no contract that never gets paid off. I been studyin' on this for a long spell. I don't aim to sit here in these Flatlands till the walls of Jericho come tumblin' down."

Then word came that no teacher was to be hired for the winter school term. Few in the community felt this so grievously as Sabina.

"We gettin' out," she stated emphatically, her mouth a defiant line. "I can stand most anything but that. You boys gonna go to school—ain't nothin' I can see counts more'n that. I don't aim to bow down in the dust of this land if my boys can't get they schoolin'. I plain won't tolerate." She banged the skillet in which she was stirring a corn pone with a wooden spoon, her body taught with anger and challenge.

Once Sabina had made up her mind, action followed swiftly. She went to call on Jeff Jackson. When she returned home, her eyes were agleam and her jaw set and she had an air of businesslike purpose.

"I done sold out," she announced. "Lock, stock, an' bale. I sold our cotton crop, such as it is—an' jes as it is. Mist' Jackson get somebody else to pick it. He takin' back the farm and all on it."

"How much he pay you, Ma?" Obey pried. "How much money you got for all this here?" His eyes bulged at the prospect of a large sum.

"I don't reckon he cheat me. I got enough to get us to Chattanooga and get us settled there."

She did not divulge what she had got for the farm, but she went about the preparations for removal with a satisfied air that, to Amon at least, was reassuring. She said Jeff Jackson planned to use the place just as it was for a new tenant. All that was required was for them to pack their personal belongings and make their farewells.

"How we gonna get to Chattanooga, Ma?" Willy asked. Sabina stopped long enough in her bustling to answer. She had to consider very carefully every expenditure, she said. Railway fare was dear. It would put a deep dent in her resources to see them all to the city on the train. "I 'llow as how jes me and the trunk and Jeb gonna ride the train. You three boys gonna hoof it. We'll go on ahead and stop off at Aunt Tatty's while I look for a place to live. I'll make a big sack of food for you-all. Ain't no harder walkin' than choppin' cotton or hoein' corn. Ain't no need you hurry, an' you ain't gonna get lost. The road straight on up there. Iffen you does get off the road, you can ask your way back on again."

Everyone in the Flatlands learned quickly of Sabina's decision to move away. The reactions were mixed. Aunt Willo was moist and blustering. "I gonna miss you for a fare-thee-well, Bina. I don't see why you wanna go off like this, pullin' up an takin' off like a kite in the wind, so sudden-like. You ain't take time to cogitate."

"Yes, I have," Sabina contradicted with vigor. "I study on it a long time. My mind all made up ever since they said they ain't gonna be school again next term."

"Well, it ain't gonna be the same with you-all gone. I de-clare. We gonna miss you somethin' fierce. Maybe you come back."

"Maybe," Sabina said, "but I ain't countin' on it."

For the boys the excitement and haste of getting ready to leave curbed any hankerings after the farm. They were sent on numerous errands—to the Stengels to give Pontella certain herb roots she had asked for; to Aunt Candy with a message that she could have the iron wash kettles if Uncle Effam would come and fetch them away; to Walt Logan's with the churn, for he had recently broken theirs. Sabina gave most of Jordan's carpenter tools to Zeke with the understanding that if he did not want to use them—and she was pretty sure he would not—he should keep them against the day when Obey or Willy or Jeb might have a need for them.

The last of the chickens Sabina cooked up to take with them on their long journey. She had used up the last of the meal in

A Trumpet Sounds

making pones, and these she divided and made into a package for each boy. The trunk was packed and tied with rope. There was an extra packing case of bedding and kettles and dishes. Ma and Jeb would each carry a crocus sack. Uncle Zeke was to carry them in his wagon to the station in Calhoun and to start Amon and Willy and Obey on their way.

All was ready and Sabina was giving the tidied cabin one final going over when Amon, standing at the open front door, saw a wagon pull up at their gate. It wasn't Uncle Zeke, for this wagon was piled high with household gear and was drawn by two mules. Sitting high on the seat with Pula Kemp beside him was Fez Babber.

At Amon's startled, "Hey, Ma!" Sabina came to the door and gaped over his head. "Well, I de-clare!" she said. "If it ain't Fez and Pula. Now where you reckon they goin' to?"

"Howdy," Fez called when Sabina came out on the gallery steps. "I hear you movin'."

"Look like you movin' too," she answered, her gaze scanning the piled wagon and coming back to rest on Pula.

"Me and Pula decide to get married and she don't wanna stay hereabouts. We goin' to Chattanooga. I heard you and the little boy goin' by train and the other three gonna walk. You reckon three boys could ride on the back end of my wagon?"

Sabina looked hard at Fez and Pula and then at the three boys clustered around her and then at the piled wagon.

"You purty well crowded right now."

"They be room in the back. Three boys don't take up much space."

"They's room, Ma," the boys urged, overjoyed at the prospect of a ride where they had supposed they would have to walk. "We can squeeze on."

"Well," Sabina consented, "I reckon the Lord sent you, Fez, an' I'm purely grateful."

"We take good care of them," Pula said. "Chattanooga be a powerful long walk."

"Yes. It pinched my heart thinkin' on it. I reckon I wouldn'ta been able to shut my eyes till I'd had 'em safe up there. Thank you kindly."

Eunice Young Smith

Sabina had given Fez a paper with the Collinses address on it where he was to deliver the boys. Obey and Amon and Willy had climbed aboard and started out ahead of Sabina and Jeb. They sat on a feather bed with their feet dangling over the endgate and watched the farm vanish from view around a curve in the road. Jubilant at not having to go on foot the long trek north but to be riding instead in the lap of a feather bed, the boys held tight to their sacks of food and settled down to enjoy themselves. They teased one another and made silly jokes and then Amon, feeling a sudden exhilaration began to sing: "Climb on, chillun, climb on de train . . . we headed for the Promise Land."

The other boys took it up. They all sang: "Lay down your troubles and climb on de train . . ."

Fez and Pula looked back and smiled and nodded and then they too joined the song: "Climb on the train . . . climb on the train . . . We headin' for the Promised Land . . . ummmm."

Part Two

Chapter 14

Amon walked along the tracks for a way and then dropped down a shallow bank to a dirt lane that ran for several blocks between the railroad bed and a jagged row of rude shanties. Stacked one against another, the shanties were a bleak patchwork of stained and rusted sheet metal, oil drums, and flattened, weather-blackened boards, odds and ends of tarpaper, oilcloth or cardboard—any material that could be converted into a makeshift roof or wall. Some of the shanties had no windows, some only small squares of cracked glass, or apertures covered by crazy shutters. Doors were rough boards nailed together and hinged with bits of rope or old harness. Chimneys sprouted from rooftops, braced and wired to keep them from falling down. All the shacks leaned drunkenly. Dooryards were littered with rubbish, and mangy dogs nosed about in the refuse.

It was dusk and lights were beginning to appear in windows. Amon could see people moving about in the shacks, many people in tiny rooms. He could hear the wail of babies, voices screaming or cursing, an occasional song.

In the Bottoms, over beyond the rail yard where he had been today, he had seen hundreds of shacks like this, hundreds of sorry-looking people. Why were all these people crowded into huts along the railroad tracks? Why the hundreds in the Bottoms and over beyond? Where had they come from? Had they once lived on farms? Had they, like Ma, come to the city thinking to better

A Trumpet Sounds

themselves, to find jobs, and schools that would stay open in a bad season? What had happened to them? What had kept them in such holes?

He came out on Tenth Street just as the street lights were being lit, but tonight he had no time to watch in delight while the man with the long stick ignited the gas lamps. He waited for the busy traffic to thin, then ran across the street and turned west. When he came to Cottage Street he cut through a vacant lot to Douglas. Two more blocks and he would be at Aunt Tatty Lou's house. Eagerness to be in out of the approaching night urged his steps, but he was not afraid. Only three weeks ago he had been a country boy, alarmed by anything strange or unexpected. Three weeks ago he had not known a thousand things familiar to him now.

It seemed to him that even on that night of their arrival in Chattanooga he had lost, in the sheer enchantment of those first moments, some part of his former self. In all his fourteen years no dream he had ever known approached the reality of their entrance into the city—he and Willy and Obey, clinging to the endgate of Fez Babber's wagon, trying to take in the lamp-bespangled streets, the maze of people, the witchery of lighted shop windows, the streetcars and fine carriages, the noise and movement. Fear was shunted aside by excitement and a burgeoning desire for participation.

At length they had found Douglas Street, and the boys had been delivered to the right address, a tall, two-storied house, unpainted, with sagging porch and missing shutters.

Amon could scarcely believe they were at the right address until he saw Ma at the door. Then quickly there was Jeb, throwing fat arms around his neck, and Aunt Tatty Lou and Uncle Hesh welcoming them, urging them in, thanking Fez and Pula and inviting them in for a cup of coffee, but being declined because Fez said he still had to find a place to stay for the night. Uncle Hesh gave Fez directions to a place that took in travelers and he and Pula went on.

Then they had met their cousins—Cream, a tall girl with smooth, light skin and a quick warm smile; Oona, who was about Obey's age, grave and sedate; the twins, Abraham and Lincoln,

Eunice Young Smith

who confided to Amon right off that they were ten, in the fourth grade and all the kids called them Abe and Linnie.

Aunt Tatty Lou stormed them with questions, and so did Ma. Tatty set them down to supper at a long table in the kitchen. It was past the regular supper time so the boarders were not there, she said, and the family could talk freely about themselves. Amon had been so excited he could neither eat nor talk.

Although he had never seen Aunt Tatty before, he felt he knew her from his mother's accounts. She was thin like Ma and talked fast and had a chuckle that made him feel good inside, although sometimes she looked at Uncle Hesh with a sharp, half-angry glance that reminded him of the way Ma sometimes used to look at Pa when he had done something she didn't like. She kept asking the boys questions without waiting for answers, and she told them all about the twins and how far they were in school and how smart they were, even though the twins were right there and could very well speak for themselves, and did. She told them Oona had won a prize for a composition and that it had been read to the whole school by the principal. She asked Oona to go and get it and read it to the boys, but Cream said, "For goodness sake, Ma, let the boys catch their breath before you ram us all down their throats." Amon liked Cream; she reminded him of Leah. Uncle Hesh said, "Let them get their bellies full, Tatty. We ain't so likely to make 'em sick on a full stomach." Everybody laughed and he felt friendly and jolly with these relatives of Ma's.

Obey and Willy told them all about the three-day journey to the city and how they had made camp one night by the side of the road, gathering corn shucks at the edge of a harvested field to bed down on, and how in the night white riders had come and routed them out and made them leave, cursing them—and how scared they'd all been, Amon sick all the night.

The wonder and strangeness of things made Amon silent, and he heard his mother making excuses for him as she used to to Aunt Willo. "Amon's awful shy, but I figures the city take some of that outta him after he be here a spell. Amon's a good boy, Tatty. He ain't mean a-tall."

"An' he real bad for the singin', Aunt Tatty," Jeb said, fondling Amon's sleeve. "You should hear him sing "My Country,

A Trumpet Sounds

'Tis of Thee" right up in front of the whole school all by his lone."

Amon had laughed and pushed Jeb away, rumpling his fuzzy head affectionately. It was good to be with Ma and Jeb again, the long journey already moving away in his thoughts.

"That's fine, Amon," Aunt Tatty said kindly. "Maybe you will want to join the choir at our church. We have a fine choir at the African Baptist Church. Your Ma been there yesterday. She ain't quite to home yet in our congregation, but she'll get used to it."

Amon had looked about the kitchen then and noticed that things even here were different than at home. There were no beds in Aunt Tatty's kitchen, and there was a great deal more of other furniture. In truth, there was more furniture in Aunt Tatty's house than he had ever seen in any house in the Flatlands. He thought it was very elegant until he heard Aunt Tatty speaking of it later. Then the corners of her mouth had twisted down and she said, "I can't do no better with what Hesh brings home," and Amon knew what she meant. Most of the furniture had not come from stores, for Uncle Hesh was a junk collector.

Uncle Hesh was slow-moving and soft-spoken. He looked as though he were sorry the furniture wasn't new.

"But I like Uncle Hesh," Amon told himself now as he hurried along. "I like Uncle Hesh. He's a dilly with the harmonica, and he's goin' to show me how to work it. He tells jokes and he knows all kinds of songs. I wish I could go along with him when he collects junk. We could sing while we go. He could play the harmonica and I could drive the horse. Ma wouldn't hear of that nohow. She's so almighty set on us kids goin' to school. What's she gonna say when I tell her what I gotta tell her now? I'll stand up and say, 'Ma, I'm a growed man now; I'm the man head of the family. I gotta work and support us.' She ain't gonna like it. She'll talk me down, I know she will. But I ain't gonna let her. We been at Aunt Tatty's three weeks now, but Ma ain't happy. I can tell. Don't know what ails her exactly, but she's awful downmouthed.

Amon speculated that his mother might not like living at Aunt Tatty's house even though it was a fine one and they had a whole room to themselves upstairs. Aunt Tatty had had to put one of the boarders out to make room for them because the rooms downstairs were already too full of furniture and people. Ma fussed around trying to help, but there wasn't much she could do. Aunt Tatty said the boarders were used to her cooking, and she didn't let Ma help much with that. Even though the house seemed to Amon very large, it was crowded. Four boarders and eight children and Ma and Aunt Tatty and Uncle Hesh made fifteen people in and out and around the place, and you couldn't spread out like at home where there had been twenty acres. You couldn't get away from somebody looking at you all the time or talking to you. You couldn't sit still and think your thoughts but what somebody was asking were you sick or something.

Amon raced the last few yards to the house. He jumped the two steps of the porch and swung into the lighted kitchen. Before the door clicked to behind him, he heard Ma's sharp retort: "I don't 'llow as how I got enough to do around here, Tatty. That's the truth." she stood with her feet planted firmly, hands on hips, talking to Tatty's back as her sister hovered over the steaming pots on the stove.

"You can do around here just like you was to home," Tatty said. "I don't care if you scrub and dust. But it seems to me like now you got a chance you'd welcome a little rest."

Amon took off his coat and cap and hung them on a nail near the door. Jeb and Willy and the twins were playing ticktacktoo at one end of the long table. Oona bent over some schoolwork. Amon slid into a chair, longing to tell his news quickly while his courage lasted, wanting to be alone with Ma to tell her and at the same time being afraid to be alone when he told her. She could talk him down easier if they were alone. He was uneasy in the atmosphere of conflict between his mother and his aunt, yet glad of it, since it distracted his mother from his entrance and prolonged the time before he must face her questions.

"Where's Cream?" he asked Oona. She looked up from her book long enough to say, "She's not home yet."

Amon knew the laundry where Cream worked was on the other side of town and that she often was late getting home. But it was necessary to talk, to divert his thoughts to someone besides himself. He asked the boys, "How's school?"

"Where were you?" Willy put his hand over the paper while he eyed Amon through straggles of hair. "You skipped, huh?"

A Trumpet Sounds

"Where's Obie?" Amon tried to distract him.

"Out sortin' junk with Uncle Hesh. Me and Jeb helped for a while."

Oona looked at Willy condescendingly. "You should say Jeb and I."

"Why?" Willy screwed his mouth and swished back his hair the better to outstare his cousin.

"Because it's correct grammar," she said primly.

"Who said so?"

"That's what I go to school for. Didn't they teach you grammar where you went to school?"

"No," Jeb volunteered. "We jes got teached our letters."

"Taught," Oona corrected. "You should say 'We were taught our letters.'"

"Oh, fudge," Jeb retorted. "Oh, fudge, oh, fudge, oh, fudge! That's what Cream says—oh, fudge!"

"Hey, it's my turn—get off the paper." Abe poked Willy.

Amon wondered if Ma would jump him right away about where he'd been. He needed Uncle Hesh there. Ma listened to Uncle Hesh. She was saying to Tatty, "I ain't used to be a lady of no work. The Lord say to keep busy and you keep happy, and I ain't busy enough."

Tatty banged the lid of the kettle and Sabina went on, "I reckon they is washes can be had to do in Chattanooga same as other places."

"Sure there is, but you ain't got no tubs to do 'em in. I can't have washes goin' on round here when I got boarders to cook for. And there ain't no room to hang clothes in the back yard with all that truck Hesh got piled around out there. Ain't no room for nothin' really round here more'n what there is already."

Even his mother's back looked grim to Amon. He wondered if his news might not make a difference in her problem. He could hold it no longer.

"Ma," he blurted, "I got me a job today." Sabina swung on him, her eyes disbelieving. "What you say?"

"I got me a job."

"What you mean? Where you got you a job?" she came toward him. "Where you been all day? Oona say she didn't see you at school. Where you been, son?"

Eunice Young Smith

"At the foundry."

"What foundry?"

"Marks and Benson Sashweight Foundry . . . over by the yards . . . where they make sashweights. They give me a job."

"What you talkin', boy? Who'd give a skinny lil boy like you a job in a foundry?"

"I'm a man, Ma. I'm fourteen. I told the foreman I was fifteen."

"What foreman you tell that to?"

"The bossman at the foundry."

Oona's attention had been drawn from her books. She slid along the chairs to sit close to Amon at the table, her eyes asking. "Really, did you get a job?" She said, "I saw you on the school grounds this morning; then you didn't come in with the rest."

"I was sortin' out my mind," Amon replied.

His mother came over to the table and looked down into his face. "How come you go to that place wantin' a job?"

"I heard some talk about there bein' this place open at the sashweight foundry, and I went over to ask about it."

He saw the disbelief in his mother's eyes, the frown, the uncertain puckering of her mouth. How could he make her understand? It was still a fearsome happening in his own mind, how he'd ever figured to be so lucky as to get past those gates, the guard, get in to see the foreman, get the words out that all the way over he had practiced saying. He had told himself over and over, "You gotta do it. Ain't no use bein' scared. You can be scared afterward . . . Not now . . . You the man of the family. You gotta be a man." Could he make Ma see?

Talk flowed around him, pushing him with questions—Willy, Oona, Aunt Tatty, Ma. Cream came in. "What's all the fuss?" she asked.

At the supper table with the boarders and Uncle Hesh and the rest, conversation was general, and Amon sank into himself. He wished he might be alone, free of the house and all those in it. There was a time when he might have fled, not considering consequences. Now he dare not. He had to show his mother, all of them, he was a man and could face up to things he didn't like.

Uncle Hesh asked him about the job, gave him some good advice. The talk was brisk about work in general, most of the boarders having strong ideas pro and con. No one seemed to know much about the sashweight factory. But above it all he heard his mother's assertion: "I'm dead set on all my boys goin' to school. Maybe Amon can work now. But he going' to get his turn at school too."

Amon's heart had leaped at her words, and later that night in their room, when the younger boys were already asleep, Sabina spoke to Amon again about his job, revealing to the boy a part of what lay in her mind.

"How come you go a-lookin' for that job, Amon?" She asked as though she had not yet had the true answer. She sat on the side of the bed that she shared with Jeb, the light from the oil lamp falling on her head and shoulders. Amon noticed that her hair was dappled with white. It struck him with surprise. "How come you do that, Amon, when all the time I figures you at school?"

"I been there very day 'til today."

"Why didn't you go today?"

"I told you, Ma. I heard about this here job, and—"

"You heard it from Tom. I don't study Tom so good for you, son—him wantin' you to go out on the town nights like he does."

"Tom's a nice guy, Ma. He don't go out on the town like you make it sound. We just meet at the drugstore and sit around and sing is all. He makes big money at the factory. He's got a girl, and they gonna get married."

Amon poured out his confidences, imploring Sabina's approval, longing for her sanction of his endeavors. He could see her face softening, and her shoulders seemed to droop a little. She looked like a young girl sitting there on the edge of the bed in her white nightdress, her hands folded in her lap. A terrible yearning flowed through Amon. He longed to reassure his mother, to put his arms around her and say things to her—little kid things, teasing things, play things. He wanted her to know how glad he was at her gentleness with him, how thankful that she was not angry; and he wanted her to be happy about what he had done.

"You knows I want you to go to school," she said sadly.

"I know."

"I don't know how you come to do it."

"I don't either, Ma. Tom's dad jes told me about this job and I says, 'You reckon I could get it; and he says, 'It don't hurt none to

Eunice Young Smith

try.' And sort of sudden-like I figured I had to try. You ain't mad are you, Ma?"

"No, I ain't mad. I reckon right now it happened like the Lord intend. You smallish to take on a man-size job, son, and I had my heart set on all my boys goin' to school. But first we gotta get a place to live."

"Ain't we gotta place to live, Ma? Ain't we here?"

"I can't abide the way we doin' here." Sabina's shoulders straightened, and her lips set in the old stiff line. "I can't abide livin' in this here house that ain't mine and where I can't do what I wants. Your Aunt Tatty's a good woman. She means well. She tends this house and that's as it should be. It's her house. But I ain't got no say and I can't do nothin' like I wants. I can't take in washes—and I gotta take in washes to earn us some money. We ain't livin' offen somebody else. Hesh works hard, but he got his own to support, and we put Tatty out of one of her boarders. That ain't right, and I can't abide it. We plain gotta get into a house of our own. I can't do nothin' without I get some washes."

"You can have what I make, Ma. You can have it all." Amon felt elated that his mother wanted a house of their own badly enough to need his earnings. It was the key to the whole situation. He sat up on the tick and hugged his knees, and his thoughts raced ahead. Sabina went on, staring at the stained wallpaper around the window. "That ain't all I can't abide. I don't want no truck with that stuck-up church Tatty goes to—them folks with all their fine airs and store clothes. That ain't the kind of church I likes a-tall."

"We can go to another church. There's a lot of churches in Chattanooga."

"No we can't. Not while I'm livin' in Tatty's house and eatin' her victuals. No we can't. While we under her roof we gotta do like she want. Go to her church and knuckle down like she say." Sabina's eyes snapped and her teeth clicked together. "And I can't abide it. I want a place of my own."

Fleetingly, Amon thought of the huts along the railroad track. He wondered if to be independent she would settle for a tarpaper shack and the stench of Newby Street.

"I reckon it's the Lord takin' care of us," Sabina said as she blew out the lamp and got into bed. "I been prayin' hard. Didn't

A Trumpet Sounds

figure the Lord could hear me over in that African Baptist Church of Tatty's, but I reckon the Lord got ears for somethin' besides the rustle of starched skirts." Amon thought he heard a sigh. "Anyways, I'm right thankful, son. You got a job and I goin' to look for a house for us. You get your chance at school—maybe next year. I gonna see to that. But right now we find a place to live and what you earn sure gonna help a powerful lot."

Amon rolled on his side under the blanket. He felt light as air. He would have enjoyed running down the street fast, his arms pumping, his feet lifting high. He would like to sing at the top of his lungs. Oh, he would work hard at his new job. He'd show them he was a man. He'd show Ma he could take care of her, that he was truly the head of the family. It was a long time before Amon could sleep.

Chapter 15

A wind had blown all night, rattling the loose shutters, moaning among the chimney pots, making Amon sleep lightly and awaken early. Long before daylight he pulled himself free of the covers and slipped into his clothes. Sabina awakened and dressed, and together they went down to the kitchen were Sabina stirred the fire in the stove and put water on for coffee and gruel. She fixed a lunch for Amon to take with him, and she gave him two nickles for carefare, for it was a long way across the Bottoms to the foundry.

With his lunch bulging one pocket Amon raced up Douglas Street to Eighth and then east to Sonderman's grocery. Few people were about this early, mostly men going to work, hunched against the cold, heads pulled down into coat collars. Distantly in the fog-gray dawn he could hear the clip-clop and rattle of a milk wagon, a window opening and shutting.

At the grocery store Tom was waiting for him. "Hi, boy," he greeted with teeth-chattering cheeriness. "Right sharp this morning, ain't it?" He fell into step beside Amon.

"Yeah, it's great."

"What'd your ma say about your job? Must be jake, seein's you're here."

A Trumpet Sounds

"She don't like it much," Amon admitted.

'She wanna stop you?"

"Not exactly. She might could even be glad some."

"Yeah?"

"She wants to move out of Aunt Tatty's house. Reckon maybe she couldn't do that 'less I got this job. You reckon they'll put me to work where you are, Tom?"

"Naw. You'll be out in the yard unloadin' at first."

While they waited for the streetcar, Amon jumped up and down and swung his arms to warm himself. Other men gathered on the corner. They talked to one another in grunts and snatches: "Howdy" . . . "Cold" . . . "Christ, ain't it" . . . "Ya look beat" . . . "Feel like hell today" . . . "How's ya old woman?" . . . "Bad" . . . They shifted feet, hunched shoulders, spit, cursed the tardiness of the streetcar, and waited.

Light was breaking along the rooftops beyond the coalyards when the rattling car came along and the crowd at the curb boarded, all the Negroes taking seats at the far back.

In muffled voices, all the way down to the foundry, Amon and Tom talked about the plans for a quartet that would include Kirby Jones and Denny Macks as bass and tenor second. They decided to call their group the Silverairs, and as soon as they had a sufficient number of songs ready they would go singing nights in the streets. Tom was certain they could make some extra money this way, and besides it would be fun. He had a special version of "Daisy Bell," which he hummed softly in Amon's ear, saying the words only loud enough to be heard above the rattle of the car. Amon giggled. He thought Tom was right smart to be able to change the words of a song around and make them funny that way.

"We can do the same thing with *"Josephine, My Jo,"* Tom said. "And we'll ring in a lot of extra harmony. We got to practice every night till we get real hot on about four or five songs. Then we'll start out. We can sing the regular version for the first few verses, see, and then come along with our own lines if they ask for more. If folks like a tune, they'll stand still for a lot of repeats. But we'll slay 'em with *our* repeats, see?"

Amon saw clearly, and it delighted him. He marveled at Tom's inventiveness. Tom had once helped backstage at a minstrel show, and it had given him some ideas, he said. Instead of men dressing up like Negroes and telling jokes and all, it ought to be real Negroes. They could do it all better. Didn't he have a pocketful of jokes? Funnier than those they had told at the minstrel show. Might need to be toned down a mite for the ladies—but funny, terribly funny—sent the boys at Brady's into spasms.

Amon had agreed. Tom could act out a joke with the right kind of sound effects, like the one he told about the preacher at the revival. You'd think Tom was the preacher, waving his arms and telling the congregation they best be good or they'd go to hell: "And that hell a place of fire and brimstone where there's weeping and gnashing of teeth." And then this old hag gets up and yells: "Hallelujah! Hallelujah! Hurrah, hurrah!" "What you so joyous about?" the preacher asks and the old lady yells: "I can't go there. I got no teeth!"

He told Amon another funny story now, adding, "And then you do this little soft-shoe, you know, like Kirb do so good . . . and all the time music . . . fast, with a hot beat. Keep everything moving fast, that's the trick . . . see?"

Tom was full of ideas that opened a new and enthralling world to Amon, a world of creation and dramatic expression. Intricate harmonizing of melodies was nothing new. He had been doing that, everybody did that right along with the hymns, the play songs, the work songs. But until now Amon had little acquaintance with the popular songs of the white people, and their fast tempo and sentimental words enmeshed him. He liked to sing them with all the syncopation and variation he and Tom and Ben and Kirby could invent.

The car stopped. Tom said, "Here's where we get off." It seemed to Amon they had arrived at the foundry altogether too quickly. He piled out after Tom and some of the other men and entered the foundry gates. Here the boys separated, promising to see each other at noon.

Amon reported to Mr. Leeper and was put to work beside a burly man with a bristling red beard and squinting eyes, named Suggs, unloading scrap iron from freight cars. He was shown how to fill his wheelbarrow with pieces of metal and carry it to the furnaces. Load up and away with it and then back with an empty.

A Trumpet Sounds

Back and forth, back and forth. Thinking about Tom and his way with songs Amon forgot himself and shouted as he ran with the empty barrow: "And you'll be sweet . . . upon the seat . . . Of a bicycle built for two." He pulled up at the freight car. Suggs was scowling at him.

"Slow down, nigger," he growled. "You ain't goin' nowheres."

A man atop the car gibed, "You keep that up, son, ain't none of us gonna last out the day. We ain't gonna try and keep up with no squirrel."

"Wait'll he gets a try at the furnaces, Barney. That'll take the zip outta him."

At three o'clock he and Suggs went to the furnaces. They stoked the fires with wood and kept them blazing hot under the cupolas. When the iron was melted, the cupolas were tapped and the molten metal came pouring out into a mortar-lined pan from which Amon was required to dip measures in a ladle and distribute them among the molders.

Suggs worked stripped to the waist, his bulging muscles glistening in the light from the roaring furnaces. He stood back, his feet far apart, when the molten metal came sputtering beyond the mortar pan out onto the ground. He gave Amon no word of warning, and the boy was unprepared for the sudden searing pain when a spurt of hot metal shot against his ankle. He dropped his ladle and screamed. It was a red-hot knife twisting through his foot.

He was taken to the dispensary and the foot salved and bandaged. The metal had burned through his shoe and deep into his flesh. He went back to his task sick from pain and shock, scarcely able to face the metal-vomiting cupolas.

Suggs said, "That'll learn you to take it easy, bub, and keep outta the way them jumping devils. You gonna stay alive on this job, you take it slow and easy-like."

Amon was subdued, his enthusiasm for the new job dampened. Going home on the streetcar, he kept wondering how he could conceal his bandaged foot from his mother. He talked dispiritedly with Tom, and Tom, meaning to be encouraging, said words horrifying to Amon. "You get used to it after a spell, Amon.

I worked them furnaces once. I got all kinds of scars from metal burns. Tell you what. You leave your shoes open, unlaced, see? So when the hot stuff comes a-poppin' out and hits your shoes, you can kick em off real quick. That way the stuff don't get a chance to burn so deep."

Tom tried to cheer him by talking of the Silverairs, but Amon did not respond, and conversation lagged. When they got off the car, it was difficult for Amon to walk. In front of the grocery Tom said, "You comin' over tonight?"

"I reckon, if I can walk," Amon said as he hobbled away.

"Be lookin' for you then."

Amon worried about what Ma would think of his job now. The searing metal had burned a hole through one of his only pair of shoes. He limped up the Collinses front steps. It was already dark, and the lamps were lit. Aunt Tatty was dishing up beans to the family and boarders seated around the supper table. Uncle Hesh looked up and grinned at Amon. "Howdy, son."

Amon gaped at the people around the table, forgetting to greet them in his surprise. "Where's Ma?" he asked.

"She done moved out, son."

Amon saw Oona look at her father with that expression that said his grammar was all wrong, but it scarcely impressed him, coming as it did along with the import of Uncle Hesh's words about Ma.

"M-moved?" he stammered. "Where'd she go?"

"You got a job," Aunt Tatty said, "so Bina want a house, and she go out and get one. Right down the street it is. She knew this here little house was empty. Ol' Mammy Ducee used to live there till she died. You know that little house next the alley? It run down pitiful. Nobody done nothin' to that house all the time Mammy Ducee live there and ain't nobody touched it since, only rats. Bina got herself a house, hah!" She plunked the dish of beans down and went back to the stove.

"Bina'll clean it up," Hesh said. "In two days she'll have that place clean as a new hoe."

"Sure she will," Cream said, smiling encouragement at Amon. "Don't you pay no mind how it looks now. Aunt Sabina's going to make it real nice."

A Trumpet Sounds

"You go on over there," Uncle Hesh said. "Your ma'll be lookin' for you. Ain't much in the way of furniture yet, but she get that soon. I'll help her. She make out. You got a job now. That house got a fair tight roof, and I'll help her fix a few leaks. Say, now, how'd the job go?"

Amon turned and ran out of the house, clumping along to spare the hurting foot. Aunt Tatty called after him, "Amon, whatever ails your foot?" but he did not stop to answer. He knew the tiny house by the alley. It had sat there, empty and bleak, ever since they had come to Chattanooga. He had passed it dozens of time. Funny how you didn't pay much attention to a place until somebody said you were going to live there. Then every edge of it stands out in your mind's eye—dark, droopy little place with a roof like a sway-backed horse, one window, one door at the front, and only part of a stoop, the siding no blacker than that of its neighbors.

There was a faint glow through the grimy window. Amon pushed open the door and went in. The room was hot and the air was heavy with smoke. A single candle stuck in the mouth of a bottle furnished light. But there was Ma, and there were the boys sitting on the floor on spread newspapers. A musty odor mixed with the smell of fried meat. Sabina turned from where she was fussing with the rusty iron stove. Her eyes were alight as they met Amon's. For a moment they stared at each other, understanding fusing between them.

"I saved your supper, son. We-all has et. Most of the food Tatty brung over. Hesh didn't get this here stove workin' soon enough for me to cook supper on proper. It smokes some, but we fix that tomorrow. I'll have it slicked up and runnin' smooth come tomorrow night." Her voice was easy, confident.

"Where can I wash?" Amon's gaze swept the one rickety table, the stove, and a single stool. On a shelf along one wall pans and dishes had been stacked. Sabina's trunk stood beneath the window, and there were several kettles and boxes on the floor, but nothing more in the way of furnishings.

"There's a pail of water on the stoop, and there's a pan out there."

The water was icy cold as Amon sloshed it over his face and

head. By the light from the candle in the window he found the soap and applied it freely. Then he rinsed, using all the remaining water in the pail, and threw the dirty water into the yard. Inside, Ma handed him a towel.

"I gonna have it so's you can wash inside tomorrow," she said. "Soon's I get a mite more time to see what Hesh got piled out there in the back yard and I get us some chairs and things. We jes make do for tonight, son."

"I plain don't see why you gotta move out so fast from Aunt Tatty's," Willy grumbled.

"I rent this house. Why should I stay at Tatty's?"

"You might could wait till we got a chair to set on."

"We ain't even got us a bed, Ma." Jeb's fat, round face was rueful.

"You gonna sleep jes fine, honey. Don't you fret." Amon marveled at his mother's cheerful tone. He took the food she dished up for him and sat on the floor beside Obey. The candlelight made flickering streaks of shadow along the walls, darting up and down the stained and sooted boards. Paper, which at one time had been pasted over the boards, was torn away in places and cascaded in tattered, filthy ribbons from the ceiling. Accumulated grime and decay lay on the floor, and there were large rat holes in the corners. The makeshift pipe that ran from the stove to the chimney fit at neither end, releasing a continuous smudge. It stung Amon's eyes and kept Obey coughing.

"What the matter ails your foot?" Sabina had seen Amon limp and sit on the floor with difficulty.

"Jeeees! It's all wound up," Willy said, poking at it.

"You get hurt over there at work?" Obey asked, moving closer to examine the foot.

"It's ain't nothing."

"Then why you got it all wrop up like that?" Jeb insisted.

"What happened, son?"

"Oh, the metal spit at me and I ain't lookin' the right way." Amon tried to sound unconcerned.

"Where you get it done up like that?"

"Over at the foundry. They got a big room there, call it a dispensary. They have a nurse there all the time to take care of the men get hurt. She fix it up for me."

"Chee, did it hurt bad?"

"Look at your shoe."

"Boy-man! That musta been a hot spit."

"It were, boy."

"What's it like over at the foundry, Amon?"

"I thought you was going to unload scrap."

"I did for a spell this morning."

"Did some iron fall on you?"

"Yeah."

"Offen the cars?"

"No, they put me at one of the furnaces in the afternoon. This here scrap gets white hot and melts, and then we let it out into a long pan, and it comes out of them cupolas so hot it could burn from here to Atlanta. Sometimes it bounces out of the pan. It sort of explodes when it hits the ground and the metal shoots every which way."

Amon had to talk for a long time before he had satisfied his mother and brothers as to all that had happened to him that first day at the foundry. Then they talked about the house where they were going to live from now on, and Sabina told of her plans. She said she had decided to rent this house because it was near to Tatty and near to the neighborhood well and handy to the community privy. Too, there was a shed out back where she could keep a cow.

"But we ain't got a cow, Ma," Obey objected.

"No, but we gonna have one. Soon's I get me a few washes to do and saves a bit of money."

"I don't see no grass out back."

"There's plenty pasture the other side of the tracks. Nobody care iffen a cow eat there. You can fetch it over and tie it up on your way to school mornings. We can have our own milk like we had on the farm. And we might could sell some, too." She sat on the stool, her hands clasped in her lap, and serenely unfolded her plans.

Tomorrow she would scrub this house from end to end. Hesh was going to help her get some chairs and a bed or two. He had collected this stove only yesterday. Wasn't it lucky he hadn't sold it yet? Parts of it were missing, and it didn't draw too well, but that was only because they hadn't located the right-sized pipe. She would get some stove polish and make it shine. She'd stop up those rat holes with pieces of tin. And before it got much colder maybe she could manage some paper for the walls. Hesh thought she could get some brown wrapping paper at the grocery store reasonable, and that, tacked or pasted on the walls, would keep the wind from sneaking in.

"Just let me get some washes," she said confidently. "It won't be hard. Tatty knows some rich folks over on Oak Street where she cooked once. But first I gotta get this here house spick-and-span. This a nice little place when I get it fixed up."

"Ma," Amon finally asked, "how much rent you payin' for this place?"

"I agreed on a dollar a week. That ain't bad now. Tatty, she stick up her nose some. But I don't mind. This is my house. I can do as I please in it. And I don't aim to go to that church of hers no more. I 'llow she been sort of shamed struttin' into church with us country folks."

"Uncle Hesh say we gettin' citified fast," Jeb offered.

"Yes, I reckon you is." Sabina's glance speared him. "Jes you watch you don't get so citified you find me takin' a bresh to your pants." She looked at Amon. "I don't cotton to some of these city doin's a-tall."

"What you mean, Ma?" Obey pretended ignorance.

"She don't like Amon going out nights like he does," Willy flipped a spiteful grimace at his brother, and Amon longed to cuff him. Why say that now when he knew it would rile their mother, and when she was so pleased with things. Couldn't he let anybody be?

Sabina said, "Amon got him a job now, he won't be goin' out nights."

Another time Amon might have argued with her. Tonight he let it go. His foot hurt too badly to care whether he went out with the boys or not. He'd help Ma a little and then go to bed tonight.

"Teacher gave us homework to do tonight," Obey said. "Where am I gonna do it?"

Sabina got up from the stool, her hands moving fast to gather

A Trumpet Sounds

together dishes and food and the miscellany on the table. With her apron she wiped one end of it clean. "You can set right there, Obie. You go bring your book and come here by the table. I put the candle up clost. Come 'long now. You gonna study hard and learn you good so's you can talk like your cousin Oona and Cream. Bring your book and let me take a look at it."

"Aw, Ma, don't do no good for you to look."

"Yes, it do. I'm gonna do a heap more lookin' from now on. Soon's I gets us a good bright lamp and some chairs we all gonna set round this here table nights and study homework. I been goin' right along with you boys. I know all the letters same as Jeb. I can read some in that reader of Willy's. And I can write most as good as him too. Oona been learnin' me."

"Why you so hept on learnin' to read, Ma? Aunt Tatty don't care can she read."

"I aims to learn so's I can write to Leah, and maybe read my Bible for myself."

"You don't need to read. You got us here. We can do it for you."

"I ain't always gonna have you here. You be goin' away like Asa—like Leah."

In the days that followed it was hard to say what pleased Sabina more—scrubbing her house from top to bottom and tricking it out with curtains and furniture, or buying two washtubs and obtaining four regular customers for laundry work, or changing her church affiliations from the African Baptist to the First Emmanuel Church on People Street. The Emmanuel Church was less pretentious than Tatty's church on the hill, more friendly and demonstrative, the service more like that to which the Sayres had been accustomed in the Flatlands. The congregation sang many songs with the choir.

Amon was quickly spotted for his unusually sweet voice and urged to sing solos. Sabina's pride in him was patent. "That's the kind of singin' I likes to hear you do," she said.

"I like it too," Amon agreed. He refrained from adding that he also liked the singing he did with the boys, the songs they sang at the drugstore and around on the street corners. And he refrained from telling her that he liked the buck and wing and the cakewalk. He could see no harm in dancing and singing, but so long as Ma objected, he felt it senseless to disturb her.

However, he was aware that she knew more than she let on. There were plenty of gossips in the neighborhood, and Ma wasn't deaf. Sometimes, when he was about to go out in the evening, she spoke of study, her tone reproachful. But as long as he came in fairly early and promised to drink no liquor, she did not pester him. There were evenings when Oona came to study with Sabina and the boys, and she would look somberly at him as Amon took himself blithely off.

Many evenings Amon spent with Uncle Hesh, learning to play the harmonica, contriving various ways to produce novel sounds, or singing some of the old songs while Uncle Hesh played the accompaniment:

> *Hound dog sittin' 'neath a crab apple tree*
> *Bow-wow-wowwwww.*
> *Howl at the moon and not at me*
> *Bow-wow-wowoooowooo.*

Once when Amon was there Oona had a school friend home with her, a girl named Julia Hurlehy, a wand of a girl a little older than Oona. Amon thought she was very pretty, but her steady, speculative gaze made him uncomfortable. He felt uncouth before this dainty girl, an unkempt lout with shabby clothes and shoes with holes and knotted laces. A wave of his old shyness engulfed him, and he became mute. When she left, he found himself thinking after her, hearing her quiet voice and her manner of speech, which was like Oona's.

Many evenings he spent with the Silverairs, for they had now become well known throughout the south end of town. They had worked up an extensive repertoire, an amusing mixture of songs from many sources. Sometimes on Saturday nights they visited the dime store and listened to the new song hits being banged out on the tinny piano, then purchased any song with a potential for ragging—one copy for the four of them.

Tom had a gift for what he called "spicing" a song, accenting

A Trumpet Sounds

the offbeat, distorting the melody into a weird, often compelling, syncopation. They ragged everything from "When You Were Sweet Sixteen" through "Molly O" and "There'll Be a Hot Time in the Old Town Tonight." They experimented with harmonies and sang "Mandy Lee" and "Chloe" as no one had ever heard them sung before. When they sang "The Cakewalk in the Sky," everyone shouted.

Then one night someone showed up with a banjo, and everyone joined in the "Bully Song," singing and dancing. Amon thought about Julia and wondered if she would have danced with him while he sang:

> *When I walk that levee round*
> *Round, round, round*
> *Lookin' for that bully*
> *Round, round, round . . .*

A fever of buck-and-wing music arose. To satisfy the demand the boys resorted to "My Gal Is a High-Born Lady" and "All Coons Look Alike to Me." And that night, when he returned home, Sabina was waiting for him with her jaw set, the line of her mouth like a rod. She waved him to a chair.

"Son, you set there while I talk to you." She clasped one knotted fist and Amon knew she was riled.

"What's the matter, Ma?"

"I don't like them songs you singin' nights."

"What songs, Ma?"

"You knows what songs right enough."

"I sing a lot of songs."

"You knows the ones I mean," she accused, pointing a gnarled finger at him. "You knows. Jes cause I ain't sayin' much 'bout you goin' out nights ain't no sign I don't know what goes on. I was there tonight in that crowd when you sing that disgracin' song."

"Which song, Ma? I sang an awful lot of songs tonight."

"You sing that "All Coons Look Alike to Me." That's a trashy, no-account song."

"Ma, that song was written by a Negro. You ought to be glad I sing it."

Eunice Young Smith

"Well, I ain't. That's the kind of Negro we ain't proud of, the kind runs down his own people."

"Hey, Ma," Amon strove to distract his mother. "Who do you think was in the crowd watchin' us tonight—besides you? Fez. Old Fez Babber. I talked to him after we quit the singin'. If you'd hung around, you could have talked to him too, said howdy. He's got a liquor store over on Corby right near the foundry, says he gets business from the men that work there. He's doing all right, he says. He asked us fellows to come over and sing at his store."

"Thas good. I'm glad Fez got himself a business he can run, though I don't look kindly on liquor."

"Ain't no worse than runnin' a still like he done down there in Georgia."

"Maybe so, but don't you try to turn me aside. I'm thinkin' about that no-account song you sing tonight. All you life you hear nice songs. Our people make the sweetest songs there is. You go around with that Tom and Kirby, and they teach you them trashy white man songs. That ain't the kind of singin' I can smile on."

"You don't expect me to sing hymns all the time, do you? Folks want to laugh and cut loose sometimes."

"Yes, I knows, cuttin' loose on that cakewalk and that there buckanwing. I see 'em. I know. I ain't lost my eyesight, neither my ears."

"They ain't much different than a shout, Ma. We used to dance in a shout. We sing some of the same songs we sang then. We sing 'Little David, Play on Your Harp.' We sang it for them tonight."

"Hah!" It was the essence of scorn. "I heared it. You ain't sing it like it meant to be sung. I scarce knowed it was 'Little David.' You pull that song apart and tear it all up and what comes out you mouth ain't nothin' I wanna hear."

Amon had to laugh in spite of his mother's doleful air. "You got the idea right, Ma. We jazz 'em up—that's the truth."

"You gettin' a long way from what I has in mind for you, boy, and I don't like it a-tall. I don't cotton to that gang you hangin' out with. You gotta come out from that kind."

"I go to church regular."

"It's what you do outside of church worrifies me. Preacher

A Trumpet Sounds

Bowles say he think you should be baptized and come into the church proper as a true member. Iffen you gonna be a preacher, you best get ready."

It was a long time since Ma had mentioned her ambition for him. At that moment he had never felt farther away from any possibility of becoming a preacher. It was nonsense to think about it. He tried to distract her.

"Well, we won't sing 'All Coons Look Alike' no more, Ma, if you don't like it. I promise. I don't like it much myself. Ben heard it somewhere and just thought the tune was good to rag."

"God give you a voice, Amon, a real sweet voice. You best use it right or might could something happen to it."

"I'll use it right, Ma. I'll sing you a song you like: 'Go to sleep Kentucky babe . . . Go to sleep and rest. . . . Da da da, dada de da. . . . sweet Kentucky babe . . .'"

"Hush now, you wakin' the boys."

Chapter 16

With many of the men at the foundry Amon was on friendly terms, joking with them, being included in their banter. He worked hard, responded to orders quickly, and accepted whatever tasks were assigned to him without complaint. After a time, even Suggs tired of baiting him, and a mild sort of ribbing replaced his former surly and often obscene taunts.

For Amon the work was made lighter when he sang, just as it used to on the farm in Georgia when he sang himself through the long hot days in the fields. He sang songs according to his mood or the need of the moment. Sometimes he hummed the play tunes he knew as a child, "Chicken in the Bread Tray" or the "Turtle Song" as he rattled his barrow, empty, back to the cars, the songs bringing to mind brief, bright pictures of remembered days.

Often, in those early weeks at the foundry, when the Silverairs could not afford four copies of a new song and the boys had to do considerable memorizing, Tom and Amon would rehearse in lowered tones all the way to work on the streetcar and Amon would arrive on his job so filled with the current song hit that it would break from his lips spontaneously now and then during the day. He would sing half the song, lost in the melody, until, stumbling over a forgotten word or phrase, he came to himself and caught the smiling eyes of fellow workers. Once the foreman did more than nod his head in enjoyment and approval. He asked Amon quite directly to keep on singing. The men liked it

A Trumpet Sounds

and did their work better when he sang. This pleased Amon, but he was so overcome with shyness he could not sing a note for days.

Firing the furnaces and tapping the cupolas was a daily ordeal for Amon. Fear of the exploding metal and the tension generated in trying to escape it often had his nerves jangled. To ease the strain he shouted the song sermons Ross used back in the Flatlands. There was one called "Dry Bones Goin' to Rise Again," and another about creation that Amon delivered with great fervor. One homily about Noah and the ark, with Noah boarding the animals two by two—"the elephant and the kangaroo . . . the little mouse and the grizzly bear . . . the crocodile without any hair"—particularly tickled Suggs. He would chant it along with Amon, feeding wood into the furnace and animals into the imaginary ark. Once Amon had shouted into the belching inferno: "No hidin' place down there, Lord . . . no hidin' place down there!" and Suggs had bellowed with laughter.

During those first months before the cupolas, Amon was burned many times, his feet and legs scarcely healing from one burn before he got another. Suggs appeared unconcerned at first, his only comment being, "Watch it, bub!" when the molten metal began to fly. But at the time of that final explosion, when a great blob of white-hot liquid burned his ankle to the bone, he had fainted, and it was Suggs, he learned later, who picked him up and carried him to the dispensary.

When he returned to work after three fiendishly painful days, he found himself transferred to another section. There he was taught how to make cores. Cores, the forms used to make holes in window-sash weights, were molded by hand, and after the furnaces this job seemed wonderfully easy and pleasant. Besides, the hours were shorter and the pay better.

In the core shop there was a new set of men to get to know, a new barrier of strangeness to overcome, and Amon again took refuge in singing, mostly a humming or whispered singing to himself. As familiarity with his work grew, the songs took on body, and after a few months he was singing as freely in the core shop as with the Silverairs on the street corners. A young Dutchman with merry blue eyes, one Lonny Bornstein, working at the same bench with him sometimes joined him in a popular tune. He had a peculiar high voice, and he sang in a crooning fashion. They became friends, Lonny often joining Tom and Amon at lunchtime to sing and harmonize.

Foreman Englebright encouraged the singing, as had foreman Leeper. Most of the men liked the singing and seemed to work better with the rhythmic tunes in their ears. But some of them resented Amon. They sneered when he approached them, making little attempt to conceal their animosity. Their remarks were calculated insults.

"Snotty little punk."

"Who does he think he is? Jenny Lind?"

"Some niggers need to be shown their place."

"You said it. They can sing a little . . . gets 'em biggity."

"Trashy little upstart. Look at him strut."

Amon felt like crawling.

"I'd sure like to shave him down to size."

"You and me both."

It should have worried Amon. When he told Tom about these asides, Tom looked glum.

"You better watch your step, Amon. Some night they'll jump you."

"Why? I ain't done nothin'."

"You don't need to do nothin'."

"They ain't gonna bother me for no reason."

"They don't like you. That's a reason."

"I don't even go near those guys. Lonny says don't pay 'em no mind."

"This the city. Ain't like on the farm. This a tough place sometimes, awful tough."

"They got police here."

"Don't do you no good. The cops is for the white man."

But it was summertime, and the uneasiness Amon felt during the day at the shop was quickly dissipated in the langorous evenings when the Silverairs went strolling and singing along blossom-scented streets in the better parts of town, in the saloons, and the restaurants where colored singers were welcome. Most of the coins tossed to them were spent to purchase new songs.

A Trumpet Sounds

Sometimes crowds of young people, standing in the streets listening to the boys sing a catchy air, would join in. Then the street would resound to "The Banks of the Wabash" or "In the Good Old Summertime."

It was inevitable that the quartet should attract other singing voices, and presently the Silverairs found they were a sextet, and at length a chorus of twelve voices. Then Tom took up again the idea of creating a minstrel show.

Early in April Tom and Kirby and Amon had gone to see the Harry Harrigan Minstrels when they came to Chattanooga for a week's run. From the back of the gallery, they had watched the soft-shoe dancing and heard the jokes and songs. Most of the songs were coon songs with a spurious dialect and accompanied by antics intended to be ludicrous. The boys concluded, talking about it afterwards, that they could assemble a show to beat it.

They decided to pool their resources and build a show that would outshine the Harry Harrigan Minstrels. They began work immediately with great enthusiasm, selecting the best voices for solos, ferreting out musical instruments and those who could best play them. They collected jokes and the most acceptable stories and repartee. They trained their chorus in an assortment of catchy lyrics with some improvised and very funny extra verses.

Tom's father let them meet for practice in the back of the store evenings after the store closed and on Sundays, first extracting a promise that they would not pilfer the oyster crackers and the cheese.

Amon worked feverishly to perfect his jokes, rehearsing with Uncle Hesh to discover just how long to wait before coming in with the gag-line. Timing was important, Uncle Hesh said. Sometimes a thing seemed funny because the listener had been kept waiting just so long for words he expected to follow, and then when some others came—no matter what they were—they sounded funny.

It was Uncle Hesh who taught the boys how to get laughs even in the event a joke should fail to take fire. He said, "You know there was this feller once used to come round here, and he was a powerful hand for speeches. He never did have nothin' much worth sayin', but he'd get up on a box and beller and make a fine speech anyways. Nobody listen to the words much. They jes stopped by to see what all the noise was about. He never did know when to stop rantin' and ravin'. So one day somebody thinks he oughta be showed a lesson, and they put a nail in his box. And when he got to yellin' holy Moses real loud, this person hooked a rope on the nail, and jes as this speecher was a-deliverin' his very best 'Yumpie-hi-diddy-I-am-the-greatest,' this feller yanked the box out from under him."

Hesh stopped to chuckle and the boys howled. "What happened, Uncle Hesh? What happened?"

"Why," Hesh finished, "it was his best speech. Everybody laughed fit to split. They laughed so hard and cheered so long he done become famous."

"You think we should work in a rope-pullin' stunt, Uncle Hesh?"

"No, that ain't why I tell you 'bout this here feller. I jes want to show you what makes folks laugh and keeps their attention from wanderin'. If you don't get the people stirred up enough with your jokes, start cuttin' the coattails of the man tellin' them, see? Or somebody in back cut his suspenders. Don't matter much what he sayin'—if his pants fall down, it's funny."

They tried this routine out on a small group of willing test patrons with gratifying effect. Some of the jokes and antics of their show were so comical witnesses laughed themselves into tears and stomach cramps. Eventually, after months of hard work, the boys had produced an hour-and-a-half-long entertainment, fast-moving, melodious, and happy.

It was difficult for Amon to elicit any words of praise from Ma for these doings even though Obey and Will and Jeb and all of Aunt Tatty's family as well as those neighbors privileged to attend a rehearsal were loud in their enthusiasm. Julia Hurlehy had been present at one rehearsal, coming with Oona in the evening to Sonderman's store. She had said to Amon afterward, "It's a terribly clever show. You are wonderfully funny in it, Amon. I do hope it's a success." Amon had squirmed with pleasure, thinking as he had the first time he had seen her, "She's the prettiest girl I ever knew." He felt less ill at ease now with her complimenting him, her eyes smiling into his. He felt exuberant, as though he could

A Trumpet Sounds

perform superhuman feats of song and dance and humor. He wanted to ask her to walk home with him, but before he could find the words, Oona had drawn away and taken Julia, and the boys crowded around him with their talk and laughter.

They had gone over and over their show until every minute of it ticked off like a well-oiled clock. At length they were satisfied that the show was ready to present to a theater manager. Aunt Tatty suggested they have some older man act as a spokesman for them. She thought they might induce Grant Rayburn, a dignified member of the African Baptist Church and a man of some presence, to undertake the mission. After attending a rehearsal on a Saturday night, he agreed that the Silverairs Minstrel Show was exceptionally good. He was willing to act as emissary, and he promised he would see a manager on Monday. They would all meet at Sonderman's store on Monday night to learn the results.

All day Monday at the foundry Amon worked with songs bubbling on his lips. The songs were from their show and were gay and witty, and the men seemed to enjoy them, especially Lonny, who for the past weeks had listened willingly to Amon's jokes, laughed at them, praised his songs, but had not committed himself on the chances for the show. And so inward-looking was Amon, so absorbed in mental rehearsals, he was for an interval removed from the obvious malice of his enemies; he was deaf to remarks and talk that might have startled him had he heard them.

On the streetcar going home, Tom and Amon talked excitedly about what Mr. Rayburn would have to say, what the theater manager would be like, when he would want them to put on their first show, and where they would take it after a success in Chattanooga. They parted with "See you soon," and Amon went home to eat hurriedly with Ma and the boys and then to return to Sonderman's store.

The families of all the participating minstrels were there, and the talk was heated and blithe and steamed on in endless channels of possibility for all the boys. No one doubted the show's quality, its polish, and they waited impatiently for Grant to appear and tell them when they were to start.

But from that second when Grant set foot in the grocery doorway, everyone knew what he had to tell. They listened pa-

Eunice Young Smith

tiently while he recounted his meeting with Mr. Gordon, the manager of the Amadon Theater. They listened submissively, like people accustomed to endless thwartings, people who had suspected all along, though they would not admit it, that their endeavor would be fruitless, but who had worked diligently anyway, compelled by some inner growing or reaching—knowing in the striving a certain salubrity, an unquenchable need for fulfillment.

Rayburn reported that Mr. Gordan had said quite bluntly that townspeople would not be receptive to a show put on by Negroes, no matter how good it was. No one would come except those Negroes who could afford tickets. He couldn't risk affronting his regular customers by offering them such a show. He refused even to witness a rehearsal, contending it was useless. Even if it was the best show on earth, he said, he couldn't put it on. That was that.

Someone suggested halfheartedly that they try another theater, that there was more than one show house in the city. This was met with apathy. They all knew that any other theater manager would say the same thing.

The boys went back to singing in the street, for the nickles and dimes thrown to them. Sometimes they sang in Fez's liquor store, and Amon saw many of the men there who worked at the foundry, and he saw grimaces of hate from some of them. Fez knew the boys' singing was good, but his shrewd knowledge of men told him that not all ears listening were friendly. A sense of foreboding came to him about this boy from the Flatlands with the voice of a lark.

Chapter 17

Autumn came again. The mockingbird scattered notes infrequently, and roosters crowed all night long in the bright moonlight. As cold settled in, chimneys spiraled gray smoke, and soot fell in the heavy air and lay in eddied patterns on streets and walks and curled in dark laceries on porches and window ledges.

Sabina brought her washtubs into the kitchen, and all day water was heating on the stove, and the house filled with the smell of lye soap and wet linen.

Bright and early she fed the younger boys and sent them off to school. And every morning at six o'clock Amon met Tom at the grocery store and together they boarded the streetcar for the foundry. Tom had had a small raise in pay, and he and Lilly were going to be married.

"We gonna live in that little shed back of the store. Lilly gonna fix it all up pretty. She got notions— Ummh-umh! That gal's a fixer, sure now."

"Lilly's okay, boy."

"Yeah, sure enough. Son, how come you ain't got a girl?"

Amon shrugged, not knowing exactly. He liked girls well enough. He was very fond of his cousins, and he really enjoyed dancing with girls. But only one girl had attracted him beyond the most casual interest. That was Oona's friend, Julie Hurlehy. He had thought of her at first simply as Oona's school friend, and he failed to attach significance to his own remarkable rise in spirits whenever he saw her, at school or on the street or at Aunt Tatty's. He thought she was pretty to look at and sweet, real sweet. But just a kid like Oona, giggly, full of nonsense.

Then that evening, after rehearsal, when she had spoken to him seriously, just a few words, but they had sent his blood racing ridiculously. That first time he had met her, at Aunt Tatty's, he had thought her shy, like himself, and some part of him reached out to her, wanting to detain her, know her. But that was all, nothing a fellow could tell anybody about. He couldn't say to Tom: "She's little and soft and she purrs like a kitten and she makes me feel good." So far, he'd not gotten up the nerve to ask her to walk out with him even. Not that he hadn't thought about her as his girl sometimes, but so far he hadn't done anything about it. He was seventeen now. He supposed he ought to have a girl. He had been working at the foundry almost three years, and his pay was three dollars for a ten-hour day—as much as many men with families earned. Ma must have a nice little hoard tucked away by now. She never spent any money that he could see, except for food and rent, and her washes took care of that. He tried imagining what Ma would say if he came home one day and announced, "Ma, I'm gonna get married. Can I have all that money you been hoardin'?" He chuckled inwardly, seeing her bridle, her dream for him shattered. He pushed the thought away.

At the shop he gave his full attention to the work at hand. He had been doing some experimenting with the formula for the cores and had come up with a new blend that he felt was superior to what they had been using. He explained his method to Warren Englebright, who in turn took it to the head chemical engineer. Exhaustive tests proved it a sound combination of elements which produced a better core under all conditions. The company, very gratified with the improvement, had put the new process into production.

Carlton Holt, the chief engineer, had commended Amon on his initiative and Englebright had told Amon the company thought his discovery called for recognition. So Amon was not altogether unprepared for the call that morning to the supervisor's office.

"Sit down, Amon," Mr. Appleton said. "I don't suppose you are entirely surprised to be here."

A Trumpet Sounds

Amon grinned, too excited to think of proper words.

"I'll come to the point. In recognition of your loyalty and service to the company as well as your initiative and interest in your work, we feel you have earned a substantial increase in salary and an advanced position. You like it there in the core shop?"

"Yes, sir, very much."

"Get along with the men?"

"Yes, sir."

"How would you like to be foreman of your shop?"

The words were stunning and left Amon speechless, but Mr. Appleton went on. "You know all the details of the work and the blend"—he grinned—"since it is yours. Even though you are very young"—it flashed into Amon's mind that Mr. Appleton didn't really know how young he was—"we feel you are the man to oversee the coremaking with the new formula. Your salary will be increased to five dollars a day." He shuffled through some papers on his desk while Amon tried to collect his scattered wits. "How does that suit you?"

Amon nodded, his smile showing all his teeth. "When do I start?"

"Right away. Your new duties will start immediately."

"But sir—" Amon fumbled with intruding doubts. "What about Mr. Englebright?"

"He'll take over Krumm's department. Krumm is being transferred to shipping." He rose and extended his hand. "We are pleased with your work, Amon. We trust you will be with us a long time."

Amon had plunged into the hall, thrilled and bewildered, his first thoughts being, Wait till Ma hears this!

Back in the shop he tried to subdue his soaring spirits. Lonny told him Englebright had just informed them of the transfer. He congratulated Amon, slapping him on the back and shaking his hand. "You showed them how to make a better core. You got a right to a break."

No one else came to congratulate him, however, and trying to appear casual he went to his own bench and busied himself there. Tomorrow a new man would take his place at this bench, perhaps a rookie in from the yards, and he would have to show him how to handle the molds and the metal, just as he had had to be instructed when he first came to the core shop.

Now, with new and extended responsibility given him, he felt suddenly diffident, reluctant to leave his bench and the procedures with which he was familiar. But his job now was to oversee the work of the whole shop and, willy-nilly, he must exert himself.

He went through the shop watching the work, speaking to this man and that one, making friendly remarks. He had been working with these men for a long time; he felt he knew them well. Yet now they acted strange with him. There was a cold reserve, a knife glance from the corners of eyes, a sullenness in men usually jovial. Ill will had swept the shop like a tidal wave, submerging the safe shore of amenity.

He knew what bothered these men, what lay behind their behavior, the degrading ancestral patterns of their thought. He knew, as only one can know who has been subject to it all his life, the emotional bias that prompted these men to resent a stripling Negro boy, no matter how competent, as their boss. To be friendly, to patronize a fellow worker or someone they deemed beneath themselves, was one thing. To countenance a Negro taking over their supervision was intolerable.

The whole day was sticky with tension, apprehension on Amon's part, smoldering resentment on theirs. He walked about as in a nightmare where the sense of fear was greatly elongated.

On the way home he refrained from telling Tom about the raise and the new job. He knew he would learn about it soon, but right now he didn't want to hear what Tom might have to say. It would be all he could do, he thought, to tell Ma.

Tom said, "You actin' mighty glum. What's eatin' you?"

"Nothin'."

"You feelin' okay?"

"I feel okay."

"Ain't nothin' wrong at work, is there?"

"No." What a black lie.

"You comin' to the store tonight to sing?"

"I reckon not tonight, Tom."

A Trumpet Sounds

"What's gettin' into you, son? You plain downmouthed."

At home he could eat no supper and Sabina was promptly suspicious.

"What the matter ails you, son?"

"Nothin', Ma."

"Whyn't you eat then?" Willy squinted at him through locks of hair, stuffing his mouth with bread.

"These here is good chitlins, Amon," Jeb assured him, amazed to see anyone refuse good food.

"Yeah, I know." Amon tried to smile at him, feeling a warm affection for this fat little brother who could go to school every day and be fed and clothed and be free of problems, and who was so cheerful and lovable.

"He got him a girl, Ma," Obey tossed out between bites. "Only thing make a guy not eat. You got a girl, Amon?"

"Somethin' sure wrong when you can't eat." Sabina's sharp eyes and sharper instincts told her it was no trivial matter disturbed the boy. She would not pester him now. Better to ask later when the other boys were in bed or at Tatty's.

"You should have been to school today," Obey said. "That'd really make you wanna eat."

"Take your fingers outta your plate. What's wrong with you at school?" Sabina spoke to Obey, but her concern lay with Amon, her thought of him held in abeyance.

"We had a test."

"Did you pass?"

"How should I know? We ain't got our papers back yet."

"Miss Burt says you ain't supposed to say 'ain't,' " Willy taunted.

"Well, she ain't here to hear it."

"Don't do you no good to learn grammer lessen you use it," Sabina reproved. "You quit sayin 'ain't' if Miss Burt say it ain't right."

"You jes said it." He laughed delightedly.

"What you supposed to say instead?"

"Aren't. That's the short for 'are not,' see?"

"Aren't." Sabina toyed with the word. "That's like Oona always says. She talks real nice, Oona do. So do Cream. Cream might could be a teacher, she's that smart."

"Well, I wish I had her for a teacher instead of Miss Burt. She's a wildcat."

"She make you learn."

"And that would take a wildcat," Willy jeered, winding a strand of hair around his nose.

"Boy-man! What a day I've had," Jeb sighed.

"A body would think you work hard or somethin', baby."

"Don't call me baby." Jeb raised his gravy-covered spoon and threatened Willy, who slapped it, knocking the gravy over Jeb's face.

"Stop that!" Sabina banged the table with her fist.

"He called me a baby. I ain't no baby."

"Aren't."

"Ain't."

"You're only in third grade."

"That don't make me a baby. Anyways, I ain't talkin' about school. See?"

"What you talkin' 'bout, honey?" Sabina cajoled him.

"Well, didn't I work hard today when I got home from school? I been all over gettin' stovewood for you, ain't I?"

"Haven't I," Obey corrected.

"Oh, for cryin' in the soup, Ma!" Amon's unhappy feelings vented themselves in a rasping outburst. "Why you gotta go scrounging round for fuel that way? Don't I make enough so's we don't have to do that?"

"Ain't no sense spendin' money for what we can pick up for nothin'."

"We don't need to do that no more. I'm making good money at the foundry. I got another raise today. You don't have to do things like that no more."

"Any more." Obey grimaced.

"You got you another raise!" Willy crowed, "Jeepers! How much you makin' now, Amon?"

"Five a day."

"Boy-man! We're rich."

"That what makin' you not eat, son?" Sabina frowned anxiously.

A Trumpet Sounds

"I can eat your chitlins if you don't want 'em." Jeb reached for Amon's plate, and Willy slapped at his hands.

"You've had enough, bub. You're so fat now you waddle."

"How come, Amon?" Obey prodded. "How come you got another raise?"

"Amon works hard, he's a good man. That's how come," Sabina said.

"Ma, I wanna go to work," Obey screamed at her. "I'm sick of school. I wanna get a job and make a lot of money like Amon does."

"You goin' to work soon enough." Sabina snapped at him. "I put you to work real soon. It's about time Amon had a turn at school."

"When he's makin' all that dough?" Willy squeaked in genuine dismay.

Amon thought, "I could tell them I've been made a foreman, and then watch their mouths fly open. They'd have a thousand things to say, things I don't want to hear." No, he couldn't tell them. He'd wait until his brothers were in bed. He wished he could tell Ma alone, could bury this news in some secret pact with her where it might stay covered, a dread thing, not to be divulged to the other boys or the neighbors or Aunt Tatty, who would accept it as one does a scandal, talking and talking, stripping the facts of whatever garments of seeming clothed them. They would rend all illusion and there would be left the naked and ugly truth.

When supper was over and the dishes cleared away, Sabina insisted all the boys get their schoolbooks out and do their studying. Amon tried to help Willy with some of his arithmetic problems, but he was so distracted by his own dire problems he gave up after a while and went into the bedroom where he sat on the edge of the bed, his hands pressed between his knees, and fell into deep brooding.

He could hear Jeb spelling his words over and over. He could hear the scratch of Obey's pencil and the wood sputtering and crackling in the stove. Out beyond the window he could hear the sounds of the city, the clang of the streetcar over on Tenth Street, the rumble of carriage wheels, the clop-clop of horses, the barking of dogs, someone's cow bawling in the pasture across the tracks—probably Ma's—a faraway train whistling across the night; and above and over all he could hear his own pulses throb, could hear the pain mounting against his temples, back of his eyes. The blood racing along his miserable nerves made more clamour than all the noises of the city.

He rose and went again into the kitchen. His mother was gathering up the ironed garments, folding them and laying them carefully in a basket, her hands curiously attentive, as though she worked among flowers, finding pleasure in what she did. "She's sure of something," Amon thought. "Inside of her she's sure, and she ain't afraid."

It was hot in the kitchen, the house too small to contain him. He took his coat from the hook near the door and went out into the night, Sabina asking no questions of him. He walked up Douglas Street to the foot of the hill. He thought of going to Sonderman's, but only fleetingly. He did not want to meet or talk with his friends. He did not feel like singing. He thought of going to see Uncle Hesh, of telling him about the job and of his fears, then abandoned that when he remembered the boarders and all the other members of the family who would be about. He began to think of Julia, trying to see her with her family, trying to see her alone with himself. He wondered if she would be a good person to confide in.

He ascended the hill and turned west on Vine Street, walking toward the Ft. Wood grocery store. Many of the young bucks made a habit of hanging around this store. It was a general meeting place. He decided to avoid the store and so turned a corner a block before he got there. It was a poorly lighted street. He could hear voices arguing in a shadowy yard, a dog beginning to yelp as though kicked.

Suddenly someone caught his arm. He swung around, tense nerves knotting his fists and crooking his arms into fighting position. Then he relaxed, looking down at the grotesque figure of Fez Babber, his crablike shadow stretched monstrously across the sidewalk.

"Oh, Fez—hello," Amon stuttered. "What you doin up here?"

"I been lookin' for you."

A Trumpet Sounds

"You know where I live."
"Didn't want to go there now."
"Why not?"
"Something I gotta tell you."

Amon made no answer but moved on up the street, Fez jerking his way along beside him.

"I hear something today."
"Yeah?"
"A lot of the men from the foundry comes to my place—"
"Yeah, I know."
"They sure enough stirred up tonight when they comes in."
"You know why?"
"I didn't at first."
"I reckon I know who they were—Lupins and Crumbshaw and Blinks."
"Yeah, they's some of them. Others too. They talkin' real loud and tough. They don't care who listens. They foamin' off about somebody put in over their heads. And brother! They purely hates this somebody. I didn't pay it much mind till Wilkie Drucker—he comes in generally with that Tate—the guy with the scar down the left side his face, you know?"
"Yeah, he works alongside of Tate in the core shop."
"Yeah, till this Wilkie Drucker says: 'That God-damned singin' nigger.' Then I starts to listen."
'What did they say, Fez? You know who they talkin' about?"
"You get you a new job or something?"
"Yeah, I got made a foreman."
"Lordy! How come?"
"Back a month or so ago I been messin' around with the stuff they make the cores out of and I figured a way to make a new formula, a better one."
"Tom told me about that. You right smart, Amon."
"Maybe not, if it just brings trouble."
"Like bein' made a foreman, eh? Ain't no Negra I knows of been made a foreman."
"I didn't want it, Fez. I didn't ask for no raise or new job."

Eunice Young Smith

"How come they done give it to you?"

"Those men high up in the company wanted to show me thanks for what I done. They reckon they doin' me a good thing."

"They don't know what they doin', boy, they purely don't."

"What am I supposed to do, Fez? Turn it down—quit—tell them I don't want to be foreman—don't want the money the job pays?"

"Them men are sure mad."

"I know, and I don't know what to do."

"They out to get you."

"Did they say so?"

"That's why I come to warn you."

"What they aim to do? Did they say?"

"I dunno. But they get good and drunk some night and they don't stop at nothin'. I gotta get back to the store now. Pula's there alone. I jes wanna let you know."

"Thanks, Fez." Amon could say no more. The fear that had sloshed around in his middle all afternoon had begun to jell, to become a solid lump.

He went home, hung his coat on the hook, glanced at Sabina copying words from Willy's speller, walked into the bedroom and went to bed. He'd not tell his mother tonight. She'd have this trouble to worry her soon enough. Anyway, there was nothing she could do, nothing anybody could do.

Chapter 18

WHEN Amon saw Tom the next morning, the news was written all over his usually cheerful face. He flopped off the store veranda and fell into step beside Amon.

"Bad news sure travel like the wind, don't it?" Amon said.
"Sure do. What your ma say?"
"She don't know yet."
"Ain't you tell her you been made a foreman?"
"Not yet."
"She hear it today."
"I reckon."

There was a long pause. No need for words where understanding was complete. After a while Amon said, "What am I gonna do, Tom?"

"Sure is a fix."
"What would you do if you was me?"
"I wouldn't take that there job. No, sir. I wouldn't want to be no foreman."
"I like the job. It pays five a day."
"That's a lotta dough, son. Sure is a lotta dough."
"I know all about the work in that shop. I made up the new formula. We make better cores now than has ever been turned out before. I used to think all the men liked me there in the shop. We got along fine. But not no more—not now."

On the rattling streetcar the boys talked in whispers, Amon

Eunice Young Smith

fearful of their words reaching listening ears. He imagined everyone on the car knew his situation and had a menacing attitude. Going into the foundry, he noticed furtive glances. Even those men with whom he was friendliest seemed reserved, their greetings diluted with caution.

In the core shop he hung up his coat and cap and went to his accustomed bench. Another man was there, the new man he had broken into the work only yesterday. He concentrated on showing this man the tricky procedure, being painstaking in all the details of the work. The morning passed and work progressed. As long as the cores turned out satisfactory in content and numbers and the men's personal feelings did not interfere with their work, he would be thankful, he told himself. Maybe in time he could ease their resentment.

Yet it became clear all too soon that time is a slippery commodity and cannot be purchased on our own terms when needed. In the days that followed, the undertow of animosity affected production. Mistakes were made, whether intentional or accidental was hard to determine—a succession of blunders which, while in themselves not disastrous, reflected on Amon's foremanship.

Contemptuous talk was rife in the core shop, some of the most bitter of the men deliberately inciting fellow workers to thwart the foreman's efforts at effective production.

Amon did not tell his mother of this friction at the foundry, but she sensed his unease and guessed at the trouble. She had been dubious and dispirited when she first learned of his promotion. She had said to her sister then, "I'm feared, Tatty. Ain't no white man gonna set for a colored boy tellin' 'em what to do."

The holidays had come and gone, without enjoyment for Amon, only filled with apprehension for the growing unrest at the foundry and his inability to cope with his new duties. He wanted desperately to justify Mr. Appleton's confidence in him, wanted to show them he would make the company a good foreman. He wanted to show everyone, himself most of all, that he was capable of performing his new duties efficiently. But the harder he tried, the more abrasive things became.

Eventually the disruptive situation became patently clear to

A Trumpet Sounds

the supervisor, and one of the troublemakers was discharged. This was a drastic measure aimed at suppressing the rebellious climate in the core shop. It only aggravated it.

When Tom heard the news, he was doleful. "Man, you in a fix."

"I sure wish they hadn't fired Stankey. The rest of the men will hate me worse than ever now."

"Yeah."

"I don't know what to do."

"You ought to get them to take him back."

"I tried. But the boss thinks discipline is needed. That's what he said."

"That discipline gonna fall on you."

"Yeah."

"Sure is bad, son." Tom wagged his head.

"What you figger I ought to do?"

"Same as I figgers when you asked me before."

"Quit?"

"Yeah, if you like livin'."

Later, at Sonderman's, where he stopped long enough to speak with some of the fellows loitering there, the advice was the same, more casually given, yet no less fervent: Quit, before it was too late. "And don't go wanderin' near any white sections of town. Stay in crowds and go home early."

It was a warm evening in late February. The thought of Ma's steamy kitchen and the tiny house crowded with brothers was unwelcome. He turned his footsteps toward Douglas Street. He wanted to talk with Uncle Hesh. He found him in the back yard sorting junk. Seeing Amon, Hesh straightened, wiping his sleeve across his moist face. "Gettin' warmish, ain't it?" he greeted.

"Sure enough."

"How's it go with you, son?"

Amon shrugged.

"You look sort of beat."

"The weather maybe."

"Could be. How's your new job comin'?"

"I don't know, Uncle Hesh." Amon picked up a small gear and tossed it into a pile aimlessly. Hesh emptied the contents of a

Eunice Young Smith

sack on the ground and continued separating rags from papers, stacking the papers in a neat pile and throwing the rags in a basket. Amon stared around the cluttered yard, across the fence to the neighbor's line of limp laundry, back to the Collinses' stoop, where every kind of discarded article was piled or leaning. The rear windows of the house peered like bleary old eyes from between toppling hills of kegs and cans and wheels and dismantled beds and store fixtures and other appurtenances of his business. A small boy came, picking his way through the litter, in quest of "Something to hold up the leg of our stove, Ma says." Hesh found a box of miscellany and fingered through its contents until he found a piece of iron calculated between them to be about the right height. He pocketed the boy's penny and came back to the paper sorting. It was almost dark.

"Have to wait till daylight to finish this, I reckon," he said.

Amon stood twisting a piece of rusty wire back and forth until it snapped.

"What's on your mind, son?" Hesh seated himself on an upturned keg. "You look like ol' Ma Gloom."

"Uncle Hesh," Amon blurted, "what am I gonna do? They ain't gonna let me keep that foreman job. They makin' it pure hell down at the foundry. Nothin' goes like it should. Seems like they all bent on makin' mistakes—on purpose. And today one of the men got fired."

"You fire him?"

"Jess, no! But I reckon I might just as well have."

Hesh rubbed his chin. "Set down, son, and tell me about it." Amon sat down on an old buggy seat and unburdened his heart. In the gathering dusk Uncle Hesh's face was indistinct, but the plant of his hands on his knees and the way he spit indicated he had formulated some strong feelings about the matter.

"You could quit." It was given out as a possibility in a tone of voice which plainly stated there was really no alternative.

"I'm makin' the best money I ever made. If I could keep goin', Ma maybe could take it easier, maybe live in a better house, maybe—"

"She don't want no better house, son. She's rather you stay alive."

A Trumpet Sounds

"I know. She's been against this foreman job from the first." His mother's words jangled even now in his ears: "They's some places you can't go and they's some jobs you can't hold." They infuriated him, made him want to stick just to show somebody, maybe only himself, but somebody, it wasn't true. It was doing your job well that counted. You did a job to the best of your ability and you got rewarded. He didn't want to lord it over anyone. He only wanted to work hard and get ahead if he could. Mr. Appleton had seen it that way, and Mr. Englebright and some of the other men high up in the company. It was the little guys, the men in the shop, in the yard, the more ignorant of the workers, he realized now, who were set most violently against him.

"There's other jobs," Hesh said. "Anyways, it don't signify. Any job you get, they feel they gotta tell you what to do. That's the white-man boss speakin'. But Amon, they can tell your outside self what to do or not do. Can't nobody tell your inside self. That's where you are boss—see? That's where you can say what is. Nobody can say that you gotta think so and so. Nobody can see inside you, can they? Ain't nobody can tell your brain what to think. That's free, real free. They can't say, 'Don't you dare have them thinks.' They don't know about 'em. Sometimes them thinks can be—" He paused for a moment and then went on. "Well, anyways, it's them thinks is goin' to do a powerful somethin' one day, you mark my words."

"How, Uncle Hesh?"

"I dunno, I dunno." He went off into his dream, gazing into the gloom. "I reckon it's what keeps a lot of us colored folks sane. We can hate the white bastards right into hell, shit on 'em, spit on 'em, kick 'em in the ass, tramp out their guts, strew 'em all over the place, hang 'em to light poles, and they can't do a thing about it. In our thinks we can change places with them, we can trample 'em down, rub their faces in the dung pile, tell 'em where they can sit and stand and where they dasn't, tell 'em they can have just what we want to hand 'em and that's all, tell 'em they don't dast to speak to us lessen we give 'em leave. We can hand out the pay and cheat 'em; we can lie to 'em and make fun of 'em and sneer at 'em and iffen they don't like it we can take 'em out and beat 'em up and lynch 'em and abuse their women. And they can't do one damned thing about it. Ha!"

Amon had never heard Uncle Hesh so moved. He was seeing him for the first time—not the shuffling, quiet, backing-away man who sat in Aunt Tatty's kitchen, but the man who was boss of his brain, even when he could be boss of nothing else. It was his soul-saver, his Saturday night binge, his opium, his escape—the secret of his toleration of white people, the salve for the wounds at their hands, the cheating, the demeaning, the patronage. Some of the venom of his words transferred to Amon. He could feel what Hesh did. It removed some of the tension, soothed him.

"I'd have to start all over where I did three years ago," he said. "I've worked hard to get where I am." He twisted another piece of wire until it snapped. "Anyway, what if I did start over somewhere else? Wouldn't the same thing happen again? I'd just get to where the job was good and the pay good and some white man would want to dress me down. Ain't that so? I can only go so far, only do so well, cause if I do too well I scare some white man into meanness. Ain't that so?" His voice was rising in excitement. "I gotta look for a job where I can stay down—way down."

"It don't signify. You gotta stay alive to work anywheres."

Amon pondered. "Maybe things will settle after a bit, after the men get used to the idea." He knew he was fumbling for courage. Every day had seen the situation at the foundry worsening. The firing of Stankey was like waving a match over gunpowder. He contemplated going to Mr. Appleton and again begging to have the man taken back. But he knew they wouldn't do that. The head office was not to be intimidated, even if he was.

"Maybe you're right."

"Yeah, sure."

"What should I do, Uncle Hesh?"

"Like I say—give 'em back the job."

"That's what Tom says."

"He's right."

"Ain't no other way you can see?"

"Ain't no other way I can see."

Amon got up from the buggy seat, the tight ache in his throat loosed a little. "I reckon I best tell Ma."

It was hard to abandon his dreams for the future, his feelings

A Trumpet Sounds

of achievement. It was hard to think of giving up so good a salary. Yet he could see there was no other way. He would give back the job. He felt a sudden great relief. He would not have to think about the hate and the terror any more. He said good night to Uncle Hesh and walked down the street and home. Sabina was still at her ironing, the endless chore that occupied so great a portion of all her days. The windows were open to the mild night, but it was stifling hot in the small room. The lamp flickered and guttered in a faint current of air. Amon slid into a chair, away from the smoking lamp, and for a few moments watched his mother as she smoothed a garment and folded it. She took a rolled shirt from the basket and shook it out, then reached for the hot iron.

"Ma," he said, "I 'bout made up my mind."

"That's good, son." She ironed a sleeve with elaborate care, waiting.

"You still study I should quit my job?"

"I study it that way, son."

"Well, I reckon I made up my mind."

"That's good. Hardest part is makin' up you mind to a thing."

"I reckon."

"That's right. It's the hardest part. It's the part we gotta get God's help for. The rest He figgers we can do for ourselves."

"Yeah."

"You'll find another job, Amon, iffen you want one. But it about time you had your turn at school now. Obey wants to work with Uncle Hesh for a spell. And I want you should go to school, son."

"I'm so far behind in school now, Ma. I'd never catch up. Even Jeb is ahead of me now."

"You can catch up, Amon. You're a smart boy."

"I'm no boy, Ma. I'm a man. I been doin' a man's work for three years."

"I know. You do work like a man, but you jes a schoolboy." She chuckled at her small joke.

"Oh, Ma, it ain't funny," he said, but he felt lighthearted, like joking. Ma's humor was catching. "Oh, well, when I get free of this job, I might could want to go to school. You got enough saved so's I can loaf for a spell?"

Eunice Young Smith

"I got enough saved," she said.

"You're the best saver I ever knew, Ma. I don't reckon you spend any money a-tall." He felt gay now, a great weight sloughed from his spirit. And suddenly he felt a deep tenderness for his mother. He got up and put his arm around her.

"Go along," she said. "I gotta finish this here bundle tonight." But her voice was gentle and the words sounded happy to Amon. He went out into the night. The air felt cool against his face. He could smell tomato plants growing in cans and boxes along porch rails. Voices came to him—laughter—a child being sung to sleep. He wheeled up the street and headed for Sonderman's. Tom would be glad to hear of his decision. He wanted to run, feeling light as new-blown cotton. He began to sing: "In the moonlight . . . uuumm . . . In the evening, by the moonlight . . . uuummm."

Some boys were lounging on the corner, and he stopped to talk with them, asking if they had seen Tom.

"Tom's gone to Lilly's, I reckon. They gettin' married next week."

"That so?"

"That's what Lilly say. She outta know."

Amon laughed. "They gonna be married sure then. Tom gonna do what Lilly say." He headed for Lilly's house, swinging along with a light step. Lilly's mother was sitting on the gallery. She said. "No, Tom ain't here. Lilly gone to church meeting tonight, Amon. I 'spect Tom's over to Ft. Wood."

Tom was probably with Ben and Kirby, so Amon decided to go to the Ft. Wood store too. They might strike up a song or two. It had been some time since he had been with the boys to sing.

When he arrived at the store, a crowd had gathered and Tom was there. Amon pulled him aside and told him he had decided to give up the foreman's job, that he was going to tell the boss tomorrow. He was through, washed up with that job and happy about it. He wasn't scared any more. Tom slapped him on the back and hugged him. He did a buck and wing, clapping his hands.

"Now you talkin', son. You usin' the ol' noodle. You get another job. Boy, I'm purely glad of them words. You had me worried plain sick. Yes, sah! Now maybe you stay alive and can

159

A Trumpet Sounds

come to the weddin', huh?"

"Sure enough. Don't you worry no more. Tomorrow it'll all be over but the dust settlin'. I be my own man again."

"Broooother that's good."

They joined the others and Amon said, "Let's scrape us up a little tune, boys. I feel a song comin' on."

"What'll it be?" They all seemed happy, catching his spirit.

"Let's do 'Oh, Baby Mine.'"

They sant it with embellishments. They sang "Danny Deever" and "Rosy O'Grady" and "My Dream Is All of You," rollicking up and down the scale, enjoying a gay inventiveness. Couples gathered and begged for more songs to dance to. The boys, feeling happy, were agreeable.

It was late when Tom and Amon finally started for home. They cut through a vacant lot at Palmetto and went along the tracks that cut obliquely across Vine and Clark Streets. There were no lights here, but the boys knew every step of the way.

"Man, you're like your old self again. It sure makes me feel good."

"Yeah," Amon agreed. "I feel good too. Jes like I got outta a tippy boat onto sound shore. I sure feel good."

And then without a word of warning Tom began to motion with his hands, sort of flapping them about—a motion that Amon felt rather than saw. Tom whispered, "There's somebody tailin' us."

Amon's first thought was that some of the boys had followed them. He was about to turn and wait for them, but Tom grabbed his arm. His voice was strained, though only a whisper. "Don't run! If it's cops, they'll shoot."

Amon was too terrified to talk. His instinct was to run, yet his legs buckled under him. His pace quickened though; thought was chaotic. Bolt—maybe they could make cover in the darkness. How many were following them? Cops or not, they could have guns. What did they want? What were they after? Him? Or just anybody? Who were they?

"What'll we do," he panted, trying to stay abreast of Tom's long stride. He could hear the quickened scuttle of the stalking footsteps on the cinders, could feel the pursuers closing in on them. He could feel Tom's fear too, loud in the darkness. There was no time to think further. The men were upon them. Both boys were grabbed and hit over the head with clubs. They went down, Amon falling on top of Tom. Only partially stunned, Tom groaned in his ear: "Don't fight 'em! God! Don't fight 'em!"

He was picked up then by the front of his shirt, and for a moment he saw his assailant. The man had not troubled to cover his face. They did not intend to leave him alive to tell any tales. Then the iron-knuckled fist smashed into his face. He fell, his arms covering his head, his senses reeling. He could hear the shotlike crack of a club against bone and Tom screamed and a muffled voice said, "This one—this here's the one." He was yanked to his feet again, and again the iron fist smashed against his jaw. A splintering pain shrieked through him. He went down on his knees as a club descended. A kick in the ribs lifted him off the ground and rolled him onto his back. A cleated boot came down like a sledge into his groin and Amon doubled over in agony. Then the boot came at him in concentrated fury, a welter of kicks—to his head and belly and back and chest and groin and face. No part of him was spared—the pain was beyond bearing—and then a great black abyss and nothingness.

Chapter 19

There was a thick stillness all about him, folds of fog through which sounds came muffled, far away, so far there were only shadows of sounds. He could faintly hear thuds of objects coming together violently—cracklings, like glass shattering—pointed, hurting sounds, minute yet piercing. He could not free himself from the din, for if he moved, excruciating pain seared him. If he lay still, the pain burned less fiercely, dwindled to long enchained circles going from end to end of him and from side to side, around and around. He wandered then, becoming lost in a wood and banged sightlessly against trees, being driven by a storm, and his eyes were stabbed again and again, spears running through his head to the back. A terrible sickness rose in his belly—a violent retching, and the movement was like a vast sea of agony—and then darkness came again.

Long after he was well, Amon would remember his fearsome journey back to consciousness. They said he was four days lying like a dead man, a swollen, battered pulp with only a trickle of pulse and lungs wheezing for air. He heard about it piecemeal from Ma and Obey and Willy and Uncle Hesh and Aunt Tatty and Cream and Oona and the twins, from Ben and Kirby and Fez and from the friends and neighbors who came to call, from the endless talk that went on around his bed.

Tom, they said, hadn't been beaten so badly. He had been able to crawl across the tracks and up to a house and tell the

Eunice Young Smith

people there about Amon. Tom's nose had been broken, but he was not in such bad shape otherwise, except for bruises and cuts.

When they had brought Amon home, he was thought to be dead. A doctor had been called, coming reluctantly from his bed in the middle of the night. He had looked at the mangled body and shaken his head. He didn't think the boy would live, but he would do what he could. He put the broken ribs in a cast and the jaw in a cast and the arm in a splint. He had stitched up the gaping wounds on face and head. He told Sabina he could not tell what internal injuries had been sustained until the boy regained consciousness, if he ever did. He gave her instructions for poultices and left.

There had been a time when the fuzzy blanket of Amon's coma folded aside and he saw, as in a busy street, dark faces all about him and mouths writhing in anger and eyes blazing with the stress of argument. He didn't catch words, only the meanings of words, and all the furious voices came together like a bellows blowing the flames of hatred, the wish to retaliate in kind—to throw a burning torch into the house of the white man—to maim and torture others as he had been . . . and Fez was there, his twisted face and disfigured body a further goad . . . and dimly the idea floated across his mind that they were talking as Asa used to . . . that Asa was there among them, urging them to rise up as a pack, as a united force, and take vengence, giving as they got, dealing out hatred and fear and violence. His sick body was dragged along in a yelling, gesticulating mob . . . and battered and pummelled and trampled by his own people because he was too weak to protest or get loose from them. Then the angry faces and the bitter words faded, and he lost touch with reality again.

Now he lay, unable to move without pain, but with his mind clear, and considered his luck. He was alive. He was lying in bed in Ma's little house, his body washed clean, his ribs and jaw in casts. One eye was unhurt. He could see the patchwork cover of the bed, the sunlight coming in the window below the half-drawn shade darting fingers of light through the amber glass bottle that held the candle on the chest. He could smell soapy water and something cooking.

Presently Sabina came in with a cup of steaming broth. She sat down beside the bed and fed him, cooled spoonful at a time. It

163

A Trumpet Sounds

was hard to swallow, hard to speak. Ma, serene and competent, her headcloth faded from many washings, her sleeves rolled back, showing the thin arms with veins bulging like ropes, her hands gnarled and lumpy, yet easy moving, soothing. "Ma!" he thought. "Oh, Ma."

"You eat all this here," she said, "It'll give you strength."

"It's good, Ma."

"That eye lookin' better, son."

"Can't open it yet."

"The swellin's gone down some."

"Can't talk with this thing on my jaw."

"I reckon. Don't try."

"Where is everybody?"

"Oh, around. Willy and Jeb totin' Miz Tucker's wash."

"Where's Obie?"

"He helpin' Uncle Hesh. He dead set on havin' hisself a job."

"Uuumm."

"Seem like the whole town been in this here room. People I don't know even. They comes before you all back to consciousness, your face all over bandage. That Lonny Bornstein you used to talk about, from the core shop you know, he come with a couple of other men. And one day the great big man, said his name was Suggs, he come. Nigh filled up this little room with him. He stood here beside your bed a long spell, jes lookin', not sayin' nothin'. Then he pulls out this little shiny horseshoe—that trinket I got tied to your bedpost there, and he lays it on the covers and says, 'It's my lucky piece. I shoulda give it to you sooner.' And when he left, he says to me, 'We ain't all damned murderers, ma'am.' "

"I like that man. Not much for talk. All them church people talkin', talkin', talkin' . . . wear you out talkin'. But everybody feel so bad, and they wanna help."

"Uuuummm."

"They comin' to see you in little bunches from now on. I tell 'em I can't work in crowds. I can't take care of you when the whole place swarmin' like a beehive with a new queen." She smoothed the sheet over him and with the hem of her clean apron wiped away the sweat that had gathered on his forehead.

"How's Tom?"

"His Ma say he be all right in a week or two. He come to see you purty soon."

"Lilly frettin' some?"

"I 'spect. They ain't gettin' married this week." She cocked her head.

Amon smiled inside. He wondered if Julia would come to see him. In a way he wanted her to come, to see him and feel sorry for him. At the same time he didn't want her to see him all battered and ugly. He imagined her there in his bedroom, sitting beside the bed like Ma was, maybe holding a spoon for him to eat, or a cup of water for him to drink, her long pretty fingers holding the cup to his lips. She would be smiling a little perhaps, her eyes kind, and the sun would come rushing in through the window there and make her skin like deep old gold, and . . .

"You rest now, son," his mother said. "Purty soon I gonna rub your back with some liniment and you sleep better."

"I can sleep now," he said. Talking fagged him. He slept for long stretches of time, the night sliding into morning and the day into night again; and it seemed his body would never cease to hurt, nor his brain to seek sleep. People came, spoke to him, brought him food, small gifts. At first they were part of a long dream, faces in a parade—Oona with tears streaming down her cheeks, Willy peering between bars of black hair, Aunt Tatty with her hand across her mouth, faces of angry men, Fez's face, Uncle Hesh bending close, struggling against emotion, women's faces, pitying.

As the days progressed and he improved slowly the parade broke up into individuals—Oona offering to read to him, Abe and Linnie bringing him a bluejay's feather they had found, a Mr. Forbes from the foundry who said he would call back later when Amon was better, Ben and Kirby bringing words of cheer from Tom, and Mrs. Drudie from next door bringing him custard.

And then one day Oona came again, and Julia was with her. Amon felt his injuries were worth something at last when he saw her eyes and heard her choked words of sympathy.

"I was here before," she said, "but you didn't know it."

"Hey," he said, trying to smile out of the unbound side of his

A Trumpet Sounds

face. "You've grown up when I wasn't looking."

She blushed, color suffusing the smooth golden cheeks. She smiled a quick, acquiescent smile, her eyes falling for a moment from his. She had done just that, he thought, and he hadn't noticed because he had been too busy with his job and since Ma had switched churches he didn't see so much of his cousins. Oona had been growing up too; she had woman signs and was knowing of them. She giggled telling Amon about school, constantly asking Julia's confirmation of everything she said. They sat beside the bed on kitchen chairs and chattered to him and to each other. Julia said she had been to the dime store and had heard the new hit song, "Crazy Joe." She sang the chorus for him, shrugging her shoulders and moving her hands to the quick rhythm of it:

> Crazy Joe, Crazy Joe . . .
> Tippy tip tapping, heel and toe
> Oh, ho . . . come a glide, then a slide
> Then tippy top
> Watch him go . . . Crazy Joe.

When Oona said they had to leave, Amon thought Julia looked reluctant. She stood beside the bed and touched his bound arm timidly, "I hope you get better real soon," she said.

And Oona added, "You hurry it now, Amon. There's going to be a sing at our church and Mama wants you to be in it. She says there's nobody in our whole church can sing as well as you. She wants you in our sing even if you do go to that old Emmanuel Brethern Church."

A week or so later this was affirmed by Aunt Tatty herself. "Hurry on and get yourself outta them casts. We needs you in our sing. Reverend Stuber givin' you a special invite. They want you to sing a solo; they want you to do that 'Ezekiel Saw the Wheel.' You sing that so beautiful, Amon." She put her hand to her bosom and throwing back her head began to sing:

> Way up yonder on the mountain top—
> Wheel in the middle of a wheel—
> My Lord spoke and the chariot stop . . .
> Wheel in the middle of a wheel . . .

She broke off abruptly, laughing at her own singing. Amon tried to smile, a crooked, one-sided smile. "The doctor don't say when I'll get out of these casts, Aunt Tatty."

"Yes, he does. He tell your Ma about three more weeks is all. He bind you up in tape then. But you be outta the casts and can walk around. You be good as new soon. Look at you now, your face almost all healed—your eye opened all the way, most the pain gone from your belly. Your Ma got more good remedies, ain't she? She know about herbs. Always was a hand with herbs. She knows what good for what, better'n a doctor, I say. You hurry it up some now. All kinds a things a-waitin' on you gettin' well."

"That's right, son." Sabina came in from the kitchen and stood beside her sister. "Lots of things waitin' on you. Miss Burt comin' this afternoon. I told her you done quit work and is gonna go to school now, come fall openin'."

"Oh, Ma, I'm not going to school," Amon groaned. "With all them little kids!"

"Miss Burt say maybe she can tutor you some—that's give you special lessons all to yourself. She say she can do it this summer yet, and by fall you might could be a grade further. It won't cost much. She's a mighty nice lady. She look like Cream and she talk beautiful. I'm purely itchin' for you to start, son."

"Well, I'm purely itchin' too, Ma, but not for school. This thing on my chest is so hot it feels like ants bitin'."

"I'll fix it," Sabina said. "Tatty, go fetch me some fresh water from the well, will you? I gonna bath this boy. I make you feel better son. I'll get you feelin' fresh as spring clover. And when Miss Burt come, you'll feel real good."

Miss Burt did come, and she talked with Amon a long time, asking questions, probing for his scholastic status. She brought some books with her and, with Sabina closely attentive, determined where to begin the lessons. After she left, Sabina came back into the bedroom looking bright and snappy.

"I'm a-goin' to study right along with you, son. I'm 'most as far as you are now. We'll do our lessons together. We can help each other.

"You'd think it was a game or something, Ma, the way you talk."

A Trumpet Sounds

"It's better'n a game, son."

About the eighth week of his recovery a man had come to see him, a Mr. Forbes. Amon remembered him only vaguely from those first half-delirious days. He was an attorney, he said, from Marks and Benson. He sat beside the bed, a briefcase on his knees. He was genial and friendly and genuinely sympathetic. He said he spoke for himself as well as the company in deploring the savagery of the incident and that he had come as the company representative to make what amends they could.

"It wasn't no fault of the company," Amon said.

"We know that," he replied, "but the company wishes to pay for your medical expenses and make some other compensation."

"That's mighty kind," Sabina said. She came into the room and sat at the foot of the bed, her hands in her lap. Mr. Forbes fiddled with the straps of his briefcase and asked Amon how he was getting along and whether the doctor was satisfied with his progress and a few other casual comments. Then he said quite abruptly, "Do you know who the men were who attacked you?"

"I only know one for sure."

"How many were there who attacked you?"

"Four, I think."

"You're not sure?"

"I know of four. There might have been more."

'Why are you certain of the identity of only one?"

"He was the one who spoke—the only one who said anything. I knew his voice and saw his face."

"Couldn't you see the faces of the others?"

"It was real dark. But that one that I heard—he said I was the one they were after. I heard it plain, and I know that voice. I saw his face, too. He didn't have anything over it."

"Someone from the shop—the core shop?"

Amon did not answer. He glanced at Sabina and then down at the covers of the bed.

"Don't you want to name names?"

"No, sir."

"We have some ideas ourselves. But of course we have no proof." After a pause he added, "Do you think you could identify this man at any rate?"

"They didn't knock me out right away. Seems like they did a powerful lot of pounding before they finished me off."

"Didn't you fight back at all?"

"No, sir."

"Why didn't you fight back?"

"They'd have killed us both. They'd have claimed we attacked them first and that they had to defend themselves."

"Do you intend to file charges against these men—this man? Have you engaged a lawyer to represent you?"

"No, sir," Sabina said, and her back was straight as a gunstock. "We don't aim to hire no lawyer."

"It would be best to be represented by an attorney if you are going to file charges. You should have legal help to handle court proceedings." He looked from Amon to Sabina, who was shaking her head and mumbling to herself.

"We don't want no court proceedings," she said.

Mr. Forbes shifted one leg over the other and rested his hands firmly on the briefcase. He spoke quietly but with a hint of impatience. "Amon says he knows one of his assailants. I've talked with Tom Sonderman. He was conscious during most of the—the assault. He says he knows two of the men, says the rags came down from their faces in the scuffle. He saw the faces plainly."

"Did he tell you who they were?"

"No, he didn't."

"I reckon we both know who the men were right enough," Amon said quietly.

"The two of you testifying in court might obtain a conviction—a fine, some manner of redress. Marks and Benson is anxious to see justice done. We are a big company. We have many Negroes in our employ. We want them to know we do not condone this sort of thing, that we will do all in our power to obtain justice. We cannot, you understand, accuse men without sufficient evidence. But if their guilt is established in court, they will of course be discharged from the company and punished. However, we must establish their guilt first, legally."

"No, no." Sabina shook her head in vigorous disapproval. Mr. Forbes stared at her in open question.

"We know who's guilty. They know who's guilty," she said.

"But it must be shown, proved, by process of law."

"We don't aim to prove nothin'. They be no need. We know who done it. They know who done it."

"That's hardly enough to satisfy a jury."

"And God knows who done it," she added, not hearing his last remark.

"Yes, but—"

Sabina went on as though he were not speaking. "We don't want they be fired from their jobs. They got families to earn for—children. It were bad enough when that one man was fired. Maybe that cause all this here trouble. I don't know—maybe not."

"It might have precipitated this assault, Mrs. Sayre. But I think the trouble was brewing earlier."

"Maybe. Anyways, we don't aim to stir up no more trouble."

"But I don't think you understand. In order to obtain any redress—"

"What's that?"

"A compensation—some kind of repair or amend for what has been done to your son. We have to establish guilt in a legal manner."

"Maybe that so, but we don't aim to do it." Her lips set in the old, familiar straight line, and Amon knew Mr. Forbes might just as well give up and go home. He would get nowhere with Ma. But the man persisted, "If the case were taken to court—and personally I would like to see it taken there—there is a good chance these men would be convicted. There is considerable sentiment against these outrages, you know. Many just-minded men abhor this kind of thing, Mrs. Sayre. I think a jury might well be expected to find these men guilty of unprovoked assault and put them in jail or require them to make restitution in some form."

Sabina had followed his words closely. "You mean them men could be made to pay us money for what they done?"

"Yes, I think so."

"We don't want their money, Mr. Forbes. We don't want none of it. We just wanna leave all that lay. Don't want to rile up nobody no more. We don't wanna take nothin' to court, nor have nobody jailed."

Eunice Young Smith

"Don't you want to see these men punished?"

Sabina shook her head slowly.

"It was a brutal thing done to your son, Mrs. Sayre."

"We knows that. But it don't do no good sendin' them as done it to jail. That don't make them no better. It might could make them worse—meaner. It wouldn't help their families none. Ain't no sense makin' their children suffer for what they daddies done. It just make them mean, too, when they grows up. We don't see no sense in all that."

"That's a very charitable attitude," he said in a manner that suggested he reserved another opinion. "Perhaps you are fearful of further retaliation."

"I don't know what you mean esactly."

"He means they might try to get even then again, Ma—maybe do this over again."

"I 'llowed thas what he mean, son." She turned to Forbes. "Maybe we is afeared. They's always plenty to be afeared of. But that ain't what's keepin' us out of no courtroom now."

"Is this your decision, too, Amon?"

Amon had been studying his mother's face with somber, thoughtful eyes. "Yes, sir," he said. "I feel the same as Ma. We've talked this all over, Mr. Forbes. The whole family has talked it over. We don't none of us figure revenge do any good. I'm glad I'm alive. I'll get me another job when I get well. I was going to quit anyway. I didn't like all the ill feeling I was causing. I had made up my mind the night this thing happened."

"Yours is an unusual attitude," Forbes said.

"No it ain't, really, Mr. Forbes," Sabina leaned toward him, her eyes imploring his understanding. "Maybe I can't say it so's you'll see. Lots of us folks feel this way. It got to do with religion, I reckon, and maybe you don't think along the same as we do. But me and Amon don't feel no hate. You rightly got to hate to want to go into that there court and testify against them four men. We feel terrible bad about what happened. It makes us sick deep down in our hearts. But we just don't figure it do no good gettin' back at them, goin' into court and all."

"It would take courage too, I think," Forbes said.

"That ain't courage, Mr. Forbes," she said with a shred of

impatience. "What you talkin' about, gettin' your nerve together and goin' to that place and pointin' them men out, swearin' they tried to kill you." Her shoulders writhed as though the thought were loathsome. "And hopin' they get punished. Maybe a jury do find them guilty. I don't know. It seem it ain't likely. But maybe they has to pay a fine or go to jail for a spell. Or maybe they don't get convicted. But they gonna be shamed just the same, and their families shamed, and their children. And that's not a good thing. They ain't no need to do that, Mr. Forbes. They gonna get punished anyways."

"They are?" It was a startled rejoinder.

Sabina nodded.

"How do you mean that? Does Amon intend to—"

"Get even, you mean? Is that what you thinkin'?"

"Well—I—you—"

"No, we don't aim to get even. God take care of that."

"Oh, I see." He settled back a little in his chair.

"Maybe you does, and maybe you don't. I pity them four men, Mr. Forbes. I don't hate them. Neither do Amon. He knows a thing. What you reckon made them do what they done? You think they to blame? You're wrong, Mr. Forbes, plumb wrong. They actin' out a long line of teachin' as been drummed into them since they babies. They thinkin' like their mammies and their pappies did, and like their mammies and their pappies told them to think. They just like most the white folks after the war—being' afeared the colored folks is gonna rise up maybe and try to even the score one day, or try to take away what they figure is theirs, or marry into their families. Bein' afeared has made the ignorant ones mean. All white folks ain't that way. We knows that. But these here sorry ones, they can't help bein' like they is. They don't know no better. They ain't growed up to where they can think for themselves. They actin' just like they learn when they babies."

Mr. Forbes stared at Sabina. She glanced away from him, toward the window, but her eyes were unseeing, inward-looking. She shook her head slowly. "I don't hate them. I'd a lot rather be in my shoes than theirs—even in Amon's shoes than theirs. I couldn't never pray again iffen I was in their shoes. I couldn't say to God 'Forgive my trespasses'—I'd be too shamed."

Eunice Young Smith

She paused then and the room grew still. The attorney sat with one elbow on his knee, his chin cupped in his hand. He sighed deeply, as one who has made a mental journey into a distant realm and returned singularly stirred by what he found there. At length he moved, taking a new grasp of his briefcase. Putting both feet on the floor he made as though to rise. "I am reluctant to leave the matter here," he said. "But I believe I can appreciate"—he said the word with a certain reverence—"your attitude. However, Marks and Benson, and the company, wish to make a gesture of compensation to Amon. It is not a matter of legal claim, you understand. We simply wish to do what we feel is just."

"They been mighty good to me down at the foundry, Mr. Forbes," Amon said. "Nobody could be any better than Mr. Appleton and Mr. Englebright and some of the other men down there. I'm purely thankful. You don't need to feel you gotta do anything for me—for us. We get along, soon's I get back on my feet."

"I'm sure you will. Your job is still waiting for you, will be waiting for you if you want it."

"He don't need that job, Mr. Forbes. Thank you kindly. Amon's goin' to school now." Sabina's tone and expression bespoke her pride and gratification in the fact.

"Really?" Mr. Forbes rose. "That's splendid. I'm glad to hear it. This will help some then, I think." He opened his briefcase and extracted a slip of paper which he handed to Sabina. "This will help on the schooling."

He turned and held out his hand to Amon, who took it with his left hand, the other being in a cast. "Good-by, son. I hope your recovery is quick now and complete." He bowed to Sabina and left.

"This check is for $400," Sabina said. "I knows my 'rithmetic enough to count them zeros." But she turned the slip of paper this way and that as though at some other position the figures might change.

"Let me see it, Ma."
She handed it to Amon.
"Hallelujah! You're right, Ma, right as air. It is for $400. What

173

A Trumpet Sounds

do you know about that!"

"Sure goin' to see you through a lotta schoolin', son," Sabina grinned.

Chapter 20

As soon as Amon felt able to sit up, Miss Burt came, bringing books and paper and pencils, and Amon's tutoring began. Three afternoons a week for two hours she coached him in grammar, reading, arithmetic, geography, and spelling. She assigned work for him to do when she was not there. Because of the lapse in his formal classwork she found it necessary to take him through considerable reviewing, in some subjects, notably grammar, to start at the beginning.

They sat at the table in the kitchen or sometimes moved to the porch steps and worked with tablets on their knees, trying to talk above the noises of the street. Sabina brought her mending and sat beside them. She listened attentively to the instruction, and in the evening, after supper dishes were done, she shooed the younger boys into the yard so that in quiet she and Amon could go over the day's lessons again. She learned the spelling words and called them off to him to write, and then she checked them against the book to see that he had written them correctly. She sat beside him while he did his reading assignment, going over and over difficult passages until Amon grew restless and impatient.

"I know it by heart, Ma. For Pete's sake, let's move along."

And she said, "I ain't—aren't got it yet, son."

"You don't say 'aren't got it.'"

"What do I say then? What do I say?"

"Haven't."

A Trumpet Sounds

"Humm."

"You work too hard at this, Ma."

"No, I don't. I like it."

"Well I don't. Not all the time at any rate. I can't study every minute. I want to do something else once in a while."

"You gettin' along so fine, Amon. Miss Burt say you're a right smart pupil. You learn quick."

Sometimes Oona and the twins came in the evening to play with Willy and Jeb, and Sabina turned their game into a spelling match, including Amon. She sat by the lamp and held the book, marking off each word with her finger, the nod of her head and the uptilt of her mouth bespeaking her delight in the proceedings. Amon felt at a disadvantage pitted against his young cousins and his younger brothers, stumbling as he did over words they knew quickly. His heart sank and he dreaded the opening of school and the time when he would have to join a class of children ten and eleven years old.

Then one day Oona came racing down to deliver a message from her mother to Sabina, and Julia Hurlehy came racing with her. The girls dallied over their errand, sitting at the table in the kitchen where Amon worked at a writing exercise, asking him questions, giggling, until Sabina shooed them away, saying they bothered Amon when he had a lot of work to get done before Miss Burt came. But Julia had seemed much interested in what he was doing and in the progress he was making, and this had given a fillip to his waning determination. He said, "Come back again soon," when the girls left; but it was to Julia he spoke, at Julia he looked.

That evening he had gone to Aunt Tatty's, saying he had something he wanted to talk to Uncle Hesh about. However, when he got there, he didn't go out back where he knew Uncle Hesh generally was to be found. He went into the house looking for Oona. Aunt Tatty was at a church meeting, Cream said, and Oona was at the drugstore with Julia. He had left then, after saying only a few words to Cream, and had gone to the drugstore. The girls were there, sitting at a table near the wall, sipping sarsaparilla.

He ordered a lemon soda and with elaborate casualness carried it to their table and sat down.

"It's really hot tonight, isn't it?" He smiled at them, thinking,

"I've got to watch how I talk now."

Talking with the girls wasn't difficult, however, because they did most of it. He hoped some of the boys he knew would drop by while he was there. Every time the door opened and someone came in, he craned to see who it was, hoping it might be Ben or Kirby and they would see him with Julia Hurlehy and maybe think she was his girl. They had so often ribbed him because he never took a girl out walking, or to the church suppers, or dancing. Julia was so pretty, he thought, sitting there with his cousin Oona, both girls in light dresses, cool, sweet as magnolia blossoms.

When they finished their sodas and got up to leave, he rose too and walked with them out of the store and down the street. He said he would see them home, taking Oona home first and then Julia. Her mother and father were sitting on the front porch, and he sat down and talked with them for a little while before he said goodnight to Julia.

It was easy after that to ask Julia to go walking with him in the evenings. She had a job daytimes tending Mrs. Rayburn's children while their mother worked at the dress factory, and during the day Amon was increasingly engrossed in his schoolwork. But several evenings a week they managed to see each other and go walking. Sometimes, after satisfying Sabina that he had all his lessons for the morrow, Amon would go to Julia's house and they would sit in the swing on the porch behind the crepe myrtle vine and talk and sing. Often they joined boys and girls dancing in the street to the music of banjo or mouth harp.

One Sunday afternoon shortly before school was to take up they walked out Douglas Street to the top of the hill, past the university buildings and on out to where Battery Place ran along the crest of the bluff overlooking the river. Battery Place intersected Lindsay, an avenue of imposing residences, and north a short distance beyond the intersection Lindsey ended abruptly. A wooden barricade marked this dead-end, and beyond it through a tangle of willow and locust and scrub oak the bluff ran steeply down to the river's edge.

"I used to come here sometimes when I was little," Julia said. "My father carried me along when he was working for the McCawleys down the street there. He'd let me play around in the yard while he trimmed or mowed or weeded and I'd walk up this far and look through those railings down to the river. Then later I came by myself and sat under these willows. No one could see me, but I could look over the hill and down to the river, and over there to Chattanooga Island. It's beautiful this time of year, isn't it? All red and gold and purple, sitting there like a jewel or something in the middle of the water. I love it. I used to run away from the other kids and come here all alone; and then when I got home Mamma spanked me because she said I had no business running so far from home and in the white folk's section. But I'd come back anyway. It was worth the spanking just to be where it was so pretty for a while."

They ate the sandwiches Julia had brought and found a grassy place where the slope leveled a little and sat down under a willow. The weeping branches screened them from the top of the bluff but allowed a view of the river. Amon stretched out on his back, his hands clasped under his head and Julia sat cross-legged beside him. He stared out through the swaying fronds at the water flowing serenely far below, at a boat churning a frothy wake with gulls dipping and flapping, at the sun dappling the hillside and stroking the broad curve of the shore. He thought the world had never seemed so beautiful, so terribly beautiful.

There had been many times in his boyhood when life and the earth had seemed a wondrous and joyous thing—a misty fall morning, birds singing at daybreak, the cotton fields in flower. But nowhere in his memory was anything to compare with the elation he knew now when, in the company of this slim, quiet-spoken girl, he could look on loveliness, could talk of things deep in his heart with a complete sense of freedom. The arms of his mind embraced her, caressing her shyly, touching the cheek and hand and hair with timid fingers, new to the ways of love.

He told her about the farm at the foot of Horn Mountain, describing things in great detail, wanting her to see them with her heart's eye, as he did, and he enjoyed the relived experience now as something shared with someone he felt he had known a long, long time. It was as though Julia were a part of all he felt for the farm, all his memories and all his yearnings, and she became inseparable in his mind from those things he loved best, and

inseparable from his hopes.
They talked of the future, especially of their plans for the future. Julia had graduated in June. She planned to work for a year and then attend Hampton Institute.
"Why Hampton? That's a long way off."
"Well, Tracy's there." Her brother was studying medicine. "He'll be through next year. But he doesn't plan to come back here to practice. He wants to intern and start practice there in Virginia. His girl lives there and they like it. If I go to Hampton, it'll be right nice to have a relative close by."
"It costs a heap of money to go to college."
"I'm saving all my money now, and I aim to work while I'm there in school—enough to see me through."
"Why do you want all this education, Julie? What you gonna do with it?"
"I want to teach. I've told you that before."
"You've mentioned it. You want to teach here in Chattanooga?"
"Maybe not. Maybe in some little place where it's hard to get a teacher. There's lots of places in the south, Amon, where Negro children don't go to school at all because there are no Negro teachers and they aren't allowed in the white schools. Miss Burt taught in a tiny little cabin way back in the hills of Kentucky before she came here. She said there is a desperate need for good teachers."
"Leah used to talk like that," Amon said. "She used to say she wished she'd stayed in school longer so she could teach. I reckon she'd be a whole lot happier right now teaching a crop of younguns than what she's doing up there on Buzzard's Roost." He was silent for a while musing over Leah, and presently he said, "I reckon being a teacher'd make more sense than being a preacher."
"Your mother talks a lot about your being a preacher, doesn't she?"
"I've heard it since I was so high. Just thinking about it makes me sick."
Julia laughed. "Maybe it wouldn't be so bad, if you were a good one. It's a chance to influence a lot of people."
"Yeah, that's what Ma thinks. She used to say to us when we

A Trumpet Sounds

were just kids: 'Lead us out of the land of the Pharoahs.' I never could figure how she expected me to do that. I can't scarce lead a mule to water. But I've thought about it a lot, thought about how I could do what she wants. I used to think down there at the foundry that if I worked hard I could make something of myself as a business man—could be sort of an example to others like me. You know how that turned out."

"I know."

"My brother Asa, he's up north somewhere now, he always said our people never would get anywhere because we were too passive, not willing to go to open war with the whites, stand up and demand our rights. He used to talk a lot back home about voting and all that, but folks just listened and didn't do nothing—anything. I don't reckon they understood."

"Maybe not. We're just beginning to get up out of that place where none of the colored folk had any education, and to think about how much we need it."

"When I was little, the only thing I was good at was singing."

"You've got the sweetest voice I ever heard, Amon. When you did that solo up at our church, there wasn't anybody there didn't have goose bumps."

"I remember my first solo," Amon chuckled. "I got up in school and sang 'My Country, 'Tis of Thee.' I had this great big feeling, so big it pushed out all the shyness and the scaredness—'Land where my fathers died. . . . Land of the pilgrims' pride.' You know, I didn't even know what half the words meant, only that they spelled something great and good, for me as well as for everybody. 'Let Freedom ring . . . From every mountain side.' And for me it did, it really did.

"I used to think when Ma got to harping at me that when I grew up maybe I could sing about our troubles, you know—the way they make ballad songs about folks' troubles and sorrow. I thought I'd tell about our people, miserable and degraded, wanting to do better but not knowing how to go about it."

"They wouldn't listen, Amon. White folks don't want to think about a lot of sorry ones."

"It was a silly idea. I never did think about it again until right now. Ma says we don't want to make folks pity us. She says we want them to respect us."

"I think she's right. My mother and father feel that way too. They say we've got to stand on our own feet and get to be somebody from our own effort. That's why they are so anxious for Tracy and me to go to college. You can't buck the white folks' world when you don't know anything and they think they know everything. I'm so glad you're studying so hard and going back to school, Amon."

"I dunno, Julie, honest I don't. I get all mixed up trying to figure things out. We all talk and talk and talk. But where does that get us? And you walk away from the talk and do nothing. You say, 'What's the use? There's too much lined up against us.' So you get some kind of job and you get married, like Tom and Lilly, and have kids, and that's it."

"Oh, some of us have to see further, Amon. Some of us have to try to make it better for the rest."

"You get so you don't care. You get paid on Saturday night and you stop and get a beer, you eat a good supper and take your girl out and everything is sort of easy and sweet—and you just don't care."

He rolled over and threw his arms around her waist and buried his head in her lap. "Right now I don't care if the world stops spinning. All I want is to be here with you."

She fondled his ears, her hands silky and cool. She bent and kissed his cheek. He turned his face to her then and she kissed his lips. He clung to her in a delirium of joy, and they kissed and kissed, again and again. They were two people alone in a room made of willow walls, velvet ceiling starlit, and the air smelling of burning leaf smoke.

When at last they walked out again into the street, into the circles of light from the street lamps, back into the world of houses and sidewalks and stores and noise and people, Amon felt like a man enchanted beyond redemption. His fingers laced with Julia's, and he pressed her arm close to his side as they walked, his emotions so turbulent he could not speak.

They crossed a corner, walking away from the light into deep shadow, then gradually out again into a corner light and then again into shadow, their footsteps sounding slow and loitering. The trees

A Trumpet Sounds

rustled autumn crisp leaves, and somewhere a mockingbird trilled a plaintive, end-of-summer melody.

Amon bent his head to Julia's ear and sang so softly it was like a whisper:

> *Oh, promise me that you will take my hand,*
> *The most unworthy in this lowly land*
> *And let me sit beside you . . . in your eyes*
> *Seeing the vision of our paradise . . .*

"I love you, Amon. I love you so much," Julia said.

Part Three

Chapter 21

PROFESSOR Sterling spun around on the piano stool. He rested his elbow on the music rack, running his fingers through his hair, and tilted his face toward Amon. "You are a singularly satisfying pupil, Amon," he said. "You have a keen ear, very sensitive to vowel and tone color. Too few pupils really have it. It's remarkable in one with no long previous voice training."

"Well, I did have a sort of training," Amon rejoined. "I learned when I was just a kid how to make my voice mock something I heard. Pa used to drill me over and over in the fields or in the woods to listen to sounds with all of me. After a spell I got so's I could make the same sounds just as he did. He was a great one to imitate sounds."

"Perhaps it was a better training than he realized," Sterling said, his fingers fiddling with the keys. He was a spare little man, unlike his chunky, clucking-hen sister, Mrs. Tabor. A reserved man, with scholarly tendencies, he had returned to Chattanooga from Oberlin and was now teaching voice and giving concerts.

Mrs. Tabor had insisted her brother hear Amon sing, and knowing Miss Burt, had arranged with her for Amon to sing a solo at the commencement exercises in June, which her brother attended. He was instantly impressed by the young man's voice and had talked to Amon later and offered to coach him. This had seemed to Amon one of those lucky happenings with which life had a way of surprising him, and although his enthusiasm was not shared by his mother—she said she thought the time wasted that

A Trumpet Sounds

might better be spent on his books where he was doing so well—he had agreed to pay Professor Sterling fifty cents a lesson and had subsequently begun his voice training.

More than two years had passed since his beating, a time of intensive study and schoolwork, of physical labor and physical healing. A period too of great joy in his association with Julia. She had been enormously proud of his rapid progress—a progress spurred on by her interest and their common love. Then she had left for Hampton, and for a while Amon floundered, seemingly at loose ends, his ambition dislocated.

But he felt himself a man now, armored to some degree by hard work and experience, although to his teacher he seemed scarcely more than a boy, very thin and not very tall, with long fingers and feet and a sensitive face with wide, expressive mouth from which came unusually beautiful sounds. From the first the professor had been enamored of the boy's voice and had invited him to share concert bookings, training him to sing suitable songs and presenting Amon on programs as his protégé.

Sterling flung off the piano stool now and strode to the window. "Very good, Amon. That will be all for today. Rest now. We'll use "The End of a Perfect Day" as the finale of our Wednesday concert. The ladies are always charmed by that." He smiled a knowing and conspiratorial smile, his eyes twinkling. "No use giving people more than they can digest."

"I hope more than ladies will attend this concert," Amon said.

"I hope so too. Our program is varied enough to please both sexes. Come sit down, son, and relax. There's time for a cup of coffee, I believe, before the next pupil." He went to the door and called, "Clara, could we have a cup of coffee in the parlor?" He came back and sprawled on the divan.

"How long have you and I been working together?"

"About a year and four months," Amon told him.

"We've done quite a few concerts, you and I."

Amon agreed.

"Not made much money, eh? But enough to defray the costs of your lessons and a bit besides, eh?"

"Yes, sir."

"You've enjoyed it?"

"Yes, sir, most of it. I'm very thankful for the chances you've given me to appear with you. I don't think I could do it alone—I mean get up and sing before people—I—I—"

"Oh, I think you could."

Amon shook his head.

"You just have to take the first plunge. Water never seems so cold once you're in, you know."

But Amon looked the doubt he felt, knowing all too well his own shyness and the panic that audiences always roused.

"We all get stage fright, even veteran artists know that. Perhaps it's a good thing. Fear puts all our glands performing at their peak, and that's a sort of tuning up. You sing better for it, once you get over those first moments of panic."

"I have that terrible feeling that I will open my mouth and nothing will come out," Amon said ruefully. "I don't think I will ever be able to face up to an audience alone."

Mrs. Tabor came in with cups of steaming coffee which she set on a small table near the divan. She passed a cup to Amon and offered him fresh cupcakes. She chattered amiably for a few minutes and then withdrew. When she had left, Professor Sterling said, sipping his coffee with relish, "I think I'll let you go to our next scheduled performance in Rome a day ahead, Amon, and let you see to the arrangements for the concert. It's important that we have a hall with some heat in it, and that enough handbills are distributed. No use going down there to a poor house and a chill. There's a train to Rome at 12:45. It's the only one, in fact. Brother Carter will meet you and see that your lodging is taken care of. He's pastor of St. John's. I've written him. I can come down then on Wednesday."

He poured himself another cup of coffee and took another cupcake. "It's fortunate school doesn't start until next week or your mother would no doubt object to your taking these two days away."

"Yes, she scratches if anything comes between me and school."

"I admire her tenacity. Not many of us stick so faithfully to an ideal."

A Trumpet Sounds

However, Sabina had been agreeable to the two day trip to Rome for the concert. She pressed Amon's best suit and polished his shoes carefully. She ironed his white shirt and sent him off to Rome with her blessing.

Settled comfortably on the train, Amon fingered the ticket, safely pocketed, and let his thoughts drift pleasantly. The extra money to be earned from this concert would be a welcome addition to what Ma was willing to allow for new clothes for school— school and his lessons with Professor Sterling. He wondered where it would all lead to. No telling, life has strange ways of unfolding, and you can't reckon what is at the center of the roll. Look at Willy and Obey, working now for Uncle Hesh—even though Willy still talked all the time of going to sea. Jeb too. Where'd they get those notions? From the twins more than likely. Ever since they'd began working on the docks, all they think about is the sea. These last two years sure have seen a lot of changes. Now Cream is married and gone up north—funny how they ran into Asa in a big city like Chicago. Asa's got a good job, Cream says, but he isn't satisfied. She says he's all the time trying to stir people up to do something better for themselves. He's worked on her man, she says. Wonder if it did any good. Cream didn't say. But her letters sure get Ma riled up . . . And Ma wouldn't rest till she's written Asa a letter. Ma's getting pretty good at letters since we've been studying together. Have to watch out or Ma'll beat me yet in school. She's sort of given up on Willy and Obie and Jeb—just like Aunt Tatty gave up on Oona. Oona was so good in school and Aunt Tatty hoped she'd want to go to college like Julie. Then Oona gets married to a guy she'd only known a few weeks—crazy in love. Well, I guess I know how that is. I'd have done the same thing if Julie had consented. But Julie is strong, and she's dead set on being a teacher. She must be working awfully hard off there in Virginia. Haven't heard from her so often lately. She's working hard. I'm working hard. Not time enough for everything. Look at me—from daybreak till noon unloading barges at the wharves; two afternoons with Miss Burt and two a week with Sterling—always a stiff drill. Then preparing for concerts and all. Doesn't leave much time for anything but sleep.

"Your ticket!" The conductor was nudging him. Amon

Eunice Young Smith

reached for the slip of green paper and handed it over and then turned again to the window, trying to recapture his reverie.

At the station he was met by Reverend Carter, and as they walked to his home he discussed with Amon what preparations had been made, the number of the handbills circulated, and the church members who were working to acquaint everyone in the community of the coming event. It seemed to Amon that everything had been thoroughly taken care of and he couldn't see where there was anything really requiring his attention. He spent the evening pleasantly enough with the Carter family and then went to bed.

The next afternoon he went to meet the train and Professor Sterling. But when the train pulled in and then pulled out without any sign of the professor Amon felt a sweeping sense of alarm. His gaze raked the track as though he expected to see the sprightly little man running back to him from the swiftly vanishing train.

He rushed into the station. It was empty save for the man sweeping the floor. He ran out onto the platform and searched idiotically among the baggage and freight. He stood disconcerted for some time before he was willing to admit that the professor simply hadn't come.

What would Reverend Carter say? What did one do in a circumstance like this? How was he supposed to explain? What would they do about all those people who had paid their money for tickets? The committee had outdone itself selling out the house. It was unthinkable to disappoint them. But what was he to do?

Amon walked along the street, his hands deep in his pockets and his heart in his boots. What *was* he to say to Reverend Carter? How make an excuse for such a failure? What could have happened to the professor?

Chagrined and miserable he returned to the minister's house and informed him of the professor's defection. To Amon's relief and amazement Carter seemed not unduly perturbed. He told Amon quite calmly that somehow he would have to carry on alone—put on a performance by himself.

"Alone! Oh, I couldn't!"

"Why not? You can sing."

A Trumpet Sounds

"But an accompanist; I need an accompanist."

"Can't you accompany yourself?"

"I can play a little," Amon admitted, "but only a little."

"Do the best you can, son. Give us a full evening of songs. Don't worry too much about the piano. It's the singing folks want to hear."

Evening came and the audience began to trickle into the hall long before the scheduled start of the program. The hall was soon filled, and they sat patiently waiting for more than an hour. Then Amon was introduced. No word was spoken about the missing half of the performing team. Amon sat down at the piano, struck a few chords, and began to sing. For an hour he sang. Each song was received with enthusiastic applause. He sang all the songs of his modest repertoire. With these exhausted and the audience still insistent, he resorted to songs the Silverairs had sung, and then, urged further, he was reduced to singing a comic song about a preacher and a bear that he had heard one night at Harry Harrigan Minstrel show.

> *Now a preacher went out a-hunting*
> *'Twas on a Sunday morn*
> *He knew it was against his religion*
> *But he took his gun along . . .*

In wheedling tones and inflections Amon sang the story, how the preacher caught a couple of quail but on the way home meets a grizzly bear. The bear at his heels, he takes to a persimmon tree. The bear shakes the tree and then climbs up after the preacher, and then the preacher starts to pray, his prayer ending: "Oh Lord, if you can't help me, for goodness' sake don't help that bear."

The preacher climbs higher and higher. He pleads with the bear and importunes heaven. The treetop sways with the burden of man and bear. It bends and swoops. The parson cries aloud for help, the chorus of the song always ending: "Lord if you can't help me, please don't help that bear."

The audience, rolling with enjoyment, by the second or third stanza had joined in, finishing the ballad and the concert on an exuberant note. After much praise and many thanks for a fine performance, they slowly dispersed, leaving Amon in an unexpected glow of satisfaction. The selections he had resorted to might not have met with Professor Sterling's approval as the most appropriate material for a concert, but he had certainly entertained the folk. And when they came to count the contributions there was almost forty dollars, twenty dollars to Amon and the rest to Carter. Amon was delighted, thinking, That's better than the pay for four day's work, and it really was fun, even though I have sung myself hoarse.

Back in Chattanooga Amon faced the professor with his remission. "How did you come to miss the train? I was in a terrible fix."

"Well, I must confess," Sterling admitted smugly, "it wasn't altogether an accident."

"How could you do such a thing? Didn't you know I'd be scared plumb to a shadow?"

"Yes, but you did come through, didn't you? You sang, didn't you—without me or anyone else to sustain you or even accompany you?"

"Yes, but"

"It was what you needed, son, a chance to prove to yourself you can face up to an audience alone. I believed you could. But you had to believe it. Carter and I connived in the matter and put you to the test. And you see, you have come through with your coattails flying. Now that you have survived this ordeal I want you to sing for a friend of mine. Mr. Erlick is editor of the *Chattanooga Times,* and an excellent music critic. I'd like his judgment on your voice. If you are free, we will go to his home this evening."

At the Erlick house a dinner party was in progress, and Sterling and Amon were asked to wait in the reception hall. Sterling left, saying he would return later. For three hours Amon sat in the hall listening to the voices and laughter of Mr. Erlick's family and friends in the dining room. He went over and over in his mind the songs he would sing. He wondered what a music critic's estimate of his voice would be. The odor of food sickened him. His palms were moist and sticky. He felt a violent revulsion

A Trumpet Sounds

for the people laughing and talking in the dining room, for their indifference, their demeaning condescension, their arrogance. He loathed them, his disgust turning his stomach sour. He longed to get up and leave, postpone this interview, come back another day—or not come back at all. He felt angry that Sterling had again deserted him, and fearful lest he not be able to sing when the time came. But something held him to his seat, and the waiting honed all his senses.

At length the guests departed, not even noticing the Negro sitting motionless in the corner of the great hall. Even Mr. Erlick seemed to have forgotten him, if indeed he had been told of his presence at all. He walked back into the drawing room and then, after a period when Amon suspected the butler had informed him or reminded him that there was someone waiting to see him, he came out again and invited Amon into his study. Two ladies there withdrew, and after a few preliminary words Amon was asked to sing something. He had prepared "The Lost Chord" and "I'll Take You Home Again, Kathleen." He sang them through without accompaniment, his unhappiness giving a haunting quality to the melodies. When he finished, he saw the ladies had returned and were sitting beside Mr. Erlick. He introduced them as his wife and daughter. They begged Amon to sing something more. He sang for them then the gay, flowery "Il Bacio." He sang it passionately, sweeping with ease to D above high C and down, with a legato Professor Sterling would certainly have approved. Amon thought he discerned pleasure in the mien of the *Time*'s editor, pleasure expressed unreservedly by his wife and daughter. Yet Amon felt he had fallen short in some way, that his voice was inadequate, less worthy than Sterling had led them to expect.

Mr. Erlick rose and went to the phonograph at the end of the room, wound the crank and put a record on the spindle. "Have you ever heard Caruso sing?" he asked.

"No, sir."

He let the needle onto the disc, and suddenly Amon was listening to singing like nothing he had ever heard before. A golden, powerful voice was singing words he could not understand, but which were enthralling to hear. What sounds! What sounds! These were not simple, sweet melodies. This was thundering, chariot-wheel sound. It electrified his imagination. This was singing such as he had never dreamed of. He listened to other recordings, Scotti, Melba, his ears and his mind bombarded by majestic arias.

But it was the voice of Caruso that enchanted him most. If only he could sing like that, he thought. If only he could sing like that! He carried on some slight conversation with the Erlicks, nodded at words said to him that he scarcely heard, thanked them courteously, and walked out of their house like a man in a trance.

His being was charged with the sounds he had heard. If only he could sing like that! Was it possible through training to develop such a voice? Did Professor Sterling think so? Did Mr. Erlick think his voice had such possibility? Why had he played the recordings for him? To discourage him? Or to show him toward what he might strive? The editor had seemed to think his voice was good, but that it needed training. He had implied that there was more to training than learning how to breathe and reach high notes. He had been reserved in his appraisal of Amon's voice. Yet he had not been altogether disparaging. He had merely shown him the difference between his voice and a truly great one. That was enough. Such a difference! And he had thought his voice was pretty good. And the songs! Those were arias from great operas, Mr. Erlick had said. Why hadn't Sterling taught him those? They were sung in French and Italian and German. "I know no German," he told himself. "No French or Italian—not even English very well. That's why Sterling can't teach me those. I want to study those languages. I want to sing like that. I want to go where I can learn—where I can develop my voice, and sing like that—sing like that! I want more than Sterling can give me. I've got to go to Oberlin where he went, or somewhere where I can learn the things I need to know. I've got to learn to sing like that. I've got to! I've got to!"

Chapter 22

"Amon! Amon Sayre!"

Amon swung around, startled, searching the faces in the crowd for the one belonging to that voice. A hand with a kerchief waved above the intervening heads as people moved slowly away from the platform and toward the tent entrance.

"Excuse me, please," Amon said to the men and women who had gathered around to congratulate him at the end of the concert. "I think I hear the voice of an old friend." He elbowed through the stream of people, apologizing, until he reached the owner of the voice and the waving handkerchief. He stood then looking down at her and the human tide parted and flowed by on either side. He caught both her hands and joy bounded into his eyes and smile and voice. "Julie! Julie! How on earth! Why, I can't believe it! Where did you come from?"

"Where did *I* come from?" Julia left her hands in his and her words came in ecstatic little gasps. "Where did *you* come from? Look—the program says Marvin Pipps, soloist for tonight." She freed her hands and fumbled with the program, which was rolled into a tight moist cylinder. It fell, and the girl standing next to her handed her another. Julia, looking up into Amon's face, took it unheeding. "Marvin Pipps! And then instead who should walk out on that platform but Amon Sayre. How come? You are the very last person I expected to see appear—the very last!"

"I'm substituting for this Pipps," Amon laughed. "It seems

he's ill—sore throat or something."

"You're not with the Chautauqua circuit then?"

"No. But Julie, how—"

"Oh, you sang so marvelously tonight, Amon. I'm still choked up from that last song. I—we—oh, forgive me, Jane, Vine." She turned, flustered, to the girls beside her, then back to Amon. "Amon, I want you to meet my good friends, Jane Fellows and Vine Saunders. They both teach here in Louisville. We're all attending the Chautauqua."

"How do you do, Mr. Sayre," Jane said. "We thought your singing was wonderful, one of the best things that's been presented."

"It was delightful," Vine agreed. "You said you are substituting. Does that mean you will appear only tonight?"

"Yes, I have another job," Amon nodded. "I just filled in for Pipps tonight when his throat suddenly went bad."

"How do you happen to be in Louisville?" Julia bubbled. "I'm so dumbfounded to see you here tonight. I thought you were at Fisk."

"I came here a few days ago. Mr. Stone—he's music director at the University—recommended me to an opera director here. But that didn't work out. I—"

"To sing in the opera? Oh—"

Amon turned from her abruptly. "Let's get out of this hubbub. Where are you girls headed?"

"Home now."

"We've been attending lectures all day," Julia said. They moved to the side of the path out of the main flow of people. Lanterns swung at intervals along wires stretched between temporary posts, their light dimmed by the swirling nimbi of moths. It had been hot in the tent. The night air was reviving. Amon mopped his forehead. The girls looked cool in their light shirtwaists, but Julia fanned herself with the program Vine had handed her and she looked flustered. She kept whirling the bag she carried by its long strings and looking questioningly at Vine. "I haven't seen Amon in four years," she said. "I want to ask him a million questions."

"We'll run on," Jane said then, taking the hint. "We know you

A Trumpet Sounds

and Mr. Sayre have a lot of back news to catch up on."

Julia said good-by and she would be home soon and yes she had her key. "I'll remember the lecture is at nine tomorrow. Don't wait up for me, Vine."

The girls walked away from them, hurrying now, their heads bent together, and Amon turned to look at Julia, undistracted. "Julie, tell me, how do you happen to be in Louisville? Do you teach here? I thought—how on earth—"

"Isn't it strange, Amon? You're about the last person I expected to see here. I came up for the Chautauqua. I'm teaching in a little school near Okolona. That's not so far from Louisville. Everyone who can wants to attend the Chautauqua, and Vine invited me to come up and stay with her. She was a classmate of mine at Hampton. She teaches here in the city. I'd like to teach here too."

"You would? Didn't you used to say you wanted a school in the backwoods?"

"You remember that?"

"Yes, and the night you said it." And suddenly Amon was remembering that summer night on the riverbank when he had lain with his head in her lap and the firmament had dropped away and love, new and overwhelming, had possessed him.

Julia caught his arm as they threaded among people. "I used to think I wanted to teach the terribly disadvantaged children deep in the country. I thought it would be a good thing to do, you know, to try to bring enlightenment to them. I had visions of going out and hunting them down and urging them to school and all that."

"You don't feel like that any more?" How crusading she had been four years ago.

"Well, I haven't changed my mind about wanting to teach children. Only I have changed about where I want to teach them. I think there is greater opportunity in the cities—the chance to influence more children. I think my teaching time would be better spent."

"Aren't the children in the country important too?"

"Oh, yes. Children anywhere are important. It's just . . . Well, I've had a lot more training than many teachers, and it doesn't get much chance to be utilized in a very small school."

"I understand. But it's rough on the rural children sometimes. I remember when our little Zion school in the Flatlands closed because Roger Fullmer, the teacher, got a better job in the city and there was no other teacher willing to take our little school."

"You can hardly blame the teachers, especially the men. They have to go where they can do the best financially. They have families to support and all." She began to talk animatedly on this subject as they walked, arm in arm, around the Chautauqua grounds.

"Julie, Julie." Amon pressed her arm close to his side. "You're the same little girl with the big dreams. You haven't changed. Four long years . . . I can't believe it . . . so much has happened . . . yet you're the same sweet Julie. And all this time I—"

She laughed nervously and drew away from him. "I really get steamed up about this teaching business. Oh, Amon, there is so much to talk about. I want to ask so many questions. Can't we go somewhere and sit down where it's quiet? We've walked around these grounds three times now."

"Where shall we go?"

"Remember that place on Lindsey Street in Chattanooga where we used to go and watch the river?"

"Here's a bench; we could sit here."

"It's right on the street."

"We could sit for a while. Are you tired?"

"People going by all the time—"

"I can't see them. I can't see anyone but you. We've four years to catch up on."

"It must be getting late, the crowd's thinning."

"I still can't believe this is you here with me, Julie. I keep thinking I'll wake up any minute."

"Oh, you're awake. Your eyes are like moons."

"Whatever happened to us, Julie? Whatever happened?"

"It's a long time ago, Amon. An awful lot has happened. I'm—"

"I know, things have a way of bunching and squeezing other things out. We corresponded for almost two years and then—"

"You weren't a very faithful correspondent."

A Trumpet Sounds

"I know. Ma says I'm terrible. She says the neighbors wouldn't know she had a son to judge from the letters I write home. I'm just no good at letters, Julie. I'm not good at writing at all. Don't you remember how disgusted you used to get at my compositions. You'd laugh—"

"I never laughed at you, Amon. To me you were the most wonderful person in the world. Sometimes when we were together and you sang to me, it was as though I couldn't stay inside myself. My heart just winged off somewhere and all that was left was an aching shell. I loved you so. I was miserable because I couldn't reach up to where you were. I had a terrible feeling that you couldn't ever be held . . . that no girl could keep a chain on anyone with a voice like yours. Remember when you heard Caruso sing and you were so inflamed with the desire to sing like he did? And you couldn't think of anything but getting off to a school where they could really train your voice. I felt then that you were meant for some grand place—away from me—away from most people—that you were headed for a mountaintop and I couldn't ever hold you."

"Oh, Julie." His voice sounded thick in his ears. "My voice isn't taking me anywhere. I had a lot of big dreams. But I've not gone far from you in these four years since we were last together."

"I remember how terribly hard it was when I left for Hampton."

"Yes, those were tough weeks right after."

"Then remember when you wrote me you had made up your mind to go to Oberlin?"

"And Ma was in a tizzy because I asked for my savings?"

"You said she didn't think you had taken enough time to think about it."

"I hadn't, for a fact. I had just come from hearing Caruso sing on some records and all I could think of was that I wanted to sing like that more than I'd ever wanted anything, and I wanted to do it in a hurry."

Time slipped by unheeded as they sat facing each other on the street bench. It seemed to Amon that Julia was more beautiful now, that maturity and thoughtfulness rested with singular grace in her expression. All the things that had happened to him in the last four years became as last season's leaves, blown about and scattered—inconsequential. Nothing seemed as important as this that was happening to him now, this reunion with Julia, this acknowledged wholeness of his being when he was with her. Time did not exist save in these moments.

Yet time still intruded, was not to be put down, for Julia was saying, "How long will you be in Louisville, Amon?"

"My engagement is up day after tomorrow."

"Then where will you go?"

"I don't know exactly. Where do you live, Julie? In that little town of Okolona?"

"Yes, I—But I'm staying with Vine now, while I'm up here. I guess I told you that. She and her husband have an apartment on Clinton Street. He works at Shelly-Plaza. Her mother lives with them. She takes care of Vine's little girl while Vine teaches. We could go there to talk, if you'd like. It's an awfully small place though."

"And we'd have to talk to Vine and her husband and her mama and . . ."

"I think they'd all be in bed by this time. It must be very late, Amon."

"I just want to talk with you, Julie, with no one else around. Maybe we could find a restaurant that's still open."

"There's one I know called Mambo Joe's, where Vine and I have eaten sometimes. If it's still open. It's quite a piece from here though."

"I don't mind walking if you don't. You tired?"

"No, I'm used to walking. I have to walk—"

"Oh, Julie, this is so wonderful. Just like old times. I don't care where we go, just so we're together and can talk—like we used to. Remember how we could talk a night through, you and I? I've never known anyone I could talk to like that except you. Let me look at you under this light." He turned her to him and cupped her face in his hands, searching with starved eyes her hair, her saucy nose, the gentle curving mouth, the smooth golden cheek. "Why did you let me stop writing?"

"I didn't, Amon. I tried. I—"

"Let's walk. There's a policeman."

A Trumpet Sounds

They walked on, arm in arm, out of the light of the corner lamp and down a shadowy street, past stores and houses and a church and across a bridge. They stopped to look down at the water and the boats moored along the shore. There was a smell of oakum from a barge somewhere in the darkness, and the sound of water lapping against pilings. The stars seemed bright and close, reflected in the water. They moved on again, and it seemed the night wrapped them about and they were alone in it, for the streets were empty. Only an occasional carriage passed, rattling some late partygoers homeward.

Julia said, "It's strange, isn't it, how few places there are in a city to sit."

"We could try someone's front yard."

She laughed. "Yes, or the jail."

"Are you tired?"

"Not very. We sat at the lectures. How about you?"

"I could walk all night—fly even."

They came to Mambo Joe's and went in. The place was empty, and the proprietor sat at a table changing notations on a menu. He glanced at them disinterestedly. "Closing time," he said.

"Oh, could we just have a cup of coffee?" Julia asked.

He looked disgruntled, then wavered, finally shuffling his menus together and slapping them down on the table. "Maybe." He got up and went to the backroom.

Amon and Julia sat down at a little table near the wall. Only one murky lamp near the cash register remained lit. A woman with a pail and map came in and began to slosh water on the floor.

"Amon, tell me about Fisk. You know I never did find out why you stayed there when you were on your way to Oberlin. It was Oberlin you'd set your heart on, because it has such a fine music school. What changed your mind?"

"Your cousin, Shean." He looked at her quizzically. "I just stopped off at Fisk on my way to Oberlin, and Shean was the first person I met there. Remember I wrote you that? He wanted to show me around his school. I'd never been on a campus before and Great Jupiter! Was I impressed! I stood in front of that Jubilee Hall and it looked like a palace to me, like a shining mansion of learning.

"He took me to the music building, Magnolia Cottage. It has a lot of gables and a little tower over the front door, and there is stained glass in the upper part of the windows. There is a mimosa in the front yard and the whole place looks like something out of a storybook. Shean took me all around, to visit every building. I'd never dreamed of a place like that—fine buildings, beautiful grounds just for boys and girls to come and study in."

"You were overpowered. I felt the same way when I first went to Hampton."

The man came with two cups of coffee and set them down on the table, and Amon paid for them. "It's after closing time," he reminded them, and Amon nodded, not really hearing.

"That's what I was, overpowered. I never got to Oberlin. I didn't have much money. I really don't know how I thought I could get very far with what Ma had given me—the money she'd saved from my earnings. That was all I had. Shean had an idea how I could make some money if I hung around a while. He took me to a preacher friend of his in Nashville by the name of Shuttleworth. This parson thought we could give some recitals around at different churches, and he and I would split the proceeds."

"Did your mother mind your going very much?"

"Yes, I think she did. But you know Ma. She won't stand in the way if she thinks it's the Lord's will."

"And she's all for education, I know that."

"Yes, with a reservation. She believes in being educated for a suitable purpose."

"In your instance, preaching." Julia twinkled at him. "Oh, I remember what her ambition for you was. I remember how glum you'd get whenever she talked about it. But education to study music—she can't see that?"

"She doesn't mind my singing, or training my voice to sing well. She just doesn't see where it will have a practical benefit. It's hard for me to see either, Julie. I don't really know why I want so much to train my voice. I can sing now better than most choir voices. I can give concerts. I gave a lot of them with Professor Sterling before I left Chattanooga."

"I know you did."

"I was good enough to be asked to join the Jubilee Singers."

"You were? How wonderful!"

"Well, I thought it was wonderful too, when it happened. I thought it was another rung up the ladder. I—"

"Wasn't it?"

"It got me dismissed from school."

"How? Oh, Amon, how could it?"

"It's a long story. Say," he turned to locate the cafe owner, "could we have another cup of coffee, please?"

"He's gone," the woman mopping the floor said. "You kids oughta go home. You wannt stay here all night?" She began clearing the floor near them, racketing the chairs and tables together in a corner.

"We want to talk," Julia explained, "and there's no place to sit down and talk."

The woman came back from her ministrations with the furniture and caught up her mop. She pushed the hair back from her forehead and stared at them with tired, speculative eyes. "Lovers, heh? Why'nt you go home?"

Julia said, "No, just friends. We've not seen each other for a long time. Couldn't we have another cup of coffee—please?"

"I ain't the boss, but I reckon I could scare up another cup of coffee if he ain't throwed it out by now. I go see." She let the mop handle fall and shuffled away to the back room.

"It's awfully late. Do you have to be up early?"

"I have a rehearsal at eleven, and you said you had a lecture at nine."

"There is a session on Home Economics I don't want to miss. You said rehearsal. You told me you sing at the theatre to accompany a movie. How do you do that?"

"It's an operatic short. I'm behind the screen. That's the only way the manager could figure to use me. I really came to Louisville to try out for the opera company. The director liked my voice, said he liked it a lot. He tried different ways to make me into a white man. But it didn't work. Then this theatre manager got the idea that he could use me behind a screen. I hate it. Sometimes I feel such loathing for the white people I could puke. Then I remember Asa's hate and I can understand it."

"I think we all hate part of the time. You can't be human and not detest the cruelty of white people—even though they aren't all that way."

"There seems to be mighty few who aren't. Even those who want to be fair are cruel because they don't do anything about it, don't take a stand to defend the right."

"Well, that makes them not so different from us. How many Negroes want to take a stand in their own defense?"

"It's not wanting to, Julie; it's not knowing how to. I think lots of us are ready and willing to battle for our cause, but we don't know where to begin."

"That's my big idea, my rallying call." Julia leaned toward Amon and laid a hand on his arm. "*In the classroom!* We can't go anywhere, climb anywhere, as ignorant lumps. We have to get education. Our real goals can't ever be accomplished physically. We have to compete mentally, intellectually—you can see that."

Amon shook his head. "It looks so hopeless."

"Well, it isn't going to change overnight. But each of us who is determined to rise above his predicament is like one grain of sand more in the mortar mix of the foundation on which one day we may stand."

"My God, Julie, how discouraging that sounds."

"Not really. No more hopeless than building the pyramids must have seemed to those dragging up the stones. Everything gets done by littles. It's hard to see, when you have a big goal, that the factors are minute and innumerable."

"It calls for a lot of self-sacrifice and a whole lot of perseverance. People in masses don't have either one. They want to see the wall give—and right now. That's what Asa wants, what he talks about getting, by force."

"Maybe we'd all like to get it that way. But there are thinking people who know it wouldn't last, wouldn't gain us anything really permanent. I think we are working the right way, you and I. We're trying to improve ourselves and maybe some of the next generation."

"Yeah, that's what I'm trying to do—from behind a screen. And I can't see any benefit except the forty dollars I earn by doing it."

"How long will that job last?"

"Only a week."

"And you don't know what you'll do then?"

"I've been offered the place of leading tenor with the Jubilee Singers when they go to Boston for a summer conference called The World in Boston. I've wanted to get to Boston, so I signed up. They say Boston is the leading music center of America."

"Boston!" Julia said, drawing in her breath quickly. "And I might have missed you."

The scrubwoman appeared with a coffee pot. She shuffled to the table and filled their cups. Then she rested back on her heels, hitched her mouth up on one side and delivered her ultimatum: "When you get that there coffee down, you don't get no more. I be done finished with my floor by then, and I plain wanna walk outta here. So you can git."

"We will," Julia promised. "Thank you." She smiled at the woman, but it appeared not to soften her. She sniffed, rubbing the back of her hand under her nose and then down her skirt before she turned away to pick up her deserted mop.

"You were telling me how you happened to leave Fisk. How did we get off the track?"

"There's too much to say. We don't have to say everything tonight. Now I've found you again, I'm not letting you go. Oh, Julie, wasn't this the hand of fate? We'll see each other a lot now."

"Silly," she chided nervously, "you just finished telling me you are leaving day after tomorrow for Boston."

"Don't spoil this, Julie. I don't want to think about Boston. I don't want to think about anything that can separate us again."

She reached across the table and touched his hand. Her lips quivered like a small girl about to cry. "Go on, tell me about what happened at Fisk. So far, I have in mind only a picture of you gaping at architecture. We can't make this coffee last all night, you know." And the quivering lips broke into a smile.

"No. Well, I wrote you about my work that summer, giving the concerts with Parson Shuttleworth. By the end of the summer, what with all the extra expenses I'd had, I ended up with just nothing, not even the money Ma had given me. I was in pretty sorry shape. There was only one good thing came out of the business."

"What was that?"

"That was meeting Mrs. Haskins. I roomed at her house. She was a nice lady, a schoolteacher, too, and she knew Miss Boil, who is the director of music at Fisk. Mrs. Haskins offered to take me out and introduce me to Miss Boil. I didn't see how that would help me much, but I went—and I met Miss Boil."

Amon stopped, took a sip of coffee and wiped his forehead with his handkerchief.

"I wish you could see her, Julie. I wish I could tell you how I felt trying to sing before that great, gaunt, stone-faced woman. At first she wasn't going to hear me at all. She looked me up and down, and boy-man, I was a far piece down.

"But Mrs. Haskins begged her to listen to me for just one minute—and that's about what she gave me. I sang 'Beyond the Gates of Paradise' with all the expression I could manage. When I got through she said—you couldn't tell anything from her face—'Wherever did they teach you to sing such rubbish?' But she asked me some questions about my scholastic rating and my finances and told me to come back next day.

"I went away with Mrs. Haskins. I couldn't eat and I couldn't sleep. I was worried and I was scared. I wrote you, I think, but I don't know now what I said."

"I do. I was just getting ready to leave for my second year at Hampton. The letter came that day and I read it over and over on the train, trying to make out just what was wrong."

"I think I was praying—part to you, part to God. Anyway, next day Miss Boil sent me to Dr. Hall's office—he's the president of Fisk. Sort of forbidding-looking. She gave me a note to hand to him that said I was an eighth-grade pupil. When I went into his office, I was scared to a frizzle."

"Did he bite you?"

Amon laughed and reached to slide the back of his hand down Julia's cheek. "No, it wasn't as bad as I'd expected. Dr. Hall was a lot kinder than he looked. He talked to me for a while and then said that because of my voice—Miss Boil must have said something for it—he intended to let me enter the lower school on probation as a special student. I would follow a course of studies designed to further my general education as well as my singing.

A Trumpet Sounds

He said he would help me get a job."

"Did he?"

"Yes, as furnace boy in Judge Bates's house, and a place to sleep over the stables. And there I was—board and room and a dollar a week wages. My college life began."

"That sounds like a wonderful break."

"It was, yes. But I had to work awfully hard that year. I did a lot besides tend furnace at Judge Bates's. I waited on table and drove the carriage and was general handyman. And their house was way across the city from school. So my legs kept nice and thin. I had to work my brain overtime on courses in the history of music and literature and language because I wasn't at all prepared in them."

"All that besides your regular schoolwork? No wonder you stopped writing. Poor boy," Julia murmured.

Amon sipped his coffee before he went on musingly, "I remember one cold night when I was firing the furnace late and it was giving me some trouble. I began to sing at it. I wanted to swear—so the singing was real loud, see. Judge Bates came tearing down the stairway in a fury, wanting to know what I meant by playing his gramophone in the cellar. Then I guess he felt ashamed for accusing me because after that he used to let me come into his study sometimes and listen to his records. He had a fine collection, Galli-Curci, Scotti, all the best singers."

"Did you work for Judge Bates all the time you were at Fisk?"

"No. One year I worked for Professor Zondos, and then more than a year for the Wheelers. He's a lawyer. They were right kind to me. But all the time I was working I didn't have any money, Julie. I got my room and board and a few dollars extra—not enough for books and paper and pencils. I was asked to do a lot of singing around the campus at school functions. Whenever they needed a soloist, they'd call on me to sing. I had a notion it was in some way paying for my tuition and music sheets and all. Nobody said it wasn't, so that's what I thought—that I was paying my way like that. Maybe I should have asked some questions. But I didn't. I was working so hard all the time. It seemed I was never alone except when I slept. I never went anywhere—just studied and sang, and come each day I said howdy and did what had to be done. I was getting a marvelous training. I knew that. My voice had grown. I could sing quite a few of those operatic arias I loved so much. I could sing some in German and Italian. Not perfectly, you know—but pretty well. My speech had improved. Miss Boil is a friend of pure diction, and I really worked at it. And then one day—"

"You kids plain gotta get outta here," the scrubwoman said, her leathery face cross and tired. "This here place closed down a long time ago. I wanna go home now, see? I'm done with the scrubbin' and I wanna lock up."

"Oh, we're sorry," Julia apologized. She got up quickly and opened her bag. "You've been kind to let us sit here so long. Thank you." She pressed some coins into the woman's hand. "Thank you."

Amon followed her out and took her arm as they walked away from the café along the deserted street.

Julia sighed. "It seems as though you possess the earth when you walk alone in the night. Everything sleeps and the stars are glowworms and the stillness is a velvet robe and you walk abroad with nothing—nothing—between you and your innermost being, and you say, 'Here I am, God.'" She caught up Amon's hand and pressed it between both of hers. "Here we are."

"It's like that, Julie. Oh, Julie dearest, dearest, I—"

"And then one day—" she prompted, pulling her fingers from his. "You were telling me about Miss Boil."

"I don't care about that now. I'm with you again. All I care about is being here with you. Let's talk about you, honey, you and me. I don't care about Fisk anymore now."

"But it's important, and I want to hear," she said with undue emphasis.

"Oh, well," he went on then. "I'd been asked to join the Jubilee Singers. I felt honored, and of course I accepted. I went to rehearse with them regularly. It was right before commencement and I was preparing for exams, too. And one day Miss Boil called me into her office and told me I was being dismissed from the university and to please return all the music I had borrowed from the library. It was like she'd clouted me. I didn't know what to say,

A Trumpet Sounds

what to think."

"Didn't she explain at all? How could she say a thing like that and not explain?"

"I asked her why. She just repeated what she had said, nothing more. I didn't know what to think. I didn't know what to do. I was stunned—felt sort of crazy, like I was drunk or something. I went to see Dr. Hall, but he didn't explain either, just comfirmed Miss Boil's decree. I was sick with despair and confusion, and I went to see Professor Stone—he's the director of the Jubilee Singers. He didn't seem very surprised, now that I think about it. He just suggested that Miss Boil might have a case of jealousy. There was considerable antagonism between the two departments of music, a deep rivalry, really. But it isn't all that simple. I found out later that Miss Boil had been furnishing the funds for my tuition and expenses all along the way, for years you see, using her own money, and begging from friends for me. And then I learned another thing I didn't know and no one had bothered telling me. By tradition the Music Department of the university and the Jubilee Singers have nothing to do with each other. I don't know why I hadn't learned this sooner, but I hadn't. And of course I know now what I did to Miss Boil. It was like deserting to the enemy, even though I was an innocent traitor. For four years I'd been her protégé, her particular achievement, and then after all that work on me, I'd betrayed her. Or so it must have seemed to her."

"Yes, I think I can understand how she felt."

"I would have apologized if she'd told me, if I'd known what to apologize for. I'd have done anything to get back in her good graces. But I didn't know, and she wouldn't talk to me, wouldn't or couldn't explain. Anyway, under this sort of fog I was asked to leave Fisk."

Amon's voice cracked over the last words and Julia put her hand back in his. "What a shame. I think she was in love with you, Amon."

"Oh, no, not me. My voice though, maybe."

"To Miss Boil it must have been sort of like raising a child, loving it, nurturing it, and then seeing it shift its affections to a neighbor. She must have cared an awful lot to be so harsh, Amon."

"Well, that's the story. Since then, I've been looking for jobs. Stone got me this one in Louisville. Where are we walking to?"

"I'm heading for Vine's. I hope they don't hear me come in. They'll think me a huzzy."

"We don't care what they think. But I don't want to cause any trouble for you. You could never explain to anyone how you could walk all night with someone you love and have it seem like minutes. I've missed you so much these last four years, Julie. Ma used to say 'Keep thine eye single.' But I've kept mine single to the point where I can't see anything but my music. I've lost sight of people and human values."

She said, "That's the price we have to pay sometimes for achievement, Amon. Perhaps it is the only way, even though we kill something in ourselves at the same time. It seems cruel, but—"

"In the end you ask if it's worth it."

"Don't ever doubt it, Amon. To hear you sing is to know that, whatever the cost, this thing attained is worth it. Here's Vine's. I never have seen it this still around here. It's almost pretty at night when you can just see the steps and the lines of the walls and gables and doors all draped in deep purple of night. It's—"

"Julie . . . Julie . . . I'm torn up. I can't say it—what I want to . . . I want to tell you . . ."

"Don't say it, Amon. This has been a night I'll hold close to my heart the rest of my life."

"But we haven't talked about you at all yet. Dearest, dearest Julie. Our talk has just begun." He took her in his arms then, pressing her body fiercely to his. He found her mouth and kissed her passionately. He kissed her closed eyes and her cheeks and her throat. She submitted to his kisses, her head thrown back, her face drained and still.

"Julie," he groaned, "I love you. I've never stopped loving you."

Don't, Amon—don't do this."

"Why not? Julie, don't you love me?"

A Trumpet Sounds

"No, no." She pushed free of him. "I have no business kissing you, nor you me."

"Julie!"

"I've tried to tell you all evening, but I couldn't. It was so sweet being with you. I wanted to talk like we used to—walk and talk and talk . . . like the old days . . . you and I together. But not this—not this! I didn't want any more than just the talk." She was sobbing now, her body convulsed and shaking.

"Julie, look at me." Amon turned her tear-smeared face up to his. "Don't cry. We're together now. We'll stay together. You can come with me to Boston. We'll find a way to get married. I'll—I'll make enough money somehow. I'll—"

"Don't . . . don't talk like that . . . It's not possible."

"Why not, Julie? You love me. Say you love me."

"I love you."

"That's all that matters."

"No!" She was shivering and her hands tore at the white bag. Tears flowed down her cheeks, and Amon tried with fluttering, clumsy fingers to wipe them away.

"Why do you make it so hard for me! Can't you see? Don't you know anything! If you'd gone home once in a while, you'd have known. Someone would have told you. I wouldn't have to say it now. I'm married! Why don't you know it? I didn't want to . . . to tell you."

"You're not! I don't believe it!"

"I am . . . I am! I live in Okolona. Seth is a farmer. I teach. We—"

"No! No!"

She fumbled in the bag for her key. "It's been such a beautiful night. Why does it have to end like this." She was sobbing so hard the words came out in gasps. "Goodby, Amon. Good-by."

She ran up the steps, unlocked the door and let herself in. The door clicked shut. Amon stood at the foot of the steps, staring up at the blank, closed door, his senses reeling, his own eyes now blinded with tears.

Chapter 23

Amon's one thought was to get out of Louisville as quickly as possible. He walked the night through, wrestling with his heartbreak. Toward dawn he returned to his room and flung himself across the bed. He slept through the hour for rehearsal, and when he appeared at the theatre for the matinee, the manager was dissuaded from his angry accusations by the stricken look on his face.

"You look like you'd swallowed poison," he said.

"I have."

"Maybe you ate something. Think you need a doctor?"

"No."

"Can you sing?" The manager was convinced he could not.

"I don't know . . . I'd beg off if—"

"At this hour? Who could I get to replace you now? But you look beat. Go get yourself some coffee and a shot of brandy. That'll pick you up."

"Yes," Amon said and went to a shop near by and ordered coffee.

Somehow he sang through the scheduled arias, an indifferent performance, but he was scarcely aware of it. He went to a café then and ordered dinner but was unable to touch it. He walked the streets until eight o'clock and then went back to the theatre for the evening show. Afterward he went to his room and slept. Next morning he packed his few things and took a train for Chat-

A Trumpet Sounds

tanooga. He wanted to see Ma before he went to Boston. Boston! The glorious opportunity! The long-yearned-for chance! It was dust in his mouth.

He berated himself for his neglect of his mother. He should have written her more faithfully these last years. Somehow he should have managed to go home oftener. Thinking back over the pinched and arduous years at school, he could not recall when he might have gone home, for he had no money at all. Still, the self-accusation held. He should have gone. Had he done so, Julia might still be his girl—not married to someone else. He would have kept track of her, known what was happening, known about Seth. Why had Julie not told him about Seth? He tried to think back over the period of their letter writing. When had it diminished? When ceased? They had just drifted, like two canoes on a fast stream, carried along willy-nilly. Could he have done anything different if he had known? He had become so involved with work and study—and his music had become an obsession. Could he have divided himself successfully? Maybe Julie knew this. Maybe she deliberately chose not to let herself be a distraction, a diluting factor to his ambition. "But you wouldn't have been, you wouldn't have been!" his heart cried. "Oh, Julie, you would have been the reason for it all."

He flailed himself with regrets and remorse and excuses. Maybe it wasn't so bad not writing to Ma often. She knew he was studying hard, and that was what she wanted, wasn't it? He'd written and told her every so often how it was, and he knew Ma was there in Chattanooga and that she was safe and well. It wasn't as though she might take off when he wasn't looking and get married—but with Julie it was different. "Young and pretty," he told himself. "I might have known some guy would come along and want to marry her. What did I think? She'd set around and wait for some clown riding clouds and living on dreams? Julie's practical, got her feet on the ground. What would she want with a dope like me, anyway? But if I'd only known . . . if I'd only known."

He found Sabina just as he expected, still doing washes, still milking her cow and tending her chickens and keeping her house immaculate. She seemed the same, her thin frame straight as ever, cheeks smooth as a chestnut. Her hair was all white now, soft about the deep-set, knowing eyes. Ma welcomed him as though he had been gone only since yesterday and she knowing all along he'd be returning at any time. She made no fuss. "Well, son, I'm purely glad to see you. Now set while I make a cup of fresh coffee and you catch me up on things and I'll catch you up."

She told him Jeb had been hired as a cabin boy on a packet boat plying the river between Kingston and some city in Georgia, but she wasn't quite sure of the name.

"Jeb gone too, eh? Seems we've all gone off and left you, Ma. When did Jeb take off? I didn't know you were here all alone."

"Oh, I'm not alone, son."

"No, I suppose not, really. You have Aunt Tatty and Uncle Hesh. How are they?"

"They're fine. But I don't see too much of your Aunt Tatty. She's busy as a stove poker in that there African church of hers, and—"

"The neighbors come in a lot, eh?"

"No, I ain't time to have much truck with the neighbors, except those I can help. But I ain't—aren't alone. I got this here." She picked up her worn Bible and held it affectionately, patting the rust-brown cover. "I got my Bible, son, and I can read it." Her eyes twinkled and her smile was smug. "I ain't—aren't never alone."

"Ma, as soon as I get settled in Boston, I'll come and fetch you. I'll get a job and stay up there after the Jubilee Singers go back to Nashville. I'll come fetch you, and you and I will make a home up there in Boston."

"You've not told me you goin' to Boston. Now, here's your coffee and there's a slice of corncake, like you used to fancy. You just commence to the beginning and tell me all about it. I'm purely cravin' to hear."

He told her then about the offer to go to Boston, about his leaving Fisk and going to Louisville to sing. He told her everything in detail, except for his meeting with Julia. Of that he simply said he'd seen her at the Chatauqua with some friends.

"Eh, she's a fine teacher," Sabina said, "if you can judge from the way folks take on about her."

A Trumpet Sounds

"I think she is. She's what they call a dedicated teacher."

"What do that mean?"

"That her teaching profession is of first importance to her—that she's devoted to it."

"I reckon she's that, sure enough. You hear her Ma talk you'd think Julia's the only teacher ever was. But they downtalk Seth. Her folks don't set much store by him. They don't see why Julia ever marry a man like him. But I do. Seth's a farmer, and from what I hears, a good one. He went to school at Hampton, same as Julia. Her folks got a notion you gotta be a somebody in a city—that country people are no-account."

"Why didn't you tell me Julie was married, Ma?"

"Law, didn't you know?"

"Not till she told me. Why didn't you tell me?"

"You didn't ask me. Wasn't you writing to Julia all the time you at school?"

"Yes—well, no. We stopped after a while. We both got pretty busy with schoolwork I reckon, and—we just lost track of each other."

"Well, young folks gets married right along. You be gettin' married one of these days."

"I won't be getting married."

"You be comin' home by-an'-by."

"No, I'm going to stay in Boston. I want you to come there too."

"You'll be gettin' married, son. You won't need me. I do all right here."

"I won't be getting married, Ma," Amon reiterated. "I've got to study and train, and it takes all my time, all my money too, just to do that and live. Anyway—well, anyway, I won't be getting married. As soon as I get a job and a little money ahead, I'll come and fetch you."

"You still a-hankerin' to make something of your singin', son? I don't like to disconvince you—the Lord works in strange ways, and maybe this is one of 'em—but I can't see as how you goin' very far tryin' to concert-sing in this white man's world. I don't like the way you sing their songs. I don't like 'em a-tall."

"You haven't heard me sing in a long time, Ma."

"No, but I reckon you still singin' like you did here with Professor Sterling. Your voice was purely white, and that ain't—isn't the way it meant to be. You got a colored voice, Amon. It's a beautiful colored voice. It's your own, the way God give it. But you tryin' to make it white, and that ain't—isn't good, son. Colored folks don't like to hear that kind of singin'. And the white folks not goin' to listen to a Negro sing, nohow. Don't matter how good he is. You just wastin' your time, son."

Ma was harping on the same old theme. His wounded spirit turned aside from added hurt. The visit in Chattanooga was not as satisfying as he had hoped. It was good to see Uncle Hesh and Aunt Tatty and to hear all about Cream and Oona and the grandchildren. He talked with the twins for a short time one evening. Abe was working at the Sessler Foundry, and Linnie had a maintenance job in the Heisman Building on Broad Street. They had grown to be tall, good-looking men and seemed to be content with life. They were getting ready to call on girls, so Amon's visit with them was short.

He went to see Tom then and found him still living in the tiny house in back of the store, the father of three small boys. He was still working at the foundry, he said, and he told Amon a little about how things were going down there. He asked if Amon had heard about Fez getting killed and at his surprise recounted the episode for him. Fez, he said, had always acted as a sort of peacemaker between the whites and the Negroes in his bar until one night there was a fight that turned into a free-for-all in which fourteen men were hurt, and Fez was killed trying to stop it, before the police got there. "This poor little twisted guy they found under one of the tables with his head bashed in."

"What's happened to Pula?"

"She's around somewhere. She sold the joint right after it happened. Didn't want no further truck with liquor, she say. She livin' with an aunt, I think."

Memories came flooding back on Amon of the times when Fez had been a critical factor in his life, and his throat thickened for a moment considering so ignominious a death for so brave and sometimes gallant a little man.

Lilly brought them bottles of soda pop after she put the

A Trumpet Sounds

children to bed, and they sat on the steps and talked about the boys and girls Amon used to know, what they were doing, who had moved away, who had married whom. But Amon felt removed from all their talk, as though he had been wrenched from another sphere too quickly to adjust now to the old pattern of thinking, the old ways of his life. He said good-by to Lilly and Tom with a half-guilty pang, certain he would never see them again, and that it didn't matter.

Lonely and depressed, he took the train to Boston. He had come to Chattanooga mainly to see Ma, needing to find her unchanged, the unswerving rock in the rushing waters. He had wanted her encouragement, the affirmation of his hope for their reunion in Boston. He had sought relief from his hurt and a prop for his flagging ambition. He had found neither.

What Boston looked like that night of his arrival Amon would never recall, for he was aware of it only as a great, humming, noisy, narrow-streeted repository for his misery. He found his way to the colored section and obtained a room with a family that lived above a meat market on Columbus Street. It was a dark, evil-smelling cubbyhole, but it afforded him privacy and a bed.

He had brought with him from Louisville a letter written by one Dr. Coffers, whom he had met after the Chautauqua concert, one of a number of people who had been impressed by his voice. The letter was to Mr. Fowler Hardy, a businessman in Boston. It had been Dr. Coffers's opinion that Hardy might be able to help Amon find a job, or failing that, might be able to recommend teachers or other means to further his career. An unsteady hope had reasserted itself, and Amon decided to lose no time in contacting Mr. Hardy.

He located his offices and went there to present his letter. Mr. Hardy received him courteously, read the letter, and asked Amon to sing a song or two for him. He was generous in his praise of Amon's voice. He asked a few questions, took him out and showed him how to open a bank account at a neighborhood bank, shook hands with him, and promised to speak to several friends in his behalf. In the meantime, he recommended Amon continue with the Jubilee Singers.

Amon returned to his room above the meat market wondering just what promise might lie in this interview. What could he expect from Mr. Hardy? What was he likely to do for a strange Negro he knew nothing about? How long would it be before he would hear from him again? Weeks? Months? He ate frugally at a saloon and then inquired the way to the Brotherhood House where Professor Stone had written him the Jubilee Singers would be staying.

The troop welcomed him warmly. He had not seen any of them since he had left Fisk. They talked freely of events there, of their work on The World in Boston conference, of the schedule of performances and rehearsals. Amon was to be leading tenor with a salary of fifty dollars a month and expenses.

The program promised to be pleasant and not too arduous. There would be many hours of the days free. These he planned to spend looking for a more permanent job, any kind of work which would enable him to stay in Boston after the Jubilee Singers finished their conference and went back to Nashville. He read advertisements, answering any that sounded hopeful of employment for a strong and willing Negro.

In the next few weeks he canvassed from Copley Square to the Common, along Tremont Street to the end of Beacon and all the streets on down to Boston Harbor, asking at every hotel, every café, every store for any kind of work, in vain. He ate and slept and rehearsed and sang and walked the streets of the great city, each day a repetition of the day before, each day bringing him closer to the time when, with greatly reduced income, he faced the improbability of staying in Boston at all. Each day his spirits sank a little lower.

He had given up hope of ever hearing from Mr. Hardy and had finally got work at the Savoy Hotel emptying spittoons and tidying the lobby, when one evening he returned to his room and found a letter tucked under the door. He opened it with nervous fingers, for the return address was that of Fowler Hardy. The letter simply said that five of the leading Boston voice teachers were willing to give him auditions. It specified times and gave addresses. The appointments were in the evening, after the studios were closed to regular pupils.

For two days Amon's thoughts were in an upheaval. Excit-

A Trumpet Sounds

ment caused him to do his work with great alacrity, singing the while. He hustled about the hotel lobby, spouting arias. Sometimes people stopped to stare and listen, lingering at the desk or lowering their newspapers. But no one asked him to stop.

The third day after the arrival of the letter Amon ate his evening meal and went to his room to wash and freshen up for his first appointment. He put on a clean shirt and brushed his suit carefully. He started out immediately for the studio on Newbury Street. It was a long walk from his room on Columbus to Professor Wilton's office, but he appeared at the door at precisely the appointed time. Wilton, a dapper man with a face as animated as a drawn shade, wasted no time in preliminaries. He had Amon sing. Then, after making a note or two, dismissed him. "We'll see what Salterborn and Finns have to say. Good evening."

One after another Amon visited the studios or offices of the five great voice teachers. Each listened to him politely and sent him on to the next. The last name on the list was that of Titus Fielding, who taught at the Boston Conservatory of Music. Fielding was tall, powerfully built, with deep furrows between his eyes and a booming voice. He gave Amon sufficient time to display his vocal habiliments and then quite directly said, "Sayre, you have a voice that would be a pleasure to train. You have subtle and unusual tone color. I believe your voice holds great promise. I should be quite willing to undertake your training if"—he exhaled a long, gusty sigh—"you are sure you think it worth your while. The lessons are costly, the results dubious."

"You mean," Amon stammered, "my voice might not justify training?"

"No. I mean that when it is trained, what will it gain you? Each of the teachers you have sung before has been impressed with your voice. They have telephoned me their opinions. Any one of us would welcome such a voice to train. They are honest men. They simply don't want to take your money when they feel there is no future for a Negro as a serious artist."

He sat slouched in his chair, gripping the arms, his eyes steel shards between the deep furrows, staring in sad silence while Amon tried to harness his rearing emotions. They had told him Boston was different, more advanced than the south, the people

Eunice Young Smith

educated beyond the constrictions of prejudice. But it seemed Ma was right again. Even here in this northern city the barrier held. The measure of a man's worth was not his gifts, not the quality of his mind and spirit, but the color of his skin and the irredeemable opprobrium attached to it. *My country, 'tis of thee . . . Sweet land of liberty . . . Of thee I sing.* If only he could sing to this land of liberty, pour out his voice in song to delight the ears and soften the hearts of men and make them free . . . free of the irons of unreasoning bias. Surely if his voice was good enough he could conquer antipathy—at least soften it. He could sing against the mud walls of ignorance and contempt and scorn and melt them piece by piece with a rain of music, sweet music, the best he could produce. He would give himself, pour out from the font God gave him all he knew to win the hearts of little people. If *only* he were given a chance.

He did not know how long he sat there in the still room thinking deeply. Titus Fielding's voice boomed through the fog of his uncertainty. "Well, Sayre?"

His attention jolted back. When he spoke, the words sounded thick and muffled in his own ears. "I want to study with you if you'll have me. I'll do anything you say. I can't stop now what I've been working toward all my life."

Chapter 24

AND SO, at five dollars a lesson, Amon had begun to study with Titus Fielding, going to his home in the evening instead of to the studio, approaching by the back door so as to avoid causing embarrassment to the family, a requirement which rankled even as he submitted to it.

After a time, he obtained a better job, waiting on table at the Hilton Restaurant on Tremont Street, where his meals were part of his pay, where the tips were good, both features helping him to save more money toward his expensive lessons. He joined with some new friends to form a quartet, and they took bookings to sing anywhere they could. One of the four, Euman Jennis, was a fine pianist, a natural musician who could catch any tune once heard and produce it on the keyboard. Whenever a piano was available, he accompanied their singing.

Money came in slowly. The hundred dollars he had put in the bank when first he arrived in Boston had dwindled to almost nothing. He was haunted by a sense of urgency. October came and the trees splashed color all along the boulevards. Cold winds swept down from the north, and chimneys began to belch smoke. Amon had changed his living quarters, for the sake of economy, to a room with an elderly couple on Washington Street. In order to supplement the meager donation of the city welfare service, Mule and Cloony Franks rented out their one bedroom while they slept in the kitchen. Mule's right leg had been severed in a switchyard accident, and he had never recovered sufficiently to work since, rheumatism and sciatica taking over after the stump healed.

Their two rooms were on the ground floor of a four-story tenement overflowing with occupants, where two rooms in most cases was home to eight or ten people. Children spilled from the doors and over the steps and sidewalks and basement areaways. The grim and ugly façades of the buildings in this district gave only a hint of the filth and deterioration of the interiors, backyards and alleys, the damp basement rooms where rats and vermin abounded and sanitary conditions did not exist. It was a daily struggle to be clean, and often Amon yearned for Sabina's immaculate kitchen, for the strong smell of lye soap. He wondered if ever he would find a decent job with enough permanence to enable him to bring Ma north. Winter was rapidly approaching, and he had hoped to have Ma with him before Christmas. He considered where he might locate a suitable place to house Ma when he did bring her. He had written her more frequently since he had been in Boston, and although her letters were never complaining, he felt she would be happier with him than alone in her little house on Douglas Street, provided he could find a better place to live than where he was now. One evening, at the close of his lesson with Titus Fielding, he voiced this feeling.

"Why don't you get your mother then and bring her here? I too think you would be happier."

Amon had to confess he couldn't pay the fares.

Fielding took out his wallet and handed Amon seventy-five dollars. "That will do it, I think." And when Amon tried to thank him he said, "Never mind. pay me back when you're flush. You'll work better, I'm sure, if you have peace of mind. You know as well as I do that our emotional life has a drastic effect on voice. You can lose yourself temporarily while you sing. But it is with the whole man that we sing. Get your mother up here, Sayre, and make a home for yourself." He brushed aside Amon's efforts at gratitude saying simply, "I'm your friend; I want to help you."

Amon left the studio with his spirits lifted. He went to his room and wrote Sabina, promising to come to Chattanooga for her the following Sunday, and asking her to be ready to return with him. He looked eagerly toward this reunion and chaffed at the time consumed in the long train ride. He expected, when he vaulted the house steps on Douglas Street and in the front door, to find Ma elated. But she was entirely unruffled, she went about the preparations for her removal as dispassionately as she had when they had moved from the farm in Georgia, giving her mind fully to the tasks immediately confronting her, undistracted, once she had made up her mind, by tangential regrets or hankerings, or her sister's forebodings.

"Amon needs me up there in Boston," was her firm reply to every objection. She had sold her cow and chickens and the furniture. Amon helped her pack the feather beds and quilts and dishes and her irons in a packing case Uncle Hesh had provided. He checked the case and their suitcases through to Boston on their tickets. He and Ma said farewell to all the relatives and friends gathered to wish them luck.

On the train Sabina was very quiet, staring from the window at the passing scenes, her hands folded primly in her lap. She looked very dignified in her black bombazine dress with the white scarf, both feet with their polished shoes planted firmly on the coach floor, her calm manner bespeaking inner repose and assurance.

Amon took her shawl and hat and laid them on the rack above their heads. "I don't reckon you'll care much for the place I'm living in now, Ma," he said. "But we'll find a little apartment of our own. You can stay with some friends of mine till we find us a place."

"Who are these friends?"

"One of the boys I've been singing with lately. I wrote you about him. Euman Jennis, remember? They have room at their house. He's a fine fellow, lives with his folks in Roxbury. They've been mighty kind to me, and his mother says to be sure to bring you out to their place when you get to Boston. Then we'll find a place of our own, Ma. You're good at that. I've just been living around most anywhere lately, where it's cheap and handy to the places I been working."

"You not gonna be working when you get back from this here spree."

"I reckon not. But that restaurant job wasn't very good anyway, long hours and short pay. I'll look for a full-time job now."

"We get us a place where there's water handy and I can do washes same as down there in Chattanooga."

"I wish you didn't have to do washes, Ma. I want to work so you won't have to do that any more."

"What you want I should do, son? Set and fondle my aches? I like to work."

"Well, perhaps you could do something else."

"I don't know how to do nothing else that earns money—not like I knows washes. I stick to my last, same as you stick to yours."

It was a long wearisome trip on the trains, sitting up all night, trying to relieve cramped positions by walking up and down the aisle, listening to crying babies, eating from the basket of food Ma had prepared, changing trains, refilling the basket, journeying on again. When they at length reached Boston, Amon was anxious to get Sabina to the Jennises. She had been uncomplaining on the trip, but he was fearful to risk too much weariness and discomfort.

Mrs. Jennis greeted Sabina cordially, the whole family extending themselves to make her feel at home. The packing case was delivered and temporarily stored in the cellar.

However, the kindness of the Jennises and the ease of their pleasant home was not to deflect either Amon or Sabina from their determination to find work and a place of their own as soon as possible. After but one day of inactivity in Olive Jennis's clean and orderly house, Sabina was restless and unhappy. She asked for directions and the names of streets in the colored section near the heart of town. And while Amon went to look for a job, she set out to find them a suitable place to live. In a matter of days she had found an apartment on a narrow court off Westminster Street. It was a tiny house, one of a double row of single-story buildings constructed contiguously with a single wall separating one unit from another. A brick path ran between the rows of front doors, and there were no yards, front or back. Although none of the houses appeared ever to have had paint, they were in reasonable repair. Derby Place, as it was called, was swept and tidy and gave semblance of respectability. Water was obtainable at the end of the court, and so for Sabina the major requirements had been met.

A Trumpet Sounds

She paid the first week's rent of four dollars and had the packing case delivered.

She went to work with scrub brush and soap while Amon made a crude bed for her from the packing case, and two small stools for them to sit on. There was a cupboard built into one corner of the front room, and Sabina placed her dishes and pans and linen in it. There was a hearth, but no stove.

The day was ending when the new quarters had been cleaned to Sabina's satisfaction. She placed one feather tick on the board frame Amon had made and another on the floor. She surveyed their home. It was cold, the wind bleating dismally around the thin walls. Without any word to Amon she put on her shawl and went out. Shortly, she returned, her arms loaded with sticks.

"Plenty of wood lyin' around up there on Westminster Street," she said as she knelt before the hearth and crinkled paper and laid some sticks and lighted the fire. As the flames grew and dispersed the deepening shadows, she brought her kettle and hung it on the crane. She laid out two cups on clean papers spread on the floor and pulled up the two stools and sat down to wait for the water to heat. Amon sat down beside her and, watching her face in the firelight, knew her content. She hugged herself, rocking back and forth, humming softly.

That night he wrapped himself in one of Ma's clean quilts and fell asleep on the feather tick on the floor, happier, more confident, and more hopeful than he had been in months. He felt that now Ma was here it would be a turning point. Something must break in his favor soon. He had Fielding to repay; he must keep on with his lessons; and he had at least to help defray their living expenses.

He started out confidently the next day, his thin coat little protection against the searching wind as he made his way from hotel to hotel, café to café, from dock to warehouse to market to stores, to the railyards and the stations, fruitlessly. Still, he was not cast down. When he returned at night to Derby Street, Ma would be there, he thought. There would be a clean house and the smell of food simmering on the hearth. There would be light and warmth of the fire—and there was always tomorrow.

He found Sabina cheerful, elated by the ready customers she had obtained, and by her shiny new washtubs. "I'm a-goin' to get a stove first off," she said. "Then I can get more for my washes, I doin' the ironing too."

Amon went to wash up in the shedroom. He sloshed water on his head and face, soaping, rinsing. While he dried himself, he sang lustily, "Trompons l'es-pérance ho-mi-ci-de ar-ra-chons, ar-ra-chons . . . Guil-laume . . . à ses coup."

"What are you singing?" Sabina asked peremptorily as he appeared at the door.

"Just rehearsing an aria from *William Tell*."

"Why don't you sing so I can tell what you say?"

"It's in French, Ma."

"Sing a song I know the words to," she said.

"What'll it be, Ma?"

"Somethin' can dandle our spirits, son. You and me'll sing together while I dish up the victuals." She began to hum and then they both sang:

> *Come on Michael . . . hold the wind*
> *Don't let it blow the world away . . .*
> *Mmmuuuuuuuuuuum Oh, my Lord.*
> *What kind of shoes do Michael wear*
> *He wear shoes walk on air . . .*
> *Muuuummmmmmmm Oh, my Lord.*
> *Look over yonder, what do I see?*
> *Two tall angels a-comin' for me . . .*
> *Mmmuuuummmmm Oh, my Lord."*

Amon sat on the stool by the hearth, warming his hands at the flame and sniffing the stew.

"You hear any good words today, son?"

"No, nothing. There seems to be three men for every job. Every time I get to a place they've just hired somebody else. I don't care any more what the pay is or what the work is, so long as I can work at something. If I don't get a job soon, I'll have to give up the lessons. I'm behind with the tuition, and I haven't been able to pay Fielding anything on the loan he made me. He's mighty kind to me, Ma. But I can't impose on his kindness much longer."

"Don't you fret, son. You gonna find you a job. I plain knows it. I been prayin'. God will find a way, son."

A Trumpet Sounds

Her confidence, well-founded or not, was reassuring.

"You getting friendly with any neighbors, Ma?"

"Yes, I met two-three. They're right friendly. Mrs. Hinchbaugh, she live next to us to the north there, she's real nice. She tell me she take me to her church come Sunday. She's a Methodist, but I'll go anyhow. I'll find me a Baptist church by-an-by. Amon, what church you go to here in Boston?"

"I haven't gone to any church, Ma."

"Why don't you go to church, son? You always liked church. You might could meet some handy folks that-a-way, in the choir and all. Why'nt you go to church, Amon? You singin' all them French and German songs and you forget the old songs you used to sing so sweet."

"I'll not forget them, Ma."

"Then why don't you sing more of them? You tell me about the songs you sing for that teacher you got now, all of them fancy arias and operas and all. Don't you sing nothing else now?"

"I'm trying to become an artist, Ma. I have to learn to sing those songs that make an artist, the great classical music."

"Humph."

"If you ever heard Caruso sing, you'd know what I mean. I can't sing simple little melodies all the time and ever become a concert singer."

"You got your heart dead set on bein' a concert singer, son?"

"I reckon, Ma. I've got to sing. I've got a good voice, you know I have. Fielding thinks I have one of the best voices he's ever trained. He told me so. I don't know what will become of it or me. I can't see much future. I get sick—sick thinking about it. But I can't do anything else. I've got to sing, the best I know how. Maybe some people will listen. Maybe if I sing well enough they will want to hear me even if I am a Negro. And if they listen to me they might listen to others with a friendlier ear—might look at us with more . . . more . . ."

"I know what you aimin' at. But whiles you waitin' to do that big somethin' you talkin' about, why don't you sing for us folks? Give some concerts for our churches same as you did with Professor Sterling.

"I didn't earn very much money with them."

"Better than none at all. You plain got nothin' to lose tryin' that door."

"Maybe you're right, Ma. Maybe I should try to give some concerts here. I could try the churches again. But"—he tilted a smile at his mother—"they're no place to deliver French arias."

"No, you best stick to our own songs. They do our hearts the most good. We don't never tire hearin' them."

"I'll talk to Fielding about it. Maybe I could even sing in a white church. He has a lot of influence, knows the directors of many choirs. I've heard him talking on the telephone often at his house, recommending one person or another."

"Why you want to sing in white churches?"

"Because they pay more, Ma, and I want to sing where I can make some money. You know we need it."

"You can't sing 'Steal Away to Jesus' in a white church. You can't—"

"Maybe I could. Why not?"

"Cause it ain't—aren't fitting. White folks got no need for songs like that."

"Why not? White folks have troubles, and the old songs could tell them other people have troubles too. Anyway, I don't have to sing that one. There are plenty of hymns that folks in all churches like. I'll talk to Fielding when I go for my next lesson and see what he says."

"Come eat now," she said. "Hot up your insides and it'll build up your courage."

Chapter 25

"SAYRE," Titus Fielding said, tilting back in his chair and tapping the desk with the end of his pencil, "I've been campaigning for you for months. In my estimation you're far and away the best voice in Boston right now. I've plagued choir directors telling them what they already know. You've auditioned for several of them. I get the same answer. They won't put on a Negro. I think they are contemptible, certainly a miserable excuse as followers of Christ. But that's how it stands."

"I've got to do something, Mr. Fielding. I've got to use my voice to earn some money, *somehow*." Amon sat with his hands clasped between his knees. He had finished his lesson and had been engaged for some time in earnest conversation with his teacher. "My mother seems to think I should try to sing in some of our churches. But I'm afraid it wouldn't net me much. And it's important I make some money somehow."

Fielding rocked back and forth and continued to scowl at the carpet. Amon went on, "I used to put on concerts with Professor Sterling back in Chattanooga. I've been wondering if I couldn't do that here."

Titus Fielding studied the floor for some moments before he answered. "I don't think it would work."

"Why not? I know there would be difficulties, but I'm used to difficulties."

"It would be quite an undertaking here in Boston. I wouldn't advise it."

"But I have to try something." Amon's tone bespoke his desperation. "It's a cold winter."

"I know. Your mother is here and you'd like to keep her; there are no soles left in your shoes; and you're in debt. But it's too soon to give a concert, Sayre. Nobody knows you here. You need to have made many small appearances first. It takes the offer of a positive reward to get people out to a concert on a cold winter night."

"Couldn't I have bills printed that would paint up the inducement?"

"That takes money. So does advertising. So does renting a hall."

"I could pay for the hall after the performance, couldn't I?"

"I doubt it. They'd make you pay in advance."

Amon pondered that. "I'd have to have an accompanist too."

"That's the least of your worries."

"I think I could get Euman to accompany me. He's a first-rate pianist—if he'd have time to rehearse with me." Amon was thinking out loud.

"Better give up the idea, Sayre. It's no good. You'd find yourself in all kinds of trouble."

But the idea had taken hold of Amon with the steely grip of desperation. He had to find a way to put on a concert. Fielding said his voice was the best in Boston. Why not advertise it as that and expect people to come to find out. He was a pupil of Titus Fielding—the bill could state that. It needn't state that he was a Negro. Surely those people who knew Titus Fielding's reputation and who respected his judgment could be induced to come to hear one of his pupils. And surely the critics would attend. Amon's self-debate was all one-sided in favor for. He knew he would be grabbing chance by the tail, but he felt he had to swing with it and try to hang on. His position was such that nothing, he felt, could worsen it.

Titus Fielding was saying, "I'll call him—see what he has to say."

"I beg your pardon," Amon apologized. "I wasn't listening. I—was thinking. Call whom?"

"Metzler. Let me try to persuade him. They need a soloist up

A Trumpet Sounds

there in Newton Center. It would be only Sunday work, of course. But it ought to net you five a week at least."

Amon rose. "Thank you very much. You've been mighty kind and I appreciate it." And he left, thinking, "I'm not going to wait around for any more directors to refuse to engage me for their choirs. I'm going to see Euman now and find out how he feels about brushing up on some classic music and being my accompanist if I put on a concert."

It was late and he went home, deciding to go to Roxbury the following night. In the meantime he would tell Ma about the project he planned and get her reaction. He walked rapidly all the way from Newbury Street to Derby Place, his feet numb, his face stiff from the brutal wind, but his mind in a ferment of plans. He realized it was a risky thing he contemplated, but he told himself the idea had a few things going for it. It was simply a matter of convincing people he was worth hearing. The bills would state that. They had to be properly worded—maybe Fielding would help him with that. He had a true friend in his teacher. The man had gone out of his way to be generous, understanding. He was continuing the lessons without pay. He now permitted Amon to come openly to the Conservatory, ignoring any criticism or jeopardy to his standing. He had held auditions at which Amon was heard on the same basis as other pupils. He was scornful of the hypocrisy of the clergy and church members who refused Amon membership in their choirs because of his color. But he was one man against a battalion. Would he continue to defend his Negro protégé? Would he write words of praise sufficient to woo the public?

When Amon voiced these questions to Sabina, she was flatly skeptical. She agreed with Mr. Fielding that it was too soon. He was not ready yet. He would be jumping off the bridge backward, she said, not looking to what was down below. "Why don't you sing around in the colored churches for a while, son. Get yourself knowed better. Don't be hasty. You gonna pull the drawstring clean out the bag and lose all your peas."

"I've got to do *something*," Amon reiterated. "My voice is all the tool I have."

"We get along."

"You always say that. But how are we getting along? We have

Eunice Young Smith

no fuel, except what you pick up in the streets, no furniture, just enough food to keep alive. That's not getting along. I've got to earn some money, Ma. I've got to." He ground his teeth and plunged his hands deep in his pockets.

Later, when he discussed his idea with Euman, his friend was barely more optimistic than Sabina. He was willing to accompany Amon, and thought they could use the church piano perhaps to rehearse. However, his lack of enthusiasm was disheartening.

Every day Amon continued his search for work, getting each early news edition and scanning the help-wanted columns. He pestered employment agencies and went repeatedly to hotels and cafés. He had a job for a short time shoveling snow from the streets and sidewalks, working with a crew of men hired by the city. He showed up for his voice lesson on Thursday so exhausted he could scarcely sing.

When the lesson was over, Titus Fielding said, "Sit down, Sayre. I have news for you. Perhaps I should have told you of it right off. Didn't think adding excitement to exhaustion would relax you. Shoveling snow all day is not exactly the exercise we recommend for voice pupils. But you won't have to go back to that tomorrow if you don't want to. I've got wind of a job for you. But first, about that Newton Center solo request. Miss Abelman says she would be delighted to have you sing with her group. They are putting on a benefit for some orphanage or other. I know Minnie Abelman—she's a real woman—I think I told you, secretary of the New England American Missionary Society. I think when she hears you sing she will want to recruit you permanently."

Amon's face brightened as he listened. Some of his weariness dissolved. Fielding went on: "Then there is this regular job of messenger for the John Hancock Insurance Company. I heard about this last evening from a friend. You may start tomorrow if you wish." He fingered inside a vest pocket, scowling deeply, and then pulled out a card and handed it to Amon. "That's the address—see Mr. Bloomdahl. Never mind—never mind—" He brushed aside Amon's thanks. He swung around in his chair and rose. "Well, that's all for tonight. Go home and get some rest."

Out again into the snowy street, his feet light, his step quick, his weariness gone, Amon suddenly wanted to speak to people as

231

A Trumpet Sounds

he passed, to greet them, to pull their chins up out of their mufflers by a cheery "Good evening, sir. Fine evening, isn't it?" He hummed to himself, "Golden slippers I'm gonna wear . . . Gonna put on my robe and cleave the air . . . Hallelujah, Lord!" The wind whipped the words from his lips, blew gusts of snow into his throat, blinded his eyes, and froze the tears starting there. His happiness was almost more than he could bear.

It turned out Miss Abelman was so pleased with Amon's voice that she arranged for him to sing the solo in the evening choir at her church every Sunday. She agreed to pay for his transportation and five dollars a Sunday.

The job as messenger for the insurance company was pleasant and easy work, taking Amon from office to office in the big building, often to the bank or the post office or some other downtown building. He could sing at his work, and he did, filling the halls and corridors with melodies. Customers, businessmen, clerks, and fellow employees got to know the messenger boy with the voice, and smiled and nodded whenever they saw him, often asking for a favorite song. Amon always willingly obliged if there was time. The job paid seven dollars a week. Four for rent, he figured, sixty cents for carfare, and two dollars for food. It left nothing for shoes or furniture. But with what Ma brought in and the Sunday singing they could manage, and he could begin to pay a little on his debt to Titus Fielding.

This fortunate turn of events had not, however, quieted Amon's desire to give a concert of his own. He sorted through his repertoire and selected what he believed would be suitable songs. He offered to sing solos in the Twelve Apostles Baptist Church, to which Ma now belonged, in exchange for the use of their piano for his rehearsals with Euman. The two young men met whenever they and the church and the piano were free.

Through his singing Amon became very popular in the church, and there were numerous requests for him to sing. These were gratifying but not very remunerating. Through the winter Amon trained and rehearsed and worked. He and Euman gave several small musicales, and from his share of the proceeds he was able to repay Mr. Fielding the seventy-five dollars he had lent him.

The cold retreated by late March, and rain and mud replaced the snow and soot. Then one night he spoke to Titus again about putting on a concert.

"If I could put on one good concert—fill a house, just once, I could pay all my debts and get on my feet." He looked at the soles of his shoes, cardboard stuffed, and grinned wryly. "Get off my feet, I should say."

Titus Fielding shook his head. "I wish I didn't have to seem a wet hen, but—" His lower lip stuck out and he stroked his chin, thinking. "But—well—if you're dead set on it, I'll do what I can, Sayre."

"If you'd write the notices. Would you do that? If you'd just do that, I'd—"

"I will. Where do you think to give your concert?"

"Shelley Hall."

"I know the manager. I'll see what I can do. How much money do you have?"

"None. I'll have to have credit on the printing, the advertising—everything."

"I'll stand for you. But mark my words, Sayre, I've warned you. What shall you do about suitable clothes. You should wear tails and black tie."

"I can rent them. Euman will take care of that."

"He your accompanist?"

"Yes, we've rehearsed all winter. I've promised him half the take."

"Generous," Fielding muttered, "if there is a take." Aloud he said, "Have you determined on a date for your concert?"

"In April, the middle of April."

"That's hardly time enough. You can't get the word around. You should contact many people, enlist sponsors, work up enthusiasm."

"I can't wait any longer," Amon said, his conviction being that if he waited longer his nerve would evaporate beyond retrieving.

Many things were amiss on that night of April 15 when Amon Sayre, the "star pupil of the celebrated teacher, Titus Fielding,"

A Trumpet Sounds

made his concert debut in Shelley Hall. It was a miserable night of sleeting rain and haggling wind. The house had not been more than half-sold, and Amon had worked himself to exhaustion all day.

Then an hour before curtain time he had received an anonymous telephone call, the voice warning that no nigger could sing in Shelley Hall. He was thrown into a paroxysm of dismay. Titus, blazing with anger, dismissed the call as the depravity of some crank and strove to be reassuring. But now fear was added to nervousness and anxiety, augmented by dismay at the turnout, and Amon took his place beside the piano tense and unhappy.

He sang the program through, the lieder of Schubert and Schumann, the romantic songs of Berlioz and Tchaikovsky and Brahms, ending with the "Erlkönig." The applause was generous, as voluminous as one could reasonably expect from an only partly filled house. Fielding found no fault with his voice or delivery. People came backstage afterward, but Amon was so sick with his sense of failure that he could not speak.

The music critics who had braved the mean weather to be present spoke glowingly of the performance in their columns next day. They seemed to think he had made an artistic success, whether it had been financially so or not.

Amon read the notices to Sabina over their supper the next night. She heard them in silence, then went to the stove for the coffee pot and poured herself a second cup of coffee. She had not attended the concert, saying it was too bad a night for her to go clean down town to hear him sing a lot of songs she couldn't understand the words of anyway. She reserved any pronouncement on the concert and left Amon to find consolation where and how best he could.

Financially, the concert had been a fiasco. Amon found himself further in debt than ever, and with no means of paying it. He brooded, trying to ferret out the crux of the failure. He went back to his messenger job deflated, unable to sing cheerily as he carried messages from place to place. He came home at night to sit morosely by the fire in the bare apartment that he had not earned the means to furnish.

"What went wrong, Ma?" he pondered. "Where did I miss?"

Sabina ladled up two bowls of vegetable soup and set them on the crate she had devised for a table. She broke ashcake into her bowl and stirred it, waiting for the soup to cool.

"You eat your supper," she said.

Amon held the bowl between his knees, dabbling the spoon around in it. He stared into the firelight. They ate in silence, the clicking of their spoons against the bowls and the crackle of the burning sticks sounding loud and sharp in the silence. The fire leaped and writhed, throwing wierd shadows on the walls and along the bare floor. They finished their supper but continued to sit there, the fire dying to embers, glowing steadily for a while and then falling apart with a sigh.

Sabina said musingly, "There is an old song my mammy used to sing before she was sold downriver. I ain't never forgot it. She had so many sorrows. She was born in sorrow, and she lived in sorrow all her days. She used to sing to me about a blind man:

> *Blind man sittin' by the road . . . Huummm*
> *Oh, Jesus, let me see,*
> *Oh, Jesus let me see . . . Huuumm*

She sang that song over and over like she blind too. But she ain't blind. I reckon she wanna see something yonder from the field and the hot sun and the daylong rows of cotton. She wanna reach down deep for why it be like it is, why God so good and kind and yet he don't get into folks' heart more. He so merciful, yet we all suffer so pitiful."

There was a long pause while she laid more pieces of wood on the embers and poked them together into a glowing nest to catch the wood quickly. "I don't 'llow as she found an answer. But she sing and sing. "Blind man sittin' by the road . . . Oh, Jesus, let me see.' I reckon nobody can rightly see with their mortal eyes, son. They ain't the eyes you see a truth with. Only God can let you see where to put your feet down."

What was she driving at? Amon wondered. He knew her disapproval of the concert would out, but it was taking a long way round.

"Maybe we think we can go 'long by ourselves. We get biggity notions. We get to thinkin' we high feathers, good as everybody

A Trumpet Sounds

else, better maybe, proudful."

You want us to be proud, Amon thought and he protested angrily: "You talk about self-respect and doing a job well and holding our heads high. Now you say it's wrong to be proudful."

"We got to pray to see, and we gotta be humble to see—like Jesus. He were better than all them that persecuted Him, weren't He? He were meek as a little child. But it learned folks, didn't it—the example He set? All them millions of people has passed away, most they names ain't even remembered. All them that's so rich and arrogant—they all gone. Nobody think about them no more. But not Jesus—not Jesus, son. He meek and lowly. He let them taunt Him and kill Him. But He ain't never died. He's mightier than all. Right today He's showin' us the way. He say the meek shall be exalted, but I don't reckon God meant we gonna get rich and powerful on this here earth. I don't see it that way nohow. There's another way—another way."

Her voice dwindled off into musing. Her lips hung limp and her eyes were unseeing. She clasped and unclasped her hands, and her mind struggled for a meaning that eluded her.

"I don't know what you're trying to say, Ma," Amon said. "I've trained the voice God gave me so I could sing—where I'll be heard. I gave a concert and it was a flop. That's all there is to it."

"Maybe it ain't—isn't a flop if it learn you a thing."

"I've learned," Amon said in a tone that for him was bitter. "I've learned you can't buck a white world. To be a success you have to be able to make some money. And how you going to do it? How you going to do it?"

"You're a colored man, son. You goin' noplace tryin' to be white. God make you like you is, and He got a reason. You got to be yourself—not no imitation of somebody else. It aren't right to throw back to God He made you one color and somebody else another. That's His business. He knows why He done it. It's your business to be your own man, full and straight and good. You no need to look on anybody and envy 'em."

"I don't envy anybody, Ma. I only want a chance to fulfill myself as a singer, as a man."

"You ain't—aren't bein' true to how God made you," Sabina persisted doggedly.

"How am I not? I don't know that, Ma."

"You tryin' for something you ain't—aren't. You tryin' to sing like a white man. You turnin' your face from God. You sayin' you don't like what He give you or how He made you. You—"

"Oh, Ma, how can you say that? It isn't true. I'm trying to use my voice the best I know how. I don't know what you're driving at."

But dimly he did, and it disturbed him. He could not phrase his knowing, but he felt a vague dissatisfaction with his singing. Something was missing, was wrong. Yet he could not name it. He felt the concert had been a failure not just financially, some other way too. Perhaps it was in the way Ma meant. But it was not clear in his own mind, and Sabina had not made it clear.

The concert did have a compensating aftermath. It had been attended by Samuel Galveston, an impresario of means and reputation. He wrote a letter to Amon saying that he had greatly enjoyed the singing and requesting him to call at a certain address. The letter was waiting when Amon arrived home from work several days after the concert.

"What you reckon that letter's about, son?" Sabina was impressed by the printed heading on the paper and the businesslike tone of the letter.

Amon read it over several times. "I don't know. Might could be just to compliment me on my singing."

"He could have done that the night of the concert, couldn't he? He say to come and see him. What's that for, eh?"

"I reckon I'll have to go and see."

And since the request for a meeting was "at your earliest convenience" Amon decided to go that very night. He ate his supper hurriedly, cleaned himself, brushed his worn suit and went to the address of the letter.

Mr. Galveston welcomed him most heartily. He pulled a chair forward and urged Amon to sit. He was a dignified, slim little man, with a goatee and a balding head.

"I was very much impressed with your singing last Saturday night," he said without further ado. "In fact, I was completely charmed by your voice. I would like to conduct a tour for you."

A Trumpet Sounds

Amon's astonishment was patent as the little man with the goatee went on to describe his qualifications as an entrepreneur and his extensive experience in introducing talented singers to the American public. His confidence in his choice of Amon as a likely protégé seemed without misgiving. "I have a very fine pianist who would travel with us and accompany you. His name is Byron Evans. Perhaps you have heard of him."

"No," Amon had to admit.

"You will find him excellent, I am sure. Now, as to remuneration, I can guarantee you a hundred a month and expenses, and then of course a percentage of the house."

Amon was astonished. Go on an extended tour with an accompanist, with this gentleman making the bookings in advance, and with a guaranteed salary of one hundred dollars a month! It seemed preposterous.

"Are you employed at present?" Galveston asked.

Amon found his tongue. "Yes, I have a job with the John Hancock Insurance Company." He assumed Mr. Galveston already knew this, had talked with Titus Fielding, and was only asking as a formality. He knew also, no doubt, how much the job paid. His offer seemed utterly fabulous to Amon.

"Our tour, as I plan it, would take us across New York State and Pennsylvania, Ohio and Indiana and Illinois to Chicago, then parts of Kentucky, and terminate at Knoxville, Tennessee."

"I'll have to discontinue my lessons," Amon said inanely, not having properly collected his wits. It sounded as if he were in need of being convinced, and he felt uncouth and foolish. But Galveston continued to smile in the friendliest way. "This is an opportunity to exercise some of your fine training," he said.

"Yes—yes—"

"I understand you are living with your mother. Can she manage without you for a while?"

Amon laughed a little. Mr. Galveston should know Ma. "Yes, she can manage, I'm sure. We have good neighbors. She's very self-sufficient." And he thought: It's I who cannot manage without her. Ma'll be all right. I can send her money, lots of money . . . all of it, for he had said a hundred dollars *and* expenses. Wait till I tell Ma that. I can't believe it. I can pay my debts now. I can buy

Ma things she needs for the apartment. There will be money to spare.

"Hallelujah!" It came out in a joyous shout and startled the little man with the goatee, but he beamed.

"You accept my offer then?"

"Oh, yes. I'm honored that you have chosen me, that you think my voice good enough."

"Fine. Fine. We will meet again, two weeks from tonight. I'll contact Byron Evans. We will want to rehearse several programs before we start. But I shall go ahead now with the bookings, and—"

"How long will we be on the tour do you think?"

"Several months no doubt."

Amon looked in dismay at his shabby suit and worn shoes and then in some embarrassment at Galveston. "I—I—you see—" he floundered, trying to word the information that he had no proper clothes for traveling and no money with which to purchase any.

Samuel Galveston drew a wallet from his pocket. "Of course, I'll advance part of your first month's salary," he said, "as a binder." He handed Amon five ten dollar bills. "I'm happy you have accepted my proposition. I'm sure we shall both find it profitable."

Chapter 26

Amon jerked to alertness at the loud knocking on the door of his hotel room. He had been sunk in deep reverie induced by the words he was putting into a letter to Sabina. "Come in," he called.

The door opened and Samuel Galveston appeared, mouth agrin above his neatly trimmed goatee.

"At work so early," he chidded.

"A letter to my mother," Amon said. "I promised I'd write every week. I thought that would be an easy assignment when I made it at the start of our tour, but—" he shrugged. "Well, I reckon you shouldn't make promises you don't know whether or not you can keep."

"Are we working you so hard as all that?" Galveston stepped into the room. He wore a belted sports jacket and cap. It was not his customary business attire, and Amon was by now quite familiar with what it portended. Galveston was dressed for a morning's walk. After some five months on tour with him, Amon had grown accustomed to seeing Samuel Galveston in hiking togs and to obeying this signal to get into his own. Because of the sedentary aspects of constant travel, Galveston found it wise to make time for exercise. He was fond of walking, especially through the countryside, and often walked from one town to the next.

"Well," Amon said, "you must admit we have no time on our hands. What do you have up your sleeve? Byron and I were going to work up a couple of new arrangements this morning, you know."

"Not this morning, my boy. I'd like to jaunt to the next town, Rogers Park, I believe it is. We'll take the train from there to Chicago. Come along, we'll have breakfast in my room." He looked archly at Amon. "Of course, if you'd rather work—" He walked to the window and peered out. "It's a beautiful day. Postpone the work."

"Let me finish this letter," Amon begged, "and I'll be along. It's a fine day. I'd enjoy walking."

"Very well. Don't keep the bacon waiting." He left, and Amon resumed his writing. He was telling Sabina about their stay in Evanston, Illinois, about the concert there to an overflowing First Methodist Church and the heart-warming response of the people. "It made me feel good, Ma, real good. I think it would have made you feel good too. Maybe you'd be proud of me now and say all my work and training wasn't wasted time.

"But it isn't all honey on this trip. I don't have to arrange for accommodations for us along the way. Galveston does all that. But in some towns when he is not able to get rooms in one hotel after another, I know what the trouble is. In one town he had to beg rooms in a mighty sorry place, and in another accept the hospitality of strangers or sleep in the station. Galveston's a real gentleman. Any place that turns me away turns him away too.

"In most of the towns where I've sung it is to full houses and mostly white people. Mr. G. is well known, and when he is backing a singer I think people take it for granted he will be good. I don't know how much he takes in from every concert. I know he's not losing money on me. I am content with my share and the hundred a month we agreed on. I'll keep on sending it home to you, and you do what you please with it. I have little need of money for all my travel expenses are supplied.

"I think I told you that Byron and I are working up arrangements for some more of the old folk songs. Everywhere they seem to take well with audiences. I really love to sing them and hardly ever give a concert now without including several. Mr. G. thinks this is good also, and we work out programs together."

Amon's thought drifted for a moment to a concert in a large

A Trumpet Sounds

city where, after the performance, an old man had come to him to say, "Mr. Sayre, I cannot tell you how deeply your singing of 'Swing Low, Sweet Chariot' tonight has affected me. I have listened to great singers in many lands, but I have never heard a voice with the rich, red-velvet quality of yours."

A rich, red-velvet voice! Oh, those days back in the cornfield with Pa teaching him to imitate the sounds he heard, when he had clothed himself in the feathers of the mockingbird and defied the other birds with—"I ain't as pretty as a red bird but I can sing better—I can sing red and I can sing blue and I can sing speckledy if I've a mind to." Back then with Pa he had learned the first lessons in vocal color. Yet he knew this faculty was not his exclusively, nor entirely a learned thing. All Negroes had it to some degree, a racial trait, a genetic characteristic, mutated from centuries of custom and emotional need. The seemingly simple, repetitious songs had a haunting, hypnotic force, sounds strung together, unhampered by strict adherence to meaning, to create a sort of incantation, a spell.

But back to his letter: "Mr. G. has come in to say he has an idea to walk part way to Chicago this morning. I only hope he doesn't decide to walk all the way. God bless you and keep you well, Your loving son, Amon Sayre."

He folded the letter and inserted it in an envelope, addressed it and stamped it. Then with it in his pocket he went down the hall to Galveston's room. He and Byron Evans were in animated conversation and as Amon took his seat at the breakfast table he launched into a humorous anecdote concerning a man he had met on a train to Pittsburgh. After Amon had finished his breakfast, the three men descended to the lobby, walked a few blocks to the railway station, had their bags checked through to the central depot in Chicago, asked directions to Rogers Park, and set off.

It was a sunny, invigorating September morning. The village streets were filled with people and a bustling traffic. As the three men gained open country, sidewalks ceased and they walked the dirt road. It ran for a distance at a slightly lower level but parallel with the railroad tracks, and then the tracks branched away to the left and the road ribboned through open flat farm land. Well-kept fences enclosed fields of incredibly high corn. Goldenrod and pale purple fall asters waved above the dusty grass at the edges, and further on bordered lush green meadows where cows grazed.

They came to a vast tract of land where many people were picking up potatoes, and they stopped to watch. All over the field backs bent and arms moved energetically.

"They work so silently," Amon remarked. "Down home this would all be a singing." He was filled suddenly with nostalgic yearnings for the north Georgia country of his boyhood. He longed to go home, to visit the Flatlands again, the dusty summer roads through the hills, the winding waters of the branch, the mill at Calhoun where he used to take corn to be ground—he, perched on old Lightning, bag of meal tied on behind, clopping home in the dusk. And he remembered the singing. It seemed to Amon that the old songs he had been hearing all his life, the field songs and the play songs, the chanteys and the shouts and spirituals, held for him a new significance, as though previously he had heard them with only part of himself, their greatest meaning and beauty lying quiescent in his mind until now.

The jaunt to Rogers Park was uneventful, and from there they continued to the city by train. At the auditorium in Chicago their performance was given an ovation, Amon called again and again for encores. Gratified but tired, Amon finally retreated to his dressing room. He shed his coat and removed the tie and was about to sink into a chair when from behind a screen in one corner stepped a figure. A short, stocky man in street clothes with the lip of his hat pulled down over his eyes. For a full moment Amon stared.

"Asa! My God, Asa!"

Their embrace denied Time its toll, denied the years of silence, denied the semblance of indifference or neglect. They rocked together. "My God, Asa, where did you spring from? I knew you were somewhere in Chicago, but had no idea how to track you down."

"I knew you was coming," Asa said. "It was in the papers."

"And you came to my concert!"

"I heard you sing. Man, you got that hall of listeners like that." He cupped his hands.

"You were out there—one of them?"

A Trumpet Sounds

"No, I got in here with the piano." He grinned. "I been hiding in the wings."

"But why? You should have been out front, in the first row."

Asa shook his head. "Just where they'd have been looking for me."

"Who looking for you? Are you in trouble?"

"It's a long story."

"The police?"

"No, no. Union thugs."

"What do you mean?"

"Don't you read the papers?"

"Sure—headlines anyway."

Asa's head reared and his shoulders squared a little. "White unions are strong here in Chicago. They scare the hell out of the bosses. That's just dandy, only now we got the A F of L fighting the IWW and that's not so good."

"Whose side you on, Asa?"

Asa's laugh was a short jerky grunt. "The A F of L won't allow Negroes in their damned union. But the IWW does, so where do you think I stand?"

"Great, you belong to the Industrial Workers of the World. Are all Wobblies afraid to show their faces in public?"

"No, but I got an extra iron in the fire."

"Yeah?"

"I'm organizing black men to have their own union. We have to unite, Amon, if we want to be heard or seen. I talk my head off trying to convince black men they'd have a lot of power if they'd get together. We could fight for our place in the work force, same as the other unions . . . Together we could stand up and face them. . . ."

The last words were asserted with a vehemence that took Amon back to those days in the Flatlands when Asa used to rant at Pa. He was the same rebel, the born crusader, only now with solid goals to travel toward.

"You've got courage, Asa. You married now?"

"No, I move around too much." He was silent for a moment before he added, "I got a girl."

"So?"

"She works for the NWA. That's the Negro Women's Association. She's trying to do for them what I try for the men." He shook his head a little. "She got some powerful tall hills to climb."

"What you both are doing sounds very brave to me."

Asa shrugged. "We say our piece is all. You sayin' it one way, we say it another. See?"

"Yes, I see," Amon nodded. "Since I've been on this trip I have come to see life, us, this land, as I never did before. It scares me, Asa."

"It scares me too, I reckon." He studied his clenched hands and a knot of nerves pulsed at his temples. "It's time we got up and got somewhere now, and I want to help to make it happen. Maybe one day you and Ma be proud of me, of what I do."

"I'm sure of it. I'll tell Ma."

"How is she? Where is she and you on this tour?"

"She's in Boston."

"Alone?"

"Yes. After Jeb went to work on the packet boat, she was all alone. So I went and got her. We have a little apartment there."

"Give her my love."

"She'll start praying for you."

"I'll take all the help I can get." Both men laughed quietly.

"Once I'm really going with my singing I can help you too, Asa. If you'll just let me know where I can reach you."

"I'll let you know."

Amon rose. "Let me get out of these clothes. We'll go somewhere for food. I eat after a concert, not before. I'm starved. We'll eat and talk."

"No," Asa said, laying a detaining hand on his arm. "No."

"Why not, Asa? It's been so long. We have so much to get caught up on."

"I know. I'd like to, but with things so hot right now, I best stay out of sight."

There was a knock on the door, and Asa jumped for the screen. It was Galveston who entered. Amon introduced his brother. In his bluff and hearty way Galveston invited Asa to join them for their late dinner.

"We'll make it a real celebration. Amon hoped to find you

A Trumpet Sounds

here, but didn't quite know how to start looking. He was a real hit tonight, this brother of yours." He put his arm affectionately across Amon's shoulders. "You may have to share him with the press and some businessmen. They are all eager to talk with him. And—"

Asa shook his head decisively. "Another time. I've got to go now."

There was more pounding at the door. Galveston swung it open to a battery of newsmen. There were eager questions, blithe rejoinders as he pushed them back with the promise of interviews later around the supper table. In the general hubbub Asa slipped away unnoticed.

The press was eulogistic. Amon clipped several of the notices and sent them to Sabina with his letter, telling her he had seen Asa, but only for a short visit. He would tell her all about it when he got back home.

Amon was reluctant to leave Chicago without seeing his brother again, but his good sense told him that to pursue this desire would be dangerous to Asa and likely realize little.

From Springfield the tour took them to St. Louis, to Memphis, and then eastward. After leaving Memphis, a restlessness possessed Amon. He thought it might be the nearness to Georgia, to the locale of his boyhood. The harvested fields, the carnival colors of the foliage, the bare strips of red clay, the endless march of crumbling shacks, took him backward in time. He stared from the coach window, chin in palm, his attention refusing to be engaged by Galveston's rehash of the previous day's experiences.

An engulfing miasma beset him, anger and frustration, disgust, bewilderment, loathing for the treatment he and Galveston had encountered in so many places on the tour. Oh, yes, there had been many warm-hearted and generous individuals, much genuine admiration for his singing, plaudits for which he was at first grateful and which he later despised. He felt himself strangely changed. Out of his timidity and fear he had emerged a truculent and often hostile man, obsessed by an implacable and rankling scorn for white people and for the obsequiousness of his own. His very gut roiled at the leering white faces that masked so thinly a rooted condescension, a smirking hypocrisy. The insufferable inequities. He was revolted by the signs everywhere! We Don't Serve Negroes Here . . . For Whites Only on toilet doors . . . Reserved for Whites at restaurants and hotels. The accumulation of affronts became a crushing weight on his spirit, a sickness invading his dreams, nightmares in which he never seemed to escape.

He recalled the night after a particularly successful performance when he had gone back to their hotel and in the shower had scrubbed and scrubbed as though somehow he could wash himself free of the unhappy repugnance he felt, lose the tensions which all along the way had been exacerbated despite Galveston's cheery optimism, despite his seeming popularity, despite everything.

Years ago—it seemed so far away now—when he was just a kid in Georgia, he had not known such feelings. He had had no well-defined brush with prejudice. He knew there was a separateness, that there were abuses by white people, inequities that all Negroes put up with. He knew there were those who, like Asa, rebelled. But as a kid he had been so happy, really, so ignorant of what injustice meant. The friction sort of ran off him as the branch water after a swim. How far away it seemed now.

He recalled the unnerving dream he had had a few nights before. He thought he saw Leah and that she spoke to him, her hands extended, but he could not make out her words. He looked to where she pointed across a jagged crack in the earth. Ma was on the other side, her face distorted. He called to her, but he seemed to know he could make no sound and she could hear nothing. He stood there waving and mouthing as the crack grew wider and wider. It widened into a chasm and Ma stood on the edge of it. He called to her to go back—go back. He woke up screaming: "Go back! Go back!" He was unable to go to sleep again that night, and the next day the dream stayed with him in the form of a senseless fear.

"You've been moping the last few days," Galveston said. "Not feeling under the weather, I hope."

"I don't think so," Amon said, "but to tell you the truth, I don't know what's wrong."

"Perhaps you're just tired."

A Trumpet Sounds

"I feel depressed."

"It's been a rugged six months. You'll be glad to get home."

"Yes, I feel I must get home."

"We'll all be glad to stop looking at timetables for a while," Bryon said. "I enjoy these jaunts, but they are wearying."

Amon nodded absently, but he told himself, "It isn't homesickness. It isn't that."

The last two weeks of the tour seemed interminable. He sang his songs without zest, not feeling involved with them, his mind continually harassed by a nebulous anxiety.

At Knoxville, with his contract fulfilled, Amon bade farewell to his two good friends and started on his homeward journey.

He had at first planned to go through Virginia and Maryland and then north. But almost involuntarily the decision came to him to go to Chattanooga and pay a brief visit to Aunt Tatty and Uncle Hesh and then go to Dalton and visit Leah at Buzzard's Roost. It might be a long time before he would be so close again, he reasoned, and a visit with these kin would give him news to carry to Ma. Leah would be glad to see him, to hear about the tour. Hadn't it been Leah who first told him about the great halls where men sang? Hadn't he fulfilled her prophecy? He felt a sting of remorse that he had not tried to write Leah and tell her so.

From Chattanooga he took the train to Dalton, and when he arrived he checked his bags at the station and looked about for a conveyance to take him to Okochogee Mountain. He found a white boy who, for an exorbitant fee, agreed to carry him to the forks in his rickety wagon. Dalton was little changed from his memory of it. He talked with the boy in a desultory fashion, asking commonplace questions and hearing commonplace replies.

Feelings of apprehension mounted as he neared the base of the mountain, unbalancing his anticipated joy. How long it seemed since he had heard anything of Leah. Letters from Buzzard's Roost had never been frequent, and in the last year or so there were none to his knowledge, unless Ma had gotten some and not told him of them. When he left on this tour, he had given Ma a paper mapping their itinerary. Yet he knew that only a cataclysm, and maybe not even that, would induce her to intercept his tour with a letter. She would be all right, she had assured him when he left. "I'm fixed comfortable and I can look after myself. I been doin' that for a sight of years, son. You go and don't you fret about me. This a fine chance for you. I'm right pleased you goin'."

Well, it wouldn't be long before he would be home again. Love for Ma, a longing to see her, swept through him. He saw her now as when he was a small boy and she was driven to punishing him—she towering over him with the birch switch, her eyes snapping, her headcloth awry, a Biblical couplet misquoted on her lips—and he fearing her displeasure a thousand times more than the sting of the switch. He saw her marching to church of a Sunday, prim, self-assured, her long feet slapping the dusty road, her back straight, her step buoyant. How beautiful he always thought her. He saw her bending over a basket of laundry, her knobby hands smoothing and folding the freshly ironed shirts and dresses. He saw her rocking on the gallery in the moonlight, with all the children at her feet. Leah there too—Leah, who had come home because she was so lonely up on Buzzard's Roost she couldn't bear it. And he saw Ma fixing things for them to take with them when they were making ready to return to Leah's home—Ma fussing over Leah, her lips trembling so she had to hold on to her mouth. He saw again with great vividness his climb up the mountain with his sister, the revolting battle of the snakes, the storm, the discovery of the guitar. How enchanted he had been with that instrument. What music he and Leah had made. Even now, so long after, he could experience again in a diminished way the spine-tingling thrill he had known as a skinny scared-rabbit boy when he had sent his songs and his strumming about the mountainside.

At the Forks he paid the youth and took the trail up the mountain. The path was wider, more traveled than he recalled. He climbed fast, sweating, panting. A pressure formed at the back of his neck, and his temples throbbed. He was disconcerted to find the way unfamiliar, strange to him, as though he had never been this way before. Halfway up, there was a string of cabins that had not been there when he visited Leah. Areas of the mountain had been cleared now and rough gardens planted. Hogs zipped snorting from the path into the brush, and chickens scratched in disorderly yards.

A Trumpet Sounds

Beyond these cabins the path became meager, berry canes and saplings entwined across it. He pushed through with a frantic sense of being hindered purposely. "You'd think Leah or Harp would hack their path clear," he mumbled. "Looks like it's not been used all summer." He spread aside the clutching briars, and they fell together behind him.

Before he reached the clearing, he was consumed by a feeling of panic. The way was too strange, too unlike what he remembered. Sweat soaked his shirt, and he mopped his face until his handkerchief was sopping. Coming out of the trees at the edge of the open ground, he was struck by a smothering stillness. Not the quiet of an isolated farm in the repose of an autumn afternoon, but the stillness of a deserted place, forsaken and dying.

Yet this place was not deserted. A horse drooped his head over the gate of a small corral, and a pair of overalls hung on the line. A yellow dog came yapping at sight of Amon. Not Bruno—Bruno would long since have died and been replaced. He spoke to the dog in a low voice, hushing it. He came to the door and stood there hesitantly, urges conflicting—one to throw open the door and burst in, another prompting him to knock first. "How silly," he thought. "We'll laugh about this when Leah opens the door."

Glad words were forming on his lips when the door cracked ajar a few inches and a hideous, incredibly wrinkled face peered at him through clouded fishlike eyes. For a moment Amon was dumb, the old crone staring at him, wordless, while the dog took up his yapping again. He struggled for voice. "Leah." It sounded like the paddings of nightmare. "My sister—Mrs. Bracket—she lives here, did live here."

The woman's toothless, sucked-in mouth opened, and her head came out far enough to spit across the doorstep. "Not no more she don't."

"Where—where is she?" Amon faltered. "Where has she gone?"

The woman squinted at him, suspicious. "You say you her brother?"

"Yes. I—" He stopped. There was no use explaining to this crone. She would make no sense of an explanation of a tour. Anyway, it didn't matter. All he wanted to know was Leah's whereabouts so he could go and find her.

"Leah Bracket. She your sister? Well, she's dead. She dead more'n three weeks now, and her man took his stuff and left. Cleared out, he did. Sold this here place to me and my ol' man. We got papers to show. We pay hard cash money for this here place—my man did. We paid too much. He cheated us—that Bracket done. Took every cent we own. He cleared out or we'd a tried to get some back. He told us this here—"

Amon had heard nothing beyond the words "She's dead." Perhaps this old woman was mistaken. Perhaps she was speaking of someone else. Perhaps she was mad—or drunk. His mind groped for a loophole. Maybe he hadn't heard right. He was tired from the fast walk up the hill. He asked her again, "What did you say?"

"I said yah, she dead all right. Monia got her. Don't reckon had no doctor tendin' her. Folks down below say she been ailin' for a long spell. Coulda been somethin' else maybe she die of, I don't know. Them doctors don't always know. They jes guessin' half the time what folks dies of in the mountains. Half the time they dies of they own booze—and they laid out and the doctors claims they die of mountain fever—he-he-he," she cackled. "Good a name to call it by as any, I reckon. But she don't live here no more. You kin lay to that. Me and my ol' man bought this here place, paid cash for it too. Got a good roof, it has, and they's a good spring of water, and—" She opened the door further now and quieted the dog. Even to her blurred eyes the stricken face of the man before her must have been arresting. "You lookin' for your sister, eh?"

"Do you know where I can reach her husband, Harp Bracket?"

"No, I ain't no notion where he gone to."

"Leah—Mrs. Bracket—where is she buried?" He still did not believe.

"Down to the Forks, I reckon. I didn't go to no buryin'. We new to these parts. Come from Kaintuck. But them folks down below there can tell you. Or the man at the store at the Forks. You goin' down mountain that-a-way you ask them. They kin tell you. I 'spect she buried in the churchyard there. But I don't know for

A Trumpet Sounds

certain. You kin ask down there."

He turned, numbed as from a blow, and stumbled across the clearing, through the briars, and down the mountain to the church at the Forks. Leah's grave was pointed out to him by the sexton. He knelt beside the mean, untended plot, grief constricting his heart and tightening his throat. "I wanted to tell you, Leah," he sobbed. "I wanted you to know."

On the trip to Boston Amon's thought drifted back and forth over the bits of information he had obtained at the Forks. He had learned that Leah was alone when she was ill, the neighbors caring for her as best they could. They had finally called a doctor, but by the time he arrived she was dead. They had brought her down mountain and buried here there in the churchyard. Two weeks later, when Harp arrived home from logging in Virginia, he found his house empty. He had paid for the burying, sold his place at Buzzard's Roost, and gone back to Alabama. It wasn't likely Harp had written Ma. Maybe no one had notified her.

When at length Amon reached Boston, his grief was dulled somewhat. He took a cab to the tiny house on Derby Place, not wishing to walk through the streets where he would be obliged to stop and talk with friends. He lifted his bags from the carriage and paid the driver. He ran up the brick walk. Not many people were outside their houses, for the evening was cool. A few boys were playing mumblety-peg; a little girl on her way to the store for milk stared at him but did not speak. He opened the door and went in, thinking to find Ma at her ironing board, for there was still light in the sky. Fleetingly, he wondered if she had made any changes in their apartment, if she had used any of the money he had sent home to fix up their place.

He found Sabina squatting on a stool before a fire burning low on the hearth. She was rocking back and forth, hugging her stomach as though comforting a pain there, and her eyes were closed. Above her on the mantel a letter leaned against the oil lamp and seemed to cry its contents aloud in that drab room.

He dropped his bags and came to sit on the other crate stool beside her. "I'm home, ma," he said. "Did you get my letter from Tuskegee? I'm sure glad to be home."

She looked at him, nodding slightly as though it were hard to focus her attention on him, and went back to her rocking.

"You've heard about Leah, Ma." His gaze flicked to the mantel and quickly back to his mother. "When I was on the way home, I went up to see her—went to Buzzard's Roost. But she wasn't there. I heard about it from an old woman who's living in the house. Is the letter from Harp?"

Sabina shook her head, not ceasing to rock. Amon rose and took the letter from the mantel. It was dated four days previous and was postmarked from Dalton. He knew its contents before he read it, although he did not recognize the name of the signer. Evidently the letter had just arrived, and Sabina was in the first shock of the news. He returned the letter to its envelope and put it back on the mantel, only flat, not leaning it against the lamp. He looked about the room, spot-less white curtains at the windows, the floor scrubbed bone-clean, the ironing board spanning two wooden boxes. A small stove stood to one side, but there was no fire in it now. There was no other furniture except the bed made from the crate and the two stools. The place was as bare, as penitential as a nun's cell. Amon pulled the stool closer to Sabina and sat down again. He could think of no words to tell her how he shared her grief. He searched his mind for ways of comfort and clumsily offered what he could. "Leah was awful lonely, Ma."

Sabina nodded slowly.

"And she was sick a lot. The folks told me she was sick all last year."

Sabina nodded dully, as though it only affirmed what she knew, what she had known all along.

"She wasn't happy up there, Ma. She's better off now. Harp wasn't good to her. He left her alone when he could have taken her with him. She was—she was—" He could think of nothing further extenuating to say.

Sabina continued to rock, and her face was a tragic mask. The squares of the windows became dark as the daylight faded and the room filled with shadow. He wanted to put his arms around her and soothe her, but he felt restrained. Ma had never looked for help, for physical solace in her times of extremity. She had always been strong, self-sufficient. Even when Pa died, she had not given way to grief. She had rallied her spiritual forces and gone on,

A Trumpet Sounds

applying herself to duties and the day's demands. Always Ma faced up to any blow life dealt her. But not this time. It made Amon ache to see her crushed, not fighting back.

He said, "Ma, you got all that money I sent home? Heh? I can't see as how you've spent any. But I'm going to spend some, Ma. I'm going to buy you a lot of things. I'm going to get you a bed, a real bed with springs, and a rocking chair—like the one you had back on the farm. Remember the one sat on the gallery and you rocked in it on summer nights? It had a squeak. Remember, you liked the squeak. You wouldn't let Pa fix it. I'll get you another chair like that, Ma, squeak and all, if I can find it. I'm going to get you some pretty dresses too, and a new hat. And I'll get you a little trunk all lined with flower buds. I made a lot of money on this tour, Ma, and I had no cause to spend any. I haven't been able to do anything for you before, but I can now, and I aim to. I'm never going to leave you again. The next tour I make, you're going with me. You've wanted to visit Cream out there in California. We can go, Ma. I'm well known now. I'll make another tour. We'll travel, you and I. I won't ever leave you alone."

She began to cry then, tears rolling fast down her cheeks. Her head dropped to her knees, and her shoulders shook. She clasped her arms around her knees and rocked, sobbing. To Amon it was an appalling sight. He had never seen his mother cry. In all his life he had never seen her cry. Distraught, he knelt beside her and put his arms around her and held her close.

Chapter 27

Now, with the successful summer tour behind him and more money than he had ever before possessed, Amon could pay all his debts. He squared himself with Titus Fielding and the manager of the Shelley Theatre. He fulfilled his promise to buy furniture for their apartment, a bed for Sabina and a cot for himself, a table and a rocking-chair for which Sabina promptly made a cushion and a headrest. He also bought her the long-desired trunk with the flowered lining.

Then Sabina called a halt. "We got all we needs, son. Keep your money in the bank for a rainy day."

Amon felt reckless and prodigal. "Ma, I like spending money. I've never had it before to spend. I never knew what it was like to look at something in a store window and know I could go in and buy it. It's a lightheaded feeling, Ma. Makes you sort of dizzy."

"Don't you go gettin' dizzy and commit a foolishment, son. One sunshiny day don't make a summer."

"Maybe not. Maybe not, but I have an idea we're going to see lots of sunshiny days now, Ma. I'm going to give another concert here in Boston, and this time it will be a success. I'm known around now. The newspaper critics have praised my singing tour. Other agents are wanting to sign me up; I've had dozens of invitations to sing—you know that. I'll make money. Ma. I'll buy you dresses and folderols fit for a queen."

"Son, you knows I don't crave nothing like that."

"What would you like, Ma? If you could have anything you

A Trumpet Sounds

wanted, what would you wish for, eh? Name it. An automobile? One of those fancy contraptions spurts along at thirty miles an hour, eh? What would you wish for? Tell me."

Sabina rocked contently in her new rocker, all shiny black and without a squeak. She puckered her mouth and looked at him from the corners of her eyes.

"Any wish?"

"Any wish."

"Well, if I could have anything, I think I'd get me a little place in the shruburbs where I could have me a cow and some chickens."

"Oh, Ma," Amon chuckled. "You and your cow. What do you want with a cow at your age? I'll buy you a place in the suburbs, but I'll get you a goat."

"I was only foolin', Son." Her voice was playful. "I'm satisfied right here."

"I'm not, but it will do for the time being. I still have to go on training my voice. I don't think you ever get through training, or get to the place where you're satisfied to stop. I want to go to Paris and study too. I want to sing all over Europe, in the great capitals of the world, train under the best teachers. I'd like—"

"Son," Sabina interrupted, "you gonna float around on them rosy clouds much, you best get you a parachute."

Amon cackled gleefully. "Ma, what do you know about parachutes? You been reading the papers?"

"I can read them," Sabina said smugly.

No warnings could trouble Amon now, nor blight his confidence. Having re-established himself as a pupil with Titus Fielding, he now went to see him regarding the matter of a concert. With extensive experience behind him in the way of public appearances, his name better known, and his voice praised in the press, he felt he could put on a concert in Boston now with reasonable expectation of success. Since his return, he had been singing regularly in the churches, both white and colored. He had been asked again to take the position of soloist in the First Methodist Church of Newton Center. He had been the guest soloist at several civic benefits. He felt he knew more now about management and was far better informed as to methods and means of putting on a concert.

"You've made a name for yourself, Amon," Titus Fielding said. "The critics describe you as unique. People are beginning to recognize your name now as that of a distinguished Negro singer."

"I have to give Mr. Galveston the credit for that."

"No, Galveston couldn't have done a thing without your voice."

"That's what Ma always wanted," Amon said reflectively, "you know, for me to sing just the way I was meant to sing. I learned a lot on that tour. A man only fulfills himself when he is himself."

"There's no guarantee the world will recognize that as an intrinsic quality, but it's the only way a man can discover his destiny. Just keep your feet on the ground, Sayre, and don't stop training. Now, let me see what can be done about this concert."

"I'm glad I have your approval on this one," Amon laughed.

Titus Fielding assured him of his wholehearted support. He offered the services of his own secretary, and together they compiled a mailing list of some three thousand names. Important people were solicited as patrons, and those responding were so numerous it became a problem how best to include their names on the program. Advertisements were inserted in the leading newspapers, a step recommended by one of the music critics who had become Amon's good friend. The concert was planned for late March, on an evening calculated to insure reasonably good weather, and one on which no other important public event was scheduled.

Amon, with Fielding's help, prepared his program with great care. He would start with a group of lieder. He would sing "Du Bist die Ruhe" and Berlioz's "Absence"—it was a song he could never sing without thinking of Julia. He would sing "L'Amour de Moi" and perhaps "Le Tambourin" for an encore. He would sing Handel's "Where'er You Walk," "The Dream Song," and "A Furtive Tear" from Donizetti's opera *L'Elisir d'Amour*. And then for a third group of songs he would give some of his own arrangements of Negro folk songs and spirituals. He made these selections thoughtfully and sang them to Sabina.

When he sang "Ezekiel Saw de Wheel" and "Oh, Mary Don't

A Trumpet Sounds

You Weep," she smoothed her apron and rocked her chair back and forth in quiet enjoyment. "Son," she said, "Ain't no sweeter songs no place than them. I think you come to know that now. You done found yourself and I'm right glad."

Tickets for the concert were sold by the hundreds, whole blocks being bought by employees of the insurance company where Amon had worked, and by neighbors and friends on Westminster and Columbus and Washington Streets and Derby Place. The people who had heard him sing in the churches and who read about his tour in the papers all bought tickets. Nine hundred dollars worth of tickets were sold far in advance of the concert date. Amon went to the offices of Symphony Hall and paid the rental fee of four hundred dollars.

Euman Jennis had agreed to accompany him. Together they rehearsed diligently. Since Amon was his own manager, the day of the concert found him deluged with last-minute details. He had rented a suit of evening clothes, but alterations were necessary. He had ordered the piano checked by a competent tuner, but the man had failed to appear and another had to be found. He fretted ineffectually about the heat in the hall and the adequacy of backstage help, and a conveyance for Ma, and the flower for his buttonhole, and the weather, and a hundred things which he could not have done anything about anyway. He was plagued by last-minute requests for tickets after the hall had been completely sold out, and he was forced to promise standing room.

People began arriving early on the evening of March 23. The orchestra and the balcony filled rapidly. Amon arrived backstage so excited and nervous he was beside himself. Fielding and Jennis did their best to calm him. He kept peering between the curtains at the gathering throng in the great auditorium. Ma sat in the front row with Mrs. Fielding. He could spot several of the more important music critics. He saw the mayor and his wife. He could hear the rustle of Boston high society. And he could see the aisles jammed with people for whom there were no seats. People pressed into the orchestra pit, and some were standing on the steps of the proscenium and even in the wings. Mr. Hardy came backstage to wish Amon luck. He said the mob outside the doors in front must be five hundred strong.

"This is your night, my boy," he said laying a hand affectionately on Amon's shoulder. "And you have my hearty good wishes."

When the curtain finally swung aside and Euman walked across the stage to the piano, Amon tried to steady himself. He felt lightheaded, and nausea gripped him. For a moment the stage whirled and he with it. But when Euman had finished his prelude, Anon made his entrance and stood poised beside the piano in singing position, his head thrown back. A few bars of music and he was singing, his eyes closed. He was alone with his voice and the things in his heart for which it must speak.

The first song met with instant, heart-warming applause. The response was tumultuous. After the first two groups of songs there was an intermission. Fifteen minutes later he opened his last group with "Litl' Boy, How Old Are You?" the poignant, lovely song of the boy Christ in the temple with the teachers. When he finished and opened his eyes, he was startled by the strange hush over the great hall. He saw Ma's upturned face, and he thought he had never seen it before with such a light. He saw Mrs. Fielding dab at her eyes, and then suddenly, thunderously, the applause broke. It was explosive. It lasted so long he was obliged to wait five minutes before he could sing the next number.

He sang "Ezekiel Saw de Wheel" and "O Le' Me Shine" and then, without any piano accompaniment, the exquisitely moving "Oh, Mary, Don't You Weep." When he sang Ma's favorite, "Every Time I Feel the Spirit," his heart smiled, seeing her sway to the rhythm of it. At the end of this group of songs the applause was a din. Wet eyes glistened incongruously above smiling lips as people clapped and clapped, stamped and cheered and called for more. Even Ma was clapping, and she waved a handkerchief. "She's proud of me," Amon thought. "She can strut down Derby Place and be proud of me

Happy now and free of all nervousness, Amon was induced to sing three encores. He was obliged to come back again and again for bows.

"I'll never forget this," he told himself. "As long as I live, I'll never forget this." His eyes roved the audience—all those milky white faces swimming around below him, smiling, cheering, yell-

A Trumpet Sounds

ing, all the hands clapping, all that acclaim. What did it mean? What did it signify? This belated recognition? One night's triumph was no guarantee of future appearances. He knew it for what it was, sensed the chimera lurking just off stage. A sudden unbidden loathing took hold of him for all the deep-rooted prejudice and arrogance and mean regard he had known, the insuperable disparateness, the endless animosities and insults; and hate possessed him so that he could not see, could not hear, could only feel, the cold awareness creeping like an insidious drug up and up and up, numbing him, darkening his joy until, for a moment, he drowned.

Then there came from the balcony a piercing whistle, and the horror fled. He had an impulse to shake like a wet dog. No matter that this success was only one step forward, one tiny rift in the barrier, it was at least a rift. Leah had once said, "Music unhates people." Maybe it did, just maybe it did. A picture flashed into his memory: himself and Leah, with an old guitar, singing on a mountaintop:

> *Green tree a-bendin'*
> *Ol' sinner done a-tremblin'*
> *A trumpet sounds within-a my soul.*

I know the trumpet sounds now, he thought, and he smiled back at the audience, willing to enjoy this night for what it was, a beginning.

Afterword

In 1920 Roland Hayes was told by the manager of the Boston Symphony that there was no place for a Negro singer in American concert auditoriums. More dismayed than angry he decided to go to Europe for further training where he studied with some of the great teachers—Ira Aldridge, Victor Beigel, Theodore Lierhammer and Sir George Henschel.

In May of that year he gave a concert at Aeolian Hall in London. The critics were acerbic, but the audience delighted and this debut was followed by fourteen other recitals and a command performance before King George V and Queen Mary.

In Spain he sang for Queen Maria Christina.

He sang to what at first appeared a hostile audience in Germany which, after he sang Schubert's DU BIST DIE RUH dissolved into one of cheering adulation. Everywhere in Germany he was acclaimed for his interpretations of Lieder.

Then on to France where he was for a time the rage of Paris, his fluent mastery of the language endearing him to the French people and earning him high praise from the French composer Gabriel Fauré. Fritz Kreisler became Roland's friend and admirer.

He sang in Vienna and elsewhere in Austria, in Graz and Budapest, Karlsbad and Prague. He sang all over England and Wales, everywhere performing the classics dear to the particular country where he was appearing and always finishing a concert with his native spirituals.

A Trumpet Sounds

He returned to the United States in 1923 and William Brennan, who three years earlier had told him he could never sing in an American auditorium, signed him to a contract for a recital in Carnegie Hall.

That year was the start of Hayes' long and successful concert career in America, where all his life he had yearned to sing and be accepted. His first professionally conducted tour was anticipated by a soloist appearance with the Boston Symphony Orchestra under the direction of Pierre Monteux. He chose from the works of Mozart and Berlioz and Gautier. On the afternoon of the third Boston concert he learned that Woodrow Wilson had just died. "I was deeply moved," he said, "and I wanted to pay tribute to a great soul, so I sang GOIN HOME with a theme from The New World Symphony arranged by William Fisher:

> Goin home, goin home, I'm jes goin home;
> It's not far, jes close by, through an open door.
> Work all done, care laid by,
> Gwine to fear no more. . . .

Grief and emotion, the song, the singer and the audience mingled in a long moment of silence at the finish.

Roland Hayes's singing cracked open the first doors of prejudice among American theater goers. Repeatedly filling halls with both black and white along the eastern seaboard, his tour swung south where racial resistance was the most strongly entrenched. In Birmingham, Alabama a municipal ordinance was required, allowing white people and Negroes to sit under the same roof. Three thousand Negroes bought up tickets and filled the first floor. The white people sat in the balcony.

From the south his tour took him west as far as San Francisco's Civic Auditorium where he sang to some twenty thousand people. In every city where he appeared there were critics assessing his voice and delivery and presence, sometimes with niggling reservations, most often with high and unqualified praise. And although almost everywhere exhorbitant fees for halls and accommodations were extracted from his managers, double what would have been charged a white singer, he still made a great deal of money, the American criteria of success.

Eunice Young Smith

In 1924, he received the Spingarn Medal for outstanding achievement among black people. In 1932 Dr. Thomas Jesse Jones presented him with an honorary degree from Fisk University. Ohio Wesleyan also gave him an honorary degree. The French government bestowed the Purple Ribbon for his services to French music. And in 1953 he was awarded a fellowship from the American Academy of Arts and Sciences.

He had a long, crowded, exhausting and rewarding career. At seventy-five he was still singing. In 1963 he gave a benefit recital in New York City for the American Association College Centennial Fund, his artistic projection still controlled, infinitely gentle, magnetic. He was told afterwards, when he was presented with the Amistad Award: "You do the human race honor to exist."